Inde-
pen-
dence

Independence

a novel

Cecil Foster

HarperCollins*PublishersLtd*

Independence
Copyright © 2013 by Cecil Foster.
All rights reserved.

Published by HarperCollins Publishers Ltd

First edition

HarperCollins books may be purchased for educational, business,
or sales promotional use through our Special Markets Department.

HarperCollins Publishers Ltd
2 Bloor Street East, 20th Floor
Toronto, Ontario, Canada
M4W 1A8

www.harpercollins.ca

Library and Archives Canada Cataloguing in Publication
information is available upon request

ISBN 978-1-44341-505-7

Printed and bound in the United States
RRD 9 8 7 6 5 4 3 2 1

To BIM, with expectations great

Prologue

This is my earliest memory: It is 1957, or 58, and I am perhaps three, four years old. Grandmother and Mrs. King are talking inside the shed roof, the back part of Mrs. King's house. Mrs. King's granddaughter Stephanie is standing next to me in the yard. Her hair is plaited. There are big blue ribbons in it. And her white dress, her dan-dan, is clean. We have received our evening baths. She smells of Lifebuoy soap and Vaseline and powder. Across from us is the pigpen. Around us the chickens and turkeys peck at the ground. In this memory, I see myself staring into the great beyond. Then Stephie breaks the silence.

"She never coming back," Stephie whispers. I see the lights in the front house, the oldest part of their home. "I know. She never *ever* coming back."

I did not have to ask whom Stephie was talking about. Even back then, she was smarter than me. She was older by six months too. I said nothing to her. She said nothing more. What more could either of us say? We stood in front of the pigpen hearing the grunts in the dusk. The older turkeys and hens were gathering unto themselves their young ones. The sun was going down. Grandmother and Mrs. King were inside the house laughing. I hoped Stephie was wrong this time. I hoped my mother would come back for me. I know Stephie wished the same for herself. But she was wiser.

Standing there beside her, I waited and waited and waited. I hoped and kept on hoping. Stephie reached for my hand. We continued waiting and hoping. Finally, she led me by the hand back into the house. I remember thinking: *tomorrow.*

Part One

Part One

Chapter One

This is the first time I recall being so confused about my best friend from birth.

"Stephie, girl," I call into the darkness. "Whuh you doing out there so late in the night?" After all, she is the one constantly claiming that I am always acting as if I'd never learned how to take care of my own self.

"Mind yuh business," she shoots back. "Yuh too fast. You should be in yuh bed sleeping, getting ready for school tomorrow." I know Stephie does not mean anything with this tone; she is good at telling me off from time to time, so mostly I don't mind. "Go to your bed."

"I ain't sleepy," I call back. Plus I know that giving herself mouth is Stephie's way of talking back to people, especially when she wants to hide something. And I know that recently she has been joining with our grandmothers in hiding certain things from me, because they say I am just a boy. "I waiting for Grand and you' grandmother to come home from church. I thought you did be gone with them to church tonight."

"I di'n't go to no church," Stephie says. "You can't see that with your own two eyes? You can be too blind sometimes."

"But when I did see you getting ready to wash up your face and hands earlier this evening, I did think you was going to church too. Where you coming from at this hour o' the night?" I am pretending I don't feel put off by the fact she now has certain privileges over me. There have been a lot of strange things going on of late. It is like one big tidal wave is washing everyone along, whether they want to go with it or not. Sometimes I feel as if I am just watching, but then, when I least expect it, the wave wants to grab hold of me too, as if I am bathing in the sea when suddenly a big wave appears out of nowhere and with it an unexpected undertow that drags everybody out to sea. Even I can't seem to escape.

"That's my business," she shouts back. "Anyway, I goin' inside now. I'll see you in the mornin' for school bright and early."

"You cryin'?" I ask, for I definitely detect something different. "Somebody hit you?"

"Leave me alone!" Stephie shouts as if she is really annoyed. I know she too good: something isn't right, not from the way she is sounding.

"You sure you okay?" I persist. Up to now, she'd always shared everything with me. And if she had to take on a special tone with me, it was usually only when she was pointing out that I was too slow to get things, which is usually true. Of late even Grandmother and Mrs. King have taken to saying how much more mature Stephie is than me.

"Mind yuh own business and leave me alone," she says, running for the paling gate. "That is what is wrong with boys like you, always asking too much questions."

"I think you was cryin'," I shout back in my singsong voice to make a point that she can't fool me. "Somebody musta troubled you."

But there is no answer. I hear the hinges of the door creak and then the rattling of the latch as she closes the door behind her. Then a scratch from a match, and a small light comes out of the darkness. Through the glass panes in the window of her house, I see what looks like the shadow of Stephie moving around. Grandmother said that is one reason she does not like having houses so close together. The next-door neighbours always know your business even before you feel like telling them. You had to be real careful to keep a secret to yourself. And that is why she is always telling me to stay out of big-people business. She says she does not have the time nor the strength to be taking on people constantly humbugging her, especially if I should go and do or say something foolish to offend people, bringing trouble between she and others in the area. "And this place is full o' vagabonds and advantage-takers. I don't want nobody, man or woman, coming to blow the roof off this little house we have here," she has repeated so many times, "just because they bigger and stronger than you and me. Lord knows I 'fraid o' trouble and I don't want you causing no trouble for me." She never stops telling me how even now at my age, thirteen going on fourteen, there are some things in life I still do not know and would not understand, for that is the way with boys and even the mens. Particularly, she says, I should stay out of woman talk and their doings. Of late this woman talk seems to be including Stephie more and more, so that even she is now leaving me out of some things involving *she*, Stephie of all people. But I am no fool: I know Stephie too good.

I remain standing at the front window, looking into the blackness beyond the edge of the light from the window. I do not hear any singing coming from next door. Singing is how Stephie keeps herself from being frightened when she is alone at night. Most times I join in with her, the two of us singing up a storm, the two of us waiting with mostly me afraid of even my own thoughts. I hate sitting alone and just *thinking*. But just then a thought strikes me and I feel kinda foolish for even assuming something bad happened to Stephie. I tell myself Stephie must have been out training for the cross-country race at school in a few weeks' time. Sports Day. That is the big event to ring down the closing of the school term. And I laugh at how foolish and forgetful I can be at times. And I find myself frowning at the thought. Boy, I think, Stephie must be troubled really bad by Ursula Payne, the only girl in the whole school that is any competition for her when it comes to running. Maybe all the talk about Ursula looking good this year and that she might beat Stephie is forcing her to practise late into the night. Everybody knows Ursula joined a sports club somewhere up in the country and is out training hard morning, noon and night. Ursula has a mother and father that she lives with; they can afford the money for training classes, for a coach and for the sneakers and the club uniform that make her look good and ready. Everybody expects a real ding-dong race this year. More than that, as the competition has heated up, Stephie and Ursula have stopped speaking to each other, something that I gather is even more important than when boys stop talking to each other or when men disagree and even fight. Maybe, I think, that is why her voice sounded funny. Stephie was out of breath from all the training and practising even after she left Mr. Lashley's house a short while ago. Now in the house, poor thing, she does not even have the breath in her body to want to sing. I feel better now I have figured out things for myself. Stephie will be okay after a good night's sleep. We can sing together another time.

The kerosene light flickers as a breeze passes through Silver Hill. The flame in the lamp's chimney starts to soot and some of it comes out at the top and adds to the residue already spreading on the cardboard overhead. There it makes its own stain, along with those of the rainwater that comes in through the many holes in the galvanize roof. The soot is spreading, Grandmother said, like all the evil that comes out of goodness. Her roof is mashing up bad but she does not have the money to fix it. The roof and ceiling are getting it from both sides: the rain on the outside and the soot on the inside. If she does not act soon, Grandmother is always saying, the entire roof, or the part without holes, will soon be as black as hell. As black, I am thinking, as this night in which I saw Stephie walking so dejectedly only a few minutes earlier.

Now there is quiet: in this house as I await the return of Grandmother, and next door too, where Stephie is also awaiting her grandmother and, like me, ultimately our mothers from over-'n'-away. After all these years, me and she have not given up hope, even though at times she can be a bit strange in her talking. Tomorrow we will wait some more and keep an eye out for Postie. Maybe he will bring a letter. On this night, I sit by the window looking out into the darkness and hoping this new breeze across the land will not blow out the lamp. That would be nothing short of a disaster. I would be faced with a bad choice: to sit in darkness until Grandmother comes home or to let my clumsy self get me in trouble. Then she would yell at me for sitting in the darkness like some moochine idiot, saying sometimes boys could act real foolish, like they've never gone to school or have no common sense, especially when they are already a thirteen-year-old high school boy. Grandmother would say it was not right for her to have to come into a house full of darkness, not when she has a box o' matches and a big able boy chile who should be able to relight a lamp if the wind blew it out. Stephie would, she'd say. She would scold me about how I have to realize I am getting big and there are some things

I have to learn to do for myself. That by showing initiative and helping her out is one way I can try to show my gratitude for all the effort she puts in every morning, noon and night to take care of me, bearing in mind she is only a poor grandmother who is the only guardian I have in this wide world. But no, she would say, she'd come home and find only darkness, causing her to stub her toe or to stumble about over the school shoes or a school bag *somebody* thoughtlessly left in the way for her to fall down over. She would say that tonight alone it was taking no time since she left church a few minutes ago for me to lick out of her soul the little grace and inspiration she did get from the Word of God, making it as bad as if she had wasted her time frequenting some dance hall or house of wuthlessness and sinning her soul, with people just carrying on bad with their slackness. And that she has to keep wondering why boys even with years on their backs can be so immature and are always so much trouble to raise, and why my mother could not have left her with a girl to raise, one who could help herself and do the chores around the house. "Stephie would have the good sense to light the lamp so Mrs. King would not have to bounce her foot at the doorstep or inside the house when she comes home. Girls always understand things more better. And that Stephie, when you notice her these days, you can't help but say how she is growing into a real beautiful young lady and ready to take on responsibility. I have to hand it to Eudene on that one. Stephie ain't no little girl no more. Soon she'll be a full woman, praise the Lord."

In my head, I hear the conversation. I kick the shoes farther under the table. The breeze is stronger, like one of those winds that has rain on it, that produce the swaying songs from the cane fields and the clammy cherry trees behind the house, that cause the bleached flour-bag curtains at the window to shift, and the light in the lamp to splutter and soot some more. I decide to close the window.

True, I could relight the lamp in the darkness if it goes out. But I know myself. In my fumbling around is even bigger danger: I might find the chimney too hot when I try to lift it off the lamp. The heat would burn my fingers, even if to hold the chimney I used my shirttail or the end of the crocus bag that is the mat at the door. As everybody done know, I can't take no pain. Grandmother is always among the first to keep telling me so: how I am always crying at the first lick or bounce; that even though I don't shed long tears anymore, I am still a crybaby, and she does wonder what I would do if I was a girl and had to deal with pain every month. And Stephie, when she is rough with me, is always saying I still soft. So I know if the chimney burns my fingers, I might just drop it. *Bradung. Crassshh.* Stephie would hear the sound all the way over there in Mrs. King's house. I would end up breaking Grandmother's chimney, the one my mother sent back from over-'n'-away these many years ago. That would be more than a disaster. For except for the picture on the side of the house, and of course me, those splinters of glass would be the last reminder of my mother in this house. My bottom and not only my ears would pay the price. I would be the one crying for sure this night. And through it all I can already hear Stephie saying, "Serve you right, 'cause with you and you' awkward self, I don't know why you woulda go and touch that chimney for." And trying to sound so womanish, Stephie would suck her teeth and say, "Sometimes I don't know about you," and shake her head.

As I close the window, my eyes again catch the greenish light coming from the front house across the road from us. Must be the television set. The light has intrigued me all night long. Mr. Lashley, whom the grandmothers refer to as Lashie, came back home earlier in the day from working on the overseas program. He arrived on a big truck with so many barrels on the back that we gave up counting them. Mrs. King in particular was waiting for him, with Stephie inside her grandmother's house looking out at the two of them talking. Mr. Lashley had asked Mrs. King to get the house wired for him when he was gone. This was because, Grandmother had explained, Mr. Lashley's mother lived too far away and he did not want her to keep having to come up by us to look after the house. Mr. Lashley's mother was a town woman, did not like the people in our village and could never hide her feelings about us. Mrs. King and Stephie looked after the house when Mr. Lashley was working overseas. When he wrote and said he wanted the house wired for electricity, we all knew what was coming. Over the last weeks, Basil the electrician had been busy getting the house ready. Sometimes Stephie was over there alone sweeping and acting like she keeping house. With all this talk about wiring and electricity, we knew Mr. Lashley could only be thinking of bringing back one thing: a television.

Mr. Lashley did not disappoint us. Among the barrels and suitcases lifted from the back of the truck was a big cardboard box with the words *RCA Television* on the outside. Earlier tonight, leaving Stephie to watch over the house, Mr. Lashley went to Enid's rum shop just as he always did the first night back. This time, there was a difference: as Grandmother and Mrs. King were leaving for church, Mr. Lashley and his drinking buddies were coming back to his home. I saw Stephie opening the door to let them in, and I thought she was also stepping out the house to leave the men alone and to join the women at church. Soon I heard the laughing and joking in Mr. Lashley's house, and a greenish glow appeared in the window. Then the noise in the house grew quiet, so much so all was silent for a long time. I was reading my school textbooks when I heard footsteps in the night. I opened the window and saw Stephie crossing back between the houses. Maybe that was when she decided to take a run to get in shape. Now everything makes sense.

Except for the music of the wind, all is quiet once again. It is just like any night in early December, like any of the nights I sit at home and wait for Grandmother's return. The exception is the glow coming from Mr. Lashley's house. People are now saying how progress has definitely come among us in this the first year of our independence. The village has its first television, making us just like town people. Now we children have something else to look forward to tomorrow. Whether Mr. Lashley knows it or not, every child in the village will be visiting him as soon as the sun sets. I plan to be one of them. I'll be joining Stephie. *Tomorrow.*

Chapter Two

I hear Grandmother's gentle knocking and her calling my name in a whisper soon after I closed the window. From where she is calling in the darkness, she must have seen the lights going out inside the house. I unlatch the door and Grandmother steps inside. She stoops just beyond the threshold to take off her shoes, while shifting to one side so I can reach past her to refasten the latch. Along with her white handbag that contains her Bible, Grandmother carries her shoes into her bedroom. I hear as she pushes the shoes under the bed. In a short while, I also hear her striking a match to light the lamp she keeps on the box beside her bed. The glow spreads, throwing off shadows. Later, when she is comfortable, she will lower the wick, partially, she always claims, to save on the oil during the night. Kerosene oil, like everything else, has become so expensive since independence in 1966. But as she says, it is oil nonetheless that, like the five wise virgins, she has to have in her lamp to keep it burning 'til the break of day.

She's been in the house five minutes when we hear first a gentle *pitta patta* on the roof and then a steady drumming, like the sound the men make on the kettledrum in a tuk band. The wind has picked up as if it wants to raise the roof off the house. As it huffs, the wind makes the house shake and causes the light in the bedroom to splutter. All of this is only to foretell a downpour is on the wind. Now it arrives. The steady beating slowly moves to the back of my mind. It remains there as Grandmother draws the curtains to undress. Placing on a hanger attached to a nail in the side of the house the sleeveless and loose-fitting cotton dress—what she calls her outside clothes— she changes into her nightgown. This is a discarded white dress, still loose fitting, also with no sleeves, but now so old she would not even wear it into the yard. With the possible exception of Mrs. King and maybe Stephie, never would she allow anyone to lay eyes on her in that house dress. Some things, she says, are for inside the house and others are for when the world is watching. Mrs. King and Stephie are different, Grandmother says, even though they live in a different house; they are like family. I fluff the bags for my bed and place them on the floor, stretch out on them and cuddle myself. From above my head and beyond the curtains, I hear Grandmother walking around and muttering to herself, and then there is the usual creaking sound as she gets into the bed.

The rain continues its steady drumming. A stream of water splatters near my head, causing me to jump at the suddenness. Another hole in the roof. Not waiting for Grandmother to call to me, I get up and go to the table just a short distance away from the end of my bed on the floor. On the bench beside the table is my bag already packed for the next school day. The texts I had used for studying earlier in the night are in the bag along with the exercise books containing my homework, one exercise book for each of the five subjects scheduled for the day. All that is missing is the paper bag containing the cheese cutter Grandmother usually gives me for lunch. I leave a space among the books for where I will place the cheese cutter, positioning it so the oil from the cheese won't grease up and soil any of the books. I make sure the mouth of the bag is closed, in case another hole appears unexpectedly in the roof, for I do not want water to leak in and soak the books. Otherwise Stephie and her grandmother would be angry. It is my responsibility to take care of textbooks when they are in my possession. That is one rule on which everybody insists. I am ready for tomorrow. Nobody will accuse me of holding them back or even making us late for the bus and school. On the table I find an old biscuit tin with bits of paper still stuck to the side. I place it where the water is dripping, and immediately there is a pinging sound.

"What's that I hearing now?" Grandmother asks from behind the curtain.

"It's another hole," I say. "I put the biscuit tin to catch the water."

"Lord, I don't know what more to expect next," Grandmother says. "This ol' house like it bre'king down over we head. Same thing with that house Mrs. King got below there. All we can do is hope and pray God keep us safe. And that the waters from what's sounding now like a' all-night rain don't wash us away this night. Faith."

I do not reply. Otherwise I might end up having to listen for most of the night. Then I might oversleep, making everyone angry at me for making them late. I grab the bag at the bottom of the bedding and drag the whole thing away from the biscuit tin with its staccato dripping sounds. The bedding is right up against the steps to the front house now. Grandmother always complains that the carpenter who built the shed roof, a later addition to the house in which we sleep, did a bad job. He did not even bother to place the floor of the addition on the same level as the rest of the house, but left it as if the old and new would never be on speaking terms. The front house with its second-hand Morris chairs, closed off most of the time, is higher than the shed roof. That carpenter, she said, was just like all the other mens she knew: just an advantage-taker and useless, and why from early in her life she had decided to have nothing to do with them, for they simply ain't no use. In the darkness of the night, we still find ourselves stumbling if we forget to step down on leaving the front house or to step up as we leave the shed. The reason, she repeats, she knows that every new development ain't progress. And now the shed roof too was leaking. So much, she says, for all the money she slaved for and saved to pay the carpenter. All the money she worked so hard for, walking up and down the length and breadth of the land, bottling all that dew by taking in so much night air, especially on Saturdays, sitting outside the main shop in the village, trying to get people to buy what she was selling, whatever fruits were in season or brought into the country for resale, and whatever she and Mrs. King could cobble together to make a few rare-mouth cents. Money that instead of she licking out on herself and having a grand time at this stage of her life, she had to be spending on this old house and on me too.

"You checking on the lamp in the front house?" Grandmother asks. "You better turn it out to be safe."

"I doing that now," I respond, hoping that with my mind drifting I have not missed other questions from her.

"Be careful. I don't want you to drop my good, good chimney and make it bre'k. Don't let no rain fall on it and crack it, you hear me, for it still hot."

"Yes, Grandmother," I promise.

"And don't fall over the few chairs in the front house in the darkness either."

"Yes, Grandmother."

"And when you come back and get into your bed, remember to say your prayers," she instructs as usual. "You shoulda been at church wid me tonight especially to hear the young people singing so sweet, but instead you had to stay home and do your homework, that way you stay out of trouble. It's better that way, anyway. After all, you is a high school boy, even if sometimes you don't much act like one. So, say your prayers before you go to sleep. Ask God to give you wisdom and understanding and to open up your brain so you can take in the learning that costing me so much money, which I ain't even got. 'Cause you ain't even got no godfather, not like some of the other children around here. Pray for education for your development, 'cause in this wide world you will need it to progress."

"Yes, Grandmother." I prepare myself for another of Grandmother's sermons, which she gives when she is in her mood or if something is troubling her; when she can go on forever talking about why she is a true-true Christian woman and how nothing in this world, including poorness or sickness, can ever shake her faith.

"And pray too that yuh mother will write soon," Grandmother says. "Lord knows I can do with some help, for the burden is heavy and I getting old. Pray that at least if she still can't see her way to send for you just yet that she will send a tra-la or two, so that I can buy a little food to put in yuh mouth when the morning come and to put clothes on yuh back. You need sustenance and three square meals if you is to take in a secondary education. So you praying?"

"Yes, Grandmother."

"Then why I don't hear anything?"

"I praying in my head. Silenty, silenty."

"Okay. Sleep good."

"Good night, Grand," I say.

"Good night. God bless."

In a short while, I hear snoring, the comforting reminder throughout the night that I am not alone. Most times the snoring is so loud I cannot sleep. That is when Grandmother says she is really overtired from too much worrying. When she says she can wake up even herself with such loud cow-bellowing, enough to lift the roof off the little old shack. This time it is not that bad. It is what I have become used to, when all is quiet in our lives.

Even so I cannot get to sleep. My mind is drifting and I keep thinking of the tone in Stephie's voice. She *must* have been crying. I am now certain, which is strange, for Stephie does not cry for nothing. Not even when she gets the two of us into big trouble. Even then she does not cry. I do. And I smile to myself as I remember something I probably will never forget, when even then she just would not cry. There is something about what happened then, what caused her to be so calm as she prepared herself for the beating that awaited her, that I still can't understand; something in how she went about shielding herself that has puzzled me all these years; something, to tell the truth, that probably shows the difference between boys and girls or, as Stephie would say, between big people and crybabies. I relive that moment, searching every word and action for the real meaning, almost every time I try to get myself to sleep. Stephie crying makes me think ever harder about when we tried to be bad and rebellious, when we almost brukout, as Grandmother would say.

"Come," I hear Stephie saying as she tugs on my hand, almost dragging me behind her. I see the two of us standing there. We are about ten or eleven years old. Already we are tired of having to be so different from everybody else. Everything is always out of bounds for us. "Leh we go."

With that I find myself dashing across the road right behind her, the plaits of her hair flapping, right into the crowd of dancers. The entire room is trembling from the tall speakers in the corners. We push through the people. The bass from the music is pounding as loud as my heart itself. My head is swinging. I know Stephie and I should not be doing this. This place is trouble, not like church. It is hot, even with the two fans with long white blades circulating overhead at jet speed. I smell the sweat from all the dancing and from people walking for hours in the hot sun. And my nose stings from the odours from all the rum and beer everybody is drinking and even splattering on the floor and on one another when dancing fast. I look around, seeing the inside of this place for the first time. Over to the side, women are selling drinks, some pouring from bottles into plastic cups, others plunging their hands into pans with ice and water for a beer or sweet drink. This is the dance hall Grandmother and Mrs. Kings always warn us about. "Never ever let me catch you in that hall," Grandmother has said so many times. "That ain't where church-going people find themselves, not in a place of such wuthlessness." From what I hear, the people in here will probably be at it, dancing and carrying on wild, well into fore day morning. They will be dancing and drinking and eating the rice and peas and fried pork chops and chicken or fish cooking in the back. It seems no different from what I have been hearing from the boys at school.

"See," Stephie says, her two arms swaying in front of her, just like one of the sisters in Pastor Wiltshire's church. "Isn't this lots o' fun?"

"Uh hum," I agree. I am giggling and so is Stephie. I have never been in anything like this. Still, I do not feel as if I can just let myself go.

"Now the children at school can't laugh at you and me no more," Stephie says, holding my hand and pivoting on her heels as she swirls around, just like the women, but stumbling at the end. "They can't keep saying that we ol' fashion and too ol' time-ish like grandmother children." She laughs as she attempts the move again, and again stumbles.

I shake my head. We are trying to act just like the men and women around us, mocking all their fancy footwork, how they sway with one another, just like the tops of trees in a strong breeze. Even so, Stephie stands out, for unlike all the other children, she is wearing a long white dress with sleeves down to her elbows, not like all the other girls, particularly those that already have real boyfriends. They are wearing next to nothing in their pedal-pushers, miniskirts and low-cut blouses. And me, I am in my regular school clothes, even though there is no school today. It is Emancipation Day. The whole island is one big celebration. People are drinking up and talking a lot about how bad it did be in slavery, but not now. *Massa day done*, the hi-fi speakers blast out, with everyone on the floor, squeezed together. *Freedom people, it's time for fun.* In here anything goes. *Dance up on she; push back on he; shake up yuh body. Ain't no fantasy, we have the legacy; This train can't stop 'til we really free. Can't stop.* For just this once, Stephie and me are just like all the other children. I stop moving and stand still, holding her hand, watching what the men and women nearby are doing to bring off these moves while still staying in time with the music. And I feel the sweat running out of my hair down my face, down my back and belly. A side of me really wants me to enjoy myself. But another side won't let me: it keeps telling me it is wrong and that I won't like the outcome. Then, sure enough, I hear a familiar voice.

"You two." It is loud and clear. The music must have stopped. I sense Stephie bristle and my heart drops. "Yes, *you* there, Stepha-nie, come this way. You too, Mr. Christopher."

I turn to look. It is Mrs. King, Stephie's grandmother, beckoning and frowning. The children standing around her are pointing at us and laughing. I feel my head drop.

"Oh loss," I hear myself despairing. Stephie sighs, pushes pass me and heads toward her grandmother.

"Licks like fire," I hear someone say. "Pure licks for Stephanie and Christopher." School tomorrow will bring more of this taunting. I follow Stephie as the people stand aside. It is a long walk to the door. I swallow and blink fast, already feeling the water rising in my eyes. Stephie walks ahead of me, her head bowed, the plaits falling forward on her shoulder. I am wondering what could get into me to make me let Stephie lead me into this trouble. Mrs. King is at the end of the line, standing between us and the only door into this place. Everyone is watching. It feels as if the entire festivities are on pause. Everyone is awaiting their resumption once this disruption is over. Once we are gone.

"You don't know I got five minds to give you one lick around your head," Mrs. King says when face to face with Stephie. Quickly her hand rises and slaps Stephie against her head. The blow makes Stephie stumble, or maybe she had, in anticipation of the blow, started to run. She dashes pass her grandmother. "And you too," she says, giving me a knock against the back of my head as I try to run too.

"Licks, licks, licks," the children are chanting.

"Your grandmother and I ain't raising the two o' you this way," Mrs. King shouts after us. We are running down the steps into the yard where more boys and girls are waiting, all smiling broadly and jeering. Even the adults are laughing, and some of them make as if to grab us. Stephie is already at full speed and I am trying to catch up.

"Not to find yourself in all this slackness as if the two o' you is some kind o' riff-raff," Mrs. King is saying at the top of her voice. "So yes, run. And you better run and hide, both of you, for when Peggy and I done with the two o' you, you'll never want to step foot in this place again." Already I am out of breath trying to keep pace with Stephie with her dress tail swishing around her long legs. But she is too fast.

When I arrive home, Stephie is sitting on the big limestone that is the step to Mrs. King's house. I do not know what to do. Maybe

Grandmother is not home. Maybe she does not know what it is that Stephie made me do. That is how I will explain what happened.

"*Christopher*," I hear the call from the neighbouring house.

"Yes, Grandmother," I answer, trying to hide the fear.

"Find your way in this house right now," she commands. "And Stephie, you just wait right there 'til your grandmother come home. Eudene and me ain't raising the two o' you to go off courting no trouble, not in some bawdy house as if you's two let-go beast like some gutter-snipe with no proper training."

"Yes, Grandmother," I say, resigning myself to the worst. "I coming."

"We are children of God," she says. I start to walk away.

"You know, all the children right 'bout what they keep saying 'bout you and me," Stephie says loud enough for me to hear.

"What that you mean?" I ask, turning to look back at her.

"That you's a grandmother child, nuh," Stephie says as if I shouldn't even require an explanation. "Same as me. You's a grandmother chile and me a grandmother chile. And that is why everybody does unfair the two o' we."

"Chris-*topher*," Grandmother is shouting from inside the house.

"Coming," I shout back. "Coming, Grand."

"A grandmother chile," Stephie sneers after me. "Sometimes I wish that you too did have a' auntie Dorothy."

"What you mean by that?" I ask her.

"So that you could go and live with her, the same as I could go and live with my aunt Dorothy," she says. "She won't be old-fashioned in her ways."

"*Boy*, are you coming?" Grandmother interrupts.

"You think your grand would let you live with your aunt Dorothy 'til your mother sends for you?" I say, eyeing the gate in the paling for the appearance of Grandmother, possibly with belt in hand.

"You don't understand, don't you," Stephie says with that tone. "It's not *me* alone. Suppose I leave you behind too? But you'd never understand anything. That is all I know."

She must notice the frown on my face as I turn and resume walking. She has always been smarter. She knows things I don't.

Sitting on the step, she must hear me crying in our house. Soon I hear Stephie singing, alone this time, waiting for her grandmother. I cannot join her singing, not this time.

Since then, nobody has ever said that Stephie and me look like we are turning out bad or rebellious. Stephie always acts the right way. I always try to follow her.

When I awake, Grandmother is already in the backyard. I hear her talking to herself as she counts the chickens and turkeys and gathers up the eggs in the nests. I jump up, thinking I must have overslept, but then I remember this morning is different. One of my chores has been eliminated. No longer am I required to walk to the beach for two loads of sand. Grandmother keeps the sand in a corner of the yard, up against the paling, in a spot where water does not settle or wash away the mound. Every morning, as she checks on the chickens and turkeys, she takes handfuls and walking around the yard dashes the sand on the overnight droppings from the chickens and turkeys to keep the flies away.

As I come out the back door, I see Grandmother with the long tin scrapers raking the pools of filth onto a piece of galvanize. When it is full, she walks out to the opening behind the galvanize paling and I hear the *clang, clang, clang* of the scraper knocking against the metal before she returns to repeat her chores in the yard. The flies are already rising out of the earth, buzzing loudly. They are feasting on the small puddles of dung, only to rise up and pitch on another as Grandmother approaches. Grandmother seems caught in a losing battle as she chases them around the yard, scooping up the abandoned droppings. In cahoots with the flies, the turkeys contribute more piles as she scrapes away others. I notice bits of dried grass and dirt clinging to Grandmother's feet. Ever so often, she goes to a patch of grass behind the paling and wipes her feet on it to clean them of the black dirt. And she moves around the yard, carefully avoiding the already stagnant water that she says might contain ringworms and even chigoes that could infect her feet.

"You see," Grandmother says when she realizes I am now in the backyard. "This is what I have to do so early in the morning: walk around this yard scraping up after these stocks. Before, we coulda use a bit of sand to cover over the spots, but the guvment up and say that it don't want people bringing away the sand from the beach no more." She says that not only has the government banned the taking of sand but it has asked the police to check on the homes. To her mind, the treatment of the sand is only the latest of a string of happenings on the island that is so worrisome to everybody. All these changes seemed to start at the same time word came that the men working on the overseas program were getting ready to come back home. "Now everything around here changing one day to the next."

It's a reprieve for me: I no longer have to walk down the hill beyond the dance hall to the beach and then walk all the way back up with the heavy basin full of sand on my head. Sometimes Stephie went with me. And as we passed the dance hall, remembering our experiences, we would try to keep our eyes straight ahead. We know that nothing good could ever come out of that place. Not even if we see all the young people hanging around. We know by now the place is where you find only wild boys and girls acting just like animals that have been penned up and are finally getting loose and behaving bad.

Not a place for well-behaved children like Stephie and me, children who one day will be flying to join our parents over-'n'-away and having to show that, after all, we have culture and proper behaviour instilled in us. If there was anything I liked about going for the sand, it was how I could sit on the beach and watch the waves beating against the shore, sometimes gently, other times so rough and threatening. I would sit and watch until Stephie would drape me up by telling me to stop wasting time by sitting and just gazing. I had to learn how to monitor myself so I would not stand there so fascinated by a piece of wood or dried sugar cane bobbing on the waves that I'd forget I had to hurry home and get ready for school.

Grandmother said it was a good thing when Stephie joined me, for walking all that distance so early in the morning and carrying the sand on her head was good training for her. It would make her legs, neck and arms strong and increase her endurance by making her lungs healthy, so she would be able to run faster and longer. All of this would happen if Stephie kept her mind on running, for she was not like me. Grandmother says I have mind for only one kind of sport. Every chance I get I would spend it playing bat and ball with all them "pissy" boys on the cricket field. She keeps telling me that she doesn't like me keeping company too much with them. She says that at least Stephie knows how to choose what she likes and still please her grandmother. "Running is something a body can do alone. You don't need company for that," Grand says. Playing cricket is all that I think about. She says I shouldn't think I'm fooling her or that she doesn't know I spend all my free time at school on the cricket field. When I should be studying my books, she says, I am competing with the bigger boys. She can't understand what boys and mens see in spending so much time and effort playing cricket, except that when they are together they are occupied and keeping themselves out of trouble. When playing, they are out of the way, no longer under people's feet or pulling their shirt tail. And perhaps it is for these reasons that she allows me the freedom of doing something that I really like at school.

"Good morning, Mother Lucas," a male voice calls from the side of the house.

"Who that calling to me so early this morning?" Grandmother replies.

"How yuh mean, who that calling to you? You playing you don't know me anymore." With that, a tall slim man with a small but knotty beard appears. He is wearing a black hat with a stingy brim and a big red band around it. The man mashes out his cigarette and moves toward Grandmother in a rush.

"Whuh God bless my eyesight early this morning. Is that you Desmond, Mrs. Smith own boy, Desmond?"

"How yuh mean if it is me?" The man throws his arms around Grandmother in a bear hug. Grandmother feigns as if she does not appreciate being held that close.

"When you come back, boasie?" she asks, acknowledging with the pet word that indeed she recognizes this man who is still a stranger to me.

"I come back in last night," he explains.

"Lord have mercy, it is good to set my two eyes on yuh again. Desmond Smith, you ain't look no different from when you left here all these years. Yuh looking good, good, good, like over-'n'-away agreeing wid yuh. You know whenever I see your mother, a time don't pass that I don't always ask she for you. I always asking she how you doing and she keep saying to me, 'I can't even hear a word from him. Can't hear one word from up there in North America.' Mrs. Smith real good at keeping her business to herself. For now you here standing up in front o' me this early morning."

"Yes, Mother Lucas. And not me alone. Meet Leila here. This is my wife. I marry she only two years now."

"Poor thing. She di'n't know no better than to marry sheself to you," Grandmother jokes. "Anyway, nice to meet you Mistress Smith. I hope this good-fuh-nuttin' man treating yuh good and proper like he should a proper wife."

"He's treating me okay," Leila says. "He's okay. We getting 'long fine. Nothing to complain about. He treats me and the children quite good." And she starts to giggle.

"We decided, me and Leila after we get married, that we want to live back home here. So she come down wid me. As I just say, we arrived last night, in all that rain. But this morning when the rain stopped, even before my mother could give me a biscuit to eat and a tot o' tea to drink, I say to Leila, 'Come, girl, we gotta go and say howdy to Mother Lucas, my godmother, to leh she know that I's back in the land. Didn't I say that, Leila?"

"Since I met Desmond," Leila says, "he's always been talking about this Mother Lucas person. So indeed I was always looking forward to meeting you, especially since he said that you were like a second mother to him. You and your neighbour—"

"True," Desmond interrupts. He sounds just like Grandmother when she cuts me off before I become too friendly and disrespectful to an adult by saying too much. "True, true, true. What you just said is the plainest troot."

"But your mother didn't even drop a word about any of this," Grandmother says. "She di'n't even let anybody know you coming back. Not even none o' we in the church with her."

"She di'n't even know sheself," Desmond admits. "It was like me and Leila, after we done get married, we decided to just pick weself up and come home."

"How long yuh in fuh?" Grandmother asks.

"Fuh good," Desmond says emphatically. "You like you don't understand, yuh. We come back fuh good, fuhever. This is where my navel string bury. I'm coming in out of the cold. Once we settled a bit, we sending for Leila two children too."

"But yuh know that things still tough around here, eh?" Grandmother cautions. "This independence thing isn't all sweetness and light. Still lots a young people, especially the young boys and mens, walking the street morning, noon and night and can't get a pick fuh a job. Things still hard for some types o' people, especially if you don't have the right credentials or the right connections; if you think you're too good for certain types o' work. Lots o' mens around here ain't no use because they can't find anybody to employ them and a man ain't a man unless he wukking for his daily bread. Nothing ain't change much in that regards since you yourself lef'."

"I know," Desmond admits. "But life's hard everywhere. Even over-'n'-away in the white man's country. Why you think *I* di'n't like to write back home, sending one dry letter after another?"

"And too besides you know you going against the trend around here all these long years, right?" Grandmother is laughing as if she expects Desmond at any moment to admit he is playing a joke; her laughter proves she hasn't been fooled. "You bringing a wife and children back here from over-'n'-away when all the time people 'bout here doing the very opposite? Is that what you telling me this morning?"

"True, true, Mother Lucas," Desmond confirms, and he appears to be smiling at the puzzled look on Grandmother's face. "What so strange about that?"

"I don't know," Grandmother says. "I just don't know." Pointing at me, she adds, "I can't even hear a word from this one here mother.

Been years now since she write and he's getting to be a big boy. Soon done school in a few years' time."

"Lord, Mother Lucas, if you didn't point he out sitting there round the corner 'pon the doorstep, I wouldn't have noticed he. That is your daughter, Thelma, boy?"

"The same one," Grandmother confirms.

"He always quiet so?" he asks. "Thelma mouth didn't be frightened for anybody when me and she did be growing up together 'round here."

"Man, he's as quiet as a church mouse," Grandmother says. "Boy," she speaks directly to me, "whuh you doing sitting there, no even saying good morning when you see a lady in yuh presence?"

"Morning," I say, standing and dusting the seat of my pants.

"Good morning, young man," Leila replies with a smile.

"That's right," Desmond says. "But you know what, I left here so long I won't even know how to recognize this boy, not knowing he is one o' we if I did see he passing on the road."

"Yes, my dear," Grandmother says. "He soon have to get ready, put on his uniform and catch the bus to go 'long to school. He is a high school boy. Looks like he got a little something upstairs in he head. Not a bad boy. If he keep up doing what he's doing, he should be able to find a good job around here when he's ready, but most of all, as I hoping, when his mother over-'n'-away send for him."

"I glad to hear that, 'cause from what I hear, we need people with brains in this place," Desmond says. "I was at this meeting up north when the prime minister did come through and was meeting with all the nationals at the embassy that we have up there. Fancy that, this little island playing it ha' embassy in foreign capitals of the world, just like we is people too."

"But *we's* people," Grandmother insists. "A lot changed in the way we see things in this island nowadays. A lot changed since you and this boy here mother gone to foreign land. We ain't British no more, yuh know."

"I know what you mean," Desmond says. He is talking less passionately. "That is why me and Leila here decide to come back. Especially when I hear the prime minister saying that the island could use the help of all the people born on this island and now living overseas, saying that there is now a place on the island for all the talents we keep sending abroad. And I thinking about my mother, and to tell the truth, how much I miss her all these years, and how she's getting on in age, and that I would like to be near her, and to feel I living among people just like me. That is why I come back."

"So what you'd do back here, boasie?" Grandmother asks.

"I really like the music business and all the music I see developing in these islands," he says, "and—"

"But he's thinking more about starting a real business," says his wife, sharply cutting him off and playfully slapping him on the shoulder. "Something in the health care business, if we can do that."

"But tell me, nuh," Grandmother asks, concern creeping into her voice. "You did ever run into Thelma? You know how she doing?"

Desmond looks at his wife. They appear to exchange messages in glances.

"No, Mother Lucas," Desmond says. His voice is low and he either drops his eyes or looks only at his wife as he speaks. "I sorry. I ain't see she for a long, long time now."

"I had hoped that you would be able to tell me something about she. And what 'bout Esmeralda, Mrs. King's daughter? Ever run into she either?"

"No, Mother Lucas. I don't see she either. It's a big place, yuh know. Really big, and people does live far, far, far from their one another. So it ain't that unusual for you to be living in one part o' the country, in fact, in one city, and not see another body in the same city. It ain't like down here at all and how we does live with we one another. In fact, if there is one thing the big countries over-'n'-away teach any o' we from down here is that we're all individuals first and foremost. You always put yourself first even ahead of friends and family, not like down here, yuh know, so it is okay not to stay in touch."

"Same thing with Mrs. King next door there," Grandmother says. "Can't hear a word; not a peep. And she got Stephie, Esmeralda's girl, to take care of. I don't know why when you young people go to a foreign land, why every last one o' you don't like to write back. You don't think about yuh poor mothers sitting here and watching the postman come by on his motor scooter. Every evening he comes and every evening as God sends he goes by, not stopping, not a letter, not a word. How is a mother to feel?"

"And how is Mrs. King other daughter, Dorothy?" Desmond asks as if purposely shifting the conversation.

"Dorothy, hum, I don't know much 'bout that girl," Grandmother says, the tone in her voice changing just as quickly. "Talking 'bout not keeping in touch, you probably know more better than me how *she's* doing. Didn't you and she used to be best o' friend before you lef' down here?"

"We did, but that was some time ago, eh," he says in a soft tone. And perhaps still feeling the sting of the dryness in Grandmother's voice, he asks, "I guess you don't see much of her these days, eh?"

"Well you'd know Dorothy before you left 'round here," Grandmother says. "She ain't change much, except to maybe get worse. 'Cause you know that Dorothy and that sharp tongue in her mouth. Even with her mother, Mrs. King; that Dorothy'd cuss anybody when she ready. So let she stay wherever she is 'cause nothing around here is ever right and proper for that *Dorothy*."

"I know," Desmond says. He glances quickly at his wife and shrugs his shoulders. At the same time, he puts his hand in his pocket and fishes out two bills.

"Here, Mother Lucas," he says. "Don't upset yuhself this morning. Buy something fuh yuhself. I would never lef' you out 'cause when I was a boy you did be good to me. Family. Always know where I could find a spoonful of food if I needed it. I can't ever forget that."

"Thank you, son," Grandmother says. "May God bless yuh."

"And, boy," he shouts to me, "this for you."

I take the foreign note from him. "Thank you, sir. Thank you."

"Hear that, Leila, he calling me *sir*. You would never hear that where we come from. The children down here still so mannerly and well behaved, not like the vagabonds we left behind. That is why I think the plan we have is bound to work down here."

"Thank you, Mrs. Smith," I add.

"That's okay," she responds in her foreign twang. "You sure are mannerly."

"Thank you," Grandmother beams. "I does try my best with him." Grandmother has to be happy with the way I am behaving. Otherwise I am bound to hear about it when Desmond and his wife are gone.

"And come to think of it," Desmond says, "now I know who he really is, this boy does look something like Thelma. Her features stamped pretty good on him."

"You think so?" Grandmother asks while I shuffle my feet self-consciously.

"Well, I should be pushing off," Desmond says. "It is really nice to see yuh."

"I hope you making the right decision," Grandmother says, sounding as if she has her own doubts. "You know bringing back a wife and children in these tough times when most people still looking to get out and—"

"I know it is the right thing to do. Ain't we, darling?"

The new Mrs. Smith smiles again. Desmond hugs Grandmother. Slowly he retreats along the path from the backyard to the side of the house and then onto the road. I go into the corner with the rocks and pebbles and pour some water from the tall can into the basin and begin bathing in preparation for school. Grandmother turns her attention to making our breakfast of boiled chocolate with coconut milk and fried bakes. Soon I hear her from inside the house, singing one of the hymns from church. *Bread of Heaven, Bread of Heaven, Feed me 'til I want no more, Feeeed me*"—her voice when it hits that note sounds as if it intends to raise the roof—"*'Ti-il I waaant no mooore*. Thank you, Jesus."

"See," Grandmother says as I come through the back door and begin wiping my feet on the crocus bag. She holds the foreign banknote by the thumb and fourth finger of each hand so that it stretches out in front of her. "Manna from Heaven. Praise God." Grandmother gently folds the note and places it in her pocket. "Just like I keep telling yuh: the wondrous works of prayer. If God don't bring yuh an answer himself, he does find somebody to send to do his works. My God always answers prayers, just as I keep telling you. He always sending a godfather or a godmother, 'cause that is the way we live around here. Otherwise how are we going to be taking care of the young children if everybody that can doesn't just pitch in and help out, family or no family ties? Otherwise what's the use of all this talk about independence?" Grandmother starts singing again, her voice strong, crisp and clear. But she pauses as if speaking to her own doubts. "Even so, I holding on in hope about you and your mother. And for Stephie and her mother too. Better must come. Now eat this little morsel here and then go and dress yourself for school. Don't keep Stephie waiting." I cannot wait to get to school and have it all over with, so that in short order I will be back home, knock out any homework I have and ready to go over to Mr. Lashley and watch television.

Chapter Three

Grandmother and I have a ritual we go through every Monday morning during the school term. It is the last thing we do together in the morning and it has to come after breakfast. I stand in front of her as she sits on the bench by the back door. This is one of her favourite spots. It is where she says she likes to think. The position by the door allows her to sit with the bottom of her dress draped between her legs. The soft rays and warm early-morning breeze create the conditions just right for her to think and to make plans for the day. And for her to look at my face and with a thumb wipe away any speck of grease by my mouth. Only then does she send me on, knowing that Stephie is waiting for me in front of Mrs. King's house. We walk to the bus stop together just as we have done for so many years now.

This morning, Grandmother places the tot on the bench beside her, for there is no hint today will be any different. The trademark KLIM is still on the tin, along with some of the original brown paint, even though the tin has long given up its original contents of dried milk powder. Darnley, the blacksmith, put a tin handle on the can, but with use, the bottom stud has come loose. Grandmother has to hold the tot by its bottom. Still, it is one of Grandmother's favourite utensils: she would not give it up. She uses it for drinking water, mauby, sorrel, ginger beer, her morning and evening cocoa-tea, coffee and occasionally, especially on Sundays, the treat she makes by mixing coconut water, a cola drink from Enid's shop and evaporated milk. As I approach her for the mandatory examination, I notice the steam still escaping from the tot beside her. She nibbles on a dry Eclipse soda biscuit.

"Look at you as you get ready to go 'long to high school," she says. I smile to myself and suppress the desire to respond to her. I have come to realize this is how Grandmother talks. Even though she might ask a question, she does not expect an answer. "Just look at you. Sharp as a tack this bless'ed morning. Doesn't that make you feel *gooood*? Only God knows how much I wish you' mother could see you now. She would be too please, 'cause she's one person that does love dressing up. Always in the latest fashion, and you too even though she did spend only a few months with you, dressing you up like some dolly. I wouldn't be surprise at all if that isn't what she is spending all her good time over-'n'-away doing right now. Man, she would be so proud to see you stepping out in style. Hair greased and brushed, with the part to the side of yuh head, uniform cleaned and ironed, yuh two shoes shining like ram goat stones, yuh belly full."

She gently holds my chin and tilts it to get a better view of my head, particularly my hair and how I comb and brush it. As she talks, she runs her hand behind my ears, rubbing away some of the excess Vaseline on my neck. Every three weeks, Grandmother makes sure I go to Mr. Evans's house, where all the old men meet and talk. He cuts my hair in the shaded side of his house or under the hog plum tree. Once I returned without a part cut in my hair. Grandmother made me return with instructions that Mr. Evans should know better. Neither Mr. Evans nor I ever made the mistake again. Every morning I apply Vaseline and water and brush my hair. This way I stand out in school. All the other boys are sporting afros, growing their hair in big balls, seeing whose is the biggest. I too want to grow mine but Grandmother will have none of it. I try to tell her that if I must cut my hair, it should be done by one of the younger men who are up on the latest styles. But Grandmother explains that I should not be running after every fad and fashion. "In my day, a young gentleman kept his hair short and tidy rather than looking too rebellious like one o' them vagabonds and criminals that never comb let alone cut their hair, so that the hair is all matted down with dirt and grease. Plus I gotta tell you one more thing if you please: long hair is for women. The Bible tells we that a woman's hair is her beauty. It don't say anything about the hair of a man."

With the inspection over, she reaches into her pocket and gives me my lunch money for bottle drinks for five days. "Now don't you go now and lose what I giving you," she warns. "'Cause if you're ever get so foolish or careless as to lose it, you done bust luck, and for the whole week at that. Use that lunch money I give you to buy some-thing proper, something nutritious, you hear me." I nod my head.

"So what you plan to do with the little thing you got this morn-ing?" she asks, bringing an unexpected change to the ritual. Normally she would end by telling me to remember to come straight back home when school let out, that I am not to hesitate or tarry with people who would only lead me astray and into trouble. The shift throws me off. I think for a moment, for I am not sure what her response will be to any plans I may have. Grandmother might be thinking of asking to *borrow* my foreign money, only to eventually say she is tired of me harping and carrying on about wanting back the *few cents she's been holding for me*, since, she would say, in any case, she had long paid me back with sweets and fruits and even lunch money. Slowly I say, "I was thinking that I will put it toward the pair o' boots I need for the cricket team tryouts. Mr. Jones, the sports master, say all o' we must start wearing full cricket gear."

"Still, how will you make up the rest o' money for the boots?"

"I'll try and save, especially if anybody gives me any money at Christmastime," I say. "I was thinking I have to go and look for my father and see if he can help me out."

"Don't bother with *he*," Grandmother says, waving her hand as if to shoo away one of the flies. "He's as old and doltish as me. I don't know why you keep pining so after that good-fuh-nothing father of you' own. Leave him in God's hand. He done do his damage when he did get you. What I hope is that perhaps your mother will send you something," Grandmother says, pausing to swirl the coffee to dissolve the sugar in the bottom of the tot and then to take a sip. "That is who you should look to for help and not to that man who is your father in name only, 'cause that is the way things work 'round here, a man like your father put himself in some way with some young girl and then run off, and you may as well get used to them ways as soon as possible. You is your mother responsibility and next to she you is mine. If we hear from your mother, we might even be able to write she back and ask she to buy and send for you some of the things you want for cricket, but I don't know."

I do not answer because I do not like it when Grandmother turns to talking about my mother, for how can I not feel I am always a burden? This is when she talks about how my mother went overseas to work as a domestic and to go back to school, with the hopes of going all the way to university. The last Grandmother heard was that after a string of jobs for various rich-people families, my mother decided to become a nurse. She reported she was starting out as an assistant in a hospital with a French name and hopefully working her way to becoming a registered nurse. That was about three years ago, before I went to the new school and started needing a uniform, books, bus fare to and from the city and lunch money. How can I not give her the money when she asks to *borrow* it? Still, I cannot believe my run of good luck when it comes to cricket. Grandmother is even encouraging me to take it up. That is a switch. It is almost as if she wants me to occupy myself with other things that men do rather than getting in the way of she, Mrs. King and now Stephie.

"Anyway God will provide," Grandmother says. "In any case, I was thinking I should give this to you." She takes the foreign note from her pocket. I try to hide my surprise, remembering Grandmother's warning that I should never be too quick to show my feelings. Otherwise people would know your weaknesses and know where to hurt you. "You can put this bill with the one he gave you. When you go by the bank to exchange them, put it all together and use the money to help with the cricket boots. 'Cause we have to remember, apart from the cricket boots, you still need a white shirt and white pants. If money left over from the boots, it can help with the shirt and the pants."

"But this was a gift to you," I say, "for you to buy something for yourself."

"I know, but I was sitting thinking," Grandmother says with a slight smile. "And I keep thinking it would really make my heart glad if I used what God sends to bless others. *Actually*, I was thinking of putting it in the collection box at church. But when I remembered you said you wanted cricket boots, I changed my mind."

"Thanks, Grandmother," I say.

"Now run along before you're late for the bus."

She waves and lifts the tot to her lips. I must hurry so as not to keep Stephie waiting. Plus I can't wait to tell her that from the way things opened this morning, I have no doubt how great a day it will be for me, a day I foresee ending with me in front of Mr. Lashley's TV.

I am the last person to squeeze onto the bus. The driver stares at me crossly as he closes the door for the final time. As if to make the point the door will not be reopened, the conductress in her blue and white uniform leans back against the door as if she is barring it from those inside as well as those on the outside. Sucking on his teeth in disgust, the driver pushes his hat to the back of his head, giving himself an unobstructed view of the way ahead now that he does not have to worry about making frequent stops. He changes gear and steps heavily on the accelerator. With a sudden jerk that causes most of us to rock as one, the bus moves off toward its final destination. Around me, I smell the early sweat of cramped bodies and of powders and perfumes, even though all the windows are open, as well as a hatch in the roof. I put my book bag between my feet and hold on to the chrome-plated handle that runs the length of the bus.

An hour later, the driver reopens the front and middle doors to let us off into the fresh air of the main bus stand in the city. As usual, I am happy to escape because of the nausea that seems to hit me every morning on the bus. But I know I am lucky. The driver left scores of schoolchildren at bus stops along the route. Many students now know this trick: the best chance of getting a place on the bus going into town is to first take a short trip in the opposite direction. They pay the extra fare for the ride to the end of the route, often having to stand all the way, in order to secure a spot on the trip back down to town. Some of the bigger girls have men-friends who are much older than them and have cars, and who drop them off at school every morning and pick them up after school. These girls dress up and act more mature, even in the way they wear their school uniform. But only the few girls who are able to hang out with these men-friends late at night and in the dance halls on weekends get this special treatment. Everybody knows they are already *full* women except they are still in school. Those without men-friends and who cannot afford to pay extra have to wait another hour or so for the overcrowded bus that passes them to make the round trip and collect them when the first rush is gone. Most certainly they arrive at school late. This is not good. They have another "late" placed on their attendance record and on the reports students receive at the end of term. For good measure, most of them get a flogging from the headmaster.

This morning I haven't seen Stephie. As I walk the short distance from the bus stand to school, I keep an eye out for her, hoping she decided to come to school early. I don't like it when the headmaster flogs girls. They cry all day—not like the boys who have to show that the headmaster can never hit them hard enough to make them cry. And then I remember and my heart feels good: Stephie must have left early to attend the special coaching the games master is now holding for the cross-country race. Part of the training is to help students build up their endurance by running the actual route of the contest every school morning. This is the first morning of real practice.

Stephie, I think to myself, is really taking this thing seriously: training so hard first thing in the morning and last thing at night. Perhaps I will see her just before the morning assembly and she'll tell me how the training went. That is when we will exchange the textbooks. She takes from me the books I will not be using before the luncheon break and gives me the ones I need for my morning classes. Luckily we are both in third form and doing the same subjects but are not in the same class. We have been sharing textbooks for almost three years. Pooling our scarce resources is the only way Grandmother and Mrs. King can afford the books we need.

I do not see Stephie at assembly. And I do not, therefore, get the textbook for French class. Neither do I have the texts for physical geography and history. My response when asked by each teacher why I don't have them is to say that I forgot the books at home in the morning rush or that I lent them to another student. The teachers are not forgiving. By lunchtime, I have received three detentions. Plus each teacher is demanding that I write "I must remember to bring my books to school" two hundred times during those detentions. I cannot let Grandmother know about the lines. She would say what a waste of good exercise book paper that costs her so much money. But I will have to tell her eventually, for the exercise books will now write out faster than we had expected. If I do not have exercise books to write in, there will be more detentions and lines, and I will be caught in a real bind. I assume Stephie is in the same trouble as me, having to waste good writing paper and getting Mrs. King angry at her and the teachers. I can't understand why she would do this to us.

The drive back home is no more pleasant than the rest of the school day. It might be better that she is not here with me, for I am vexed and I would be asking her why she got me into trouble, and we would probably just argue. On top of this, having missed the bus for schoolchildren only, I had to squeeze into this one with the hawkers with their heavy baskets and trays after a day of selling around the bus stand. I am glad I do not have to travel so early in the morning with them. In the baskets covered with bleached white flour bags are the nuts, candies and assortment of fruits the hawkers will repackage overnight so as to be ready for the return trip on the first bus to town. Some of them and their baskets take up a seat that normally holds two or three people. Luckily I was early enough into the bus to get a seat, but maybe because I am hungry or my hand still cramps from writing all those lines, the drive home seems extremely long. The passengers are too noisy and seem to be talking about everything under the sun and laughing a lot, as if they know one another personally. When Stephie and me find ourselves in this situation together, we usually laugh at the people around us and at what they are saying, especially when they start arguing about politics or cricket. But I am in no mood to laugh anyway.

Finally, we are out of the city and into the suburbs. The driver is grinding the gears as if trying to make up time. One of the women reaches overhead and pulls the chord, setting off a loud ringing. "Let me off here, skipper," the woman says. The driver gears down. "'Cause all the same I don't know why you have to be driving at such a breakneck speed for," she says. "And when you got schoolchildren in the bus too." I notice her looking at me, and I look around and see one girl who might still be in school, but she is not in a school uniform.

The bus comes to a stop and those on the outside begin to gather up their possessions from the ground. The door flies open and the woman that pulled the chord drags her heavy basket to the entrance. She steps outside and says to one of those waiting to get on, "You young fellows there, give me a hand here with my few tacklings here, to lift the big-able basket on my head." Meanwhile, she takes a long piece of cloth, rolls it like a rope and wraps it around the extended thumb and little finger of one hand to form an oblong ball with flattened sides. She places this pad on her head and braces her neck. One man standing outside helps another inside to lift the basket through the door and place it on the woman's head. She balances the basket and then secures the empty board tray under an arm.

"Thank you," the woman says to the men. "God bless yuh." Calling back into the bus, she says, "Good night, Mavis and Clorine. See yuh all bright and early on the first bus going back into town in the morning if God spare life." Only then does she allow the incoming passengers to get on the bus. She steps off, head erect and steady. For the rest of her walk, she won't even have to touch that basket to keep it balanced on her head.

At almost every stop, this same scene repeats itself. Those women who are more fortunate get the assistance of a relative or two waiting for the bus's arrival to help carry the baskets and bags. That's what I do when Grandmother goes into town on Saturdays. I time her arrival at the bus stop in the afternoon and am sure to be on hand to help her carry her baskets back home. Grandmother buys enough to resell to people in our area only once a week. She does not sell in the city, not like these women who make a living in the city every working day. Grandmother says that you can find some of these same women with their loud behaviour in one dance hall or the other every Saturday night. Like Grandmother, they too are often the only working adult in their homes. There is no man in the house. On this evening, most of the women walking away from the bus are carrying their load alone.

The distance between the stops is getting longer, and we are back in the country. I am not in a good mood when I walk through the door and fling my bag on the floor. I am about to call to Grandmother and complain about what a wretched day it has been for me, and to tell her it was all because of Stephie, when I notice Grandmother talking in the backyard.

"Good evening, Grandmother, and good evening, Mrs. King," I call from a distance so they don't think I'm creeping up on them. I do not want Grandmother to accuse me of listening to what does not concern me or trying to stick my nose in big people business. And because Mrs. King is here, I dare not let on about how I feel about Stephie and all the trouble she put me in. There are some things I am permitted to discuss with Grandmother only. Even though Mrs. King is as close as family, I still have to be respectful. I still cannot fly past my nest.

"Why yuh so late this evening?" Grandmother asks.

"I dunno," I lie, because of Mrs. King's presence.

"Good evening, young man," Mrs. King says. She then turns back to Grandmother and says, "I had to say it is true that it is better to be born lucky than rich. Which o' we won't thank the Lord for sending a real good godfather for any o' these two children we have here?"

"But just look at that, nuh, girl," Grandmother says with a tone of approval. "We can never tell when we can expect a little goodness. I was only this morning telling that little boy there about how children like he and Stephie could do well with a godfather, and look what you are now telling me. God is really a good God."

"For true," Mrs. King says. "And that is not all. Lashie brought back quite a number of nice, nice dresses for her. So many T-shirts and bodices, pants and undies too. Shoes and even a gold chain to wear around she neck. I had to say that he must have spent a pretty penny on her. But when I tell him that, he just say that we wasn't to mind that, that he was blessed to be able to go up north and work on the contract every season and to make good, good money, and that every man 'round here wasn't that lucky to get the chances that he got."

Mrs. King seems so happy and enthusiastic, clapping her hands in elation. I walk back into the house but can still hear what they are discussing, though they seem not to care. They continue to talk loudly, not behind their hands, whispering to stop their voices from carrying.

"Lashie said he felt blessed to be able to buy all these things for my Steph'nie," Mrs. King says, "and that that was what he was thinking when he was getting ready to come back home, that what he was doing was the least he could do knowing I does be looking after his house when he's away, especially since he ain't so sure he wants his own mother to keep coming around the place and making noise with people. So that with me and now Stephie looking after his house when he's away, when he comes back down, the house ain't smelling musty from being shut up all the time. Too besides, he says, every man done know a house ain't a real house far less a home if there isn't a woman in it, no matter how young she is, and she will learn and in a short time she'd be looking after the house when he is out trying to make a few cents when the time comes, and that is the way he thinks things always did be on this little islan' here. And besides he said as a man he is different from other men."

"I glad he's grateful for what you are doing," Grandmother says. "I glad he finally decide to act like a big man and to settle down and to stop fighting the ways of the world. Faith, it is time he just be natural like everybody else."

"And one of the things he bring back 'specially for Stephie is one big radio that you can also play records on like all the records the boys and girls 'round here trying their hand at," Mrs. King continues. "When I first did see it, I did think it was a grip or a valise or something so. Or one of those things you does see the lawyers down by the courthouse carrying 'bout their papers and briefs in. The thing is really big fuh true and loud, loud, loud. The thing holding six o' them big-able batteries that we can get from Enid shop, or it could work off 'lectricity if I decide to put it in the house, if I can see my way to afford it. And Steph'nie say when she turn it on over at his house, with the electricity, my dear, the radio can pick up stations from here and the next place, from all over the world. Last night, she tell me she was up all hours of the night 'cause the pain wouldn't let she sleep and she say she was listenin' to some radio station from all the way in South Africa, talking 'bout now the Englishmens turn against them South Africans so they can't play cricket wid the rest o' the world no more. Things she learning 'bout at school. She say she listen 'til the pain went away and she dropped off to sleep."

"What causing she not to sleep?" Grandmother asks, seriousness in her voice.

"How would I know, nuh?" Mrs. King says. "You know these young people of today. They quick to bawl out at the first little juck or pain they get. Especially the girls o' today. They ain't like me or you when we was them age. If they had to take pain the way we did, I don't know what they would do. That is why she didn't go to school today. Why I really gotta try my best and really toughen she up if she is to become a proper woman and know her way in the world."

"Not that time of the month for she, nuh?" Grandmother asks.

"No. No. Nothing so. Just she saying she getting these pains all of a sudden so. But she will get over them soon. Might be some infection or the other. I gave her some warm ginger tea, just in case it is gas cutting her belly, and I tell she not to go to school today if she ain't feeling too well. But I am a little concerned even at this age she is still a little too softie, softie. I won't want to know she is the kind to grow up in the world and let some man make a fool o' she and to have his way with she. That won't be right, so she gotta start getting tough real soon. Still, I talked to Lashie and he says I should take her to his doctor and that he might give she some tablets to take, but he don't think it is anything much to worry about."

"Still, it is good Lashie looking out for her," Grandmother says. "I always did know she was a lucky chile. And you know who was the first to say that? My own Thelma. You know she and Esmeralda was best o' friends, not like she and Dorothy who couldn't get along at all. And when your Esmeralda find sheself in that way I did know, if we all weren't careful enough, it was going to be only a matter of time for Thelma and then, *bram so*, just like that, she come home and tell me she pregnant too. Everything in life, like they planned together. The result is that Stephie did come into this world six months ahead o' Christopher, and I remember Thelma, she own self just starting to show, coming home from the baby-lea and saying, 'Ma, that is one purty girl fuh so Esmeralda got there. She sweet fuh so.' She tell me, 'I took one look at that infant laying down there and not crying atall and I done tell Esmeralda she is going to have to be careful, careful, careful, for that little girl gine break a lot of men's hearts when she grow up.' *Hehehehheh.* Them is the said same exact words she did say to me. And, despite what you're saying, I think it is still true."

"Yeah," Mrs. King says. "Them two children as babies did be like a twin. The two o' them sleeping in the same bed, wearing the same clothes and eating the same food. Remember how he get christened at the parish church in the same outfit as Steph'nie?"

"Of course, I do," Grandmother confirms. "Esmeralda was his godmother too, the same way Thelma is for Stephie. And remember how the two o' them did use to laugh and make sport with one another, saying when the two children grow up, Christopher Diego belongs to Stephanie Ariand and the two o' them were destined to be one."

"Even so, having a child on their own wasn't what we wanted for them two girls still so young," Mrs. King says.

"Still, once you look at the young infants, them looking so innocent, how can you remain angry with them girls?" Grandmother says. "That's why you and me still trying to help out by letting them go overseas to make something of themselves and without burdening themselves with a child right away."

"So true," Mrs. King says. "But now, we don't know where on

God's good earth to find them two girls o' we own." The joy and laughter have slipped from her voice. "Something keeps telling me the two o' them still together, they still looking out for one another," she says slowly. "'Cause the two o' them know how to survive in any place different from down here, even in a man's world."

"If *they's* still alive," Grandmother says, dropping her voice.

"Lord, God, Peggy. Don't say that," Mrs. King exclaims as if to drown out Grandmother's voice. "No. No. NO. Don't even think, far less mouth, them things."

"Yes, you right," Grandmother says. "Lord forgive me," she quickly adds, asking pardon for taking the Lord's name in vain in the way, she always insists, I do. "But not knowing, sometimes all kind o' strange thoughts come into yuh head. Suppose they find themselves with a strange man, one that must always have his way or nothing, and the two o' them living in a strange land, different from down here. Suppose that is the case; that they got husbands or boyfriends that won't let them be, won't even let them write the two o' we, or to send and ask about their children. We're only human. It is so hard not to know about them."

"But God does answer prayer," Mrs. King says, the words gushing out, "for He didn't have to speak to Lashie heart when he was up there and get him to buy all them things fuh Stephie and to get him to understand the ways of the world and what a man is supposed to do for the good o' heself and for others too. He ain't family to she, so he di'n't have to spend his money on her. But he did and I have to be thankful. Plus Lashie keep telling me he is a responsible man, that he won't be doing anything too drastic too soon since he have a few good years still on the program, for he done know what he is doing and that he won't let me down."

"Praise the Lord," Grandmother says. "And He didn't have to send along Desmond this morning with that little tra-la that I could put toward the cricket boots."

"So," Mrs. King resumes speaking in her normal voice, "Lashie say Stephie can come and visit the house any time and if she want to watch the television, she just gotta come over."

"And what Stephie ha' to say about all this niceness?" Grandmother asks.

"What you expect, nuh?" Mrs. King says. "After all, she might be big for her age and fulling out in she body, but inside she is still a chile. So she behaving just like a chile on Christmas mornin'."

"Good fuh she," Grandmother says.

"I going over now and light the lamp 'cause I think she already over there taking her place in front of that TV," Mrs. King says. "I just hope she remember tomorrow is a school day. So, I gone for now, darling love."

I decide this is the time to make my move. Stephie is already over at Mr. Lashley's, and by going there I will get a chance to ask if she is now becoming like some other girls we know. I will ask her straight up if it is because she's having all these things happening in her life that she thinks she is now so big she can miss school, and without even putting me on my guard. I will remind her them girls she's now patterning herself after soon find themselves having to miss school full-time when they find themselves in the way and that she better be careful. I cannot wait to have it out with her. Plus there is the television. I am almost through the door when I hear: "Ah hi, hi, hi, *hi*." Grandmother clears her throat in the usual menacing way. "And *where* you *think* you going now, *mister* man?" I freeze in my step, one foot about to cross the threshold of the house into the yard. I had expected something like this. But still my heart drop.

"I planning to go and watch TV," I say.

"Look, boy, sit your backside down in this house here, yuh hear," Grandmother says as harshly as I have ever heard her. "What the France you think this is? Next you'd be running around out there with all them wild boys like they don't got no owner when you could be doing something useful for yourself."

"But everybody—" I start a reply, the one I had been playing out in my head all day in anticipation of this moment.

"Everybody *what*?" Grandmother cuts me off. "You ain't *everybody*. 'Cause the next thing I gine know is that I'll be finding you down there at that dance hall all hours o' the night. No. No. Not you. No, you sit your behind down in here and study your books for school."

"But that is all they does be talking about at school," I try. "Even the teachers. They saying we should be watching the news on TV and on the *radio*"—I drop in that word to remind her of what Mrs. King had said so approvingly—"to learn what is happening on this island and in the rest of the world."

"And do they tell you that when you are in this piece o' house we have here I can keep an eye on you? I can know you're safe?" Grandmother says. "That way nobody can unfair you and take advantage of you just because you have me alone to protect you. No, you stay in this little shack here and keep yourself out of trouble. No TV for you."

I pull the chair up to the window and look out at the boys assembling at Mr. Lashley's house. And then I see Stephie moving in the house and a thought strikes me.

"But Stephie's over there," I explain, pointing, "and Mrs. King ain't stopping she."

"What Mrs. King does do in her house is she own business," Grandmother says. "What we does do over here is *mine*. And too besides whatever Stephie doing or not doing these days in Mrs. King house or over there at Mr. Lashley ain't none o' your business. You hear me?"

"Yes, Grandmother," I say, dropping my voice. I have no more arguments. So it is back to these stupid books.

"Good," she says, but she must see the dejection on my face. "You stay right there with your books for school. It is better for you that way. Otherwise you can come along with me to church this blessed night. I can keep an eye on you there. Do you want that?"

"No, Grandmother," I answer quickly. Church would be too boring. Plus everybody knows that church during the week is only for children in houses so strict and cut off from the rest of the world they can't do anything else.

Grandmother steps out into the night, leaving me at the window to watch her walk down the road and the boys swarming to the green-ish blue light in Mr. Lashley's house just like the bats and beetles to Grandmother's lamp. I will now have to wait until tomorrow to find out from Stephie how she feels about what is really going on with her these days and why nobody, not even she, telling me anything.

Stephie does not attend school the next day. Once again, I find myself in detention and getting home with the sun setting. Stephie does not go to school for the entire week. By mid-week I have written so many lines in my exercise books, Grandmother has to buy me another four books. I cannot even get close to Stephie to talk to her. So I am having this growing feeling of worry in my stomach. I've seen her only in the distance, such as when she crossed the road to Mr. Lashley's house every evening, pushing past the boys assembled outside. They gath-ered as soon as the television came on at 5:30 p.m. and stayed until the first strains of the national anthem and the announcer saying it was the end of programming and good night. No girls came to watch the television, or those that came at first quickly stopped or would stay for only an hour or so. Stephie alone was allowed to enter the house and to pull up a chair. All the others had to watch through the windows and the door to the front house. Some climbed the ackee tree by the side of the house to get a better view, even if they could not always hear the dialogue. When Mr. Lashley closed his windows and doors and said it was time for the children to go home and go to bed, some of them remained behind, peering through the flaps to the windows and doors and through the cracks and the knot holes in the side of the house. And they stayed even if it rained and chilled the air.

Only Stephie was free to stay inside the house until the television went off the air. She was the only one of our age to be in the house when the men from the area came over to drink the Beefeater gin, vodka and the Johnnie Walker whisky Mr. Lashley brought back from over-'n'-away. They would be eating the ham, the smoked meats, the tinned sardines, piltchers and salmon Mr. Lashley had brought home. I would stay at home and hear the men talking loudly and arguing as they relished the respite from drinking the locally made rum and in quantities they could usually only afford on Saturday nights when they got paid and took over the rum shop until early morning. Through the window, I would see Stephie looking at the television, or getting up to close the windows and doors when it started to rain, or opening them when she wanted to let some air in or even to give the boys on the outside a clear view.

Only me, of all the boys, did not watch the television. Instead I had my homework to do, especially all those big words the games master, Mr. Jones, is forcing us to learn to spell in his English composition class, before getting to bed at what Grandmother called a respectable time. Not only must we learn how to spell the big words, but we must learn how to slip them into regular conversation to show we are maturing and learning how to use proper words the proper way, as befitting the young people of an independent nation. This week, I was perhaps the only person still at school who did not know about the Cartwrights on *Bonanza,* about Eliot Ness and *The Untouchables* and *The Fugitive,* about anything, for that matter, that had to do with television.

When Stephie is not over at Mr. Lashley's, I hear her singing at the top of her voice in Mrs. King's house. But the songs are different now and I couldn't join in even if I wanted to. They are not the hymns from church or that we must learn at school for morning prayers and special occasions. Neither are they any of the old-time music we've heard the old people singing nor any of the banja music, which Grandmother and Mrs. King call the special calypsos with all their slackness, the ones they say are more suited to the dance halls and for foul-mouthed children. As Christians, they would not have us singing such music in their houses. The songs Stephie is singing now along to the radio Mr. Lashley brought back for her are strange to me.

This is the longest time Stephie and I have ever gone without talking. By Wednesday evening the following week, Mrs. King brings over all the textbooks in Stephie's possession and says Stephie won't be going to school for a few more days. I don't understand. It's not like Stephie to not share with me what is going on with her. I keep telling myself she is okay, that somehow Stephie always manages to take care of herself.

Chapter Four

O nly now that Stephie is not around do I realize how much I depended on her. Saturday I keep hoping she will help ease the pressure on me by showing up ready to do her share of the chores we have in common, but to no avail. Stephie remains in the bedroom, listening to her radio, and does not even do her early morning chore of sweeping the house and preparing the utensils in the kitchen while I wash down the pigpen with the water from a big tank next to the pen.

During the week, I noticed that all of a sudden she had stopped singing—something I could never have imagined happening until it did, *bram*, just so, without warning. As if she was really starting to believe all this talk about how she is now too big for certain behaviour. But being big does not stop Grandmother and Mrs. King from singing or, in fairness, me from having the same work cut out for me every Saturday. When it rains, the tank collects the overflow running off Mrs. King's house, but most times I have to fill it with water from the standpipe close to the bus stop. On Friday night, surprisingly, the task of filling the tank and preparing Mrs. King's kitchen for the next day fell solely to me. Nobody told me why. Stephie just didn't show up to join me in marching to and fro along the road with the heavy bucket on my head. The same was true for the preparations. All the ground provision and the rest of the food had to be washed and stored away in the kitchen before bed for the weekend business Grandmother and Mrs. King carry on together. Me alone was left to deal with the changing circumstances. And Stephie not even bothering to tell me anything. Just playing her music loud, loud.

As I was bringing the water, the boys from just about every point in the village were already assembling at Mr. Lashley's house. I was soaked from head to foot by the water splashing from the bucket with each step I took. I did not feel any better when I noticed, through Mr. Lashley's front window, Stephie there drawing up *sheself* in front of the television and laughing out loud, loud, loud at all the jokes and fight scenes. The shouts of *"Aie, aie, aie!"* from the gathered group followed me to and from the standpipe. These were the sounds of the over-happy children shouting when someone landed a cuff, or when there was a shoot-out scene, sounds that only taunted me.

I made sure not to let Grandmother or Mrs. King hear me grumbling, for they might have said I was just jealous of Stephie's good fortune. Too many times they have told me that a heavy heart makes heavy work and that I must learn to accept my lot in life without grumbling. Grandmother thinks that none was ever more vain than all those young men crowding up Mr. Lashley's front house windows just to stare at a TV when they should be out helping their mothers and families doing housework, studying their school books or reading the Bible. Of late, whenever I ask them anything, Grandmother and Mrs. King simply respond that I am a boy and not yet ready to understand certain things of the world.

Now, on a Saturday, the busiest day of the week for our two houses, and after everybody should have had a good sleep, Stephie is again not on hand to help out. I have to be doing her work as well as mine, which only makes me more cross. But I know I must keep how angry I am feeling to myself. Grandmother, I believe, would want it that way; she would approve of how I am adapting to the circumstances. Otherwise she would tell me I am not learning fast enough how to keep my feelings bottled up in me.

My day began early, as is usually the case on Saturday mornings—at least in that regard nothing had changed. Life is just one routine after another, although, obviously, not for Stephie anymore. Saturday's routine begins with the sound of Grandmother's voice, which wakes me up. For a little while now, I have been having my own personal issue to deal with—if only privately. I have been dreaming during the night and then waking with convulsions and spasms around my back and waist to find myself lying there feeling all that wetness on my belly and legs, warm and then growing cold and sticky. I have to get up and quietly clean myself off to prevent Grandmother from knowing. This morning I felt about me and relaxed as I discovered nothing this time. I could hear Grandmother, who was up, as she would say, before foreday morning, preparing for her trip to town. She had already fed the turkeys and chickens in the backyard, cleaned up part of the yard and packed the bamboo-plaited basket for the trip. Before leaving, she called out, as usual, in a strong, clear voice to Mrs. King next door. It was this calling that awoke me.

"Just shouting yuh, good mornin'," she hollered through the back door when Mrs. King responded to her first call of "You up yet?"

"Yes, long time now. You know what day this is," the reply came back. It is the same conversation almost word for word they have every Saturday morning. "Just the same, I here holding on in the name of the Lord."

"Okay then," Grandmother said. "See yuh when I get back. This boy in here should be up soon doing what he know he gotta do every Sat'dee. Don't forget to be strict with him if you feel you gotta be." I rolled over and yawned, telling myself a few minutes more and then I'd be up.

"Okay. I'll keep my eye on him fuh yuh," Mrs. King said. "Everything should be all right as usual. He's a good boy and you know that." I told myself to sit up so I would not fall back to sleep, making Mrs. King call and wake me, and then report the whole incident to Grandmother when she got back home.

Giving me instructions up to the last moment, even as she was stepping through the door, Grandmother disappeared into the half darkness. For a brief while, I heard her shoes on the stones and gravel between the two houses. Then the silence returned. I always felt lonely when Grandmother was not in the house. It was almost as if the house was too big for me alone. The wind made everything creak. And I heard the blinds flapping in the wind at the window. There were always sounds that I had never heard before, as if the house was deliberately springing new things on me.

Grandmother said it was the ancestors' way of talking to me and that I could only feel them in the spirit. That was why, she said, I should always remember to leave a little of what I eat or drink for them, no matter the amount I receive, for these ancestors make themselves known to me in a special way, which perhaps only I know about. She said these ancestors seem only to speak to me when I am inside the house, and that if I do not want them bothering me, I should keep myself busy outside in the open air most of the time. She laughed and said perhaps that was why you always found all the mens of the area walking up and down the streets, walking from pillar to post for the whole long day and at nighttime too, never feeling comfortable in a house for too long. She said these mens seem to only want to be in the house when it is time to eat and to sleep. A house for them is only a place to rest their heads at night. Otherwise these mens of the village are always congregating together in the rum shop or, when they run out of money, standing underneath the street lamp in front of the shop at night, or gathering under some tree or at the side of the road during the day. They are not, she said, like the ummens, who most likely do not mind the spirits talking to them. Even Mr. Lashley, she said of late, was coming to fully understand he can't make anything of a house without a woman in it. Woman and house go together.

I rolled over on my side and sat up on the floor. Truthfully, I do not like Saturday mornings. They come with too much work. Saturdays keep us going non-stop, doing the same things over and over until we crash back into bed with exhaustion. Not like Sunday mornings. As I looked around me, trying to remember where I had placed my clothes the night before, I recalled what Grandmother always says about welcoming the challenge and opportunities of a brand new day that is like none other before or that will come again.

When Grandmother is home on weekday mornings, she sings at the top of her voice, *"Morning has broken, like the first morning,"* as I lethargically go about my chores in the backyard. As I come near her, she breaks off singing to explain that we should always begin the day by thanking God for his goodness, even when we are not deserving of his tender mercies. The biggest mercy is to be at the beginning of something new once again. That is what is important: that God is giving us another chance to shape anew, to change our behaviour to reflect a break with the previous day. Eventually, she and Mrs. King would be singing together, Stephie and sometimes me joining in this big-people custom.

I began to say the Lord's Prayer silently, and then I improvised and thanked God for a good night's sleep and for bringing me through the darkness; I asked him to give me strength and to keep me strong so that I would be able to do the things necessary for me to do to be happy. I felt like I was acting by rote, and half-heartedly at that, for even though Grandmother was not around, I felt her presence and her eyes watching me.

That I should take the initiative and not wait until someone called to me to do what I knew I had to do was another thing Grandmother was always drumming into my head. Doing so would be one way of showing I am really becoming a man and that I am grateful for all she has sacrificed for me. I should just want to do the things that I know are right—that is the kind of man she is hoping to make of me.

I should always act, I have come to realize, as if I know what it means to be mature and to be free, without waiting for anyone to school me or to stand guard over me, telling me all the time what is right and wrong. Grandmother reminds me that at thirteen, I am a big boy, at least in size if not always in ways. My actions as well as my thoughts are what should separate me from the rest of the boys, even if I still have the desire to play with them. She tells me I must be careful with my time, and that even if I have my heart set on joining them standing under the open sky, exposing myself to the nighttime elements—what Grandmother calls "bottling dew"—or spending every night simply watching television, I should be putting my time to better use by studying my books, polishing my shoes for school or just resting my body and soul for what only God knew the next day would bring.

Another way I am different from those boys is that I have my responsibilities and duties to perform on Saturday. I too have to work for my daily bread, especially to help her to make the few pennies that I long out my hand at her to receive Monday to Friday each and every week. I cannot, she insists, be slothful. That is not the kind of young man she can see me becoming. I too must show my independence.

With these admonitions ringing in my head, I placed the bags and the bedding in a pile and put them underneath Grandmother's bed behind the curtains. The lamp was still burning on low, giving a pale glow even in the soft light of the early morning, casting an elongated shadow on the side of the house, one that moved as I advanced on the light. I blew into the chimney to put out the flame and noticed that the oil in the lamp was low, just as Grandmother had reported. And I remembered her special plea to me to always handle the chimney with care, so I let it cool down before I did anything. I stepped into the backyard and placed the bedding on the rocks for their weekly airing out.

I hoped Mrs. King was not looking into the yard. I felt a gaze, eyes pinning me down and even correcting and scolding me. A chill ran up my spine and the hairs on my legs, arms and back stood on end, each in its raised goose pimple. I felt as if someone had crept up on me and was breathing gently between my shirt collar and my back, the air flitting cold and eerie all the way down to my waist. Quickly, I ran back into the house, but the presence was still with me. That is another reason I do not like staying in the house alone. I never feel it is just me alone in there. I can't feel really free or even private.

On the table, I found the tot of cocoa where Grandmother left it under the pan for a cover. The four biscuits that she left out for me were also under the pan and I took them up and started to eat. Noticing the opened can of milk nearby, I poured a long dollop into the tot for an extra treat, knowing that Grandmother would disapprove of my using so much milk on top of what she already used. The cocoa was still hot and I blew into it, feeling the steam rising to my face, before drinking as quickly as I could. Now I had to get to my chores.

I took the two lamps into the backyard and cleaned them and filled them with kerosene. I took them back into the house, carefully placing the one with the short, round frosted chimney and the words *Home Sweet Home* on a stand close to the front window in the front house. In this position it not only gives the most light, but it is always on show. The second one—taller, narrower and plain—I placed on the box by Grandmother's bed, beside the white handbag containing the Bible. The matchbox had enough matches, so I did not have to remember to buy any. Now things inside the house were just as perfect as the eyes watching me demanded. There would be no quarrelling here.

With these chores finished, I sat on the solid limestone step at the back door and waited until I heard Mrs. King moving around in the house—my signal that Mrs. King and Stephie had tidied up themselves and had had their tea for the morning. Only then was it appropriate and mannerly for me to join them. I would not be intruding on their privacy, just as we would like them to treat us. I ambled over to the spot within the paling with the pebbles and the basins and washed my hands with soap. I could only imagine what Grandmother would say if Mrs. King were to report that I turned up at her house with my hands smelling of kerosene oil.

"Good morning, Mrs. King," I said at the back door to the kitchen.

"Good morning, Christopher," Mrs. King answered. "Had a good sleep last night?"

"Yes, thank you," I said, no different from the way I was taught from my earliest of times. This is how I must speak to an adult, especially someone who is not only older and wiser than me but who is really my guardian as well.

"And you finished all the things your grandmother left you to do?"

"Yes, please."

"Good," Mrs. King said. "Let we get started, for it done look like we have a long day ahead of us. I'll get the things ready and you can start off by yourself. Stephie might come and join you later. She's still in her bedroom."

"Yes, please," I said and positioned myself at the table with the coconuts, sweet potatoes, cucumbers, onions, thyme, marjoram, peppers, limes and the container with the blood already turning black. On the floor beside the table was a large tub in which the pig intestines were already soaking. A whitish film covered the water. In another pan beside it were the pig snouts, ears and trotters, all soaking in vinegar, lime and salt water. At any moment I expected Stephie to come out of the bedroom and join me on the bench, so I left room for her to sit. I knew what I was supposed to do and how I was to carry out my duties and responsibilities in unison with everybody else. As I was to discover, Mrs. King was not joking and she was not wrong when she said it would be a long day. And without Stephie to help out, the day felt longer by the minute.

Gratering is always hard work. Most Saturday mornings, before all this talk about how Stephie and I are now so different, we would divide the task between us. One of us would take care of the sweet potatoes and the cucumbers for the pudding and souse; the other the coconuts that would make the sweet bread. And I would gather up the skins, rinds, bits and pieces of food and the dish-washings to feed the pigs. Stephie often chose the potatoes and cucumbers, and she would sit on the bench by the table with the pan between her legs. She would take the sweet potatoes one by one and with a sharp knife remove the reddish skin. Underneath were the white potatoes and sometimes the milky juice. Not too much juice would be a sign the potatoes were still good, even if picked when young or green. Then she would cut the potatoes into smaller and more manageable pieces and place them on the table, where they would begin to turn a faint bluish black. I took over from there, gratering my share.

Next, Stephie would turn her attention to the cucumbers and onions. The skins from the cucumbers would be added to the pig food and, taking the big grater and standing at the table, Stephie alone would grater the cucumbers and onions in a large pan. All this gratering she did in short order, her hand quickly hitting a rhythm that got things done quickly. With her long, thin fingers, she is not as clumsy as my fat-fingers self. Then she added salt and vinegar and squeezed the limes into the water. She carefully cut up the peppers, using a fork to hold each pepper on the cutting board and using the tip of a sharp knife to pare around the core, so that the centre remained whole with the seeds on it. She diced the peppers by wielding the knife and fork, never touching them with her hands. The peppers—now dots of red, green and yellow—floated in the water with the lime juice, onions, vinegar and salt, a marinating mixture ready for the meat to draw in after it was cooked.

I like to watch Stephie at work. On many occasions I have heard Mrs. King and Grandmother compliment her. Stephie moves around the kitchen with a confidence that I do not have. And she has a liberty sorting and arranging I am sure I do not have, not unless I am out in the back taking care of the outside chores.

My job would be to crack the dry coconuts on a big stone in the backyard and to capture in a can as much of the coconut water as possible. Then I would use a knife to husk the coconut and place it in a tub. When all the coconuts were treated this way, I would sit beside Stephie, and the two of us would set about our tasks of gratering them. Most mornings we hardly talked, at least not with our mouths. Our eyes and the positioning of our bodies were enough to tell each other what we felt. Most of my work consisted of lifting and carrying over to the shop the pots, pans and the coal pot and coals in the evening after all the cooking and baking inside the house was done, and before the women got into the swing of actually selling.

Today, without Stephie, I have to do her job and mine. I am well into the potatoes when my arm starts to give out. Still, there is the big and seemingly unchanging pile ahead of me. At the same time, I have to start making plans to head off to the bus stop to meet Grandmother on her return from downtown. She will need help with the goods she bought. I will need the strength in my arms and in my neck to lift the heavy basket and bags from the bus stop to the house—a chore that I have long grown used to doing, while Stephie skilfully finished her inside work.

"Morning, Mrs. King," a voice hails at the side door to the shed roof.

"Mrs. Smith," Mrs. King says. "You early this morning. Whuh happenin'?"

"Nothing too much," she says. "I just thought that I would begin my rounds early this morning. The early walk will give me a bit o' fresh air. It will help to clear muh head from too much thinking."

"Good morning, Mrs. Smith," I say when she is fully in the house. Mrs. Smith is wearing a multicoloured dress with a white apron tied around her waist. A black straw hat with a white band covers most of her head. When she talks, it appears as if her voice is coming out of the hat. She dusts her feet on the bag at the door and slips out of her well-worn sneakers. The backs of the canvas shoes are mashed down for comfort, making them look like slippers.

"Boy, you up early this morning," Mrs. Smith says, which is strange, for she sees me sitting here every Saturday morning when she comes by at about this time. "Good morning to you."

"Good morning to you, Mrs. Smith," I say. She stands next to the framed picture of Esmeralda on the side of the house. In the picture, Esmeralda is leaning on a red car in front of a large house with big glass windows. Around her neck is what looks like a fur collar or what I think is a scarf. It is a picture of her in the foreign country. She sent it back soon after she went over-'n'-away. Mrs. King told us the house was where Stephie's mother worked minding children. I have seen this picture countless times—when we were very small, Stephie and I used to stand and stare at it—but only now do I realize how *girlish* the woman in the picture looks, almost as young as some of the senior girls at school, and so much like Stephie now. A baby with a pink blanket in a pram and what looks like a little boy buttoned down head to foot standing beside it are in the bottom corner of the picture. I always think the pram and the boy are waiting for her, the boy watching with his legs apart, looking as if he wants to go and pee. Esmeralda's eyes seem to be looking not only at the camera but also at them.

"Well, at least one person is up early," Mrs. Smith says. "That son of mine, Desmond, and the wife that he say he got there still in bed all this time if you please. They like they think they livin' at some hotel or something."

"What you mean?" Mrs. King asks. "And why you fretting up yourself so with the young people for? You should be glad to have your own son wid you this morning. And that he would bring 'long his wife too. You can't want anything more better than that."

"Li'l boy, shut yuh ears fuh me, yuh hear, my son," Mrs. Smith says, bringing an air of importance and even defiance to her voice. "Don't mind me, yuh hear, l'il boy. What I'm about to say is for big people." Turning to look directly at Mrs. King, she says, "It's not that I ain't glad to have Desmond back, after all, as you say, he is my own son, he rolled 'bout in my belly for nine long months, but I'd like things more better if he did come in for only a short time and was leffing soon. Then things can get back to them usual self soon enough. We could stop acting as if we have visitors just visiting."

"You mean that he really come back down for good?" Mrs. King asks. "That he ain't walking 'bout pulling we foot with all this talk about stayin' down here?"

"Girl, I gotta believe it is fuh good. At least that is what he keep telling me whenever I ask him serious or in joke how long he staying for. And that is what got me worried. I ain't seeing he or the wife that he bring back doing one thing to feed themselves. They like they expect it all to fall on me and his poor father. Like he don't know that Bertie ain't the strong Bertie that he did leave back here when he went up north all them years ago. Things change, and people too; people get old. His father getting on."

"But they need time to catch themselves," Mrs. King says. She walks from the kitchen into the shed roof to stand in front of Mrs. Smith, all the while drying her hands on a small green towel. "The wife gotta get 'climatized too. It ain't like she is from about here, like one o' we or we own kind, and can step back into the swing o' things easy so. She different, so you gotta gi' she a chance to catch she bearings."

"I'd say so," Mrs. Smith says, sounding as if she is indeed wise to the ways of the world, and even of her own family members. "So different that she like she can't even wash a glass when she done use um. And she is the first one to be going into the cabinet that Bertie placed there fuh me in the front house to take down my lovely glasses and my other wares that I does keep only for use on special occasions. Them ain't for everyday usages and everybody know that. But not she, she have to be using my good, good cups and the knife and forks too, the same ones that he, when he first went up north, as a son, did send back fuh me as part of a set o' utensils fuh the house."

"You know," Mrs. King says, "'cause you is a woman o' the church, you know what the Bible done teach and instruct us as Christians 'bout strangers and visitors that come among us, especially the women, how we must reach out to them and help as if they're we own sisters. So I gotta say that since you know better, something else is bothering you this morning. Faith. For I don't think I am hearing the real, real Mrs. Smith this good morning, but someone that looks and sounds like she."

"Not a thing different ain't bothering me," Mrs. Smith says, but there is less conviction in her voice. "I is the same body that you did always know. Just that some things you have to get use to, and I don't see he and the wife helping out at all. It is just that he just come and disrupt everything, all the patterns and ways that I did have in the house. Even his father like he lapsing back too, and what would become of the order and ways that I depend on in the house? Anyway, you ready for me this morning? I still have to collect the sou-sou money so in the Lord's name we can help out we one another as partners."

Mrs. Smith is talking about the women's own banking system. Everybody throws in the same amount every week and then waits for a turn as the pot moves around.

"Well, sounds to me like you have your crosses to bear," Mrs. King says, feeling into her pockets.

"And plus when you say anything to that wife of his," Mrs. Smith says, taking the stub of yellow pencil from behind her ear to make the recording of Mrs. King's contribution, "well, soulie gal, the first thing out of her mouth is how she can't wait to have she two children that she left over-'n'-away join she and to be living with she."

"Well, then she must be thinking about having a house o' she own then," Mrs. King says, pausing in her actions to emphasize the importance of this bit of information. "She must be. 'Cause she can't be thinking of having them living with she in that house that you own over there."

"I don't know," Mrs. Smith says and sighs resignedly. "I don't know. 'Cause she like some setting fowl looking to protect the chickens when they hatch when she talking about her children, even when Dessie is telling her that things take time and that, as we does say around here, taking time ain't laziness. I hear he telling her how thirsty ox does drink dirty water. I don't think she sees things that way."

"When is my turn now?" Mrs. King asks, reaching back into her pocket to take out two separate rolls of bills, each held together by pieces of black thread. "This is one long turn for the payout to get to me, and with Christmas coming, I could do with my turn right now. This house could use a good painting to spruce she up, and the roof leaking real bad when the rain falls."

"Everybody would like them turn now, now, now," Mrs. Smith says indignantly. "And that's another reason why my soul vex so these days." She takes a folded exercise book from the pocket of her apron and opens it. "You know that you' turn ain't coming 'til well into the new year, God willing."

"That long?" Mrs. King asks, pretending this is news to her.

"And the same thing with Peggy, before you up and ask," Mrs. Smith says, "so don't start." She turns to the back of the book to a schedule with names. "She is the week right after you; you the third Sunday in January."

"Why I couldn't be the lucky somebody to get my turn now, right in time fuh Christmas?" she says, handing over the money.

"Why? Because you know that everybody can't get them turn the same week," Mrs. Smith says. Somehow she seems more irritated than usual, for other Saturday mornings she would brush aside such comments as if they are to be expected when running a sou-sou with friends. "Every week the same thing. Everybody asking fuh them turn even if it is outta turn for them, and I gotta keep explainin' that isn't how things work. I getting tired with all this explainin' and it ain't like I getting anything extra fuh acting like a banker and adviser and bookkeeper."

"You know I was only making sport," Mrs. King says. "What happen, we can't crack a joke anymore? We never used to be like that. We could always make a joke on we one another without taking offence. Ain't that how we does live 'round here?"

"I know," Mrs. Smith says, dropping her voice. "I know. How many turns you paying for yourself this week?"

"As usual, just one," Mrs. King says and raises an index finger. "Christmas is just around the corner and I ain't got no son that just come back down, so money short, at least for me this Christmastime. The other one, as you know, is for Peggy. She left it with me for you. So make sure you mark she off as paid in the book and not as me paying two turns and she none."

"Right, right." Mrs. Smith makes the marks. She closes the book and smiles.

"And as I done say," Mrs. King says, throwing a hand around her shoulders, "if you ever want to really talk about anything bothering yuh, this door here is always open, for that is the way all o' we always live around here as Christian women, helping to carry one another burden when it getting too heavy."

"I hope so, soulie gal," Mrs. Smith says. She slides her feet back into the mash-down shoes. "I'll come back some time, when you and Peggy home and not too busy." For a moment, we hear the slip-slop sound of her shoes and then she is gone. Mrs. King starts humming and returns to the kitchen to join me at the table. Stephie has missed all of this. I do not even have her to make eyes at as we laugh silently.

"But looka this thing here today," Mrs. King speaks at the top of her voice, seemingly to no one in particular. Dropping the knife loudly on the table, she starts to blink quickly and then to rub her eye with the back of her hand. "Look how I as a big woman going to blind myself this morning. That Devil does not take one day's rest. We always got to be so cautious." I stop the gratering but can only look on helplessly. "A big woman like me, who should know better. You would think that I would be the last person, seeing that my hand touching up all these peppers here, that I would be the last to go and stick my finger in my own eye. But then I did, like some fool, without thinking first and then acting. Now it's burning me like fire. *Wuuuhlaw*, boasie. Enough to make me want to cry iffen I wasn't a big, hard-back woman already."

She walks into the yard and reaches into the water barrel to bring up a big tot. She pours the water into a basin and begins splashing it on her eye. After a few minutes, she wipes her face on the skirt of her dress and returns to the house. All the while, she keeps rubbing the eye with the back of her hand.

Mrs. King resumes cutting the peppers into small pieces, but unlike Stephie, she holds them with her hands. When she has a sizable pile, she runs a sweet-drink bottle over them to crush them and release more of the juices and then she dumps them into the pickle. This is the last batch and she stirs the water to make sure the grated cucumber and the lime, salt, vinegar and peppers are thoroughly mixed. She tastes and, obviously, approves. This time she is careful to dry her hands in the green kitchen towel on the table. Mrs. King takes the big pot from the fire and pours out the boiling water. Several times, she replaces the water in the pot and, when the temperature is right, she reaches in and takes out the pig trotters one by one. With her hands, she breaks them into small pieces and drops them into the pickle. Next, she turns to the snouts and pig ears and, using her biggest knife, cuts them into small wedges, making sure every piece has some of the gristle. They too go into the big pan.

"The men at the shop going to like this souse tonight," she predicts. "I can just see them there licking back their waters drinking the alcohol and asking for more and more souse. The pepper is what the men like, lots and lots o' pepper. And tonight, they ain't going to be disappointed. Rains this time o' the year, making the peppers plentiful. My eye can swear to that." Mrs. King adds several sprigs of parsley leaves and sweet marjoram. Then she spreads a bleached flour-bag over the top of the pan and allows the souse to draw, so that by the time she and Grandmother set up their coal pots and start selling, the meat and vegetables will be marinated and taste of acid, salt and hot peppers.

"I don't know what it is about over-'n'-away that seem to turn we people dotish," Mrs. King says. I can only assume she is remembering Mrs. Smith's visit. "You think you know why that is so?"

"No, Mrs. King," I say, taking a break from grating the potatoes. Mrs. King sits beside me and begins helping with the potatoes. She moves through the pile just as fast as Stephie usually does, and seems to be taking less effort than me as I lumber on.

"You ain't read anything about that in them books you and Steph'nie does study at school, eh?"

"About what?" I ask.

"How it is that when we own people seem to go over-'n'-away, something strange like it does happen to them. They lose themselves and the real them just disappear. Once they're up there, you never hear one word from them. Then, the next thing you hear a whole lot o' them gone offa their head. They gone mad. They ain't no use to themselves: don't know where they come from, don't know where they going, don't know which god they serving. What you think does cause that?"

"The cold?" I guess.

"Can't be just that 'cause everybody don't go mad and the cold does hit everybody up there the same way. Look at your mother there. And the mother o' Stephie too." With her head, Mrs. King gestures toward the picture on the wall. The young woman smiles back, the same way Stephie does, curled lip, big dimple and all. "All I got is that picture. In the house she got above there, your grandmother, all she got to remind her of your mother is a lamp chimney. Them is all we have of them two girls. They can't be too righted in the head. Why wouldn't they write and tell the two o' we what's going on in their lives up there? And them used to be two good, good, good girls when they were down here. Wouldn't they want to know what's happenin' in the lives o' the two o' you, their very own children that they gave birth to and brought into this world of sin?"

"But everybody ain't like that," I say. I feel strange that now it is me having to explain that things will not always be this way. "A lot of fellows at my school have their mother and father overseas and they does send money and clothes and things for them. They might still send for Stephie and me. I mean, almost every day, I does hear of somebody or the other in the school going off to join their mother or father overseas."

"Ah, them is the real lucky ones," Mrs. King says. "And that is the way things should be. Their parents are the same as when they left these shores. They still remember their broughtupcy and how to think as if they did still be living back down here. And that is good for the children. That is goodness and light all around. Not like you and Steph'nie not knowing what is what. It isn't as if either of the two of you can depend on your two so-called fathers down here. I mean, I can't think of the last day that man came around to say howdie to Stephie. We *gotta* battle on we own. That's the way it always has been 'round here, ever since I did know myself. And it is tough to think that way."

"Why is that the case?" I ask.

"Read your Bible," she instructs. "It's right there in the Bible. The thoughts and deeds of man are evil. There is evil in each and every one of us. That's not to say that we ain't starting off being good, it is that evil will overcome the good quick, quick so if we don't be on the lookout and guard against it. That is why we no longer in the Garden of Eden. It is because of the evil in the heart of men, all that badness you can never see because it is hidden away in the heart. That is the story we keeping learning even up to this day: how the good you want and even pray for is no match for the evil in man's heart."

"But some people say that right here where we live is a Garden of Eden," I say, teasing her. I expect her to object to any political argument that appears to run contrary to her religious thinking. "They saying that now everybody getting independence, we can turn this place into a real paradise so that we own people won't have to keep running away to a next country."

"I hope they right," Mrs. King says, surprising me with her response. She doesn't start cussing the politicians as she does when talking with grandmother or Mrs. Smith and the other women. "We as a special people always on a journey; we are a sojourning people. Like back in Africa, when we had a Garden of Eden, 'cause as you as a high school boy should know the cradle of civilization is Africa. That is where as a people in the very beginning we're from. The next thing we know all o' we like you and me living in this land here, brought out of paradise into a land of bondage, and we have never been able to get back. Not since that day."

"Do you want to go back to Africa?" I ask.

"*Me?* Nah, not me." The response is sharp and quick. "See me, I quite happy and contented to spend my last few remaining years here in this the land of my birth. I love it here. This is my own Africa, my Little Africa, if you please. I ain't got a place to go or to set a foot anywhere outside of this island here. The stories I hear about the real Africa are enough for me, how we manage to keep all them things in we memory all these long years, so I already know what is necessary for we to have goodness and righteousness in this the land the Lord our God giveth us."

She bangs the grater on the side of the pan to knock off the residuals. This signals the end of the conversation and a return to matters at hand, for she says approvingly, "It looks like we're making some headway, don't you think?"

"Yes, Mrs. King," I say. Indeed, we are making progress. The mound of potatoes has almost all become paste in the mixing pan, and I have already started on the coconuts. I look at the door to the bedroom. Still no sign of Stephie. I wonder what she would make of me and her grandmother having such a talk.

Mrs. King gets up, takes the container from me and empties the grated coconut into a larger pan. She shaves two whole nutmegs and some cinnamon sticks into the pan as well. The sweet fragrance of the nutmeg floats around the kitchen. I feel better if only because, for the first time, I can envision an end to the day's grating and the stripping of the skin from my fingertips and knuckles.

Mrs. King stands by the table cleaning the pig intestines by letting a solution of water, lime juice, vinegar and salt in at one end and squishing it through to the other end. So caught up are we in our chores, we do not see or hear Grandmother approaching. For the first time, I forgot to meet her at the bus. From the way Grandmother cuts her eyes at me, I know this also has to be the last time.

Chapter Five

Sweat rolls down Grandmother's face. She bows from the waist and, with the help of Mrs. King, removes the basket from her head and pushes it across the floor, out of the walking passage. An older man, Cyrus, is behind her with two long bags that look like stuffed pillowcases. His hair is well greased with a part on the side, and he is smiling broadly, as if there is something funny but hidden in everything he would say or think and do. Cyrus is wearing what looks like a brand new dungaree shirt, as there are still creases from the folding in it, and his sleeves are folded back at the elbows. His pants look, from the sheen, like they were recently pressed with a very hot iron, as the creases along the front and back of the trousers are extremely sharp. Only his shoes are scruffy. I can tell that the bags he hands to Grandmother and Mrs. King contain the salt bread rolls from the bakery in town. Grandmother and Mrs. King will resell them later in the evening as part of the meal with the black pudding and souse.

"Lord, it's hot out there, nuh," Grandmother says. She shoots a quick glance at me as if to ask whether I have been behaving in her absence. I soak the grater in the water and continue with my chores, hoping that if there are to be any reports, they will come from Mrs. King. "And you shoulda see all the people them down in town this day. They already on a spending spree. Like money giving 'way. People buying up everything they can lay hands on and set eyes on. I don't know where they getting all this money from all of a sudden and what new spirit have gotten into these people. I had to stand back and watch them while I pick up my usual things, 'cause I ain't got the same kinda money as what I did see lickin' 'bout today."

"It's all o' that back pay money from the sugar cane crop and the civil servants and teachers that government giving everybody who is anybody," Cyrus says. "Sister King, you in for some o' this money too?"

"*Me*? Not me," Mrs. King says. "That money ain't for the likes of me. It is for people who holding down a job that they does go to every morning. What me and Peggy does do ain't a job. We gotta live by we own wits and get by how best we can. So I ain't in this back pay money thing."

"Well, Mistress Bee," Cyrus says affectionately, "I too expecting my li'l piece o' change. This is one o' the blessing o' independence. This year, the civil servants like me so are not only getting a good back pay too, but they still entitled to the bonuses they does get every year this time 'round, and on top of that, they can still ask for an advance of up to three full weeks' salary now it is Christmastime. Nobody didn't have to tell me twice: I was the first in line to fill out my forms this week. That's why I thankful for my li'l night watchman job down there at the guvment headquarters. Everybody down there saying independence making things too sweet already."

"What independence got to do with back pay?" Grandmother asks.

"Everything. This wonta happen unless we was in charge of our own affairs, if we were not now our own political bosses. I mean, I was listening to the prime minister speaking on the radio when he announced the back pay. And what did he do? He said that this year we had a bumper sugar cane crop. Must be all this good rain we've been having, especially since the big rains on independence night. Everything coming up good, good, this year. Plus, if you look around the island, it full with all them *touristses* from over-'n'-away, all them visitors sunning themselves down here on we beaches now that it so cold where they come from. And more o' them passing through the harbour every day on them big cruise ships. So he said this year he imposing a windfall levy on all the exports, and that levy is the said same money he giving back to the workers. You don't see that is why all the union people praising him? Why they all saying it's a good, good thing somebody is looking out for the poor man."

"That sounds like a good thing," Grandmother says, "but I still can't see why you saying it's because of independence."

"Because you ain't see how we all living like one now?" Cyrus explains. "Even the politicians, them in government and them in Opposition, them in Parliament and them outside, all o' them now saying that since *we's* a country, we *gotta* stop all this bickering and fighting and pull in one direction. What is it the Opposition leader said? All o' we in the same boat now and we all *gotta* paddle together, otherwise we all, pardon my French there l'il boy, up *shit* creek." He slaps me playfully on my leg with the recognition of my presence during big people conversation. I look at Grandmother and figure she must be thinking that with the slap, Cyrus is treating me as if me and he are the same company, as she would say, as if me and he does pitch marbles together. Cyrus sits in the doorway and continues smiling broadly. I pull in my foot, for the slap makes me feel self-conscious. I did not expect this kind of attention.

"Cyrus, boy," Mrs. King says, laughing. "You sure you ain't going into politics, yuhself? Sounds to me like you already got yuh speech all mapped out in yuh head. Must be come from working at the government headquarters. Sounds to me like you is a budding politician yuhself there."

"*Me*, Mrs. King?" Cyrus says with feigned disbelief. "*Me* sounding like a politician? No, man. It is just that I's a man that does listen good, good, good and, as you know, everything 'bout here is politics, or *politricks* as I like to call it. You *gotta* know what is really real and not let people fool yuh, for they got a lot of people walking 'round this place here fooling people good, good, good with their sweet words and no actions."

"Well, you still sound like yuh already on the flatform begging fuh votes," Mrs. King says. "Come and let me check the book fuh how much yuh owe we for the food you done trust from me and Peggy on credit, and it is fuh more than just last week. How about for three weeks running straight? Why yuh so bad so?"

"See what I tell yuh," Cyrus says, laughing. "I done learn all my badness right here. I never stepped foot off this island."

Cyrus and Mrs. King slip into the backyard. Grandmother stands in the kitchen still catching her breath and wiping the sweat from her face, surveying the amount of work that still has to be done before we are ready to meet the men by the shop. "*Whew*, it's hot," she says, fanning with an open hand. "I hope that don't mean no rain this evening, 'cause rain would only frig up things and keep the mens at home, where they'll only create more trouble for everybody. We need we share o' this back pay money before everybody lick it out at all them big stores in town. You had anything to eat?"

"Not since the cocoa-tea this morning that you leff me."

"Okay," she says. "Hold on. I gine put on the pot now. I got some lovely okras in town and they will make a licking cou-cou with a piece o' the same salt fish that I buy this morning for the fish cakes we'll be selling tonight. Just give me a chance to catch muhself first."

We hear Cyrus's goodbyes and then Mrs. King returns to the house and resumes mixing the pan into which she poured the grated sweet potatoes. She stirs in a generous helping of salt and black pepper. Then she adds some chopped onion, garlic and shallots, stirring some more. Taking several leaves of broadleaf thyme, which we call poor man's pork, she folds them and slices several times before chopping them into small bits over the pan.

"Give me a hand here with the black pudding, Pegs," she calls.

"Okay," Grandmother says.

"You stir while I pour."

Grandmother takes the big stick and begins mixing up the contents of the pan. Mrs. King pours the first measure of pig's blood and Grandmother stirs it in. The mixture begins to turn dark, and I remember Mr. Jones at school saying that our former colonial masters, the English, would always say that one thing about black pudding was that it made everything black and common, even the white potatoes, when you were finished with it. Another thing about black pudding he had said, which I remember whenever I see the women stirring, was that it used to be slave food in the bygone days.

Mrs. King empties the last of the blood. Grandmother stirs feverishly and then signals she too is finished by knocking the stick sharply on the face of the pan to clear it of any of the pudding still on the stick.

"Now," Mrs. King says, "Christopher, come here and give me a hand with the pig belly so that yuh Grandmother can occupy sheself with that piece o' cou-cou that she was just talking about. Lord knows, I hungry, hungry, hungry. I would really, as people like to say, *endorse* that cou-cou right now if it did be ready fuh eating at this very moment."

"I know," Grandmother says. "Just let me get out o' the way. I'll soak the piece o' dry codfish that I pick up at the supermarket in town. Price was good and it will make a good butter gravy-sauce for the cou-cou. Straight from Nova Scotia this said same week, or so the advertising in the supermarket say. You *shoulda* see the people gobbling up this shipment like they never see good Canadian salt fish before."

Grandmother fetches the salt fish from the basket and places it in a bowl with water. She cuts several long okras into small pieces and adds them to the pot already on the fire. Taking a small slab of codfish from the bowl, Grandmother breaks it into small pieces, searches for bones and places the meat on a plate. She heats some lard oil in a frying pan and adds onions, tomatoes and thyme and whatever else she can put her hands on in the larder that she feels will enhance the gravy-sauce. The sizzling sound of the vegetables hitting the heated fat is followed by the sweet smell of fried onions, making me feel even hungrier.

"Boy," Mrs. King says to me, "watch what you doing. Pay attention how you holding the pig belly. You gotta be more delicate in what you're doing, not as if you are outside in the yard and being rough." Normally it would be Stephie doing the holding.

"Yes, Mrs. King."

"He like he still don't know that you can't do two things good at the same time," Grandmother says. "You got to concentrate."

I try to pay attention even though I am suffering heavy white squalls from the hunger. I hold one end of the pig belly open and, with a spoon, Mrs. King dips out the black pudding and stuffs it into the intestines. She makes sure there is enough air in the intestines so that they will not burst when they are steaming in the pot on the coal-pot fire. My mind keeps wandering, sometimes lingering on what Mr. Jones had said about the origins of black pudding and souse and the days of slavery, about how cou-cou became our national dish, but that it too was a meal for slaves. I pictured Jonesie standing in front of our form and saying time and time again, "In times past, bearing a yoke on my shoulders, of wood unshaven, I carried my loads of fish from Argos to Tegea town." And I wonder if any of that fish from Argos was dried and salted and smelled so stinky when the water dried out of the pot or boiled over into the flames.

Stephie would understand what I am thinking. Like any of the students in the school, she would laugh and identify Mr. Jones as the one we all associated with the claim that ours is a long history, as old as any other of which we could think in the whole world.

Grandmother takes heaping spoonfuls of butter from a can and stirs it into her gravy-sauce. The can, partially opened with the tin bent backwards, has on it a picture of a black and white cow eating on what looks like a green pasture. Underneath the picture are the words *New Zealand Butter*. From another Commonwealth country just like our own. Grandmother adds water to the frying pan and soon its contents are bubbling gently.

"How yuh doing there, girl?" Mrs. King calls out.

"Coming along. You know cou-cou is a funny thing to cook. You always gotta make the sauce first and have it ready. You can't go just changing the order of things for changing sake. No shortcuts neither. But once the sauce done, you almost home." I notice that the stinking smell of the codfish water boiling into the fire has disappeared completely.

Grandmother pours cornmeal into the pot with the okra, stirring constantly to make sure there are no lumps. Occasionally, we hear a loud puff as the stirring releases air trapped in the mixture. Both Grandmother and Mrs. King stop talking in order to concentrate fully on their particular jobs. I do likewise, watching the rows of what look like big sausages circling at the bottom of the pan. When we finish filling each one, Mrs. King ties knots at both ends.

"Stephie eating wid we today?" Grandmother asks, reaching for the bowls in the larder.

"I guess so," Mrs. King says. "That is, if she got any appetite today, for I don't know what's wrong with that girl."

"She will," Grandmother says. "A piece a cou-cou, steaming hot and with lot o' sauce, will do she good. Watch and see."

"I hope so, 'cause to tell the truth I don't like it with she drawing up so, like a sickly chicken that got a pip on its tongue that 'causing it not to eat. I don't like it."

Grandmother dollops the cou-cou into four bowls. She places a spoonful of butter on top of each mound and uses the spoon to make a big indentation on the top of the cou-cou. Then she puts generous amounts of sauce and fish and vegetables into the bowls. When she finishes, the cou-cou looks like a yellow mountaintop with moss and other vegetation on it, and with bits of green jutting up out of an equally yellowish sea.

"I ready fuh yuh now," Grandmother says.

"Just in time," Mrs. King says. "The two o' we here just finishing up. *Stephie! Stephie!* Come and put something in yuh stomach, dearie. That will make you feel more better. *Stephie?*"

Stephie comes out of the bedroom and joins us. She does not sit on the bench beside me but at the table with the grandmothers. The four of us sit eating silently, the only noises coming from the sounds of the spoons hitting the sides of the bowls as we scoop up portions of the cou-cou, the sauce and the vegetables for each bite. We race to finish eating while the meal is still hot and palatable. Cou-cou must be eaten hot. If not, it becomes too stiff. We are ravenous, for this is the main meal for the day.

Outside, the wind is up again and blowing sweetly through the house, cooling and offering a brief respite from the tropical heat trapped underneath the galvanize roof in the middle of the day. What we do not eat—which is not much—we scrape into the bucket with the pig food. We wash the utensils in the backyard, put them away in the larder and get ready to resume our various tasks. Stephie returns to the bedroom. Not once did her and my eyes make four, even though I tried.

Mrs. King lights the fire in the coal pot and places the biggest aluminum pot on the grill. So big is it that she has to carefully position it so it will not tumble off. Into the pot, she has poured cold water and placed the coils of black pudding. She closes the lid and asks me to keep watch before going into the shed roof of the house to start filling trays with the nuts, mints and other sweeties and various fruits that Grandmother brought from town. Soon Grandmother will join her, and they will sit and make the final preparations for the execution of their business. This is the time of the day that is always quietest in our houses on Saturdays. It is the point at which Stephie and I would be allowed to take some time out for ourselves.

Before joining Mrs. King, Grandmother now takes full control of the kitchen. She stirs most of the grated coconut into some flour and, standing at the table, smoothly kneads the mixture into dough. In the overflowing bag of garbage at her feet are eggshells and to the side on the table are the bottles of almond and vanilla essences, baking powder, the paper with what remained of the fresh butter and lard, along with the unused raisins, salt, sugar, nutmeg and baking powder. I watch Grandmother kneading and then cutting the dough into slabs, in her hand making them into an elongated shape before dropping them into a pan that she has already greased with some of the lard and dusted with flour. She and Mrs. King will also be selling this sweet bread later this evening. Grandmother takes a knife and makes three slanted cuts in the top of each loaf. Into these openings, she places a mixture of grated coconut, essences and sugar and then pinches shut the dough.

She brushes on a heavy mixture of brown sugar water and sprinkles sugar granules on top before putting the pans in the heated oven. At this point, she turns her attention to making the fish cake batter in a tall white plastic bucket with a top that fits snugly over it. We will transport the uncooked batter to the shop, and Grandmother and Mrs. King will fry the fish cakes to order, so they will be fresh and hot for the customers.

As I watch Grandmother, I hear the steady hissing of the pot with the black pudding on the fire in front of me. Ever so often the steam lifts the lid slightly and some froth overflows the sides, leaving trails in the discoloration that is building on the sides of the pot. I am listening for any popping sounds, which might be an indication that we stuffed the pig belly too full and it's now bursting.

When Stephie and I were small children, Grandmother and Mrs. King always made us keep quiet during this time of the day. They told us that if we talked too much, or if we ran around the house and were playing too loudly with friends, we would make the steaming black pudding burst and spoil. The slightest noise could do great damage. Some of the sausages tend to burst, spilling the ingredients into the water. Once the good sausages were removed, Stephie and I were rewarded for our good behaviour with the contents in the pot: we could eat as much as we wished of the black pudding stuffing and water.

As we grew older, our friends would come over around that time to play and they too would have to abide by the rules and be quiet. We would share the black pudding water with them, and, over time, quite a number of children would be spending their Saturday afternoons playing with us and hoping that the sausages did not come out whole from the pot. If some of our friends were noisy, Grandmother and Mrs. King would ask them to stop coming by when the black pudding was cooking, but they were free to join us when the pot was being shared.

During the week after school, Stephie and I were not allowed to play too much with the neighbourhood children, which did not make us happy. Grandmother and Mrs. King said the other children fought too much. And when children fight, the parents and guardians get involved, taking up for their children's fire-rage whether right or wrong. Neither Grandmother nor Mrs. King wanted any trouble with these people, so they said it was best to keep us out of harm's way. As much as we wanted to, we could not stop to play or mingle with the *wild* children. Stephie and I had to be enough for each other. If we were to play with outsiders anytime, they had to come and visit us.

These days, most of the children hang out at the dance hall or the beach on Saturday evenings. They have taken to doing all those fun things that I only hear about on Monday mornings when I am back at school. They are too big now for sharing pots. I feel so deprived by missing all the things that the other children do. Stephie does too, or at least that is what she used to tell me until she changed. But Grandmother and Mrs. King have always insisted that by staying home and helping them out, Stephie and I are learning how to take care of ourselves in the real world. I cannot go to the dance hall like the others, and now I don't have Stephie either. Maybe I'll ask Grandmother to let me spend some time on Saturday afternoon watching the men play cricket in the local village leagues rather than sit here alone. Still, I am glad that the pace of the day has slowed and I can rest a bit before I have all the carrying to do for Grandmother and Mrs. King and, more immediately, the pigs to take care of.

Sitting here alone on the back door steps and thinking, watching the wind unsettle the top of Mrs. King's mango trees, our clammy cherry tree, and the cane tops and stalks in the distance, I suddenly feel a throbbing in my jaw. It is a low but constant pain, and it tells me that while I was eating, some of the food got trapped in the hole in my bad tooth. The pain is constant enough that I cannot ignore it, but not so bad that I have to do anything about it right away. The pain is sure to go away soon. When the pace picks up again, the work will no doubt put it out of my mind. Saturday night is not a time of rest, and as our grandmothers always say, many hands make light work. If only Stephie would start back doing her share and not leave it all to me.

Chapter Six

Cyrus returned just as we were ready to leave home and offered to help carry some of the heavier stuff. "Hold strain, young boy," he said to me, "I'll come back and me and you can carry the rest." I nodded.

But he must be lingering. As I wait for Cyrus to return, darkness is approaching quickly from the east, shrouding everything in the same colour and mood. I hear the crickets chirping with growing intensity and certainty, the sounds coming from a distance, from out of the groves with the fruit trees and from the cane fields, noises that seem to prey under the watch of night. At the same time, and seemingly contradictorily, there is a heavy silence, as the ways of the day retreat, and as one world seems to change into another, without much meaning and without any clear limits of one thing from the other. Only the bats, darting around feverishly, appear not to mind this heaviness, or maybe it is the oppressiveness of the evening that causes them to come out so early, even before the skies have given up all of the sun's light and a new way of doing things is in place.

Only the bravest of the turkeys and chickens appear unwilling to give in to the new regime and take straightaway to the branches in the trees or to their nests. They want the freedom to linger. Or perhaps they are the hungriest of the lot: those who just have to risk a struggle with the darkness as they search for yet another morsel of food. Maybe they are the most knowledgeable and wish to benefit from knowing the precise number of minutes between when the sun actually disappears on a particular day and when the last of the sun's light goes out. Mosquitoes buzz around my ears and neck, and I slap my cheek as I feel the sting of one of them. Over by the tree, I see the first fireflies as they flit around showing anyone paying attention that there is always light in any darkness.

"Hey, boy," a voice calls softly to me. "What you doing there all by yourself?" The speaker sounds like he just wants to start a conversation rather than question me. Out of the darkness, Cyrus materializes.

"Nothing, Mr. Cyrus," I say. This time, I notice, he has not announced his arrival with a loud voice. It is as if he wants only me to be aware of his presence. Cyrus stands close to me. I hear him breathing loudly, possibly from the walk, and I smell his cologne and the pomade in his hair.

"*Heh-heh.* What's this Mr. Cyrus business you getting on wid?" he asks. "You's a big man now, you don't have to call me no Mr. Cyrus anything." I remember Grandmother saying I should be grateful for any attention from Mr. Cyrus.

I do not respond, for I do not have a quick answer. I am still not sure how Grandmother would react to my not calling an elderly person mister or mistress. Indeed, there are times when I simply feel foolish referring in such a manner to some people. I feel caught between two different worlds. Mr. Cyrus is right: there are times when I am allowed to act like an adult. There are times when I get away with calling adults by their first name or by their surname, or even—and this depended on the person—by their nickname. I heard Stephie calling Mr. Lashley by his first name, Wendell, when she and Mrs. King were talking. But I know Grandmother still insists that I do not address some people by their first names. Cyrus must know this. He must understand my hesitancy to call him by his first name. There is so much I find confusing and uncomfortable about Cyrus. I look across the road and wonder how the boys and girls over there would react to him here, with his loud breathing, the heavy cologne smell and his standing so close and whispering.

The last of the turkeys finally takes to its branch in the tree. This gives me a chance to move away from Cyrus and make as if I am preparing for another chore elsewhere in the yard. Suddenly I hear a plop on the ground and know there will be at least one pile awaiting us and the flies in the morning. Around me, it appears as if the darkness has consumed the paling so that there are now no boundaries, merely the darkness of the night that merges everything into one, the trees with the turkeys and chickens, the houses, the cane fields and everything else up to and beyond the horizon. At that moment, it seems that all light has been extinguished, except for the glow across the road at Mr. Lashley's house, to which my mind and my eyes are always returning. I see the shadowy outline and hear the loud breathing at my side, as the steady tempo of the distance, the chirping sounds and the stillness continue to intensify the announcement of themselves and their dominance for the next while. Beyond that, I see the stars forming all the familiar patterns in a cloudless night. Suddenly, it is as if I have been wrapped in a big blanket, head to foot, and that in it the air is still hot, humid and sticky. A breeze makes the sweat on my neck feel cold; it enters the short sleeves of my shirt and chills my underarms. Again I look across at Mr. Lashley's house and Cyrus notices.

"So I see your little friend Stephanie taking man full-time now," Cyrus says to me. "*Heh-heh-heh.*" My heart leaps into my mouth. I feel the anger boiling up. It takes over my tongue. My neck turns hot as if I am wrestling and somebody is choking me.

"*Whuh,*" I stammer, "what that you say?"

"I mean that your little friend got a man to take care o' she, ain't it?" Cyrus chuckles. "And you know what that means. All I'd say is that it's about time since she must be seeing she own blood long time now. *Heh-heh-heh,* nuh. 'Cause my boy Lashley like he got heself fix up real good with a good piece o' young meat."

I want to tell him that Mr. Lashley is only a godfather. I want to repeat to him some of the things I heard our grandmothers saying. But he is just laughing as if I am talking foolishness. Maybe I am sputtering something back at him, for I don't like the way he is talking about Stephie.

"You playing that you ain't know what's going on?" Cyrus says. "We talking here as man. Man to man. Ain't you a man too?"

I have to admit that perhaps he is right. Only me, of all the people in the world, appears not to know what is happening. And I am angry: at Stephie for not telling me anything, for we were never like that, and now I don't even have a good response for Cyrus and his wuthless nastiness; and also at Grandmother and Mrs. King. I feel like asking them why nobody never tells me anything, and if what Cyrus is saying is the reason all this work now falling on me alone. But Grandmother would only get angry at me, telling me I must not be grudgeful-minded, and what would I do then? And Cyrus too, I am angry at him. Why does he have to make me hear all these things? And most of all I am particularly mad at myself for being just so foolish. I suck my teeth loudly, mainly at myself for being such a foolish fool. As Grandmother would say, I am a real foolie the fifth.

As we walk toward the lights in the near distance, I know it is going to be a long night. I take another glance at the greenish-blue light coming from Mr. Lashley's house, and I tell myself Grandmother is right that what happens in one house is no business of anyone else, even in a neighbouring house. I must not be bad-minded. People have to learn to mind their own business and not to be bothering themselves with what ain't got no calling to them. Except that it does not seem so right when it comes to Stephie: we did always be so tight with each other and there still ain't anything I won't tell *she*.

"So then, what you doing tonight?" Cyrus asks, leaning in to bounce my shoulder.

"When I finish here," I reply, stepping back, "I going to feed the pigs in the pigpen, and then I'm going to help carry the trays and the rest o' things down by the shop."

"I see." He sounds as if I have missed something in what he asked. But he does not explain. It feels a bit creepy.

I walk over into Mrs. King's yard and take up the bucket with the pig food. I hear his footsteps behind me and feel the annoying heat of his presence. The handle of the bucket is still warm from the sun as I lift it, taking care that the contents do not splash out. The heat from the afternoon sun appears to have affected the pig food; I hear fermentation bubbles bursting to the surface. Apart from the peelings and skins from earlier in the day are banana skins from when Grandmother and Mrs. King had been snacking while they talked. The swill smells sour and I do not want it to splash on me. Into the bucket I throw some growener, the brownish, dry pig food that comes in small pellets, which supplements the scraps.

The pigs started grunting loudly as soon as I touched the bucket, and their squealing turns more feverish the closer I come to the pen. Reaching over the railings, I throw the contents into a long wooden trough, once again taking care not to let any of the pig food splash over the sides. Quickly, the pigs bury their snouts into the trough and I hear the crunching sounds as they hungrily chew on the various skins and peelings. With the noises of their grunting, chewing and slurping following me, I walk to the drum that collected the water for the animals and take out two bucketfuls. I throw the water into the trough. This should be enough to keep the pigs through the night. The last sound I hear from the pen is of the two pigs falling heavily into their usual spots in the far corner, with one pig resting its head on the other's side. Then I hear Cyrus talking to Grandmother and Mrs. King.

"Let me give yuh a hand there," Cyrus says. Coming into the light, I see Cyrus helping to lift a tray onto Mrs. King's head. He winks at me as if to indicate I should keep our talk secret. Then, to prevent her from stooping, he hands Mrs. King the stool she will be sitting on for the rest of the night. Mrs. King steadies the tray on her head and turns around to watch Cyrus helping Grandmother with her tray and her little bench. Both women are wearing white aprons.

"Leave these," Cyrus says. "As I say, I'll help the boy to bring 'long these things. You go along and set up until we come."

"God bless yuh," Grandmother says. "You're a whole lot of help tonight."

"Ain't nothing," Cyrus says, "I glad to help out."

On the first trip, Cyrus and I carry the two coal pots, a bag of coals and the bucket containing the fish cake batter. On the next trip, we carry the covered pans that contain the pudding and souse. Finally, I return on my own for the bags with the salt bread rolls and the sweet bread loaves. I am about to turn down the lamp as usual when I think that Stephie might want to return to the house and if so, will need some light. I leave it on for her. I latch the back door and step outside.

"Let me give you a hand there, and this time don't call me no Mr. Cyrus. I'm just Cyrus for you, you hear." I hadn't realized he had followed me back home and was waiting in the night.

"Yes, sir," I say. Surrendering one of the bags to him, I walk beside him silently into the darkness, trying to remember from memory the locations of loose stones, potholes and the sudden indentation and rising on this track leading to the main road and the only real shop in our village. For a good distance, the music from the television follows us. The wind must have changed direction. As usual, the night is full of its silence. Darkness seems to absorb sounds and make the world formless and the same. In the mood I'm in, if anyone told me Stephie might not be having life easier than me I would say they are lying. For I can see no evidence of this. To me, it appears that she has graduated to other things in life, leaving me stuck behind. When next I see Stephie, I will ask her if what Cyrus told me is true and if she knows that people are already talking about her.

Pastor Wiltshire and the members of his Emmanuel Church of Zion are spreading a big white sheet on the ground as we pass by them on our final trip. The group of worshippers is preparing for a night of journeying at their open-air meeting. The worshippers are forming a circle around the sheet by linking hands. On the sheet, the pastor has stationed a big butane lamp that gives off a white light and whose steady humming could be heard some distance away. Next to the lamp, he places his big black Bible and a large brass bell with a black handle. On each corner of the sheet, the worshippers position a stone about the size of a folded fist. Pastor Wiltshire takes up the bell and goes to each corner, to the four points of the compass, bows over the rock and rings the bell. *Belang. Belang. Belang.* He touches with the tips of his fingers one of the many folds in the scarf neatly wrapped around his head. In the fold on his forehead is a silverfish star that shines brightly in the butane light. He is dressed in black, the gown reaching down to his ankles, almost hiding his shoes. A white band circles Pastor Wiltshire's waist and the two ends hang almost to his knees. On his chest is a big wooden cross, held in place by a necklace of black beads. With enthusiasm he rings the bell, letting the sounds travel out into all the crevasses and points of the globe, summoning back all of those who have travelled away from the heart or centre of the assembly.

Pastor Wiltshire begins to sing loudly while ringing the bell. Open-air service always begins with the spiritual "Let the Power Fall on I."

As one, the worshippers take up the singing. The majority of voices are female and they ring loud and clear, while the few men fall in with their bass and baritone. Pastor Wiltshire keeps going from one point to the other, stopping only briefly to ring the bell. He returns to the centre, takes up the Bible, holds it high above his head and then rings the bell some more. Each ring seems like a lash; as he raises the bell over his shoulder and appears to be throwing it again, to be flogging himself.

"Oh, let the Word of the Lord go out from this place here tonight," Pastor Wiltshire says. "Let it go unto the four concerns of the earth. And let our praises ascend to the Heavens to the most high." By now, the women, each dressed in a white gown reaching down to the ankles with her head tied in a white scarf, are swaying rhythmically, as if pulled and pushed by the exact same force, each of them producing the same response as the one beside her. "And let not your word return unto us empty," Pastor Wiltshire says. "Let our praises reach up to you. But let us be a vassal for you, Dear Lord. Let our ways be your ways. Let there be justice for all. And fairness, dear Lord. And let your word lead others to the correct way, for we know ours is a difficult task, for there will always be more sinners than saved; more unjust than just. And he or she that is called to be among the just and the redeemed must be willing to part company with the many and to start walking with the few. Lord help us who are your elect."

"Amen," the members intone.

I walk quickly pass the site of the open-air meeting. A few onlookers are already standing around. Some of them are eating the black pudding and souse. Some are laughing at the rhythmic movements of Pastor Wiltshire's congregation as the spirit takes hold of them and causes them to sway, twirl, bounce and eventually fall on the ground. Some slither like a snake, and they moan and groan and sing praises to the most high and pray for the damned.

"Pastor Wiltshire like he drawing a good, good crowd tonight," Cyrus says to me.

"It looks so," I agree.

"I wonder how many souls he'll save tonight, though," Cyrus says. He has not left my side much since coming back to help out.

"I don't know," I say, not even trying to hide my feelings. But he is an adult and I must be respectful.

"I don't think too many," Cyrus says. "'Cause you know we people. We's Anglicans, most o' we. We ain't too much into this African religion business. We ain't too much into this mixing. We's people that mostly does leave our religion for Sunday mornings and perhaps Sunday school in the evening, and then Sunday night church service. And we ain't for all this hollering and bawling all night long."

"I guess not," I say, keeping up the conversation but not fully committing myself. "Not even the church that Grandmother and Mrs. King does go to, the Pentecostals. Them is mainly Sunday go to church people."

"All the same," Cyrus says, "Pastor Wiltshire *gotta* do his thing. There has to be a place in this society for everyone. Just as long as Pastor Wiltshire and his church know what is theirs, that is fine with me. As long as they don't cause any trouble or try to disrupt things, that is fine as fine can be."

Pastor Wiltshire is swaying in the centre of his assembly. The butane lamp sounds ferocious, as if getting angrier by the moment. One by one, the members of the church start to testify. One by one, they condemn the wickedness in high places, the injustice of man to man and woman to woman, and are calling on everyone, all the fornicators, adulterers, wickers, bullers, malicious people and evildoers within the hearing of their voice to repent, for God will not always wait, he will not tarry and he is coming again soon. And they dance and dance. Cyrus laughs loudly and walks off.

A red airplane-back Rambler with leather seats pulls up in front of the shop, and five men in white shirts and pants get out of the car. Some of them are carrying cricket bats and others the sets of long white pads they use to protect their feet.

"What happen?" a voice calls to them over my shoulder from inside the shop. "Wunnuh lost another again? Don't tell me wunnuh get beat *again*."

There is no answer. The men pass me on their way into the shop. Boysie, the husband of the shopkeeper, drives up, and then a smaller car arrives. The remainder of the cricket team gets out, carrying more bats, pads and gloves. The men store their club gear at the shop between games.

I hear someone loudly suck his teeth and call out, "What I hearing *atall*." When there is still no answer, he says, "Wunnuh done lost again. It is true. I can see it on wunnuh faces. 'Cause I don't know what *kinda* cricketers all you say you *is* these days." The man is Henderson

Brathwaite, Mr. Lashley's best friend. "*Oh man*, I can't wait to hear what really happened to wunnuh backside." The usual spectators that follow the team around to away-games will soon arrive back on the next bus and will give a full accounting, without fear or favour to any of the players, of all that happened.

"Wunnuh ain't nothing like when we, the boys of old, used to play, when I was captain," the public admonishment continues. "Check the scorebook there if you think I lie. Ain't another club in this kiss-me-arse league that could hold a match to we. That is a real tradition, man. We used to meet here in this very shop and celebrate every Sat'dee night. Back then, every manjack pulled his weight on the team. We did be *proud*." The cricketers all seem to bow their heads. They would have expected this much. They must know how to take their licks on and off the field. Tonight will be no different.

"But wunnuh, you young people o' today, you ain't no use *atall*," Henderson says. "Wunnuah can't even win one game. I don't know why all o' you don't give up playing the cricket and just join the old fellows like me here drinking rum rather than running all 'round the island and getting beat each time."

There is no response from the cricketers, but there is a lot of laughter. The cricketers bundle the bats, gloves and pads with the scorebook on top of them in a corner. They reach for the clean glasses on the counter and begin to explain why their best made plans did not work out. It is not true that they have been losing every match. It is just that expectations in the rum shop are always high for them and any loss is a major defeat for the entire village. And whenever they do lose, to hear them explain it, it is usually for the same reason: some umpire made all the wrong decisions, sometimes even conniving with the opposing team to make calls that are contrary to the rules of the game.

The men in the shop are all waiting for the real reports from the spectators still travelling back. They want a true assessment of the players: Who can't do anything, not even catch a cold, far less a cricket ball? Which one lost form with the bat and couldn't even time how to hit the ball or have the patience and concentration to bat long? Which one is now just a sweet-water bowler incapable of getting the wickets of the opposing batsmen?

When the cricket team does win, there is a celebration for the conquering heroes, and even me, sitting out on the steps but still in hearing of the voices in the shop, can become so caught up that Stephie has to tell me when Grandmother and Mrs. King are calling me. Tonight, there is no celebration. Tonight, there is no escaping for me.

As I sit on the steps of the shop, I hear the sounds of the open-air meeting in the near distance. I am close enough to quickly answer should Grandmother or Mrs. King call to me. My job is to have the supply of coals ready to replenish the coal pots. But my position also allows me to see what is happening inside the shop. Nothing out of the ordinary is going on. On one side, the women line up at the shop counter to conduct their business, mainly shopping for groceries. On the other, a small section of the shop with its own door for entry, the men meet and drink and discuss politics and cricket, emerging ever so often to visit Grandmother and Mrs. King, or to pee in the gutter in the darkness. Few women or girls dare to enter the men's section of the shop. Even when a girl comes to call her father home, it is expected she will stop at the door, or on the concrete step, and shout out her instructions to those inside. The same is not true for the boys, no matter how small they are. The grocery section of the shop is an area as much associated with the women as the bar is with the men, although a boy will occasionally be seen there. Even the conversations in the two sections of the shop are different. As the night progresses, the men tend to lapse into long periods of silence. They look out into the darkness forlornly or start a fight, which usually results in the spilling of the blood of one or more people. Women come to the shop to drag the men home. They might even suspend the men from coming back to the shop for a night or two, until the men can show they can hold their liquor without fighting.

By the time the shop closes, most of them will be drunk and will have to find their way home, tottering in the darkness. Stephie and me usually sit together, listening and laughing. Other people could look right at us but through us, not even seeing us, but I would know I am really somebody because we had each other. But not tonight. Not tonight.

Already many of the usual characters are in the rum shop and they've started on several pint-and-a-half bottles of rum. I can just hear Stephie laughing at the foolishness they are talking and I smile to myself. I see the bottles on the counter, next to the unused glasses and the plastic bowl with the cracked ice, which the men have the option of adding to their drinks. Also on the counter are the gallon bottles of water, still showing the chill from the icebox and with rivulets forming on the outside. Mrs. Enid Watson, the shopkeeper, has also opened three bottles of cola and two soda drinks. She enters in the notebook in the pocket of her apron the names of each of the men who order. This is in keeping with the standard rules of the bar: those who order are liable for payment even if others consume more than they do.

As usual, each of the men has chosen a glass, which will be relinquished only at the end of the night. Each man holds on to his, whether the glass contains a drink or not. This is his *spoon*, as the men call the glasses. Each of them will use the same spoon several times to drink the available *waters* or *soup*, which is what they call the rum. Mrs. Watson, a middle-aged woman with turtleshell glasses who looks plump and prosperous, befitting her social and economic standing in the area, flits between the two sections of the shop, between the bar with the men, where she alone serves, and the general groceries section, where two women in their early twenties help her with the dispatching.

The heat from the evening and also from the two rows of fluorescent lights that run across the roof of the shop causes Mrs. Watson to sweat as she keeps order. The perspiration runs out of her hair and from under the cap she is wearing and drips down the sides of her face to her neck and bosom. As they talk, the men twiddle the glasses in their hands, take big sips or simply cradle the glasses to their chest until it is time to refill them. Over by the door, Mr. Lashley's best friend, Henderson, and his wife, Mrs. Brathwaite, share cigarettes from a box and light up from the same match Henderson strikes. Their puffs join the stale smoke already present. Over their heads, the radio hanging low from the roof has long been silent, especially since they stopped playing local music. The stubby jukebox in a corner waits for someone to deposit coins and make a selection. The voices of the men rise steadily as their number grows and the alcohol takes effect. Sitting on the step, I hear their sounds mixing within the songs and preaching from Pastor Wiltshire. From where I am, it is as if the two lifestyles are locked in a struggle for dominance.

I notice that one of the coal pots is burning low, and without waiting for Grandmother or Mrs. King to call to me, I get up, brush off the seat of my pants and attend to the fire. With my bare hands, I reach into the bag and pull out several handfuls of coals, which I place on the red embers, turning the palms of my hands black. Later tonight, I'll walk over to the standpipe and wash the coals from my hands, and I'll have to give my fingernails a good cleaning before school on

Monday morning. But for now, the dirt does not matter, as I will be called upon several times before the night is out to put my hands in the bag of coals. By putting my all into my duty, I cannot be accused by Grandmother of acting as if I'm ashamed to get my hands dirty.

Grandmother and Mrs. King's stools are set on the flat in front of the three concrete steps that run the length of the shop. Already a small crowd is forming around them. Their trays are placed on top of two boxes in front of them, and to the sides are the two coal pots, one in easy reach of each woman. Between them is the tall plastic container with the fish cake batter. The frying pans are on the coal pots, the oil bubbling gently in them, awaiting spoonfuls of fish cake batter. As soon as it is dropped into the hot oil, there is a fizzing sound, and the baking powder in the mixture causes the batter to fluff out into a ball, brown and crispy. Beyond the women is the darkness, where the light from the shop ends, just about where the gutter with the weeds and grass starts at the beginning of the main road.

Most of Grandmother and Mrs. King's early business comes from the women who come to the shop for their weekly supply of groceries. They stop to buy some black pudding and souse and fish cakes, carrying them back home in their own Pyrex dishes and plastic containers for a special treat for their family. The women wrap the filled dishes in a cloth and knot the top, so that the glass cover won't fall off or slide out of position. Later, the business is supported primarily by the men.

I return to my place on the top step of the shop by the door. Once again, I feel trapped. I wonder what Stephie would be telling me now if she were here with me watching all this going on around us, and I wonder what she is up to tonight.

Chapter Seven

"So what you drinking tonight, Lash man?" a voice calls out at the bar. I look up from where I am sitting on the step and see Terrence Willey pushing through the crowd at the bar. He is one of Mr. Lashley's oldest friends, and everybody knows that as two members of the government-run migrant worker program, they tend to move around together when they are at home. They grew up at opposite ends of the village, went to the same school and were selected for the program at the same time. However, they went to different countries, Terrence to the United States to work with sugar cane, and Mr. Lashley farther north to Canada to pick fruit and vegetables in the summer. Once or twice in the times they were back, I had seen Terrence arriving at or leaving Mr. Lashley's house. "Let me buy a drink for yuh to put yuh in the Christmas spirit, man. What you drinking?"

"I ain't really drinking anything too strong tonight, man," Mr. Lashley says in almost a whisper. "I off the liquors for a little while."

"But what you telling me," Terrence asks, his voice still loud. "You know what you're doing? Don't forget when you go back up that you can't get a proper rums like what we can get in this shop here. So you better drink up now, and while we still have a few cents left in we pockets."

"It ain't that," Mr. Lashley says, still keeping his voice low and glancing around to indicate he wants the conversation kept between the two of them. "It's the doctor, man. I under doctor orders for the last few days."

"What you mean, man?" There is concern in Terrence's voice and he does not speak as loudly. "I hope it ain't nothing too serious. Nothing to stop you from passing the exams so you can go back up in the new year."

"No, no, no. Nothing so," Mr. Lashley says, dropping his voice further and flashing his hands to signal that what ails him is of no real consequence. "Just something that I either pick up just before I come back down or that I got here. You know. But I should be all right for my medicals when the time comes. I'm on penicillin."

My heart quickens. I think of the public hygiene class the school makes us take every Friday morning.

"You know how you got it?" Terrence asks.

"Must be *offa* the toilet seat or something," Mr. Lashley says, sniggering. "You can never be too sure 'bout these things. But I should be okay. I'll be good."

"Boy, you *gotta* be careful. You know how them people getting so particular about any little sickness. Everybody gotta be taking so much blood test and chest X-rays. You can't even afford to cough too hard before somebody in the ministry asking yuh what happenin,' as if yuh have consumption or something."

Maybe this is why Stephie is acting so strange: because she is carrying a secret for Mr. Lashley.

"I know, but I'm okay," Mr. Lashley says. Then he corrects himself: "I *gine* be okay."

"'Cause I got a friend who used to work with me, a good, good worker, and last year he came down, looking good yuh know, man, took-in sick, and that was the end of him and the contract. The doctors won't pass him for the program. No more contract fuh he, and fuh the rest o' he life. Good night nurse. All he now doing is walking 'bout here, with nothing to do, no money in he pocket, when he could be up on the program making himself useful and gettin' paid for it. You can't be too careful."

"I know," Mr. Lashley repeats. "I will be all right man, just as long as I stay offa the wagon fuh a little bit."

"What the doctor tell you?"

"It ain't what he tell me; it's what he's doing. Dropping some good and hot injections in my arse every morning, man. I can't even sit down properly these days. Big arse needle he using. Gotta be scotching on one side of my arse when I sitting down." He starts to laugh, mimicking the difficulty and pain of trying to sit. "Why you think I here standing up the whole night now; can't even rest my backside on that bench over there?"

"No shit," Terrence says.

"I have to go to the district hospital every morning for the next week or so for these damn injections. Plus he give me these big-able white tablets to take twice a day. He give me about two or three times the amount o' the same tablets and say to give them to anyone I seeing, to take. But if there is anybody I seeing regular he tell me he wants them to come and see him. I hope she won't have to get them hot-arse injections sheself."

My eyes must be popping out of my head. That *she* can only be one person. And I remember Mrs. King telling Grandmother about Mr. Lashley saying she must take Stephie to his doctor.

"And then he take me off the drinks while I taking the tablets and getting the injections," Mr. Lashley explains. "For now I drinking B&G soda water. I'll be back on the drinks fuh Christmas though. Plus all that medication can make a body feel so listless and drowsy like you only want to sleep."

So that must be why Stephie looked so drained when she came out of the bedroom to eat, why she could not even help out as usual. Now I am more than angry with Mr. Lashley, and I understand why Stephie did not want to discuss certain things with me. I feel sorry for her. But I am not as anxious now that I know what's happened and that she is taking medication. Stephie will be back to her old self when she is better. Mr. Lashley doesn't seem to be too concerned. Stephie will be back at school soon, and I try to feel better for her.

"Good, good," Terrence says. He sounds less apprehensive for his friend. "You'll still be able to do the work on the house this week, right? You keeping the promise to the grandmother, right?"

"Yes, man. I's a man of my word," he says. "I done give she my word. I'll fix up that old house for her. I gine buy the paint Monday morning bright and early, right after I see the doc and get my injections in my ras, and me and you and a couple of the fellows that say they gine help me can get started on Wednesday, if not before, so that we'll have the two jobs lick-out and done by Friday self."

"Good. You know you can count on me. Want me to come with you Monday to pick out the paint?"

"You can if you want, but you don't haf ta," Mr. Lashley says. "We already done decide on the colour and the trimming, so choosing the paint shouldn't be too much trouble. After that, I plan to go down by the hardware store there on Main Street in the city and order some sides o' lumber and some galvanize for the two roofs. This is a job that they agree to give me a free hand, 'cause you know how it is with women, especially when it comes to a house. They will do anything fuh a house, no matter how small um is. So the best I can do is spruce up things and get a feather in my cap."

"The way you thinking, like yuh really in the Christmas spirit, eh," Terrence says. "Me and my old lady like we ain't hitting it off too hot, so I ain't decide yet if I doing one blast for the house that she live in. I might just decide to let it stay the way it is, no repairs, no painting, no nothing so. And as fuh the children, I might just decide to leff them out this year too, 'cause they ain't showing me no blasted respect since I come back down. So I may as well put my money to good uses and leave she to contend with her children in that house I done pay for already."

"That don't sound too good, man," Mr. Lashley consoles. "I hope things work out for yuh. I mean, when a man been away on the program and he come back home for only a short time, the least his woman and she children can do is show him some respect. At least they can pretend 'til he's gone."

"I know. But don't let we spend no more time talking 'bout them things. She can keep the blasted house if that is what she want, for all I care. Still, the way things bre'king for you, I gotta tell yuh that I glad fuh you and, as man, I'll come and help you out during the coming week. At least it will get me outta the house from under the blasted woman foot, and from around them children that she got and who ain't got no knowing. But what can yuh do; the woman come wid the children, so I either gotta accept the children with the mother too, or leff out both the woman and she children and end up losing the house in the process."

"I know," Mr. Lashley says. "I don't envy yuh man. Not one shite. Ain't a house around here any man can say belongs truly to he, not, as is the case with me, unless the man does live alone by hisself and does do his own washing and cooking for himself. Otherwise a man making bare sport if he's walking 'bout here thinking any house he put a woman in belongs to he anymore. That is the gospel truth. Why do you think I dida hold out for so long? But a man can hold out for only so long, unless he is a buller or something. Plus, in my case I gotta say that this one I checking, she's fine and young, not some hard-back cut-open cow that done bruk out and know the ways of the world. She's somebody that I think I can train, so that if she treats me good, I'll treat she good too."

I hear myself sighing in relief. Cyrus, after all, is wrong. Mrs. King is right when she says Mr. Lashley is different from other men and that he would not let Stephie turn out like so many young girls we know. I need not worry. I am beginning to like Mr. Lashley again. But at the same time, I don't like what they are saying about this *she* person, who they treating as if she doesn't even have a name.

I see Desmond Smith and Leila standing in front of Grandmother and Mrs. King. He accepts a plate with souse from Mrs. King and takes out what looks like a part of the pig's knuckle and begins sucking on it. Leila takes a piece from the plate as well and gingerly puts it in her mouth, chewing slowly. Grandmother hands her a salt bread roll with several slices of black pudding in it. She bites into the bread and again chews slowly, before giving the bread to Desmond, as if to indicate she does not like it. Mrs. King reaches into the tray and hands her a few of the fish cakes, which Leila begins eating as if she is much happier with them.

Desmond and Leila head into the section of the shop where the men drink. An uneasy hush settles among the men. When they resume their conversations, they are more stilted. Desmond pours a rum and Coke for his wife and another for himself. Together, they move to the farthest fringe of the group and some of the uneasiness shifts with them. Finally, they walk off into the darkness on the road that leads to the dance hall. As I remain seated on the step, I once again become aware of a steady throbbing in my mouth, though the pain is not great enough to cause too much discomfort.

Pastor Wiltshire rings the bell once again. From what I can see, he is ready to call it a night and dismiss his flock of worshippers. By this time, the crowd of onlookers has dwindled to a handful. The singing, clapping and swooning in the spirit has grown less frenetic as the meeting turned solemn with Pastor Wiltshire's altar call. As is usually the case, nobody has answered. Nobody has broken out of the darkness and gone to the centre where the Bible is still open and the butane lamp hisses furiously. Pastor Wiltshire's ringing of the bell has grown less enthusiastic and his voice has become less hectoring as he accepts that another night of toil has resulted in no saved souls to show for it.

Mrs. Watson closes the main part of the shop, plunging most of the area in the front into darkness. Off to my left, where the big ackee tree is casting a long shadow from the shop's light, the lovers are still dancing to the music of the jukebox, a man singing "Cry Me a River." It is like they can't wait for the dance hall to start. At the end of the song, one of the young men goes to feed a number of coins into the jukebox. The Blues Busters begin wailing their hit tune "Behold." He must have chosen this nice, soft hold-me-close tune to please the women. He could scarcely be acting on his own.

Everything is winding down, but slowly. Through the big cracks between the doors, I can see the bags of sugar and flour piled high, but nothing is moving on the inside.

"How it's been?" Cyrus says, stooping next to me. He sounds tired. There's a young man with him who is about two or three years older than me. He too sits on the step.

"I doing all right," I say.

"Getting late, eh?" Cyrus says. "Gonna need any help taking the things back home?"

"I guess so," I say.

"So, Cyrus," says Mr. Lashley's friend Terrence as he stumbles through the door, "where you been all night long? I've been looking for you, man."

"I've been around," Cyrus says. Turning to the young man beside him, he asks, "Neil, you want something more to drink?"

"I guess so," Neil says nonchalantly. "I could do with a Coke or something."

"Here," Cyrus says, hurriedly pulling a note from his pocket and handing it to the young man. "Go and get yourself a Coke and keep the rest o' the money for your bus fare back home." Neil takes the money and is about to walk off when he turns back to us.

"Any o' you want anything?" Neil asks. I shake my head.

"Not for me, either," Cyrus says.

"Nor me," Terrence says. "I've had enough to drink for one night. All I want now is my bed and somebody to hug up with. I see you looking for the same, eh Cyrus?"

"He's from downtown," Cyrus explains, nodding in the direction of Neil. "From near my workplace. He came up here to visit me for the night, but he gotta get ready to catch the last bus when it's coming back down." Neil returns with a Coke bottle dangling from his fingers and sits beside Cyrus.

"The bullers like they all gone now," Terrence says. "Like they all gone home."

"Why you don't leave the people alone?" Cyrus asks angrily. "You never hear to each his own and never trouble trouble 'til trouble troubles you?"

"I ain't troubling anybody," Terrence says. "I ain't trouble one soul. So don't be so touchous. I just calling it as I see it. Anyway, Cy, you looking forward to Christmas."

"So, so," Cyrus answers. "I ain't no touchous. But Christmas is just Christmas for me. No big thing, especially now that I does live on my own, no wife, no woman, no children, no nothing. What I'm looking forward to is the new year. I can't wait for the new year to come and for cricket to start. I'm going to be at cricket every single day."

Everyone knows how much Cyrus loves cricket. But from the way he is now talking, it appears as if he is in a hurry to shift the conversation to a more comfortable subject.

"I think next year is the start of great things for our international cricket team," he says. "I think we're about to begin a long, long run as cricket champions o' the world."

"What make you think so?" Terrence asks, sounding tired or a bit too boozy.

"It's because of young people like this one here," Cyrus says, slapping my shoulder. I almost faint: Me and cricket? Nobody's ever said that they've noticed me playing cricket. "I have a lot of confidence in the talents that we have right here among us. That is one thing that independence is going to bring out in the people, that we can be champions all over the world, just as long as we grow and develop the talents we have, just like Christopher here. What you think, Christopher?"

"I hope so," I say modestly. I am not yet at an age where the men in the rum shop would dream of mentioning my name when talking about the young aspirants for the village team. I look up and notice that several men from the shop have come outside and are listening. The jukebox is quiet and my answer seems amplified. "I hope so, 'cause I just like to play cricket any time I get," I hear myself saying. At the same time, I hear Pastor Wiltshire wishing everyone a good night and promising to return to the same place the same time next week, God willing. Just then, the bus pulls up to a stop in front of Grandmother and Mrs. King. The driver alights from the bus through the main passenger door with a bowl in his hand.

"That's the spirit," Cyrus encourages. "And that is the winning spirit. Just watch and see how the West Indies team will perform in the new year. England, Australia, New Zealand, India, we beating them all, you watch and see."

The driver returns to the bus and shifts into gear.

"The bus leaving," I say to Neil. "You're going to miss it?"

Neil hunches his shoulders. He does not move and I say nothing more. Grandmother calls to me. She is already throwing water on the fire in the coal pot, the surest sign that the night is ending for us. The lovers are wandering off and suddenly there is quiet. I get up, brush my pants and head off in the direction of Grandmother and Mrs. King, hoping Cyrus is right about one thing: that the new year will bring us some more exciting cricket.

This time, not only do we have a helping hand from Cyrus but his friend Neil as well. Yawning, I pick up one of the coal pots by its wooden handle. We walk home silently in the darkness. Even Mr. Lashley's house is all darkness. Cyrus and Neil say good night to us and head off into the night. I cannot wait to spread my bedding and close out what feels like the longest day in my life.

Chapter Eight

When I get home from school on Wednesday, I find Mr. Lashley and several men from the area still at work on Mrs. King's house. Though they are talking and laughing more than they were when I left this morning, they are still occupied with measuring and planing more lumber and cutting out the hardened cardboard for the repairs. They had started this morning by rigging up the long carpenter's bench to the eastern side of Mrs. King's house. Spread now beneath the bench are the curled shavings from the boards, along with piles of sweet-smelling sawdust and pieces of discarded wood. The men have been working mainly on the side of the house that gets the most rain, the side where Stephie's bedroom is. So far they have removed the rotting shingles-and-board siding and replaced part of it with new boards, starting from the ground sill up. Only the upper siding up to the galvanize roof is still open, and through it I can see the men have also fixed the partition to the bedroom inside the house and replaced the cardboard ceiling. The old cardboard, stained from the rain and years, is in a heap underneath Grandmother's clammy cherry tree. At one end of the workbench is a tray with a bowl containing what's left of the ice, mainly water, and a large pitcher of water to go along with the seemingly untouched gallon bottle of rum and some glasses. From what I see, none of the men is drinking yet; no doubt they will when the sun disappears and they knock off work and gather in the early darkness to plan for the next day.

"Good evening," I say, as I come up to Grandmother and Mrs. King.

"Good evening, son," Mrs. King answers. The two women are standing in the walkway between the two houses, talking and offering unobtrusive advice to the men as they see fit, when they are not talking softly to each other. They seem to be trying not to be too distant but also to not get in the way of the men working. "I hope you had a good day at school."

"Yes, I did, Mrs. King," I say. "School was okay."

"No trouble with the books today?" she asks, half-jokingly.

"No, Mrs. King," I say. "I had all the books today. So no detention this time." Mrs. King nods her head approvingly. Some of her long plaits of hair bob around her neck, others occasionally fall over her face. Her hair is mostly black with a few white hairs, and I notice that it is shiny and that she has fresh grease on her scalp. She and Grandmother normally get together in our backyard in the afternoon and wash each other's hair over the large enamel basin. Mrs. King sits on the back doorstep as Grandmother painstakingly pulls a comb through the full length of her hair to remove any knots and tangles before turning her own head over to Mrs. King.

I like to see the women *playing*—as they call it—with each other's hair. Their fingers work nimbly through the stands, smoothly making braids. Mrs. King has the fuller head of hair, and I think Grandmother particularly enjoys playing with it. What I do not like is the smell of singeing hair from the ironing comb, which arises even when they apply a good amount of La India hair pomade.

I am excited by the sounds of the sawing and hammering and of the men racing against the sun to complete as much of the job as they can before nightfall. I like the fresh smell of the sawdust. Its fragrance always reminds me of something new. It reminds me of the start of sugar cane season, when the smell of fresh bagasse from the factory is first on the air. It is like the good times when I go mashing trash with the boys from the area, searching among the leaves in the sugar cane fields for any canes left behind after harvesting. We would suck so much cane, our bellies would be too full for dinner.

Standing alone and off to one side is Stephie. She appears to be just as eagerly taken up with the goings-on as I am. But she looks so alone, disconnected from the other women and at the same time not quite part of the working men group. There is something in the way she looks, or maybe it is how she is standing, that does not appear quite right to me. It's as if she suddenly grew much older and *mature* when I wasn't looking. Her hair also looks like it has just been combed. Grandmother says she inherited her *good* hair from her grandmother. It reaches down below the sides of her face and her neck. Underneath the plaits, there is sweat on her face and neck—not the kind that comes from labouring, but that comes from standing in the warm afternoon sun, especially after taking a bath.

Stephie is wearing one of the new T-shirts that Mr. Lashley brought down from overseas for her. It is black with some pictures printed on the front, and she is wearing it tied in a big knot at the waist, just above the white shorts that were also a gift from Mr. Lashley. To me, Stephie looks prim. I am used to seeing her walking around in the backyard barefoot, but she is wearing a pair of slippers that Mrs. King said also came from Mr. Lashley.

"How you doing?" I ask as I come up to her.

"I okay," she responds brusquely, before quickly glancing in the direction of our grandmothers. There is so much I want to ask her. She has missed yet another day at school, yet from what I can see, apart from the strange way she is carrying herself and the new airs about her, she looks well, physically fine, with no lingering effects from the medication. As we continue talking, she does not ask about school once. Even though she keeps glancing at Mrs. King, I know instinctively that it is Mr. Lashley who is really the centre of her attention at that moment. He is scraping cracked and sun-blistered paint from the wood at the front of the house, while Cyrus is on the roof with a can of tar, inspecting for holes. Mr. Lashley comes upon a knot in the wood and clears the paint from around it before applying some putty to keep the knot in place. When he finishes, he uses the end of his putting knife to smooth over the patch. All the while, he keeps up a running commentary about painting and his outlook on life, which is what clearly interests Stephie the most.

"Everybody can't be a painter," he says. "The same way that everybody can't be no doctor nor lawyer either. It got to be a calling for them, something that you born with, something special, in the wrist and in the nerves in your hand, from the way you hold the paintbrush to the way you dip it in the paint. Everybody can't do that."

Mr. Lashley is wearing a sleeveless vest-shirt and overalls that have dried paint on them—*old clothes*, he calls them, from the days before he joined the Overseas Workers Program. Those were the times, he is recounting, when he was employed outside of the sugar cane crop season as a full-time painter, mainly at the island's airport. Mr. Lashley, when in the mood, would boast about his painting. On many occasions in the shop, he talked about some of the big jobs he had painted, the number of hotels and government buildings he had worked on on the island, now all monuments to his greatness, before he decided to pack it in and go for the money that the Overseas Workers Program offered. Today, even though his audience is much smaller, he is still trying to impress from his perch on the ladder.

"This is going to be the *purttiest* house around here when I done finished with she," he boasts. "Mrs. King, girl," he says, "you gine be real proud of me when I finish this masterpiece here. It gine be pretty fuh so. Just wait 'til I come back down in the new year. You ain't see nothing yet."

Mr. Lashley goes on to talk about how he might even go into business for himself, maybe with his childhood buddy Terrence, so that he won't be employed by anyone nor be answerable to anybody. He would work for himself, picking and choosing which paint jobs he wants. Boasting, he says he has no doubts whatsoever that people will be willing to pay him good.

"How was school today?" Stephie finally asks. There is a smile on her face as if she knows a secret I don't know. "Anything new happened, at school, I mean?" It is as if she is talking to a boy much younger and inexperienced in the ways of the world—as if I am just another *pissy* boy, as Grandmother and Mrs. King calls them.

"Not really," I say. "Just that everybody talking about the big cross-country race Wednesday, if you're going to run since nobody ain't seen you at school all this time."

"Of course, I will," Stephie says. Suddenly I have grabbed her attention. I see a brief tremor of her lips. I wait but she does not explain further. She bites her lips and continues staring at the house and the men. I am relieved that she at least still wants to run. I was beginning to fear that she thinks she is too big or grown up for things such as school and racing.

"It's just that your *friend* Ursula saying that she thinks that you frightened for she this time, that you know she'll beat you this year," I say, hoping to provoke Stephie into saying what she really feels and to explain what is happening in her life. "That is why, she says, that all of a sudden you stopped showing up at school, just at the time for the big race. She says you too afraid to show your face 'round the school, 'cause you know you're going to get a good trashing this time and by she, Ursula, of all people."

"Nobody don't mind Ursula," Stephie snaps. "She couldn't beat me, Stephanie King, not even in my sleep."

"Well, I don't know," I say, trying to tease more out of her, "but you know she's been training really hard, and I ain't see you've been doing anything lately, certainly not training, except for the other night when I did see you all outta breath and sounding as if you've been crying. If you're going to beat Ursula in the big race, I tell yuh, you can't be so all out of breath. People all 'bout the school say that Ursula's training hard, hard, hard first thing in the morning before school and that is the last thing she does do each and every night. I don't know what you thinking, but you might have another thought coming."

"Ursula is nothing," Stephie says, almost shouting. "*Nothing.* And I don't *gotta* do no whole lot a training like she to beat she. I got my ways. I've beaten Ursula and I am the best in that school there every single year that we run the cross-country together in we division, and I don't plan to stop now. I don't care how much she training. Everybody knows I got the best lungs in the whole school when it comes to running and that I don't ever get out of breath, at least not like any o' them other girls at school. And in any case, when you did see me I wasn't *even* crying, so I don't know what you are *talkin'* about."

"In any case," I say, "you know how I feel. Me and Ursula in the same house at school, and if she wins that will be a whole lot of points for my Set A. We might even win the sports cup when we carry forward the points to next year. So . . ."

"Don't bet your heart on them points," Stephie warns. "Set D will be collecting all o' them points. If you want points, you will have to go and run for them in the boys' race, 'cause Set D done got all them points from the girls a'ready, even before we run the race. I'll deliver them again. Just like all the times before." With that, she flounces up herself.

"Stephie," Mrs. King calls. "Stephie, you come here now. Come along over here with me and Peggy here, or find something to do with yourself in the house."

"And yes, you Christopher," Grandmother says in her special tone, "you ain't got *nothing* to do?"

Stephie walks off. As she passes Mr. Lashley's ladder, he stops her. They talk softly for a brief while before she disappears inside the house. Mr. Lashley continues scraping dried paint from the boards and removes cracked putty from the edges of the glass panes in the window. He seems to be watching me. Maybe Mrs. King and Grandmother are right, I tell myself. Perhaps this is not the right time for us to talk about all the things I want to ask her. At least that's the message I got from Mrs. King's and Grandmother's words and tone.

"Played any cricket at school today?" Cyrus calls down to me from the roof as I make my way over to where Grandmother is standing.

"Is *that* a question you asking he?" Grandmother says. "A day don't pass without that boy there not playing cricket. Morning, noon and night. That is all he wants. I does got to ask him if he think he is Sobers or a Kanhai when it comes to batting."

"He might be better than the two o' them," Cyrus calls back. "You ever see that grandson o' your'wn bat yet? Pure grace self, sweet, sweet timing, with everything coming off the centre of the face of the bat, like he did born with a bat in his hand. Everything natural, natu-ral, natural about him. The footwork and the timing in the wrists: like one o' them great dancers." This is how I often hear the men in the rum shop describe the best cricketers down through the ages. They are the qualities they look for when evaluating who should get picked for the team or who should be dropped. I smile to myself.

"Let me tell yuh now," Cyrus says, "that young man is a somebody that all o' we around here should be watching, 'cause as I keep saying, it is in the cricket that we as young nations will prove *weself* to every-body else in the world. It's the cricket, man, cricket, and we music too, that will set us apart in the world. And it all starts with talented people like that boy you got there, the next generation. All he needs is some good coaching, for somebody 'round here to take him under his wings."

I follow Grandmother into the house. Now that the sun is disap-pearing bit by bit, the tempo of the work is easing. Soon both the sun and the men will be gone. Grandmother takes to counting her chick-ens and turkeys as usual. I sit at the table in the shed roof and begin working on my geometry. I also have Spanish homework and the new set of big words that Mr. Jones wants us to learn to spell.

I feel a strong air of excitement and anticipation for the coming days and for Christmas. I feel it in my bones, and it gives me a tin-gling feeling all over. These feelings must be, as Mr. Jones keeps telling us, to do with being young and having the world laid out before us. I cannot wait to enjoy being young in the coming days.

Chapter Nine

As the excitement bubbles among us, Mr. Jones steps to the front of the assembly and raises his hand above his head for silence. When assembled like this, instead of coming together as a single unit, we must look like four separate divisions of an army, making ready for inspection or battle. At first, nobody seems to notice him, so he waves his hand frantically, as if he is doing a war dance for his group. When that still does not get him the attention he wants, Mr. Jones takes up a sweet-drink bottle and starts hitting it with a key from his pocket. The tinkling sound stills the youngest members of the school at the front first, and then the wave of silence sweeps over us in the middle range and eventually makes its way to the senior students at the back.

At the front are the eight set masters and mistresses. Each division has its own master and mistress. They are all dressed in the colours of the school's four divisions. Behind the set masters and mistresses are the prefects, then the captains and, finally, the set members, all in our set colours. This gathering is a highlight of the school term and is matched only by the cross-country race itself. Only an occasion such as this could get Mr. Jones out of his usual black tie and white shirt and into an open-necked shirt of many colours with images of palm trees, hibiscus flowers and the long-beaked birds that people overseas call hummingbirds but that we call *doctor-boobies*.

This is one of the few times during the year when we meet as an entire school, but we are not in the usual forms based on age and learning. We are assembled on the playing field at the back of the school in our sets. The set monitors are standing in front of each group. The male student leaders are dressed in their school uniform, a white shirt and grey flannel pants, while the female leaders wear a sash that runs over the shoulder and around the waist. The buzz starts again and Mr. Jones raises his hand to keep us under control.

"Good afternoon, students and set masters and mistresses," he begins.

"Good afternoon, sir," we all bellow, with what is the first and final show of unity among all sets until the end of term.

"Tomorrow," Mr. Jones says, "is the day so many of us have been waiting for. We remember how in ancient Greece and in Roman times, a good education was more than what we now call book learning. It involved much of what we will spend the next day doing. Much of the learning back then had to do with developing what we call a person's virtue. Some people were good at book learning; some were good at running, jumping and shooting arrows; some were good at talking and debating, that is what we call *rhetoric*; some were good simply at supporting others as part of the team. We don't use arrows these days, and I still think we should find a place in our curriculum for debating and rhetoric as part of our civic lessons, but we still want to see who can run the fastest and longest, jump the highest and who is the strongest. In my mind, we don't have fancy gymnasiums—we can't afford them—but we are making Olympic champions, starting them from early and making a statement to the world about our ability as a people. That is what we are involved in here. This is fun and games, but it is also part of our nation building. This is part of the bigger picture now we are an independent people. All of these things are part of the spirit we will be exhibiting tomorrow. Sports and games are important parts of our social life. They help us to understand how we should live with one another as part of a wider community. That is what education is about, to teach us morals, how to conduct ourselves and how we should behave toward other people. So tomorrow, we ain't just running any old race: we are practising a culture that aims for excellence itself. Just remember the words of the national motto and our national pledge of allegiance. How we treat the children of this our young nation, how we protect, nourish and nurture them, that is how we want to be judged by the world and how we will judge ourselves. And you, dear students, are all the children and the future of this nation."

The ringleader at the front of Set D begins singing, "*Lions. We are the Lions. We know we shall win.*" and the entire set joins in, singing and swaying like Pastor Wiltshire's followers, all of them moving in unison, swinging back and forth, to and fro, like the treetops and canes dancing in the breeze. "*Set D are lions. We know we shall win. Just hear the lion roar . . .*" One voice is missing from this group. But nobody seems to care or even notice. Maybe they will tomorrow when the race is about to start.

"Come on," our set leader shouts. "Let's show them what we in Set A can do: "*Strong, young, independent and black.*" Now our set is also swaying in unison, and the two sets are competing with each other, trying to drown the other out. Sets B and C are less worked up, which is partly an indication of where they feel tomorrow's competition rests. They know the competition in cross-country is between Sets A and D, and that it is a struggle between two runners. But gradually Sets B and C get into the spirit too, and they sing their theme songs. "*Ursula, Ursula, Ursula,*" the chant goes up around me, to be met with the rejoinder: "*Set A is a pussy cat, meow, meow, meow, tweet, tweet, tweet.*"

"As I was saying," Mr. Jones says, shooting a playful disapproving look in the direction of the Set D ringleader. "This is an opportunity for us to put on display the virtues we have cultivated all year long. We can learn *patience,* for as we know it is not always the fastest that wins a marathon but he or she that runs the good race and endureth to the end. For another virtue, we can think of tolerance, for every long-distance runner needs that, *endurance,* so that the aches and pains that we encounter, just like all the different types of people we meet in life, we've got to show tolerance toward. Then we think of *respect* for our fellow competitors. We respect them knowing that on some days they may defeat us, but that in so doing they are simply challenging us to do better next time, to dig deeper. Another virtue we would consider for tomorrow is that of *acceptance,* and here again we are not talking about complacency but about knowing that despite our best efforts, as in life, there are some things that we cannot control. For example, it may rain tomorrow and that would require running a different race than if it were dry outside. *Humility,* another of the virtues dear to us, teaches us to accept our lot gracefully, whether we win or lose. And of course we must have the virtue of *fortitude,* to be strong and be able to strike and, finally, we cannot forget, the virtue of *kindness,* which we must always show to our fellow competitors, as in life, in the hope that others would show the same kindness and mercy to us."

"No mercy," the ringleader for Set D starts. "We showing no

mercy. We show no kindness. We winning. We winning. *The Champions. The Champions.*"

"*We are young, strong and black,*" Set A's ringleader retaliates. I too am singing at the top of my voice. I can hear everyone roaring and the noise becoming louder and louder. The four male leaders and their female partners are in front of Mr. Jones, dancing, shuddering, advancing on one another and retreating, moving in a circle, as a unit and as the circle itself, shaking their fists, clicking their heels, twisting and kicking. Each leader and partner is moving slowly and distinctly, making small, slow steps on the ball of their feet, moving as if they hear a special rhythm in their heads, a distinctive beat of one, two, one, two, beat, one, two, one, two, beat. Each step forward or backward is followed by a distinctive twist, a high kick with feet flying, with the toes pointed inward at the beginning and outward at the end of the beat. Each of them appears to hear at the same time, each giving the same response to the call. They move and they stalk. When side by side, the boys and girls move forward or backward together; when facing each other, the girls move backward and the boys follow them. They circle and we sing, clap and squeal.

"Just think of those things," Mr. Jones says when he regains control of the assembly. "Those of you who are taking part in this important race tomorrow, make sure that you get to bed early and get a good night's rest. Remember there is a role to play for each and every one in each and every set. If you are not running, cheer as loud and as long as you can. Those of you who are running, I wish each and every one of you the best. And in the morning, I want you to make sure you arrive at school with a full belly. So," he turns to speak to the teachers at the front with him, "set masters and mistresses, take hold of your charges. I think we will have a good day tomorrow, God willing."

My set begins running around the playing field with Ursula in the lead. Instinctively, I start running with the crush of the crowd. "*Stephie in the garden hiding, hiding, hiding,*" the ringleader sings out. I stop suddenly in my tracks, unable to bring myself to join the taunting. "*Stephie in the garden hiding, hiding from Ursula.*" Stephie isn't here to defend herself. In the past, Stephie would always be at this assembly, in good voice, singing and leading the charge. For not only is she the best long-distance runner in the set, she is perhaps the best singer too.

The entire assembly leaves the schoolyard and heads toward the bus stand. "*Stephie, where art thou? Stephie, where art thou?*" So, the others *have* noticed her absence. And they seem to be suggesting more. Perhaps they're right. Stephie yet again has not shown up at school. And this is a day, with all its boasting and challenging, that is as great as the day of performance itself. Maybe Stephie is not as confident of herself as she had pretended to be. Or maybe she is just sick and does not want to tell me, or anyone else for that matter. I hang my head low. As the singing roars on, the members of Stephie's Set D, for the first time in a long while, have no adequate response. Neither do I.

Mrs. King's house looks majestic in its new coat of pinkish-red paint with white trim. The new sheets of galvanize gleam in the late afternoon sun. Grandmother's house, in comparison, now appears to be even more badly in need of fixing up.

Mr. Lashley sits on the veranda of his house, listening to Christmas carols on the radio inside the house. I wave hello and Mr. Lashley waves back. Inside our house, Grandmother is sitting on the bench by the table.

"Good evening, Grand," I say.

"Good evening, son," she answers. "You hungry?"

"A little bit," I say.

"Go and take off your school clothes and I'll share your food for you," Grandmother says.

"Mrs. King's house looking good, eh?" I say.

"Oh, it's wonderful," Grandmother says. "I *gotta* say God really did bless her. She's really blessed. I'm too glad for her, 'cause she really deserves it. I don't know what some of us on this island would do without a kind-hearted godfather."

I do not respond but concentrate on changing into my home clothes. The evening is free for me. With the next day devoted totally to the cross-country race, there is no homework. Indeed, I should really be celebrating, for there will be no more homework for the rest of the year. Yet I keep hearing the taunts of my own set ringing in my ears. And I do not like the way they make me feel.

Stephie does show up for the big race and nobody is as happy or more relieved as I am. I had been dreading the worst when I came to the field, for there was no sign of Stephie at the bus stop when I was leaving home. For as long as I've known her, Stephie has lived for racing. Sometimes we would talk about what life would be like if she was fortunate enough to get a scholarship to run overseas. We thought that if her mother sent for her, she would get the best running shoes and clothes to help her, for the track and field equipment would be cheap and plentiful over-'n'-away, and we doubted there were any athletes abroad who did not start with the best in gear and facilities. At least that was what we saw in the magazines. By joining her mother, Stephie might even be able to become a member of an athletic club and get a trainer to coach her. I was beginning to think that those dreams existed only in the past.

So it's a great surprise to see her already on the field when I arrive. A large group from her set surrounds her as she stretches. I can see that she has been working up a sweat as well. Seeing her, I start to run in her direction, but then I remember what day it is and that the two of us are supposed to have different interests and to want different results. Yet I can't bring myself to join the Set A supporters around Ursula. I feel a heavy burden lifting from my shoulders, but at the same time I still feel some of the anxiety from the day before. Stephie looks like the runner of old, the one that I knew. There is a bounce in the way she moves, and if she has any concerns about Ursula, she is not showing them. Her supporters won't allow her to even think about losing; they are following her around, singing all their songs and chanting slogans. As usual, Stephie is leading the singing. I feel good.

Now they are at the starting line. Stephie stands out, especially in the way she is dressed: she wears black shorts and a blazing red T-shirt with the words *Highland Farms Your Christmas Shopping* emblazoned big and bold across her chest. On her back is a drawing of what looks like a farmhouse, with smoke escaping from a long brick chimney. Stephie is wearing a brand new pair of red and grey sneakers, and her white socks are turned down and folded at her ankles. Mr. Jones walks over to the starting line and waves for all the runners to assemble. Stephie takes her usual position in the middle of the pack, while Ursula in her white running shoes and T-shirt and tight red shorts goes to the front, as is usual for her. On both sides, from the starter's position and all the way from the school to the main road, students have formed a corridor.

"Is everybody that running this race here?" Mr. Jones asks, looking around as if he expects some straggler to bolt from the darkness that is the inside of the school. Nobody appears. The voices of the students nearest to the starting line roar their opposing cheers.

"Everybody to the starting line," Mr. Jones commands. "On your mark," he calls, as all the runners but Stephie and Ursula put forward a bare foot, toes touching the imaginary line. "Get set, ready." I notice Stephie's sneakers among the feet. "Go."

The stampeding feet move through the corridor on the way to the main road. In the midst of the crowd, Stephie in her red shirt stands out. Ursula is in the lead. I find a position on the sidewalk on the edge of the schoolyard and the main road. I know it will not be long before the first runners appear. If this race is like any other before, by the next time the runners come into view, Stephie and Ursula will be out front, with Stephie increasing her lead until she breaks the tape. One thing I know about Stephie is that she is a strong finisher. It has never mattered who is in the lead at the outset.

As I wait, I think of what it would be like if Grandmother were to hear from my mother that she is sending for me. Would I be happy or sad? I am not sure. I know for certain that I would be happy at the prospect of finally getting to know my mother, my own flesh and blood, and being with the person that brought me into the world. I am sure my mother would take good care of me, and she and I would hit it off right away, just as soon as we set eyes on we one another. Both of us would be so happy that we would just run into each other's arms at the airport, just like I had seen in the theatre. My mother would grab me and we would swing around and around as if we dancing; my mother would be crying and saying how happy she is seeing me, and that she would never ever, ever leave me again, not on her life. Now that I was with her, she would take that as another chance to be a good mother to me, to be the best mother there ever was and ever will be, because all mothers want to be the best mothers for their own flesh and blood, and she would never let anything come between us again. I would tell her everything about how Grandmother was always so good to me, but how happy I was to be with her and that it is only right that every child should be with its mother and, maybe father too, but particularly its mother. And I imagine my mother taking me to a big house with some of the best furniture, a house just like the one in the picture in Mrs. King's house, like the ones I see in the theatre and on the mobile cinema the government sends out so often to entertain us on the elementary school pasture, a house with a big table, and my mother would give me a big plate of food at that table, where I would sit in a high-back chair, with a knife and fork and spoons in the right positions, just like in any fancy house.

In the distance, I see the first runner. It is Kelvin, who usually wins the boys' race. Everything appears to be breaking as expected, with a pack of the fastest boys leading the way, and the fastest girls and medium-speed boys coming next. I get up from where I am sitting and join the corridor re-forming on the two sides of the road up to the finishing line. When all is done and finished, I expect that I will be running around the field, joining Stephie in the singing. Kelvin breaks the tape held by the head boy and head girl across the corridor formed by the students. He takes a lap around the school pasture and stops in a crowd of Set A supporters, bending at the waist and panting for breath. The sweat is running down his face and he is laughing between gasps. Soon I see Ursula coming, and her long, loping strides appear to be getting stronger. As she swiftly heads for the finishing line, a big crowd accompanies her, and she jumps in the air as she makes one last joyous burst to claim victory. The chorus goes up: "*Set A beats them every day, hallelujah; Set A beats t'em everywhere, hallelujah.*" As she takes her victory lap, I stand in shock as the second runner, then the third and fourth cross the finishing line. There is still no sign of Stephie. A full ten minutes after the winner finished, Stephie shows up, the soles of her sneakers torn away and flapping. By now, the taunts are heavy. "*Ur'sla beat them all today, hallelujah. Stephanie is stinky and poor, hallelujah.*" I run beside Stephie. Except for those jeering, most of the other students have moved on to something else; some are playing marble cricket, others road tennis or pitching.

Then I notice that something is definitely wrong with Stephie, for as soon as she crosses the finishing line, her legs wobble. As she is about to fall over, I dash in front of her and hold her up, her weight falling heavy on me, her hands hanging down listlessly. The set masters and mistresses notice and two of them run over to help. Mr. Jones comes loping over too.

"Oh, God, Chris," Stephie is gasping, "Ah feel bad. I feel real bad."

I hold her. Her new T-shirt is soaked with sweat. Just as the teachers reach us, Stephie lunges forward, but the teachers catch her and hold her up. "Lord, I feel real bad," she repeats. And then, as her knees buckle again, she once more lurches forward with her upper body, and from her mouth spews out watery and slimy vomit. Stephie, of all people, is crying, and there is nothing any of us can do to help. The teachers hold her up as she, bent at the waist, vomits a second time, and then a third, and a fourth. Though she continues to retch, nothing more comes up. A female teacher gives her a white handkerchief to wipe her mouth and someone comes running with a glass of water. Stephie is sweating even more, but at least she stops vomiting. As the four teachers take her into the school, I hear the chant from the field, "*The champions, the champions.*" Someone starts singing, "*Set A rowed the boat ashore, hallelujah. Stephanie is stinky and poor, hallelujah.*" Stephie and the teachers disappear into the staff room, which is off limits to students. She remains there until the end of the school day.

As we board the bus for home, I allow Stephie to go before me and to sit beside the window so she can breathe the fresh air. I hope it will make her feel better, even though she seems to have improved from earlier in the day. She is sullen and doesn't want to talk too much. I understand that the disappointment of losing is really great; even though I am in the set that won, I can still feel what she is going through. It is not easy to have students mock and jeer at you. Seated on the inside, she is shielded a bit from the other students on the bus. Stephie slumps in the seat as the bus pulls out of its bay. I am settling in for what I hope will be a quiet ride home, when pain shoots to my brain. It feels as if someone is pushing a hot, sharp spike into my bad tooth. I hold the side of my face.

"What happen'd wid you?" Stephie asks. I cannot answer. I sit holding my face all the way home. It is pain like I have never experienced before. Finally, I have the chance to talk to Stephie and I can't even open my mouth.

"What happening to you that you coming in here like some draw-up chicken?" Grandmother says when I come through the back door. I point to my mouth. "Oh, that rotten teet again?"

I nod my head, for that is all I can do because of the pain.

"Come here and let me see it."

I walk up to her and open my mouth. She looks in.

"All that foolish toothpaste that the school making me buy every month ain't worth one damn thing," she says. "You go in there and keep yourself quiet and see if that would help." I sit on the bench and place my head on the table. It does nothing to help the pain. "You want anything to eat?"

I cannot answer. Just about when the sun is setting, I look outside and notice Stephie crossing the road to watch TV at Mr. Lashley's. The agony starts to wear off, but I cannot bring myself to eat. Merely opening my mouth causes the tooth to throb. Mrs. King comes over and joins Grandmother in the darkness of the backyard. And with what I hear, and my tooth hurting, my head starts to spin and a funny feeling takes hold deep inside my belly.

Chapter Ten

"What we're going to do with these two children the two o' we got to bring up 'round here, nuh?" Mrs. King says.

"You tell me," Grandmother says. "Now I have that one in there drawing up with his bad teet hurting him. I gotta make up my mind to take him before long to the district hospital there to see the public dentist. But who you know like going to the dentist, especially the ones we have around here?"

The voices, though low, travel to me in the house. Although I cannot see Grandmother and Mrs. King, I know from the sound of their voices where they are standing: just far enough from the clammy cherry tree to be safe from the droppings of the chickens and turkeys, but far enough away from the houses so that anyone passing on the road cannot hear them. The fact that Mrs. King has come over at this time is an indication that something is worrying her, for usually when the sun goes down, she and Grandmother retreat into their homes, shouting across to each other if they want to discuss anything routine.

"What we two fuh do?" Mrs. King asks again, not with an air of resignation so much as a tone of expectation, as if she has an answer she wishes to share with Grandmother. "Sometime I does wonder if this independence thing we now have wouldn't be a real good thing if it would mean none o' we won't have to send 'way the boys and girls from 'round here anymore."

"All I can say is deliverance better come soon," Grandmother says. "'Cause it's real hard work people like me and you doing, especially all the thinking and worrying yuh head so much. I mean you and me, we already bring up a generation, and now we have to be bringing up a next one. And at we age too."

"What you going to do tonight about the boy and his bad teet?" Mrs. King asks.

"I don't know. I going to pour a little of the camphor and oil I have in that bottle there in his head and noint down with some candle grease the jaw that's troubling he, as I think I did notice a little bit o' swelling beginning on the side of his face with the bad teet. I hope that will help."

"Don't forget to let him hold a little bit of strong rum on the teet," Mrs. King says. "Over-proof rum best, if you have any. To numb the pain."

"I know," Grandmother says. "You got any?"

"Yes," Mrs. King says. "I can give you some o' the rum left back, just a draining, tho,' from the men still working on the house. That should be enough to last you out for the night. You come with me and I'd give you a little of what I got."

"All right," Grandmother says. I can imagine the rum burning my mouth and even my throat, but I don't care that much, just as long as it helps with the pain.

"I tell yuh," Grandmother continues, "this is the last thing any o' we could want: two children coming down sick on we hands, and at the said same time. With the school all but let out and Christmas just over a week away, nobody don't have time to be worrying their head about Christopher bad teet and Stephie not feeling too good. I feel sorry for him, 'cause you know these young people: as we done know they can't take pain, not like we generation. So, I don't know."

"I think Stephie's feeling a little better," Mrs. King says, "'cause when she came home I did give she some ginger tea as you did say, and now it looks as if she feeling a little brighter with herself. I had to say to myself she must be feeling better if she can be out watching TV, but I didn't say anything to either he or she, 'cause I don't know what to make of all this bad-feels and vomiting, and he keeping telling me how he's a big man and he knows everything is all right. I don't know what to make of it. I don't want to have to take her to the doctor again, even if he paying."

"You don't really think anything *happen'd* to she, eh?" Grandmother whispers. And then I remember what Mr. Lashley and Terrence said at the rum shop. But I suspect we might be dealing with something very different than whether Stephie has to take more tablets or even injections.

"Lord, God, I hope not," Mrs. King says. "That would be the last thing I would want to happen to she. Not to me. What would I write and tell she mother if something did ever happened? Lord, God, no. Don't even think that way, Peggy, girl."

"I know," Grandmother says. "I just asking a question. You know I does be here for you through thick and thin, and I only want the best for you, the same as I would want for my own self. But to tell you the truth, when I hearing about the bad feels and the vomit on top of all the other business you did tell me about, just like when we two girls start taking sick on we hand back then, I have to say in all truth the thought did occur to me, and I say to myself I may as well ask you about if she—"

"No, girl," Mrs. King cuts her off, raising her voice as if she is no longer mindful of who might be listening. "Don't *even* mention the word. Don't even think it, for things in our lives first begin with we thinking about them, and then if they are bad or evil they always happen just as we did think them up." I swallow, for I agree with Mrs. King. I don't want anything bad to happen to Stephie, not like with all the young girls around with one, two or three children and they can't even help themselves. And straight away, I put out of my mind any other thoughts about what could be happening to Stephie.

"If you say so, Eudene," Grandmother says. "But I still have to ask you: She see her time o' the month yet?"

"You know these young people," Mrs. King says. "They don't know nothing. They just big with themselves, looking like they're more woman than they actually is. So I asked she if she late, and she said she ain't know, that she used to count the days, but then she lost track and stopped because she couldn't bother with all that counting and kind o' thing, too much work and remembering, but I have to think it is because she is new to that kind o' business and she body's adjusting. That is why I thinking of taking her back to the doctor, to see that everything is all right, so that she can be back in school full-time real soon."

Now, not only my jaw, but my entire head is hurting. I rest my head on my arm on the table. I don't want to think. But I cannot stop hearing all this woman-talk, all these issues and concerns that aren't intended for the ears of men, let alone a boy like me who can never understand certain things, who might hear or see something happening and then panic, letting his thoughts get the better of him.

"Yeah," Grandmother says. "I did be thinking the said same thing. It's because she is new at doing what she now doing, and she body only recently started to feel the effect o' the moon. You and me only gotta remember how we mothers did try to steer we onto another course and what happened?"

"Yeah," Mrs. King says. "Still, there's a lot of people like me an' you around this place. A lot o' people still trying to find them true self."

"And there's a whole lot o' people that ain't as lucky as me and you to find we one another and to be living in we own houses sides by side," Grandmother says. "At least you and me are independent. We live on we own and we get to do the things that please us without anyone telling us when to come or go. It is just the children we have to look after. Otherwise we're we own bosses, that much I'd say. We *gotta* be grateful for things like that and the fact that at this stage in life we don't have to worry about any man bothering we out. We don't have to care what the people 'bout here might be saying."

The pain is stubborn, and they talking so long, I go to the larder to see if there is anything to help with my tooth. I reach up and run my hand on the ledge near the roof where Grandmother keeps the stick of candle grease, an almost-empty bottle of Vicks and a phial of Canadian Healing Oil in a box with a torn flap, but there is nothing else.

"Anyways," Mrs. King says, "why don't you come with me for the l'il rum for that boy teet in there?" I sit back down, taking no chances, for they must have heard me moving around. "Then, I going to read my Bible and go to my bed. I don't think I waiting up for Stephie to come home tonight. She can sleep over there for all I care now."

"No," Grandmother says. "I won't have you saying that. 'Cause you know you don't mean it. But anything that happen'd, you know that you did only aim to do good. That is the goodness of your heart. So don't be saying them things. Not now. You do the same thing that you did tell Mrs. Smith. You pray and hope, you hold on tight, tight, tight 'til deliverance come. Don't even think of letting go. Hold the strain. She's still a young girl and still your charge until her mother comes back and gets her."

"I guess so," Mrs. King says. "You right. You know me good enough, and you know what is in my heart."

I hear the footsteps on the rocks and gravel between the two houses and then the distant voices coming from the house next door. Grandmother does not return right away, and while I wait, the pain in my tooth subsides enough that I fall asleep. When I awake, Grandmother is over me, pouring camphor and oil on my head. She has lighted a long, thin stick of white candle, which has a funny rawish smell, and is applying the heated oil to my jaw, chin and neck.

"You want the rum for the teet?" she asks.

I shake my head and crawl on the floor into my bed. Fortunately, Grandmother had spread my bedding. I fall back off to sleep, leaving the rum from Mrs. King in the glass on the table.

It's the final day of the term, but neither Stephie nor I can go to school. I do not know for sure why Stephie is staying away, but my case is clear to everyone. Sometime in the dead of the night, I awoke to a pain that seemed to be breaking my jaw, so much so that I started crying loud, loud, loud.

"Margaret, wat's going on over there?" Mrs. King called in the darkness. "You okay?"

"Is this boy here," Grandmother called back. "The bad teet got he can't sleep. Like it hurting him real bad fuh true, 'cause I ain't seen him cry like this in a long time."

"Maybe you should wake up Lashley," said a small voice. Stephie came into the light cast by the lamp. "He did give me some tablets from a bottle he did bring down from over-'n'-away, so he might be able to give you one or two."

Grandmother and Mrs. King looked at each other with wonder, as if asking themselves why did they not think of Mr. Lashley.

"All right then," Mrs. King said finally. "*You* go and wake he up if he's sleeping a'ready and see if he got anymore o' them tablets left."

We heard Stephie walking from the house and crossing the road. Her muffled voice came back to us in a short conversation after knocking on the door. Soon she was back with a big bottle with the name *Bayer* on it. She gave the bottle to Grandmother.

"He say that you can keep as much as you want and that you can give he back the rest in the morning," she said.

"You should crush up another one o' them tablets and let he put it in the hole in the teet just to be safe," Mrs. King said, as I gulped down some water and tablets. "Good, Good, Good," she said as Grandmother carried out her instructions.

"Now go inside and try to sleep," Grandmother ordered. "You go and try to get some sleep. I soon come." I wiped the water from my lips with the back of my hand and returned to my bedding, leaving them outside in the darkness. Eventually the pain grew numb and I was soon sleeping again. When I did get up, it was late in the morning, and I was startled, for I thought I had overslept and would be late for school. Grandmother told me not to prepare for school, that she planned to take me to the district hospital down by the coast road to let the public dentist have a look at my bad tooth. The main reason she had kept me home was so that I would not play cricket in the hot, broiling sun and making my toothache worse. Now it is afternoon, and the sun is cool enough that Grandmother says we can leave home.

"We going along now," Grandmother shouts to Mrs. King on the way out. "Look out for we while we gone. Last night I don't think I did get one wink o' sleep over this boy. So I going to see what the public dentist can do for he."

"Walk good," Mrs. King says. "May the good Lord go with yuh, 'cause you know how them dentists down there can be."

We walk, the two of us hardly talking, to the district hospital. It is the end of the workday and the infirmary is not too busy. An older man with white hair and a doctor's coat is writing on a card at his desk. My heart is pounding hard, hard, hard. Without saying anything, the man turns away from his writing and comes over.

"Open you mouth and let me see," he says softly. I do.

"Hum," he says and turns back to the desk. "You've had injections before, right?"

I shake my head no.

"Well, it doesn't matter," he explains, turning back to me with a needle. "Open again. Wide." He massages the outside of my gum. "You'll feel a slight stick and then the side of you jaw will start feeling heavy. Don't mind that." I wonder if this is what they told Mr. Lashley or, and I blink hard, *Stephie.*

I feel the stick and the pressure of his hand on my jaw. I must wince, for out of the corner of my eye, I see a funny look on Grandmother's face. The dentist sends me outside to wait while he calls in a woman and injects her too. She comes out and sits beside me. The side of my face is getting heavy and Grandmother stands over me, staring, looking at the woman and then back at me, nobody saying anything.

"Open your mouth wide," the dentist says, still in a soft voice, when the nurse calls me back in. "You may close your eyes if you want to." I do moments after seeing him reach for a silver instrument that looks like a pair of pliers. "Open wide. Wider." I feel the pressure of his hand inside my mouth and the coldness of the instrument. I open my mouth as wide as I can, my heart running faster now, and I feel the instrument seizing my tooth. *Creausk,* the instrument sounds. *Creuskkk.* He adjusts his wrist. *Creaussssk.*

"Hold on now," the dentist says. "I soon finish." I feel greater pressure on my mouth and then his wrist twisting from side to side. He gives a sudden tug and then I no longer feel the pressure and weight of his hand. I open my eyes to see a ball of cotton in his hand, which he places in my mouth. "Bite down now," he commands. "Bite down hard." I do and I taste the saltiness of my blood.

"He can go now," the dentist tells Grandmother, who is standing against a wall by the door. I hold my jaw in my hand and walk out ahead of her. An older man is making his way into the dentist's chair.

Grandmother takes me to the beach, which is a short walk from the district hospital. She tells me to wade into the water and to wash out my mouth with the sea water. She says that the salt in the sea will be good for me. I fill and empty my mouth several times until all the blood is gone.

"What you doing there?" a voice calls to us. I look back and see Desmond Smith and his wife, Leila, standing at the edge of the water. He is wearing short cut-off pants and she is in a one-piece black swimsuit. Her hair looks thoroughly soaked and a few strands cling to her face. "We were taking a sea bath a little further down the beach when I thought I recognized the two o' you there, and I said to Leila, let we go over and see what's happening. Why he's spitting so in the water?"

"The dentist," Grandmother explains. "He went to see the dentist."

"What's happening?" Desmond asks.

"He had to get a bad teet pull out," Grandmother says.

"What?" Leila says, wincing and holding her hand to her jaw.

"They still doing that foolishness down here?" Desmond says, sucking his teeth in disgust. "This is modern times, 1967. They still being so barbaric, pulling out people teeth like that? And then you washing out his mouth in the sea water, with a hole like that in his gums, suppose he catch an infection from the water and—"

"What you mean?" Grandmother asks in wonderment, laughing at what to her is his obvious confusion. "What you mean if they still pulling out bad teets? What they're supposed to do when you got a bad teet that hurting you so bad that you can't even sleep at night?"

"Not pull it out," Desmond says. "This must be the only place in the world where they still pulling out poor people teeth like in the bad old days. You people never heard about root canals or fillings? Never heard of development and progress? Of keeping the tooth no matter what, so as to keep the jaw strong and give the face its shape? Nobody any place else in the world does pull out people good teeth anymore?"

"But it wasn't good." Grandmother is losing her patience. "How many times I have to keep telling you that the teet did be *bad* and that the boy couldn't sleep at night, that none o' we did sleep last night. You think I would bring he to the dentist to have a teet pull out if it was good? And the salt in the water, everybody done know all the long years, is good for any wound or cut, so it can heal. You forget?"

"And this is what you want to bring your two children to?" Desmond says, turning back to Leila, who is still watching me with that funny look on her face. "This is the kind o' treatment you would want for them? In this day and age to have all their teeth pulled out? It makes no sense. I tell yuh."

Leila holds Desmond's arm and nudges him to move on. The two of them now appear to be arguing. When he is gone, Grandmother says that she now understands why his own mother and father cannot put up with Desmond anymore. She understands why she's heard that he and his wife aren't seeing eye to eye too much these days. Everybody, she says, should have known something was wrong with Desmond when he just showed up without warning on the island with his pockets as empty as his two long hands, bringing with him a wife without one cent to her name even though she is from over-'n'-away and lived among rich people all her life. And then all he can do when he gets her here is to take her from one dance hall to another right across the island.

"All I can say is that that boy like he really turned real foolish for true." Grandmother keeps mumbling to herself as we resume walking back home in the now fading light. "And I don't want to put my mouth on him, but if he don't watch himself good, he gine have real trouble with that woman if she stay down here with he. What a fool, talking to me that way about bad teets. Anyway, now you can see for yourself what the real world is like, what kinda dotish people you will have to contend with as you become more of a man."

Exhausted from the ordeal, I quickly go to bed after taking two more of Mr. Lashley's tablets. Somehow I manage to sleep through the night without waking.

Part Two

Chapter Eleven

B esides how bad my jaw ached, and the fact that the postman never stopped with a letter from our parents, there were other things I was still trying to make sense of at the end of the old year and the start of the new. For one thing, by the end of that disappointing and frustrating final week of school, Stephie appeared to be back to full strength, so that on the Saturday, with a burst of energy, she helped with the chores. With my optimism, I was perhaps the only person not accepting that Stephie would never be quite the same again. I guess it is true what people say: the more you look, the more you see only what you want to see.

I did notice a few things, however, and they stayed with me. It was cold outside, the temperature falling much lower than usual at night. People talked all the time about what all this coldness meant, about how they had started sleeping in an extra shirt or pants, the women in extra dresses, and even scarves. They said they could now understand what Mr. Lashley and the fellows on the work contracts meant when they talked about the cold up north. It felt like the cold spell would never end.

In many ways, nothing was making sense anymore. Everything was just coming up strange—that is the only way I can describe the mood that came among us. Everybody was just acting *so* different, especially Mrs. King on the Saturday morning before Christmas. I noticed that she was not her usual self as she waited with Stephie and me for Grandmother to return from downtown. She just stood around, as if lost in her thoughts, and sometimes grumbled to herself, often sucking her teeth. She'd look at Stephie and frown or shake her head. I noticed that Stephie was not talking much. It was like she and her grandmother couldn't bear to catch themselves looking at each other. Even when Mrs. Smith, accompanied by her daughter-in-law, Leila, dropped in for the week's sou-sou money, Mrs. King didn't have much to say.

Leila told Mrs. King she was looking forward to spending her first Christmas on the island, and Mrs. Smith proudly let it be known that she and her daughter-in-law would be baking and cooking together. Leila said that she had promised to bake a great cake the way her folks back up north did traditionally and to prepare the ham for Christmas just the way she would if she was back home. Mrs. Smith also reported that Leila had taken out the old sewing machine that she kept in the box under her bed all these years, especially since the arthritis began to slow her down, and was beautifying the house with new curtains and blinds for Christmas. Too besides, she said, her boy Desmond had bought paint and, even as they spoke, was sprucing up the house inside and out, just as she had asked him to do, and as she and Leila had discussed and agreed. When they got back home after collecting the turn money, she and Leila would see how he was making out, for you know men, how they would run off and do strange things if somebody wasn't around to keep an eye on them.

Mrs. Smith declared that Mrs. King and Grandmother did not know how lucky they were to be both the women and the men in their own homes and not have to depend on anybody for anything or beg anybody to do this or that to make their own house look good. Leila, Mrs. Smith said, was making sheself useful and even knocking out the two dresses that she and Leila would be wearing to church for midnight mass on Christmas. By then, the two of them would have completed all the baking, including the great cakes with the fruit that Mrs. Smith had ground and been fermenting in the strongest of rum and some ruby port wine from the distillery in town, the yellow pound cake with the raisins and red maraschino cherries stirred into it, and the coconut sweet bread.

All of them in the house would go off to church. They would sing all the carols at the top of their voices, listen to a word or two from the reverend, all the while hoping that he wouldn't be too long for a sermon. They would wish everyone a merry Christmas and then come back home to a small sampling of all the baked goodies before falling asleep just to rise a few hours later to begin in earnest an entire day of feasting. Yes, Mrs. Smith admitted, even the Mister of the house was saying the activities reminded him of the good old times, when he was a boy and Christmas was so special. But that was so, Mrs. Smith said with a wink, because she and Leila were smart enough to put their two heads together.

"What *happen'd*, Eudene?" Mrs. Smith asked. "You not in the Christmas spirit?"

"*Spirit*, what spirit?" Mrs. King said. She sucked her teeth. "I don't know 'bout no Christmas spirit this time around. The Christmas spirit like it passing me over this year from the way I feel."

"But what you mean?" Mrs. Smith says. "You can't just not be in the Christmas spirit. Look how you have this almost brand new house here, with the new bedrooms and everything looking so nice. You have real cause to be thankful, thankful."

"Me—" Mrs. King appeared to catch herself. "I thankful all right. I thank God for his small mercies to help us to progress bit by bit. Still, I glad to hear things working out for you. It sounding to me like you and your house going to be having a good Christmas. So I'm glad for yuh. Maybe I'll get more of the Christmas cheer after tonight, after we finish up down by the shop and see how business going. Now all I'm doing is concentrating on getting things ready for tonight."

"All right," Mrs. Smith said. "If you say so, my dear. But try and enjoy the Christmas season and remember that, after all, Christmas ain't for the big people so much as it is for the young ones. And you still have a few young ones here to think about."

"*Young*," Mrs. King said. "I don't know about that. I don't think any o' we 'round here going be young for too much longer. That is all I know. So when you use that word *young*, don't fool yuhself by taking a six for a nine." I thought I heard Stephie breathe louder, but she did not look up from the gratering.

"Still, enjoy the Christmas," Mrs. Smith said.

"See yuh next week then," Mrs. King said as the two women left the house. "And you are right," she shouted after them, "Merry Christmas. I *gotta* try and get into the spirit."

Stephie did most of the gratering, as usual, and I took care of mixing the pig food and feeding the pigs and the chickens and turkeys for Grandmother. On her return home, Grandmother once again boasted how she found these long and thin okras so lovely looking for the cou-cou she was about to stir. But this time, she had decided to go for two tins of mackerel from Canada, if only because, as a run-up to Christmas, apparently, the price of the dried codfish had gone up again and did not deserve the money the supermarkets were demanding. As a special treat, Grandmother boiled a large red-skin potato, peeled it when it was cooked and gave each of us a generous slice of it with the cou-cou. We ate in silence. Even the flies in the yard appeared to be less annoying than usual. A cool, continuous breeze from the sea fanned us lazily, as if knowing the exact moment to rise up, the instant when the heat became a bit oppressive, causing the slightest of things to get on our nerves.

Later on, with the sun setting, the four of us set out early for the shop. Grandmother and Mrs. King's business was brisk, and they sold out of everything. Indeed, we could have returned home early had not Grandmother and Mrs. King made us wait for the last bus and their regular customer. Eventually the last bus from St. Patrick's pulled up. The driver got out with his large enamel bowl under his arm, leaving the engine running as usual. He gave Grandmother the container and received the last of the black pudding and souse that she had kept for him.

"I *gotta* thank you for holding this for me," the bus driver said. "You don't know how much trouble I *woulda* get from my missus if I did come home without the regular black pudding and souse. Lord, she wouldn't let me sleep. Christmas won't be Christmas without this here little treat."

"Oh, lord, Merton," Grandmother said, humouring him, "why yuh does joke so much. Things ain't that bad." She took the money and reached into her apron pocket for the change. "And say Merry Christmas to the wife from me and Eudene here. Tell she that we hope that you treating her good fuh Christmas."

The arrival of the bus for the city was the signal for Pastor Wiltshire to ring the bell one last time at each corner of the gathering, to loudly wish everyone a merry Christmas and to invite each and every one to come out and hear him on the last Saturday of the year. He said that those who did not have a church to attend for Christmas service were more than welcome to come and worship with his flock. The worshippers shook hands one last time, hugged, wished one another a merry Christmas and slowly drifted away into the surrounding darkness. The bus drove off loudly, leaving a void and an odour, as if we were in the process of turning a page but still waiting for that act of turning to stop.

In the bar, some of the men continued to drink. But in most cases, the evening had ended. By then much of the back pay money, the Christmas bonuses and remittances that had come in from overseas had changed hands, and a fair share was now lining the pockets of the two large aprons worn by Grandmother and Mrs. King. They should have been happy and feeling the Christmas spirit. Stephie had left us, saying she was going over to Mr. Lashley's to catch the last show before the television signed off for the night. From the way they watched her leave, it was obvious that Mrs. King and Grandmother could not bring themselves to be of good cheer. And this is what I recall most about that night: a feeling hanging heavily in the air and seeking to cloak us as if it were a blanket. Something seemed to be holding that blanket and chasing down every last one of us and demanding that we give in to it. It wanted to cover us all, just as any of Grandmother's sitting hens would cover their chicks when they hatched and the rain was falling. What I remember too is that we did not leave right away to go home. Even as the main section of the shop closed, as the last shoppers made their way home with heavy baskets on their heads, even as the various groups went about their business under the cover of the night, Grandmother and Mrs. King remained seated on their stools, talking and listening to the music from the jukebox, seemingly trying to enjoy the calming evening breeze, but succumbing to the pall enveloping everything. They sat in the darkness with the millions of stars above shining down on them as they talked and made plans for our Christmas.

Mr. Watson kept feeding coins into the jukebox to supply an unending stream of Christmas music. A rich baritone voice with a lilt just like ours sings one of our favourites, "Mary's Boy Child." The music created a quiet mood, and even in the rum shop, there was a reverence, not too much talking and certainly no arguing or fighting. The men just held on to their glasses, even the empty ones, waiting. We were all touched by the anticipation of what would come next. All around us was that feeling and that hope that everything was good and that all of us were just happy with ourselves as one.

And yet something was awry. As I now remember it, there must have been a mixed feeling, like what I think of when I hear the story about the very first morning, the birth of creation, when everything was just right, or at least so it appeared, like when something is covered by a new coat of paint, hiding the old and rotten underneath. Such elation, such sweet smells and sounds to make the heart full, but something odd still pulling at the heart strings. It was just as it must have been the night of independence itself. That was when, Mr. Jones liked to say, we dragged down the Union Jack for the last time and the people cast their eyes toward the sky to see a brand new flag fluttering in the breeze, as if playing with millions of stars in the distance—when, I am thinking, the people sighed and asked themselves, "What now?"

When finally Grandmother and Mrs. King were ready to leave, I tried to brave the chill of the night by telling myself that the cold was nothing like what I would experience when my mother sent for me in the new year. Despite the way things looked, joining her was still my hope. My mind turned to thoughts of welcoming in the new year of 1968. I reminded myself that I had my fourteenth birthday to look forward to. Maybe I would finally get to spend a birthday with my mother, if she *did* write, if she did send for me. But suppose she didn't? Would I have to look out for myself more? And what if Stephie kept on acting so strange toward me, leaving me to spend so much time on my own, having to spend more time worrying about her own self? Who would I have to talk to now that she didn't even like singing with me anymore, like she was too grown up for singing with me, even though Grandmother and Mrs. King still sang along with each other, especially when it was drizzling and they were sheltering in their separate houses. Or maybe Stephie, poor thing, didn't have the time or the mind for singing. So much of this new thinking going on in my head only started when Mrs. King asked me all those questions back when Stephie first started acting sick and *stupid* toward me.

Grandmother is gently shaking me awake, saying Merry Christmas and telling me that she has a surprise for me, a very special gift.

"It's from Cyrus," she says. "He asked me to give it to you, from him first thing Christmas morning. And he says he'd be dropping by later to share the Christmas cheer, but that he really wanted me to surprise you with this. Merry Christmas," she says again.

"Thanks," I say, rubbing my eyes. "And Merry Christmas to you too, Grannie."

"God bless you, son," Grandmother said. "The *onlyest* thing better would be if your mother over-'n'-away did at least send you a Christmas card. But not a word. So let you and me be thankful for life, that we live to see another Christmas, praise the Lord."

I took from her a brand new cricket bat. It was indeed a merry Christmas.

Chapter Twelve

Like a malicious duppy fleeing before the rising sun, postman Simpson glides along the road, stopping not even once, leaving our hopes once again smothered in the bluish-white smoke of his motorcycle. It is almost as if he feels guilty for our disappointments, for he keeps his head straight, eyes steadfastly ahead of him, not even glancing our way to acknowledge our presence as he rides by. As if he cannot face up to the unavoidable heartache that comes with him, a hurt we pin as squarely on him as if he has deliberately withheld our letters. On this day, he has no friend among us, who blame him. With his mere presence he raises our hopes, only to dash them so callously.

It has been like this in the two months since Christmas. These are the daily trials every one of us with expectations of deliverance from abroad go through. Postie, a man not yet in his middle age, born of circumstances similar to ours in another section of the wider area in which we live, has to know full well the desires of our hearts. He knows the importance of his job in satisfying them. Yet he fights us day after day, as if his job is to disappoint us rather than bring deliverance.

Mr. Lashley is out in front of his house, tending to the flower garden that he started at the beginning of the year. Perhaps he has come out because he too heard the motorcycle in the distance, or by coincidence spied from his window the postman a ways out. Either way, Mr. Lashley, just like everyone else in the houses around him, has decided to check on something outside at the very moment the postman is going by.

Mr. Lashley pulls at the grass that has sprung up among the roses and at the weeds challenging his young snow-on-the-mountain trees, which he hopes will be in full bloom by next Christmas, when he plans to be back. He keeps his mind preoccupied, letting his hands guide his mind.

The size of the plants do more than speak of their own health; they also indicate how long it has been that we have been waiting for the postman to stop. The plants are a measure of Mr. Lashley's despondency as well as our unhappiness in a new year. In the first week of the year, Mr. Lashley borrowed a fork and prepared the garden, clearing first the dry grass with the centipedes, Christmas worms, millipedes and slugs. He told Mrs. King and Stephie that he wants the flowers to be in full bloom when he returns from over-'n'-away, for that would be the best time for him to do the *thing* that everybody's now been wondering and talking 'bout. Such would be a sight for his eyes: the roses in full blossom, the petals falling to the earth and newer ones appearing on the scene; the white tops of the special trees; the hibiscuses and bougainvillea; the croton in colours of red, green and yellow. They will all be coming forth from the land he tilled so that, on coming home, he will be greeted with lush vegetation and with flowers that he can cut and place in a vase on his centre table. He will seek out a special vase when he is overseas, perhaps from Honest Ed's Emporium, where they all went shopping just before hopping on the plane back home. The vase would celebrate *next* Christmas and be something that he and a brand new Mrs. Lashley would keep forever 'til death they doth part.

For after all, Mrs. King has shared with Grandmother how Mr. Lashley keeps telling her how he is getting on in life, how a man can only do so much running around and *tireding* out himself before it comes time for him to settle down, and how, as man, he can't help but to feel his time is catching up on him, that somebody finally got his number. So he has to make ready. The time is approaching fast and he can sense it in his bones. There can be no other explanation, Mr. Lashley boasts. His intention is to do the *thing*, but the *proper* way, as man, with money in his pockets.

Once he is gone back up—and he expects to fly away any time now, in a week at the most—he will leave the tending of the garden to the two best people in the world that he could leave in charge. In the meantime, he has developed a routine to satisfy his mind and make himself useful. Otherwise, he says, the devil finds works for idle hands. Five days a week, he is, as if by chance, wetting the plants with a large watering can or pulling at weeds that might choke the plants at the same time the postman comes by.

Each evening, in our separate houses, Mrs. King, Stephie, Grandmother and me have watched him with hearts that have grown heavy as the plants have matured. Today Mr. Lashley does not even bother with the watering can, and still Postie Simpson does not stop. He does not even look at Mr. Lashley on his knees, not in prayer, but pulling out the weeds that might choke his young plants. After Postie goes by, the man on his knees gets up, wipes his soiled hands on his pants and kicks one of the flowering plants. We know he does not mean it. He is not a man of violence; of frustration, yes. In these special times, we know, his actions are not consistent with his desires and wishes, or with his training. We know the action is not the natural extension of his heart. But it is difficult for us not to have sensed the sudden drop in his heart when he too realized there was no letter for him, just as there was none for any of us—not for me or Stephie with mothers over-'n'-away, and not for two mothers with daughters overseas. But we are not Mr. Lashley. His stakes are higher and his disappointments more recent. Our disappointments are smaller and more easily forgotten in the routine of life. We can wait for another tomorrow. At the moment, all of us are following the particular saga of disappointments that have of late befallen Mr. Lashley.

"Another day and still no letter." Mr. Lashley says the obvious. He is now standing to his full height, and for the first time, he speaks with both anger and pain. He makes a few quick steps as if rushing to seek shelter in the house, but then abruptly changes his mind and walks back slowly to the edge of the road that runs between us. "Maybe tomorrow," he says, looking in the direction from which he knows the postman will once again materialize. As he speaks the divide slips away, for we are all now in the same despondency, all looking to another day to bring us relief.

Hard times are indeed upon all of us. Nobody can doubt this. Even Stephie and I know it, now that we have fallen back into our regular pattern of going to school and helping out at home, with me helping Stephie to catch up with her school work. Except now that Mr. Lashley has promised to do this *thing* the right and honourable way when he gets back, and with he telling everyone that Stephie will be the true queen of his house when he is gone back up north, the two of them are more open with each other. Grandmother and Mrs. King have had to cut back on the amount of black pudding and souse and coconut bread they make on weekends. Nobody is buying any-thing, Grandmother says, even though the hunger in their bellies is just as long and even wider than before. Their mouths have become even sweeter when they come begging for credit. Grandmother tells me often that things all around are looking brown as the fields when there is no rain and the sun dries up all on which it shines, as brown as the trash on the already ripened canes in the fields around us. Things are so brown that most days our food is the same: boiled rice with fried salted codfish, or rice with the salt fish boiled down in it. Occasionally we have a soup made with yams, potatoes, eddoes and pumpkins when they are available. Sometimes we have some fresh fish when Grandmother has the money, or a few strips of chicken or beef in a stew on Sundays for a break from eating the same thing every day. So brown are things, Grandmother and Mrs. King are refusing to sell on credit, for they need cash to buy the supplies they need to make something to sell to the few who can still buy. I start to watch them more closely and I am beginning to pick up on some things that I did never notice before.

I realize things are so brown that even Mr. Watson has gone back to driving for the man who owns the largest fleet of taxis, rental cars and open-sided Mini Mokes for the tourists arriving at the airport or the harbour in town. Mrs. Watson said she spoke with the wife of the man who owned the taxi fleet, and the wife told her to dress up Boysie in the old taxi uniform—a clean white shirt and black pants—and send him along, for she would ask her husband to take Boysie back as a driver, at least for the next while. Mrs. Watson is complaining that things are so bad she has to acquire on credit from the *thiefing* whole-salers in the city the goods she needs to keep the shop open. She says she has to keep her regular customers at the bar in check. The men can no longer afford to pay for the rum they would have drunk was she foolish enough to grant credit to everyone that asks. Now when they meet in the bar, the men merely stand around talking and keep asking Mrs. Watson if she can help them out. They ask her how much they have left in the pump with her, and whether things are already so dry she cannot see her way to ease them just a little bit. Couldn't she allow them to go over the agreed limits without her having to tell anybody, leaving it to the two of them to clear up the extra, without the missus at home or anybody else knowing and getting vexed with them? By taking smaller and less frequent nips, they stretch any bottle of rum they can afford or that Providence supplies by sending a politician or government worker their way.

From inside the bar, these men gaze out at the world, hardly talking, their useless hands holding their glasses against their chest. They pretend to be listening to the radio hanging over their heads, waiting for that special announcement that everybody knows can only come from the government. I hear some of them talking softly to one another off to the side, saying they do not recall any of the government announcements they hear by the time they leave the shop, for they have not heard any that really matters. They confide to one another that all they know is that unlike the oil of old, the rum over which they prayed silently in their hearts has run out; how it is like they are still trapped in this long place and time where nothing happens. The men who were once seamen admit it is just like trying to cross the wide Sargasso Sea.

Grandmother warns me to keep clear of the men who like to cuss real stink and to blaspheme by taking the Lord's name in vain for no reason at all. They are the same ones who say they have long given up on any messiah coming. They are too old for that; they just want one period in the breadth of life to come to an end and to let another start, so that in the sameness of their living there will be the blessings of change. Grandmother says they would cuss anybody who so much as mentioned that they should all just try to hold on and not to lose faith. She says they should not be so angry with themselves or go looking to pick fights with poor-arse people just like themselves and end up putting themselves in the hands of the police and the courts. My task, grandmother keeps drilling into my head, is to watch and learn, and not get in the way of big people. I shouldn't go putting my nose in people's business by telling them what I think about anything. So I watch and learn, and sometimes Grandmother and I talk when we are alone at home at night, listening to the wind howling and the galvanize creaking as it contracts after the all-day bleaching by the sun.

What I am noticing is that in these times, brown as they are, everything is in the hands of the women: Grandmother says it is they who have saved what little money there is to see a family through these times. For she says women are the ones most familiar with times and cycles. If they have to, the women will find an argument to persuade Mrs. Watson or even Grandmother and Mrs. King to give them a little credit. They tell one another that we should all have hope, as sure as there is a God in the heavens above, and that we must simply trust in Him and in life itself. They will find a way to settle the accounts at a later date. If they so desire, they whisper to Mrs. Watson their approval for her to give their man a rum or two, though they impose strict limits for the credit in his name at the bar. The women find a way to give assurance that someday the men that live in their houses will find something to make themselves useful. The women know how to see to that, whether it means nagging the men in the night when they want to sleep, or reminding them of the calypso, "No Money, No Love."

Most nights before going to sleep, Grandmother and I talk. She has asked me whether I've noticed how the early hope for a difference with a new year has long faded. But she says I shouldn't give up hope; for those of us with real good expectations deliverance will soon come. I still have the hope of a letter from overseas and the prospect of one day going away. Only with the postman's connivance can the extended sameness be broken. Now that life has returned to its normal routine, the women are the ones keeping hope alive. The men think and dream not of what is, but of what ought to be, and with nothing to do, they are simply lost. With each morning, I am getting up, as Grandmother would say, one day older and wiser. I think I am waking with a better understanding of most things in life. That much I now know.

"I don't understand why things taking so long to happen," Mr. Lashley laments, bending over to nurse the plant he so foolishly kicked.

"Don't lose heart," Mrs. King calls across the road to him. Stephie, still in her school uniform, is at the window with her grandmother. I am outside waiting for Cyrus to meet me for another practice session. "The letter will come. Just have faith in the Lord."

"I know," Mr. Lashley says. "It is just that it ain't like my boss to wait all this long time to write and to say what is what. All like now I was hoping that I would be getting the call to go back up on the program. That is what does happen every year all like now so. In fact, a number of the boys from other farms in the same area of the farm I does go to already done get their call up and going back up in a few weeks' time. I just don't know: it ain't like my boss, not at all. And I did leave him on a good note. We left on good terms. After all it is now eleven good, good years that I've been going to him. And he did say that he would be requesting the same crew again this year as always and that my name would be top o' the list."

"It will come," Mrs. King promises. "I think sometimes it is all them lazy people that they got working at the post office that does be holding back people letters all the time. I wouldn't be too surprise if it ain't them inside workers taking their good sweet time sorting one letter today and another tomorrow, and all the time they got people like you so waiting for important mail while they playing the fool when they say they're working."

"I don't know," Mr. Lashley says. He does not sound too convinced by Mrs. King's words, if only because he has heard much the same for weeks now. "All I know is that it better come soon. I could do with a piece o' change. That is why I went and sign up for Newton plantation up the road there earlier today, as a cane cutter. I decided to put down my name on the register, just in case the sugar cane crop season get started and I'm still 'round here. Just in case. 'Cause I don't know what to make of this getting no letter, and as far as I am concerned money is money, when you're in need of a piece o' change in yuh pocket, like now. If you can't ride donkey yuh best ride cow."

"Don't mind the sugar cane crop," Grandmother says dismissively. "'Cause as Eudene done say, I don't know why you worrying out yourself so much for. You ain't gine be cutting no canes this year. You're too good for that. Cutting cane is for people who can't even get on the overseas farm program. It's for people that ain't got no ambition or no knowing. It's pure hard work in the hot, broiling sun all day long, morning 'til evening, like we still living in the days of slavery. But *you's* a regular on the contract and, as you say, I am sure even if your farmer don't come through this year, whatever is the reason, something else will bre'k for you with another farm. You will soon be gone from 'bout here. Mark my word. But I don't know 'bout this cutting sugar cane business. That would be like going backwards for you, if you ask me."

Coming round the corner and advancing toward us is Cyrus, still wearing the navy blue pants and khaki shirt that is his government-worker uniform. Mr. Lashley sucks his teeth loudly. Then he tells

Grandmother and Mrs. King he is going back into the house and will be passing the time listening to local music on the radio until the television comes on. As he is closing the door behind him, Cyrus calls to him and he reopens it, steps outside and begins chatting with him. Soon he closes the door behind him. Cyrus waves to us.

"I gone now," I say to Grandmother and Mrs. King.

"Just remember you still got your school work to do," Grandmother says, "so don't go and stay out too late this evening saying that you practising and sweating up yourself this evening. A good education is still everything in this world."

"Bye, Grand," I say. "I soon come back." I take up my bat, and Cyrus and I walk off toward the field where the others are already practising. I might not be the same age as the other men on the field, but I know I can hold my own and even size up with them. From the way the men eye me on the field, and how they are starting to talk with me, I can feel I am more than coming into my own.

Chapter Thirteen

Everybody stops to look as the strange new motorcycle roars past. Pastor Wiltshire stops preaching and also lets off ringing the bell. The deacon stops beating the drum. The women in white dresses and head ties stop singing, clapping hands, swooning. The men in long black robes halt their bass or baritone rumblings. I cannot remember, in all the many years, anything or anyone silencing Pastor Wiltshire. When in full flow, his words came out in torrents, magically rhyming in time with the movement of the worshippers.

The motorcycle is a scrambler and it is very loud. On the back are two riders, and we immediately know they are foreigners by their bodies, their long, straw-like hair bleached by the sun and sea, the multicoloured dyed clothes they wear, their faded and torn jeans, and the sandals on their feet.

"Hey, you two there," Tyrone shouts from the rum shop. "You ain't see proper people carrying on a church service? Why you have to go and interrupt people so? Like you ain't got no manners?"

"It's the Peace Corps people," says a boy helping his mother with a basket. "It is Mr. Smedley who does teach me at school."

"And who's that with him on the back?" asks his mother.

"That one is who we does call Miss Tamara," the boy says. "She does teach in we school too, the class four boys. She's newer to the school than Mr. Smedley, since she only come to the school two weeks ago. We like them because they bring to school a lot of what they does call candy but what we call sweeties, you know, chewing gum and them things from over-'n'-away for us. And particular she is always saying how much she like to hear the boys singing, and she does make we sing a lot."

"I don't give one blast who they is," Tyrone says. "And if *they's* teachers, they should know better, especially if they're teaching the children 'round here. They *shoulda* know better than to ride some loud-arse motorbike like that right through the man's church service, even if it is only a' open-air meeting. Them things ain't right, man. Ain't right at all. No damn culture, they ain't got no blasted training?"

"So why Pastor Wiltshire don't say something to them?" one of the other men in the bar asks. "If it did be any o' we from 'round here so, he would be already calling down the curses from heaven on all o' we. We would be hearing all like now that all o' *we's* a hard-hearted people with no broughtupcy whatsoever."

"What you're saying is that something different going down?" Tyrone asks.

"Of course, something is different. Look who disrupting his service. Two white people from over-'n'-away. And we saying we is an independent country. Still, we having people coming among us and carrying on as they like. I bet you that if it did be any of the young people from 'round here keeping all that noise that the police woulda long time have them under arrest and throwing some good hot lashes in them in the police van or down at the station."

"I know what you mean," Tyrone says. "They should know better. They shouldn't come and impose themselves on the way we do things."

"I'll go and tell them blasted Americans that this isn't the way to do things down here. Otherwise they can go back to where they come from and behave with this uncouthness."

"Only one is a *'Merican,*" said the boy with the basket. "The other one is a Canadian."

"Oh," the man says, as if that explanation has changed his mind.

"No, man," says the boy's mother. "You should still go and talk to them. But be careful. Don't get yourself in no trouble. Don't get too excited. In fact, why you don't take Wendell Lashley with you? He does spend a lot of time in Canada. He knows how to deal with them Canadians."

"Let we go, Lash, man," the man calls out. Mr. Lashley stumbles out of the bar, and he and the man go over to the scrambler. They talk a short while, and then the two foreigners totter away from the edge of the open-air service and approach the shop. They park the motorcycle on its kickstand and return to the open-air meeting. The man digs his fingers deep into his jeans and pulls out some bills. The woman takes up the bell and hefts it. The man peels off several of the notes and throws them on the white cloth in the middle of the open-air service. The woman softly taps the drum with her fingers and giggles. Pushing aside the hair from her face, she wobbles toward the shop. Pastor Wiltshire resumes preaching and ringing the bell, and the deacon beats the drum. They eye the dollars among the collection, and their smiles seem to say that the loudness and interruptions were worth it, after all. Even Tyrone seems to agree.

"Thank goodness for them two foreigner people," Grandmother says to Mrs. King. "Without them, tonight would be a real bust for the two o' we. Not a person was buying a thing until they come along. If you ask me, this crop season definitely taking too long to start. People so br'ek they can't be br'ek no more." The voices from the bar are unusually loud and strong for this hour of the night.

"With regards to tonight," Mrs. King says, "as you like to say, if God don't come himself, he'll send someone. And talking 'bout being br'ek, tomorrow, Sunday morning bright and early I gine be finding myself at church, 'cause I really gotta put Lashley in God's hand. I really *gotta* pray for he, because this letter foolishness taking too long and things getting too hard now. We need prayer for divine intervention."

Grandmother does not respond. When we are almost half-way home, Mrs. King picks up from where she left off, as if we had been stuck in time. "'Cause I done tell you already, you'd think that a big able man like he, Lashley, would know how to protect heself without putting anybody in trouble." She halts talking and I can hear her breathing heavily. "Still, I gine see what the doctor at the district hospital tell we next week when I take she along there. And I gine pray to God this is just a case of things coming a bit late or that the body ain't have a regular pattern yet and still missing a month here and month there. 'Cause the Lord knows I couldn't deal with no trouble right now. Not with what all the malicious people around here would have to say, how they already talking and just washing their mouth on all o' we. But we shall see. I'll trust in Christ, for he is my deliverer. Still, I think that, trouble or no trouble, the best thing that could happen is for he to get that letter and go along about his business back up north for now."

Mid-week, the mood around us has changed. The large dark cloud has rolled away and a soft, vibrant sun is shining through. People are friendlier; they're joking and lingering to talk more. Everyone, men, women and children, walks with greater purpose.

"Seems like the government announcing the start of the crop season," Cyrus says. "There was quite a lot of activity at the government headquarters when I was working, and now I hear that the announcement coming tonight on the radio and TV."

He is right. The official announcement comes during the government-sponsored community bulletin board program: the crop is beginning on Monday two weeks' time. Men and women should report for work at the plantation. Apparently, even those who did not register with a plantation during the dry season are assured of work this year. Grandmother and Mrs. King say the delay of the announcement did a lot of harm to people, but now there is a chance that things will get better. All the people who owe them money for what they purchased on trust should be able to see their way clear to settling their debts.

Grandmother must believe that people will be spending money more freely, for she sends me off to Mrs. Watson's shop to purchase some additional sugar and flour and a pound of salt meat for a soup she plans to cook the next day. In the rum shop, the men are drinking more freely, and some of them are dancing and singing along with the local music the radio is playing in celebration. Some of the men are talking loudly about the coming season. "When pigs dance expect rain," Mrs. Watson says, smiling. She too appears to be in a better mood. I order the groceries and make my way home, feeling the extra energy that seems to be recharging life all around. It feels as if something old has been laid to rest and something new has already risen in its place. As I turn toward the houses, I see Stephie crossing the road to Mr. Lashley's house. She wasn't at school again today. As usual, all the boys are present for the night's television shows. Stephie passes through them like a queen, as if she is boss of the house and everything in it.

In the backyard, Mrs. King and Grandmother do not seem to be happy at all, despite the good news about the crop season. They talk softly, occasionally hugging each other, once in a while blowing their noses. Mrs. King, in particular, looks like things could not be worse. It must be a burden that they cannot carry alone.

Chapter Fourteen

In the half-darkness of the evening, Mrs. Smith silently approaches Grandmother and Mrs. King in the backyard. She pulls up a bench next to them and, leaning forward, begins to whisper.

"So I said to myself," Mrs. Smith says, speaking louder and leaning back, "I said that is what *you* think. Do I ever got news for *you*. Do *you* think I going to sit down here and let you disown your very own son? And to have your son, your very own flesh and blood, now fighting, *fighting*, like cat and dog with his own wife. Well, not as long as *I* have breath in this body of mine and strength in my arms and two feets to take me wherever I want to go. That's what I tell him, but only in my mind, though."

"I can't believe it," Mrs. King says. "That don't sound like the Bertie I know, yuh."

"That is what I'm telling you," Mrs. Smith says. "You can never tell with these men. They can be so dotish, every last one o' them. I mean, *he* up and tell me that for some reason or other he's been thinking a lot these days and that he feel that he havetah make his way right with his Lord and saviour, that he know that he soon dead and he want to set things right with all his children first. And you know what happen when you have these men thinking. Well be Christ, wanting to make yuh way good with your maker before you dead is one thing. It is another to give away the very inheritance that you should be giving to your child of a marriage. Thinking and doing: two completely different things. So I tell him that it was *me*, Desmond own mother, who did walk up the aisle in my wedding gown for him, with Desmond big in my belly a'ready, and that it was still *me* that did walk back down with him at *my* side, and that any chile he got from me is legal and legitimate. But no, he tells me I don't understand what the good he's trying to do. He saying I don't understand how much he realized he wasn't as good as he should be to his four outside children. Now he wants to either provide for them in his will or to make things right at once by selling off a couple o' the houses that he did have in his family for the longest of time and does rent out to various people when the month comes. He thinking of also selling off a good-able piece o' the land he own, and to give whatever he gets from the sale to the four outside children. Now, these is children that don't ever come to visit him. Children he did get from a host o' young ignorant girls, not even women at the time, and who couldn't do nothing for he as a mature man. Them children and the mothers don't make a cup o' tea for he when the morning comes. They don't know or care if he's living or dead, and as far as he is concerned, to them Sunday could come on a Monday. And now he wants to give them the land and property that when he dead should be going to we only child."

"So what you're going to do?" Grandmother asks.

"Mouth open, story jump out," Mrs. Smith cautions, shaking her head. "So I ain't saying *nuthin'*, not one thing to anybody. Only *me* know what I going to do. I ain't even telling the two o' you here so, even though I know I can trust the two o' you as sisters in my church and as women to women. All I would say is I have plans to fix he good, good, good as a cent. Watch: I gine fix his business for him real good, just watch and see."

"And Desmond, what he saying 'bout all this?" Grandmother asks.

"What he saying?" Mrs. Smith says. "You know how powerful foolish these men can be, with all their pride and stubbornness. He saying he ain't got nothing against his father's wishes. One thing he says he learned when he was abroad is you don't rely on anybody, not even on family. He says that he knows that if what I just tell you is what Bertie wants that, after all it is his father's houses and land and his father can do what the hell he wants with them. He even saying this foolishness that as far as he is concerned his father ain't bound to even give he, Desmond, anything, 'cause he done learned how to be independent on his own, that his father could cut he outta his will, if his father was going to be acting this way. And that, in any case, all he wants is only a recording studio so he can carry out his plans. I tell yuh, men, no matter the size or age, they can be so *foolish*."

"But what cause all this bassa-bassa?" Mrs. King asks.

"What caused it? Just because the poor boy did ask his father to lend him some money." Mrs. Smith shifts the way she is sitting. "Money to start up a business he says he planning, or I should say that Leila planning, 'cause she is the one with a good head, and he wants a l'il bit more money to support these children that he gone and tek up overseas. He asked him to use some of the land to allow him to borrow some money against it from the bank so he could get things started as a business. That was when all this foolishness started, when his father started talking about what he would and wouldn't do to make up with his outside children and to put all his affairs in good standing. That he may as well liquidate everything right now and share off everything now he's still alive."

"Yes, you don't mind that son o' your'wn," Mrs. King cautions. "You know these men does get big in size only, but in some ways they still act like children. Sometimes you gotta be asking yourself who you really dealing with at all, man or child? Just like that one Lashley over there in that house across the road. I have no doubt Stephie in there so will wrap him 'round her finger when she ready for him. 'Cause I don't know why he don't hurry and go 'long from 'round here 'bout his business. I mean you shoulda hear he talking some foolishness the other day about becoming a cane cutter."

"A what?" Mrs. Smith asks. "*Cane cutter?*"

"Ask Peggy here if you think I lie," Mrs. King says, sucking her teeth.

"Lord have mercy, Miss Mary." Mrs. Smith's laugh is dry. "A *cane cutter*, and in this day and age. That is what he thinkin' about offering a young girl like she in there for a future? Lord have mercy. I ain't hearing right this evening. I tell yuh, these men."

"That was why," Grandmother says, "I had was to set him straight quick, quick, quick, tell him that would be like going in reverse, bare backwardness."

"These men like they don't hear and understand the saying from the political platforms," Mrs. Smith says. "Forward ever; backward never."

"Well you know me and Peggy here had to fix him real good," Mrs. King says. "There's a time and place for everything under the sun, and a time did come for the two o' we to speak *real* stern. We had to turn *acid* on he."

"In fact, it was because of all this going away that I have the trouble I have now," Mrs. Smith continues with mock disapproval. "When Bertie used to come back home from working at the munition factories up north and picking fruits like tomatoes and oranges back then in his day, especially during and after the war, he used to have a woman with a child for he almost every year. He say that he got four outside children, but I won't be surprise if they ain't more. I keep telling him to check his memory good, for when he's dead I don't want nobody showing up at my house bawling them eyes out and saying he or she is a' outside child and they coming for their inheritance. As far as I am concerned, Bertie got only one child, and that is by way of marriage. Only one child should be provided for in his will."

"But Maisie," Mrs. King says, "you really meaning what you saying? 'Cause you have to remember your own son, how he gone and pick up a woman with two children that ain't his own. What he's to do?"

"Well, that different, for I say that if a man make up his bed, he got to be ready to sleep in it," Mrs. King says. "He did know what he was getting into. He went in with his eyes wide open. Desmond can have a relationship with Leila two children and they can become like his own. Not like outside children that you never really ever had anything to do with until you reaching the end o' your time and everybody coming running to you with them hands long out."

"But how you did let things come to this?" Grandmother asks. "I mean, how old you was when you did married to Bertie? You did always be younger than he, your brain fresher and did be sharper, so what happened to let he get to this point *now*?"

"That is the point I always making," Mrs. Smith confides. "This is what happened when you married a man too old. It might look good when you young and he in his prime and he can provide for you and the children. But when he gets old, and you still young, all these strange things does happen. Everything you didn't know or was too frightened to ask about back then does come out of the woodworks.

That is why I keep on saying if I had was to advice the young women and especially the young girls they have around here, I would tell them don't ever marry no man more than seven years older than you."

"You can't be saying that in all cases," Mrs. King says. "You can't mean—"

"Seven years and that's it, *be Christ*," Mrs. Smith says, clapping her hands. "Not one day older, and perhaps no younger either. But seven years is enough of a difference. Any older and he'd only be thiefin' yuh youth from yuh."

"*Shhh,*" Mrs. King says, putting her finger to her mouth. "You never know who might be listening and might take offence. Things aren't always that easy so."

"In my case, I done know what to do," Mrs. Smith says. "Me and Leila will fix him up good. We'd fix his business for him. Leila making sure Desmond done get that health care building she always talking 'bout."

"*Leila?*" Mrs. King asks. "What *she* got to do with any o' this? You want a foreigner person in your business?"

"But what I've been telling you? Remember she's a woman too," Mrs. Smith says. "She ain't foolish like that piece o' son I'd give birth to all these long years ago who would give up his own sweet inheritance just because he and his father can't 'gree. But not his wife, Leila: she ain't for that kinda foolishness."

"If you say so," Mrs. King says. "But she is still a *foreigner.*"

"Anyway I have to go," Mrs. King says, rising. "I have to give he his Complan and tea for the night so he can sleep. I don't know why he don't call them outside children he now wants to make things right with to come and mix his Complan for him and to give he to drink. I tell yuh, next time we meet, hum, things will be very different."

"Walk good," Mrs. King says.

"Don't mind that man that you got there. Don't let him make you sin your soul," Grandmother adds.

"Next time too," Mrs. King says, raising her voice, "when me and Peggy here done with *him* too, things gine be quite different too in that house there across the road. You ain't hear cat piss and pepper yet. He, right there across the road thinking and thinking, will soon know good, good, good which god he serving when we done with he."

Mrs. Smith leaves Grandmother and Mrs. King to lapse back into silence. Knowing what is best for me, I get up to light the lamps, taking care not to harm the chimney. I hesitate a bit so it doesn't look like I am taking a cue from Mrs. Smith's departure. I do not want them to know I was listening to their woman talk, especially with them being in such an acid mood.

I wait for Stephie at the bus stop at the start of a new week. Looking down the road, I notice the men gathering in front of Mrs. Watson's shop. They are dressed in ragged clothes, old pants and shirts, and a few of them are wearing worn shoes for this first day of the sugar cane crop season. Only the day before, every church in the area was overflowing with people giving thanks. Pastor Wiltshire devoted much of his open-air meeting on the Saturday to the start of the sugar cane crop season, and many of the men in the rum shop quietly agreed with his message that there is no shame in hard work.

In the distance, a siren blows a number of times. This is the factory sending a signal around the area: the ritual beginning of the season. Women dressed in cast-off clothes, many with straw hats on their heads, begin walking in small knots of twos and threes, calling to one another as they go to work. But even after the siren finishes blowing, the men continue to wait. Only when everyone appears to be accounted for, do the men take up their cane-cutting bills and machetes and begin walking along the road, so much like soldiers in double file on parade. They shout out to those of us at the bus stop and to the other men and women, particularly those who are employed in the civil service or as domestic workers, teasing that they do not know what it really means to work hard for their daily bread. The cane cutters move through the village as if they want this moment—between the end of uncertainty and hard times and the cutting of the canes—to last as long as possible.

Mr. Lashley is the last to appear. He comes out of his house when the men are some distance on. And he walks behind them as if he is no longer sure of himself or what is expected of him, as if he is still looking for Postie to show up with his letter, even though he does not come until evening. Stephie does not show her face, not for the bus and certainly not at school.

"*O God, our help in ages past . . .*" Out of the quiet I hear a familiar voice singing, soft at first but then rising. It has been so long since I last heard Stephie sing that I lift my head from reading to listen. "*Our shelter from the stormy blast . . .*" The lamplight flickers as I look through the window and see Mr. Lashley's house in darkness. For the first time since he returned with the television a few months ago, the annoying bluish-green light is not there to taunt me. From what I've gathered, Mr. Lashley went into town earlier in the day to meet with the people running the Overseas Workers Program. Grandmother and Mrs. King are out somewhere. I know they are not at church, because Grandmother did not take her white handbag with the Bible. "Me and Eudene," she said as she was leaving, "we just going down the road to check out something." She did not say what, but I suspect that wherever they are has something to do with Mr. Lashley and what they promised Mrs. Smith they would do.

"*A thousand ages in Thy sight,*" Stephie continues, "*are like an evening gone.*" Her voice is as sharp and free as it was in old times, and it sounds as if she is speaking to just me. I am enthralled, and I close my exercise book and walk over to the window. Picking up the tune, I join in: "*Short as the watch . . .*"

I hear Stephie laugh and feel the warmth of the blood cruising through my veins. It is like old times: only the two of us are home, in different houses, the one across the road is in darkness, the streets are deserted and we are keeping company. It has been so long since our voices joined as one between the houses. When we finish the hymn, Stephie begins another that we have been singing at school as part of the independence celebrations. At school, we students sing as one first thing in the morning and for an hour or so on Friday afternoons before breaking for the weekend. Stephie laughs again as we end the song, and then there is a long pause. I do not know what to expect. Maybe Stephie is fooling with me. Will she switch on her radio and sing along with it, excluding me, since I don't know the songs? She doesn't. Soon we have gone through four, five, six hymns, me and she just singing. And when we are out of the spirituals, she turns to some of the national songs they have been teaching us at school. I join in singing "Island in the Sun." I am having fun.

"Hey you two in there," I hear a man's voice calling from the front of the house. Stephie and I stop singing, surprised. I listen, my heart beating fast, and I think I hear someone knocking on the side of Mrs. King's house. But someone is also knocking on our house.

"Yes?" I hear Stephie answer somewhat suspiciously. "Who is it?"

"Christopher, boy, open the window and look out here," the voice calls. "Man, the two o' we want to talk to you two. I never heard sweet singing like that on this island. You two ever heard how you sound singing together?"

Desmond Smith is standing outside. I look over at Mrs. King's house and see Leila standing on the step. Stephie is holding the window open.

"The two o' you can come outside?" Desmond Smith asks. "I want to talk to you two. I want to ask the two o' you to come out to the dance hall this Saturday night coming, when me and Leila having a competition for the young people." He explains that until he can get enough money to open the businesses that he and Leila want to set up, he has come up with an idea: he will ask the television station to devote a half-hour every Saturday evening for a talent show, where young people can sing and dance. Then they can watch themselves perform instead of watching programs like *Teenage Dance Party* and *Opportunity Knocks*, which come from overseas. If the competition goes well—and he has no doubt it will because of all the talent he has come across since returning to the island—he could see the day coming when there would be a national competition and a cultural festival that the island could put on for independence celebrations each year. All the songs could be recorded and sold not only here on this island but overseas, for people the world over are always looking for new talent.

"But I have to help Grandmother and Mrs. King down by the shop," I say, "and in any case, I don't know if *anybody* really wants to sing with me these days."

Stephie sucks her teeth. "Nobody don't mind you, Christopher," she says, but I can tell she doesn't mean anything bad. This is her way of being friendly.

"This is so beautiful," Leila says. "The two of you singing into the night. Is this the way you keep company? Is this how you take care of one another when you are alone?"

"Me, I just like singing," Stephie says. "Me and he always sing together."

"Whenever I pass this way," Leila says, "something new always makes me wonder about my own boy and girl, except they can't sing. But it's all so sad, not right."

"All I know is that I can see you two singing either alone or as a duet," Desmond says, ignoring Leila. "You have the voices."

"I would think as a duet," Leila says. "The two of you just sound so . . ." She raises her hands to her head to indicate she does not have the words to explain.

"But the dance hall," Stephie says. "You would have to ask our grannies."

"Let me talk to them," Desmond says. "I can talk to them. But they can't keep talent like this under a bush. Maybe me and Leila will come by tomorrow self. Let me talk to them." And he does not have to wait long. As we look down the road, we can see by the light of a passing car the two women and Mr. Lashley approaching.

"I got to go," Stephie says, closing the window and plunging the area in front her house into darkness.

"Me too." I follow suit.

I hear Desmond and Leila walking toward the three approaching figures. I wait. There is no talking between the houses now. When Grandmother enters the house, I pretend to be engrossed in my reading.

"That Desmond Smith and his wife just stop me and Mrs. King, saying they want to talk about you and Stephie and some *stupid* singing contest," Grandmother says, mashing off her shoes. I sense anger in her voice. I hold my breath.

"Something he says about the two o' you singing together. We tell him that right now we have too much on the mind to think about any ol' singing." My heart drops. It would be fun to go to the dance hall and be in the competition, even if we didn't win. Grandmother walks behind the curtain to her bed.

"So we tell him to come back and talk to we in a day or two when we have the time to listen to him. They say they will drop by in the night tomorrow." I close the book. I tell myself there is still hope. In bed, I cannot sleep. I can only think about tomorrow.

The next evening, I sit at the table wondering how soon Desmond and Leila will turn up, and whether Stephie and Mrs. King will be joining us, or if there will be separate conversations. Stephie was not at school again today, so I couldn't ask her what she really thinks about it. If she is still the same Stephie I've known all this time, though, I know she is just as eager as me for this meeting. Imagine all the talk at school if we entered the competition. Imagine if we actually *won*.

Grandmother has placed rice and peas and fried corned beef and onions under an enamel cover for me, and it is still warm. Beside the plate is a jug of mauby for me to drink, but there isn't any ice in it. Still, I pour a good amount into my tot and drink it down, feeling the heavy sweetness against the back of my throat and the bitterness on my tongue.

Grandmother and Mrs. King are sitting together in the backyard. It looks like they've been that way for most of the afternoon. Occasionally, Grandmother holds Mrs. King's hand or Mrs. King places her head on Grandmother's shoulder. Once, it looks like Mrs. King is crying, but I can't tell for sure. I keep my distance. From the look of things, they wouldn't want me mixing up myself in big-people business. I eat the food Grandmother has left for me. Soon Cyrus will come and we'll walk over to the playing field for cricket practice. I hope Desmond and Leila come before then. Otherwise I will have to wait until I return to find out what happened. Maybe Stephie will tell me all about it when I get back.

Now that the crop season is in full swing, we are beginning the practice sessions at least an hour later than before. This is to allow the players to get home from working in the field, have a quick bath, get something to eat and rest up a bit to catch their strength before coming to cricket practice. I hope Desmond and Leila do not let this extra time go to waste.

What time we lose by starting training late because of the crop season, we make up at the finish, so that most evenings the practices end in virtual darkness. I don't mind because I am in good form. At school it is usual for me to bat through the entire lunch break. My hopes are high that I will make the school team. Games master Mr. Jones and the cricketing coach at the school are encouraging me. Though they haven't told me directly, I can tell from the way they smile and talk with me that I am in their favour.

Every morning, I take my new bat to school, and during the spare time between classes, I clean and varnish it with linseed oil, just as Cyrus showed me. At night when I sleep, I keep the bat leaned up against the side of the house nearest to my head, but out of Grandmother's way so she does not trip over it as she moves around in semi-darkness. The bat is the finest I have ever used; it is of the right weight and size, and the black rubber on the handle gives me a superb and confident grip. Just feeling the ball hit the centre of the bat, even when I am poking a defensive shot, is a thrill. Intuitively, I know when I am in the right position—the bat and pads close together, my head over the bat, my eyes seeing the ball onto the very centre of the bat—and then I feel the reassuring thud of the impact and hear the *plix*. Even more gratifying is when I execute a full-blooded drive or a square cut, a hook or even a pull shot, especially when I get them off the centre of the lumber and we pause to watch the ball speed away to the boundary. This bat is the most precious gift anyone has ever given me.

I know I'll be ready to turn out for the school team, should the selectors give me a chance. I just have to finish saving up for the cricket boots that I see every day in the sports department of the main store in the city. But with Postman Simpson still not stopping, I am more certain of making the school team than of getting the shoes in time. I worry that if I do not have all the right gear, the selectors will not give me the chance they might otherwise believe I deserve.

Grandmother says she is trying her best not to lose any sleep worrying about how we can get this cricketing gear. I am making do with my white sneakers, which I lace tightly. I wash them every Saturday and place them on a piece of galvanize to dry in the sun. Later, I add the whitening to the canvas and rubber parts of the shoes. There is one problem with the sneakers: they do not give me as firm a grip as a proper pair of cricket shoes would with the spikes in the bottom. I keep hoping my mother will send money to help me get the right outfit to represent the team—if they pick me, of course. I still need the white shirts and long pants, and I don't know where me or Grandmother would get the money to buy them. Perhaps winning, or even placing, in the talent contest would help with this problem.

Cyrus really pushes me at practice. There is still so much more, he says, that he wants to bring out in me. He says my technique against the fast bowlers and the spinners is getting stronger, especially as we work on me playing with my bat and pads closer together. Most of all, he wants me to concentrate on my stance at the wicket and how I shift my weight on the front foot or the back foot to play a stroke. These are issues of judgment, he explains, and being caught on the wrong foot when I'm batting at a crucial moment can be disastrous to me and my team. "Remember we ain't playing little boy cricket no more," Cyrus frequently reminds me. "This is playing with art, not only heart, yuh hear me. So use that head that God gave you." He tells me I do not have to play every shot in the book within the first fifteen minutes of getting to the crease. Instead, I should be building up my concentration and willpower by training myself to occupy the batting wicket for as long as possible. "Temperament, my boy," he is always saying. "Taking yuh time ain't laziness." The key to progress is learning to control my exuberance. I must learn to grind things out, to exercise discipline and think of the greater good of the team. "Once you do that, once you set about playing yourself in and not acting too rash right off the bat, the runs will come." Cyrus frequently chides me to think beyond myself and put the team first. "You have to keep remembering if you get yourself out because you went and play a thoughtless shot, you won't be able to make any runs later. Now the team would be without one of its best batsmen, which would only make thing tougher for all the others who probably can't bat as good as you."

Sometimes Cyrus walks me home after practice and carries the bat. The last time, he said something that caught me off guard. "You want to come 'round by my house with me before going home?" he asked. "The two of we could just go walking. That way I can continue to demonstrate to you some things that I still want to show you." The way he smiled made me feel he was talking about more than just cricket.

"Maybe a next time," I said, for I did not like the softness in his voice. "Maybe another time. I have my homework to complete."

Sounding disappointed, he said it was all right, that what he wanted to show me could wait. "Still I hope you have sweet dreams tonight," he almost whispered. "And when you think of the bat, I hope you remember me, all the things I want for you. Maybe next time, eh."

I push aside thoughts of Cyrus and the way he was acting that night to think about Desmond and Leila's promise to come by. I cannot wait to see how this evening will unfold.

Suddenly I hear someone loudly sucking their teeth. The sound of annoyance has come from the backyard. I look out and see that Mr. Lashley has come home from the cane field and, as usual, is calling over to Grandmother and Mrs. King. Something is bothering them so much, they can hardly respond. "We just cooling out," Mrs. King says. "Waiting in the name of the Lord."

"Me too," Mr. Lashley says. "These days what else can you do, but wait, wait."

"I was thinking I would like to have a quick word with you," Mrs. King says, rising to her feet. "'Bout what we find out today. Something for we to talk about." I see Stephie at the back door of her grandmother's house, but she does not come out. She sees me but she does not speak or even wave.

"Okay," Mr. Lashley says. "Just give me a chance to get out of these blasted sweaty clothes. Let me catch a bath and fresh up. Then we can talk." He unlocks the door to his house.

"Okay," Mrs. King says, but there is no enthusiasm in her voice. Stephie disappears back into the house. Mr. Lashley enters his.

"*Wuthless brute,*" Grandmother says from the backyard as the door closes behind him.

When Mrs. King returns from Mr. Lashley's house, she rejoins Grandmother in the yard. They mutter some more to each other and Grandmother sucks her teeth long and hard, which is an indication that she radically disagrees with what she is hearing. I sit up and strain to listen. I hope they are not in this teeth-sucking mood when Desmond and Leila come to talk with them.

"You tellin' me *that* is all a big man like he can say for himself?" Grandmother says. "That is *all* he could tell you in defence o' heself?"

"Yes, boasie," Mrs. King replies. "That's all I could get outta he. I try. What yuh want me fuh do? What can *anybody* want me fuh do?" Grandmother rubs her back, and they revert to whispering.

As usual, Mr. Lashley comes out of the house at the appropriate time, picks up his watering can and occupies himself with the garden until the sound of the postman's motorcycle has long disappeared into the distance. Grandmother and Mrs. King do not leave the backyard at the first sound of the motorcycle's arrival in the area, which is unusual. Stephie remains out of sight as well. There will be no commiserating with Mr. Lashley from this side of the road today. Mr. Lashley, it seems, is on his own. Grandmother and Mrs. King seem to be finished talking even with each other. But the calm is suddenly shattered by a strangely familiar voice shouting in front of Mrs. King's house.

"*Ma-mah*, where you *is*?" The voice is accusatory, as harsh and exacting as that of any judge. I look through the door and see Dorothy Inniss, Mrs. King's eldest daughter, standing in the road. She is extremely fair-skinned, what we call "red-skin people," so different from the jet-black features of her mother, and she is wearing a black skirt and white bodice, the typical uniform of wait staff and receptionists at the hotels and guest houses along the coast. Standing beside her is her husband, Arnold, a tall man with a knotty beard and close-cropped hair, as if he is already going bald. He too is wearing the white and black uniform. "*Ma-mah*, where you is this evening? You home or you above there with that woman friend o' your'wn?"

"Oh, Lord, here comes trouble now," I hear Grandmother saying. "Just play it cool, Eudene. Just be cool. Don't let that daughter of you'own upset you any more this evening. You got enough on your mind already without she making things even wo'ser."

"Lord, I don't care what the foolishness the two o' you still getting on wid," Dorothy says, "'cause that is the two o' you nasty business, and as a Christian woman, I don't have anything else to say to the two o' you. What I want to know is what the two o' you doing to my sister daughter? That is what I come up here to find out for myself." Dorothy is talking at the top of her voice; she sounds as though she is not only talking to her mother but to all the neighbours for good measure.

"I behind here," Mrs. King says, her voice not as loud. "What you want from me this good, good evening?" I smile to myself, wondering what Stephie is making of all this. Dorothy is given to exaggeration, which is one of the reasons the grandmothers say they can't get along with her. Her visits are infrequent, but Stephie and I always like it when she drops by unexpectedly and lively up the place. I look to see what Stephie is doing, but there is no sign of her. I expect that Dorothy will make her presence felt and then disappear.

"What I really want to ask you is, as a mother yourself, how you think Esmeralda would feel knowing that you take her nice young daughter not even fifteen years good yet, and you give she to that hard-back man over there so that he could breed she up? I was at my work, not troubling a soul, when the gossip catch right up to me. Every Tom, Dick and Harry, every man, woman and child I know talking 'bout how you carrying on, how things only getting worse in this little Sodom and Gomorrah, and that you now have this poor child in trouble, and she is only just a child."

"But Dorothy," Grandmother shouts across to her, trying to modulate her voice so she sounds more reasonable, elderly and respectable, "why you have to be carrying on so as your mother says on this good, good evening? Why you have to be like Satan coming in a whirlwind after going hither and thither in the world to inflict abuse on your poor mother so? Why you have to be so brawling like your mouth ain't got no cover and letting out your mother business for all the whole wide world to hear, no privacy, so that you gotta be scandalizing everybody?"

"Yeah, Dorothy," Mrs. King says, seeming to find the strength to respond, "why if you have anything to talk to me about that you don't have some manners even for a big woman with she own children and come behind here and talk to me to my face and in a proper and respectable manner instead of standing out there in the middle o' the road and carrying on so disgraceful?"

"Look, don't let the two o' wunnuh so get me even more acid with this talk about scandal," Dorothy says. "'Cause I ain't come all the way over here to make no sport. So don't vex my spirit anymore."

"But it is you creating all this ruckus like some federation gone bad," Grandmother says.

"'I don't know what the two o' you think this is," Dorothy says, dropping her voice slightly, and talking slower as if catching her breath. "Miss Lucas, how much longer you think you and my mother can hide this from the people that already done know? So don't come talking to me that way, 'cause it ain't me causing no scandal."

"Dorothy," Mrs. King says, "please, I beg yuh for your own sake: do me a favour and try and behave yuhself. If not for yuhself, think o' the children that you have back at home, even if you never bring them for me as grandmother to see. Don't give the people 'round here anything else to talk about yuh."

"It ain't me that give the people 'round here something to talk about," Dorothy says. "I tell yuh, you and that Wendell Lashley over there can hide and buy land, but you can't hide and work it. As true as there is a God above, whatever you do in the darkness will some day come to light. What I want to know is now that she's in the way, what you're going to do when that poor little girl in there belly start swelling up big, big, big to she mouth, when she start to be really showing? You think you can ban down she belly forever?"

I sit up. And without knowing why, I kick the school bag under the table. All I can think is *no, no, not Stephie too. Why does this have to happen to she, Stephie, of all people.* In my mind it is as if something hovering so long in the darkness has finally reached out and grabbed her, just as it keeps snatching so many girls of our age. I've heard Grandmother and Ms. King talking about other girls finding themselves in the way. Now it is Stephie everyone in the world is talking about. *Poor Stephie!* Why did this have to happen? What did we do wrong? I look again for her, but there is still no sign of her in the house. I am worried about what will happen next, how Stephie will manage life. I can't wait to talk to her and hear what she thinks.

"*Shhh,*" Grandmother says. "You, Dorothy, mind yuh mouth. Why you gotta come by here and act so, as if some red ants bite yuh. You don't ever come around here, not even to say hello to you own mother, not even to see if she living or dead, and now you here with your own brawling self. Really, you should know more better, Dorothy."

"All I know," Dorothy says, "is that the two o' you behind there conniving together with that big-able man Wendell Lashley over there in that breaking-down house, so that you got my little sister daughter here, who ain't no more than a child sheself, but the two o' you got she tekking man every night and day that God send, and as if she is some big, able, cut-open cow. And from who? Old-arse Wendell Lashley, who ain't nothing these days but a damn cane cutter, who can't even get back up on the program, and who ain't got two bad cents in his pocket that he can now rub together."

"Don't bother answering she back," Mrs. King says to Grandmother, but now talking loud enough for anyone listening to hear. "Save the breath God done give yuh. She's my daughter, but you know how she is. Let she talk 'til she ready to stop. 'Cause when she ready, she would cuss God himself."

"I mean he ain't even a man with a future that can do anything for she. *Wendell,*" Dorothy calls out at the top of her voice. "*Wendell Lashley,* open up the window to that piece o' old house you hiding in over there. *Wendell Lashley*, why didn't you go and pick on somebody your own age, on a' experience woman of the world to put yuh in your place?"

"But looka this thing now," Mrs. King says. "Now she gone and troubling the poor man. I hope that he don't come outside and put himself in any trouble with she. 'Cause when she's in she spirit, you can never tell what she will do next. She might even go and hit the poor man first, and then he will gotta defend heself and hit she back. Next thing we dealing with police."

"Yes, *Wendell Lashley*," Dorothy is shouting, "I talking to you and I talking loud, loud, loud so that everyone in the presence of my voice will hear me and know what wuthlessness you's up to. You don't got to be frighten o' me, so you can open up the window and talk to me. What you doing to my sister pickney ain't right or proper. How you, a big able man, how you a hard-back, good-for-nuthing, wuthless man can go and rob that poor girl of she youth? Tell me that? What you going to do for she when the baby done come?"

"Oh, Lord now," Mrs. King says. "There she goes telling the whole world all o' my business. There she go now as if she ain't have no shame."

"Shame?" Grandmother repeats. "You know when it comes to shame that daughter of your'wn ain't got none, that shame is one thing she never did have none of. Maybe you should give she a few cents to go and buy some shame bush so she can at least get a little bit to show."

"I mean," Dorothy continues, "I am sitting at my station doing my work and people keep saying, 'But Dor'thy what the hell you' mother and Wendell Lashley say they getting on wid, though? Why you don't go up there and say something before they ruin the life o' that poor little girl that does call you auntie?'" She sounds now as if she is talking to the world in general and pleading for anyone listening not to find her as culpable as those she is holding responsible. "And I keep telling them that I will, but that because me and my mother don't get along too good, we don't see eye to eye from the time I was a little girl, I tell them that I don't want to go and juck my mouth in anybody business. And I keep waiting and now I hear the news today. As soon as the doctor did done seeing that poor little girl today. Even as he must have been telling the two o' you the hard facts o' life. One o' them blasted malicious nurses, for that is how they does stay when it comes to talking out people business, one o' them nurses did come out and whisper in somebody ear."

"That's right," Mrs. King says. "I done think it was she own self they did tell." But what Dorothy is saying is answering my own questions.

"And the next thing I know," Dorothy continues, "people like flies on shit coming up to me and saying some more, 'Dor'thy, girl, how this could happen,' and that she is only a child *sheself.* So *Wendell Lashley,*" she is screaming again, "open up the *blasted* door in there and look out. I ain't making no sport. Be accountable. I want to hear from yo' own mouth about your aims and intentions for my sister little girl, and why you had to go and do this to she."

The windows and doors to Mr. Lashley's house remain closed. Dorothy goes to the front door and pounds on it, but still Mr. Lashley stays inside. Finally, her husband pulls her away from the house, and they walk into Grandmother's backyard. Dorothy is breathing loudly. Mrs. King looks up at her and makes as if she is going to stand, but Grandmother holds her hand and pulls her back down.

"No, 'Dene," Grandmother cautions. "She ain't worth it. Don't let she make you sin yuh soul this evening. You already have too much to bear. And after all, you still have to treat she as a child, for she did roll 'round in you' belly, and no matter what, you will always be the mother and she will be the child."

"But what about poor Stephie?" Dorothy says softly, as if she is now speaking only to those in the backyard. "Who is going to take care of she now that she's in the way? What kind o' training she getting from her elders? You and this one Miss Lucas here ain't no good example with your living. Everybody saying that you, as a grandmother, who should know better, how you done sell out the poor girl just so that you could get a few new boards on a house and some galvanize on yuh roof. That you up and sell she off. And for a paint job."

Mrs. King and Grandmother do not respond. Arnold Inniss positions himself between his wife and the other two women. He says nothing.

"Where is she?" Dorothy asks, no longer shouting.

"She's inside the house," Mrs. King says. "But what you want she for, after you done bawl out her private business in front of the whole world? You may as well now go and put it on the radio to broadcast it."

"Ma, you know this ain't something that anybody can hide," Dorothy says almost in a whisper. "What about her school? You think 'bout these things?"

"What about them?" Mrs. King asks.

"How much longer you think they're going to keep her in school, eh?" Dorothy says. "And when they kick she outta school, what she gine do? Walk 'round here so that stinking, *wuthless* Wendell Lashley could keep pulling at she, especially now that he's off the program and ain't got anything useful to do? She can't ever make anything of herself, 'cause she never did start to live. Is that what you want for her by giving she over to Wendell Lashley like that?"

There is no answer. The women seem as if they have exhausted all they can say.

"I want she to come and live with me," Dorothy resumes. This time she is talking softly, pleading. "I done talked to Arnold here, and

I tell he it would be best for Stephie to come and live with me. And Arnold says it is okay with he, that whatever I wants and feels right for the little girl is fine and right with he. We can arrange things around the house so that the other children can share one bedroom, and we can give Stephie a bedroom, nothing too fancy, for sheself. At least she can stay there with the two o' we and the children until she time come. So what you say?"

"I ain't got nothing to say," Mrs. King says. "At least not anything that would get in the way of what is good for that little girl that I love with all my heart. You, as she aunt, can do whatever your sweet little heart tell you is best fuh she. 'Cause I ain't know *nothin'* no more. I too tired with everything. I can't keep carrying this burden all by myself no more."

"Okay, then," Dorothy says. "I'll go and tell she to pack she clothes and to come 'long with me. What we can't carry now, Arnold can come back for a next time."

"So you say." Mrs. King consents.

"And if I may say so, that doesn't sound like too bad a' idea," Grandmother concurs. "At least she can stay with you for a little while, 'til things quieten down 'round here. I think that is the best, Denie. So don't cry. I support you in that."

Dorothy and Arnold walk over to the back door of Mrs. King's house. I notice that Cyrus has arrived and is standing in front of the house.

The last I see of Stephie, she is walking in front of Dorothy and Arnold toward the bus stop. Stephie's head is down, as if her chin is touching her bosom, her hands reaching down gangly as she ambles along. Arnold is carrying a small valise held together with some string in one hand and Stephie's school bag in the other. Dorothy is carrying the radio that Mr. Lashley brought back. Dorothy appears to be doing as much talking as she was before, but not loudly, and Arnold, as usual, is doing just as she instructs him, as they run into her old friend Desmond Smith and his wife, Leila.

I do not enjoy the cricket practice this evening, for I cannot concentrate. By the time I get home, Mrs. King is alone in her house with the lamp already turned down low. Grandmother has turned in for the night. As I take up a book to read, I notice the unusual silence that has settled over all of us. It takes me some time to realize the cause, or at least a significant part of it: Mr. Lashley's house across the road is in complete darkness. For the second time in months, I do not see the bluish glow coming from it, and the boys are not over there. There is no sound of laughter. And in the absence of that light there is no singing either. Nothing is the same. And I don't know if Desmond and Leila visited.

Eventually, I give up trying to read. Grandmother is snoring loudly, like I've never heard before. Between thinking and Grandmother's snoring, it is impossible to sleep.

Chapter Fifteen

Ever since Dorothy came and took Stephie away six weeks ago, a heavy presence has haunted us. It is like none I have ever known or heard about. To me it is a spirit—not of a ghost with its strange smells of smoke or sweet perfume; and not of the ancestors, those who have departed and who remind us of their existence by causing cobwebs to brush our faces in the night, or galvanize to crackle in the house, or a spoon or fork to drop from the table. Grandmother teaches that even though the spirits of the ancestors are always around us, they know their place and when to keep their distance. The spirit I am feeling now is of someone living but whose presence we cannot see, taste, hear or even smell. If I observe closely enough, I can hear her laughter. I hear Stephie getting angry with me when I bug her, such as when we were little children and she told me not to touch her or breathe near her. I remember her special smile, her way of showing that she knew everything, the look on her face when she crossed the finish line and knew that yet again she was the clear and indisputable winner. I remember the times when we would sit under the trees in the backyard, when our grandmothers wanted time for themselves and we had to do something to occupy ourselves, the times when we would join the other boys and girls at play, when the tar road would be our pitch. We were small then. Now we are big, and our lives have taken a quick and funny turn.

Most of the time I smile when I remember, but some memories still make me cringe. Like the evenings we set up four large stones as bases. It was boys versus girls at rounders. Standing between the first and fourth bases, a girl would throw the ball in the air as if serving at tennis. She would cuff it with a folded fist and scamper for the first base, and we boys would field the ball and throw it at her as hard and as fast as we could. She would jump in the air to avoid the ball, showing her puffed-leg bloomers. And if the ball missed her, she would round first, second, third and fourth base to safety. But if our throw was too straight, too strong and the blow too hard, we would *cork* her, and she would be unable to hide the pain, to prevent herself from crying. We boys would laugh, for in either case we had won: either by seeing the bloomers or by making the girl cry. With her speed, Stephie always rounded the bases and got home before anyone could even take a good aim. Plus she could jump high when threatened. And Stephie soon learned how not to cry, how to protect herself, especially when she made up her mind about anything, like when she took me that one and only time to the dance hall. Stephie became tough to hide her feelings, even when she stumbled between bases. She was tough, not like me. Still, I sometimes thought that it might just be a matter of time before one of the bigger boys caught up to her. There was always something out there just waiting to pounce, to make her just like any of the other girls, to turn me into any of the other boys. A person can be careful for only so long.

Grandmother reminds me, as patiently as she can, that Mrs. King and Dorothy are not on speaking terms, not after Dorothy had the gall to blackball her very own mother in front of everyone, and so we too aren't having anything to do with Dorothy, not until she and her mother make back up.

"But I just thinking of going to see *Stephie*," I clarify, "not her *auntie*."

"When things are good and ready, you will see Stephie," Grandmother says. "But I can't agree to letting you find yourself on a bus all by yourself travelling all the way over there to see anybody over there."

"But I travel on the bus to school every day," I say. "Nothing don't happen to me then, so I don't see why—"

"In any case, once you get there, what you'd ask Stephie? What you'd do? What can *you* do for her?" Grandmother asks. "No, you let things work themselves out without you interfering. If me and Mrs. King hear anything 'bout Stephanie, I will let you know."

"That makes no sense," I persist. "Stephie ain't doing nobody anything, so I don't see why I can't go and see her. Plus everybody at school keeps asking me for Stephie and I don't know what to tell them."

"I know," Grandmother says. "But sense or no sense, I am the one around here that decides things."

But for me, this is not the final word. I would like to go and visit Stephie, but I cannot afford to get Grandmother angry with me. I plan to bide my time.

Sitting by the table, the flies buzzing in the house, I watch the rain falling heavily, each drop adding to the ever-widening puddles. The world is as grey as the clouds that are blocking the sun all day long. What can we do with it raining so, when it is so depressingly damp and cool? Stephie and me used to jump in the puddles, slide in the dirt and get ourselves into all sorts of trouble as we ignored everything our grandmothers told us about catching colds from getting wet in the rain, and about not dirtying up our clothes by playing in the mud. We liked to play hopscotch when it was dry and we had a piece of chalk to mark out our hopping squares, and when it rained and we could draw the squares with our toes in the mud. Thinking about Stephie and how we used to play, how we even got our licks together as punishment when we chose not to listen and found out that if hard ears won't hear, then bum-bum would feel, I can't stop smiling to myself. I can't stop thinking about Stephie and wondering what she's doing on this rainy evening. There is no escape from her absence, which weighs so heavily on us. And though I smile, I know I am not happy. In my heart I think I know why Dorothy took Stephie: it was to get her away from all the bad spirits that only make things worse for us, that seem to be watching us from the day we are born, ready to leap on us the first chance they get. What I don't understand is why taking Stephie away should mean leaving everybody behind.

Everybody except Grandmother and Mrs. King seems to notice how Stephie's absence is affecting me. Even Ursula. Today at lunch, as I was walking over to the canteen to buy a drink to have with my cheese-cutter, she appeared in front of me.

"So what's happening with Stephanie?" she asked.

"What's it to you?" I said, taking a defensive tone, for I did not want to deal with any more of Ursula's gloating since the race or her laughing at what has happened since.

"Nothing," she said. "Just asking. I thought you'd know something. Plus you look like you have something bothering you."

"I don't know a thing," I said, holding my head high, hoping she would leave me alone. "Not one friggin' thing."

"You know I feel sorry for Stephie," Ursula said. I was surprised she still wanted to continue the conversation. "Them things ain't right."

"What's that you saying?" I asked, not sure whether to believe the remorse in Ursula's voice. After all, she was the one benefitting the most from not having Stephie to compete with.

"Yes, I real sorry fuh she," she said. She was not laughing. I began to think that she might, in fact, be serious.

"My mother and father did be talking at home about what happened to Stephanie," Ursula said, looking me straight in the face as if to read my reaction to the news that the talk was this widespread. I tried not to show anything. "And my father said that if a man like that Wendell Lashley did as much as touch any o' his three girl children, the police would have to come for him and lock him up in prison when he done with him."

"Oh, yeah," I said, trying to hide my bewilderment.

She opened her sandwich pan. "For my father say that it is men like Wendell Lashley that does give all the men on this island a bad name." She paused to look at me to see how her words were sinking in. "And then my mother looking straight at me joined in saying that it wouldn't be Wendell Lashley that she would be dealing with alone, for after she done string he up by his two balls, she would be dealing with me, yes me, and that the police would have to come for she after she done with *me*. That if I was to be ever so foolish like Stephanie and—"

I snapped at that word, *foolish*, which was proof she was only pretending to care. "But what you know to judge? You different," I said, not bothering to hide my annoyance. Remembering our grandmothers' explanation, I added: "You don't need no godfather. You got your own two parents. You different."

Ursula took a bite of her sandwich and chewed but did not swallow. "You right," she said finally. "That very true. And that's why it's wrong."

I was totally surprised by her words. All along I had thought she hated Stephie so much she would never say anything to make Stephie look good in anybody's eyes.

"Want the other half of my sandwich?" she asked, extending the pan to me. I took it. It was ham and a special type of cheese. We smiled. "I made it myself," Ursula said. "My mother makes me make my lunch every morning. Says we have to be independent and responsible. You like it?"

"Yeah," I said, taking another bite. And I did like it.

"Good," she said, returning the cover to the pan. She looked at me and I could feel myself smiling there like some fool. I did not know what else to say or do, but it seemed like she was waiting for me to do something.

"Let me go and see if I can get a knock with the boys playing cricket over there." I gestured toward the playing field. "Lunchtime's soon over and most of the boys already out there on the pasture ready to play."

"Maybe we can do this another time," she said. "Or maybe after school, you can come by and visit me at home. Maybe some time when you don't have cricket."

"Maybe," I replied. I did not want to commit myself, for I didn't know how Grandmother would react to me going off and visiting anyone in the evening, especially a girl like Ursula. Plus what would I do if she were to turn around and say she wants to visit me at home? Grandmother wouldn't like that one bit: having strangers knowing her business. She would accuse me of taking away her privacy, for having people coming and staring into her morning, as she would say.

"Go. They playing," she said, pointing to the field, breaking the awkwardness. "See yuh later, then." I ran off, hoping to stake my chance for a spot high in the batting order before too many of the boys beat me to it.

Little did I know what Ursula meant by *later*, for after school, there she was, walking to the bus stand the same time as me. We talked until we had to take separate buses home.

"Denie, you *gotta* eat something, otherwise the maw worms gine get yuh as good as a cent," Grandmother says, standing over Mrs. King and me at the table, her hands akimbo. All along Grandmother has been telling me she does not like how Mrs. King is pining away over Stephie since she left and never ever once looked back to say hello to her own grandmother.

"I know," Mrs. King replies. "I know what you're saying, but it's just that I don't feel like I have any appetite. My mind just keeps resting on that poor little girl and how I might have let she down and fail she and her mother at the same time."

I flip open the book Ursula has lent me, for now I am relying on her to share books with me. She gave me it during lunch. It is now part of our regular pattern to spend the first minutes of the break together, and she gives me the sandwich that she makes especially for me each day in addition to her regular lunch. I keep telling her she should not bother herself with this extra work, and she keeps saying that it is no bother to her, that it is just as easy to make two sandwiches as one, and that, in any case, she likes what she is doing. So I eat the sandwich as we talk, until the boys start gathering for a quick game of cricket. After school, Ursula and I walk to the bus stand and I tell her about cricket practice. She has to hurry home, change her clothes and be ready for her father to come home and drive her to the club for athletic practices. Occasionally, she asks me about Stephie, but I do not know anything new.

One day, Ursula told me she wants to be a doctor. "A doctor?" I had said. "But they ain't too many women doctors around here."

"Well, that's more the reason to become one," she said, laughing. "At least that is what my mother tells me I should say to people. She says that is why we have independence on this island." Ursula said that if she couldn't become a doctor, she would like to start a business, like her mother had, but that her preference is to help people. "And what you want to be?" she asked.

I told her I hadn't given the idea much thought. It is easy to talk with Ursula; I can tell her things that with the exception of Stephie I would feel foolish sharing with other people. "I'm still waiting to see if my mother will send for me," I said. "I guess that is when I will decide. But I have to wait and see first. Maybe something in sports."

Now hearing the grandmothers discuss eating, I wonder what Ursula will bring me tomorrow, for she is quite good at providing something new and tasty to add to her sandwiches. I find myself smiling.

"Just that you got to remember you can't go around blaming yourself for what happened," Grandmother says, her voice pulling me back. "You tried your best, and as you said, you needed the help from Wendell Lashley, 'cause things did be hard for all o' we, not you alone, and he did come along and promise to take good care of her. 'Nough young people around here does have to rely on a godfather, even those that have a mother or father, far less people as poor as me and you. That is the ways of this island since Adam was a lad. So you can't blame yourself for that. Otherwise a lot o' we people around here would have to blame themselves too. Not when you did be acting out of the best of intentions and you did only mean good for everybody."

"I know," Mrs. King says. "I know."

"Not when he did come and tell you how he different from other mens and how he is a steady worker and he is always the first man the farmer does ask for every year. Plus he would be gone for most of the year, anyway. Anybody would think that all like now his arse would be up in Canada where he belongs working, not 'round here waiting for the postman like some loupy dog with no owner every blasted day God does send; not 'round here soring up his hands cutting canes and trying to keep you at bay. You couldn't expect such disappointment from *he*? That's why these mens can't be trusted. Why I don't know what else to say or do to make you into your old sweet self again."

"I okay," Mrs. King says.

But Grandmother and I know she is not. Though Grandmother has been trying her best to rouse Mrs. King, she's been drawing more and more into herself. She doesn't even bother to spend any time talking to Mrs. Smith when she passes by. Now Grandmother and Mrs. Smith do all the talking while Mrs. King just listens, often with a blank stare on her face, or a scowl, as if she has heard something she disapproves of. And when we were alone earlier this evening, Mrs. King seemed worried. More than once, she called me *Steph'nie* and then corrected herself. She said I shouldn't pay her no mind, she was just a little preoccupied. And she asked me, trying to laugh, if I ever notice how sometimes people of a certain age, like her, tend to mix up the names of the people they love. Grandmother never calls me *Stephie*, but she is always talking about her. For the first few days after Stephie left, one of the first questions Grandmother would ask on my return home was whether I had seen and talked to Stephie at school.

"I don't know how to help you," Grandmother says, and puts her hand around Mrs. King's waist. "But at least you know I sharing your burden with you too." Better, Grandmother reminds her, must come. Eventually Stephanie will get in touch. Perhaps she just needs more time to adjust to the new surroundings. Otherwise she would have come back to visit or sent word, just to let everybody know she is okay. Or maybe it is her aunt's fault: she must be telling Stephanie to remain at home much longer than she would want, ordering her to rest.

Sometimes I get the feeling that Grandmother and Mrs. King are afraid of me finding out something, some truth they themselves do not want to confront. I believe that is why Grandmother remains so firm in forbidding me from going anywhere near the house of that Dorothy Inniss.

It is the final day of another school week, and it's been raining all day. I am helping Grandmother and Mrs. King prepare the ground provisions and other goods necessary for Saturday's cooking and baking, when Henderson Brathwaite, Mr. Lashley's best friend, drops by to place his usual pudding-and-souse order. Suddenly Mr. Brathwaite says he has to speak his mind about his old-time friend Mr. Lashley, for he cannot help noticing all the differences he has been witnessing in him of late. He reminds Mrs. King and Grandmother of how, until now, Mr. Lashley lived *day to day*, as he called it. He prided himself on being so transient, seldom buying any groceries that would last him more than a week at the most. For he was forever telling the boys around him how he always had to be ready to just get up and go so that, as he said, when fame or fortune called he would never be found wanting.

Mr. Brathwaite recalls that it was on the Saturday, just four days after the cussing and lambasting he received from Dorothy, that Mr. Lashley appeared to have changed his mind. It was like he came to his senses. That Saturday evening after work, as soon as he received his wages, Mr. Lashley dragged himself to the rum shop like the rest of the men. After a few drinks, he belched hard, 'cause as a bachie, with no woman to cook for him, and since Mrs. King had stopped sending over his food in the evenings, he was drinking on a half-empty stomach. Mr. Lashley took a few very deep breaths, picked up his cane chopper and begged the other men to excuse him. The men watched him, wondering what Mr. Lashley could be up to. To their amazement, he went over to the other side of the shop and ordered several pounds of flour, sugar, so many pints of rice, some lard oil, some Irish potatoes, some cans of corned beef, so many packages of macaroni, a big hunk o' cheese, and several pounds of salt beef and salted pigtails. It was as if he was preparing for a hurricane to strike. Nothing about Mr. Lashley's buying, Mr. Brathwaite says, appeared to have the right proportions; he was ordering either too much of one thing or too little of the next. He did not seem to understand how one thing complements the other, and how they have to be in specific proportions to be in balance, not just thrown together all haphazardly. At least that is how his order sounded even to the men, but then they could all have been wrong, as there was not one man among them who could have done any better on his own. If they went shopping, they would have to rely on a list given to them by their missus; none of them would have been brave enough to attempt something as treacherous as shopping on their own.

Mr. Brathwaite says that as Mr. Lashley ordered, he appeared to be not only a changed man, but a broken man as well. He was talking slower than usual and there was an air of resignation about him, as if he was attending a funeral or something. The men in the shop, sensing something was wrong, listened carefully as Mr. Lashley also ordered a pint-and-half bottle of rum and two cases of mixed sweet drinks. They wondered how he would be able to carry home all them groceries as well as two heavy cases of drinks. The man wasn't thinking straight; he didn't know how things were done domestically. Suddenly it dawned on the men that he was storing up all these goods for a long haul, just like the wise old ant that was not a sluggard. Their hearts sank for Mr. Lashley, and they wondered what could have caused such a big change in attitude. It all seemed so tragic. Mr. Lashley paid, and as he stepped outside with the box of goods on his head and the cane bill in one hand, they all had to fire a quick rum to steady their nerves for him. Mr. Lashley hollered back to Mrs. Watson to keep an eye out 'til he could get back for them other two cases of soft drinks he had to leave behind.

Mr. Brathwaite says that it would be proper and correct for Wendell Lashley, as man, to go over to Dorothy Inniss's house and have a quiet word with she as the woman of that house. For although the girl is young, she is now a woman, and Mr. Lashley should recognize that he was the one who made her a woman quicker than her time would have allowed. He should recognize that with her being so young, he has the chance to make something out of her. He can make her a respectable woman—Mr. Brathwaite and his missus were just saying so the other night. Wendell Lashley should be man enough and go to Pastor Wiltshire, or any other preacher or priest that he liked, and set the date and make things proper. He should put the ring on the little girl finger, and call everything wally and say that he done with all the foolishness and wildness that he used to do before, especially now that it looks like the old life of flying here and there and everywhere seems to be finished with him.

This is exactly what the women want to hear. As Mr. Brathwaite leaves, I hear him calling to Mr. Lashley. But he does not stop at the house with the bluish glow and the children peering through the glass panes and the holes and cracks.

On Monday, Mr. Lashley is back among the gang, both as a cane cutter in the field and then in the rum shop afterwards. All week, he remains inside his house when he is not working or drinking. And maybe because, like the other men, he is so tired from the bending and rising in the cane fields, he has stopped weeding and watering the plants in front of his house in the evening. If it didn't rain, those plants would not have a drop of water all week long. As the postman passes through the village, Mr. Lashley can be seen peeping through the slats of the closed window, but that is all.

Grandmother and Mrs. King appear to accept these circumstances. Mrs. King promises she will wait for Mr. Lashley to make the first move, to see if he will really come to his senses in the way Mr. Brathwaite thinks he should. She says she hopes he is talking to and listening to well-adjusted men like Mr. Brathwaite and taking their advice. She will give him as much rope and time as he needs, and in the meantime, she and Grandmother are remaining out of sight. They are keeping to themselves in the houses or in the backyards. Now that it is raining again, they have been forced into the house to plait and style each other's hair. They seem to be seeking respite in the silence. They too are waiting.

Perhaps it is because of the rain that we do not hear Mrs. Smith coming. Or maybe it is because we are not expecting her, or just that everybody is preoccupied elsewhere. But she is almost upon us, entering the house and stopping to shake the rain off her raincoat, before we realize what is happening. Mrs. Smith takes off the plastic that covers her hat, and there is something about her action that seems to brighten her attitude, even though all around us it is glum and ugly.

"What you doing out in all this rain?" Grandmother asks. She gets up from where she is sitting and offers the seat to Mrs. Smith. "I hope you ain't out for the sou-sou money already. 'Cause you'd be too early."

"No. No," Mrs. Smith says. "Nothing so. I come to ask you to do me a favour when you go to town. There is something I want you to buy for me in town."

"Sure, sure," Grandmother says.

"But first, any word about the little girl?" Mrs. Smith asks.

"Not a word since she left," Mrs. King says. "But you know how it is."

"Nothing from that brute for a man living there across the street, neither?" Mrs. Smith asks.

"Not a word from him," Mrs. King says. "But I waiting for he good enough. I leave him in the hands of my Lord and master. How's your husband, Bertie? He okay? You got things back under control yet?"

"Yes, my dear," Mrs. Smith says. "I left he at home there waiting for me. But he's okay. Right now, the way I got he now, he don't even know what o'clock *a strike*."

"How you mean?" Mrs. King asks. "You settle things with him and get him to change his mind about the will?"

"I done take care of all that," Mrs. Smith reports. "And I got Leila to work with me. I just call up that lawyer in town we got introduced to a few years ago, and he whispered something in my ear. So I got these forms and I put them in front of Mr. Smith and ask he to sign them. I got Leila to witness it and then I asked she to personally take them to the lawyer. So said, so done. Now everything done fixed up proper, proper. I just hope all this would mean that you know who as husband and wife in my house would start back living proper and stop all this foolish quarrelling and fighting among themselves."

At that moment, we hear the sound of a motorcycle and instantly know it is Postie Simpson making his rounds. As usual, we collectively hold our breath and, based on the approaching sounds, mentally follow his progress. We hear the sound of the motorcycle growing louder and then stopping in front of our house. I look through the door to see Postman Simpson getting off the motorcycle and walking up the path to the front door of Mr. Lashley's house. We are all watching. By the time he gets to the top step, the door flings open to reveal, Mr. Lashley standing in the doorway, without a shirt on and smiling broadly. He takes the long, official-looking envelope from the postman and the two men stand talking, the rain running off Postman Simpson's heavy black raincoat. The postman walks back to his motorcycle, wipes the rain from his face, remounts the machine, revs up the throttle and quickly disappears. Grandmother, Mrs. King and Mrs. Smith look at one another but say nothing.

It is only later, when Mrs. Smith should be almost home if she had not stopped to deliver the news to those who did not know, that Grandmother realizes Mrs. Smith did not tell her what she wants her to buy in town.

Chapter Sixteen

It is as if everyone has let out their breath. As if they all knew that the fear of this time was misplaced all along. The ways of the world are starting to make sense; indeed, all is good. Everywhere, the tension has lifted—except for a few touchous points with a few people—and there is a joy to living again.

Pastor Wiltshire is as eager as ever to spread the good word and to make his own contribution to the air of excitement. As we make our first pass by him on our way to the shop, he is already set up and ready to go. He begins with a rousing rendition of "All Things Bright and Beautiful." He is ringing the bell louder and longer than he has for a while. Gone from his face are the scowls of judgment and brimstone and chastisement, and in their place is a pleasant smile of acceptance and forgiveness. Even in his words, for at least this one evening, evil is banished from the world. Once again, we are all whole. The men are working again. Expectations are running high in the land.

Grandmother puts down her tray on the box in front of her bench by the side of the road, and I place the coal pot strategically between where she and Mrs. King will be sitting. On my final trip back to the shop, the entire area is in full swing. Some of the lovers are holding hands as they walk by, while others are propped up against nearby trees or walls. The mothers and their daughters—those not ripe enough to take man, as the men in the bar say, or at least openly and with parental consent—are busily passing to and fro between their houses and Mrs. Watson's shop, most of them conversing loudly and laughing, while young men, those whose piss the women say is too young to froth, run behind them carrying the heavy boxes and baskets. Every man or boy in women's company is doing as he is told and putting his arms and back to good use. All around, it appears, as they say in the church, that the body and soul are as one in full agreement.

"*Christopher.*" I look up at the sound of the female voice, as young as Stephie's. I see the hand waving from the brown Hillman Hunter as the car goes by. It is Ursula and her family, probably out for a weekend drive-out. I wave back and feel foolish doing so, wondering who is watching me. I must get back to my duties, for Grandmother might call on me more frequently tonight, especially with Mrs. King still acting so withdrawn.

We are all under a cloudless sky with a million stars far above our heads, though they appear close enough to listen to our every conversation. The feeling that we are one is back with us again. In the distance, the breeze rises and falls now and then, loudly rustling the trees and the grass and occasionally lifting a hat from someone's head. Closer by, the butane light is burning and hissing as brightly and loudly as usual, and the women and men of the flock are in the spirit, dancing and swaying, clapping their hands and shaking their cymbals, their heads wrapped in what look like brand new pieces of cloth. Pastor Wiltshire is already dancing and speaking in tongues.

From inside the shop, the sound of the jukebox playing the popular calypso "Big Bamboo" is in fierce competition with everything else, but like the crickets in the grass at the side of the street, mindful of traditional boundaries and limits. Only Mrs. King still appears out of sorts, unable to cope with what is happening around us and to get into the right spirit. I think that if Stephie was around, she would find a way to make Mrs. King laugh and to ease the growing pressure on all of us. Then everything would *really* appear right in the world.

When I finally take my usual spot on the steps to the shop, I notice Mr. Lashley is already in the bar, with a bunch of men crowded around him. Off in a corner, some of the men are playing dominoes and draughts and listening to the radio with one ear and to the conversation in the bar with the other. They are undoubtedly waiting for the announcement promised with such joy by the cars with loudspeakers on their tops all day long. This announcement promises to put flesh on the bones of the rumours of an important speech, which everybody is now awaiting. According to the talk, the message will be clear: it will explain to every man, woman and child what it really means for us to be living in an independent country, and what we have to do to take our future in our hands.

On the counter across from the men and the radio are at least four pint-and-a-half bottles of rum. Mr. Lashley must have bought them, because whenever a man wants to pour a drink, he gestures toward Mr. Lashley by nodding his head or silently lifting his glass toward him. Mr. Lashley consents, usually by returning the same gesture or telling the supplicant, "Go ahead, man, fire a good, strong one on me." He does not have to issue the invitation twice.

"But, boy, as I was just saying," Mr. Lashley says over the radio when the jukebox is waiting to be fed more money, "I got to give it to all o' you fellows that got to make it in the cane fields every blasted day, yuh know. Christ, I have worked hard in my life, but to tell the truth I did forget what real hard work was like 'til I was back in them damn cane fields. And with them overseers in them cork hats breathing down yuh neck, as if they counting how many canes you cutting by the minute, and getting on yuh arse if you fall short by a single cane or two for the whole day. And the *money*! Lord have mercy, I don't know how anybody working in the sugar cane field can live on them wages the plantations does pay every week."

"So when again you going back up north, now?" Henderson Brathwaite asks. He pours a large drink and downs it. Then he pours a finger of water into the glass, looks into it as if he is discerning signs, swirls the water around and swallows it in one gulp. "What day now you moving out?"

"In two days' time," Mr. Lashley says. "Tuesday afternoon self."

"But didn't you say some o' the other men done gone up long time a'ready?" Henderson persists. "And isn't it that if you going up now that you going up only for the six-to-eight week harvesting, that you ain't no more like one o' the long-term fellows that does be among the first to go up near the beginning of the new year and the last to come back down when it is almost Christmastime? Ain't you now like a new *beginner*?"

"*Hee hee hee*," Mr. Lashley laughs nervously. "From the way you questioning things, you like you know the program more better than me, who has been working on it for eleven straight years and now going up for my twelfth."

"No man, don't take no offence," Henderson says. "We here among friends, as I said I chose to stick around here and fire a drink for the road with you instead of going into town with the other fellows so strong about the politics."

"Right on the button," Mr. Lashley says, swirling his glass. "Every man in his own place, if you know what I mean."

"All the same," Henderson says, "and if you don't mind, I hope you will be able to send back down a few things for me when you coming back down here. One of the things I want this time is a TV, just like the one in your house. My missus keeps bugging my arse, telling me that is what we should get, how if I did ever get a pick on the farm program all like now she would have TV too. She tells me a TV would keep the children at home and, in any case, anybody that is somebody 'round this island having a TV in their house, and it is about time we catch up too. So you can send back down one for me?"

"I guess so," Mr. Lashley says, somewhat hesitantly. "I mean it does come in a big box to carry from the store to the plane and all o' that. But I'm sure that is something I can do, just for you, Hendy. I could possibly pick up a reasonably priced television for you when I coming back down and add it in with the rest o' my luggage and thing."

"No, I don't want to wait for so long," Henderson says. "You probably won't be coming back 'til almost Christmas if things work out for you. My missus was saying I should ask you to pick up the television as soon as you get up there, within a day or two maybe, and since we're good friends, and for you to send it down in a barrel or something so. I don't want you to wait all o' that time 'til you're coming back down."

"*Oh*," Mr. Lashley says, the hesitancy and uncertainty returning once again to his voice. "I see. You want me to buy the TV as soon as I get up there and to use my own money to send it down to you right away. As man."

"Right on," Henderson says. "I'm sure you can find a good TV that's cheap, not like down here where everything always so expensive, expensive you always have to be paying an arm and a leg for them. And then what you get for all the good, good money: a piece o' shit called a TV like the ones they does sell down here, always br'ekking down and you always gotta have it in the repair shop and only costing you more money on what you already pulled yuh pocket for in the first place. The missus tell me best way is to get a TV that would last and for you to buy and ship it down here."

"I see," Mr. Lashley says. "Well, I guess I'll have to think about that and see how things are when I get up there. Then I can write and let you know what is what."

"But you think you can do it?" Henderson demands. "Tell me straight up, as man, if you think you can send down the TV or not."

"Well, I don't see why not," Mr. Lashley says, taking a drink, his hand trembling.

"Well, in that case," another of the regulars, Michael, says, "make that two TVs, 'cause my mistress would want one too if she ever did to hear about these arrangements."

"And me too," another voice says. "Same thing here. Same arrangements."

"Add me to the list," another says.

"And me too," a voice in the back shouts. "Only this time I want one that comes with a special stand."

"Seeing that it is so many o' we putting in orders, why don't we make a list?" Henderson says.

Mr. Lashley's eyes are popping out of his head. I think it must be because of the great happiness he is bringing to so many of his friends.

"And what about some o' them shirts you can buy up there so cheap?" Michael asks. "Put down an order for a few long-sleeve shirts for me. I can get some good short-sleeve ones down here. And a good dungaree jeans pants, add that in too, under my name. I could use a good jeans pants, just like them cowboys does wear on the same TV we'd be soon watching."

Mr. Lashley watches the formation of the list. Under different names are orders for underwear, sneakers, jeans and just about anything the men or their wives and girlfriends perceive to be cheaper and of better quality up north. Mr. Lashley takes another big rum, straight, and wipes his mouth with the back of his hand. "What the arse I seeing?" he says to himself, stepping outside. "*Wha'* they think going down?"

It is at this point that he notices me.

"And you, Christopher, my boy," he says, almost stumbling on me on the step, "you want me to bring back down anything for you when I coming back home? You's good-good friends with Stephie, right? I gotta see she before I go up. But with that aunt she got and now living with, I don't know."

"No, nothing I can think of right now," I say. "Not unless they does sell cricket gear in Canada. But then I heard you say some time back now, when the men were fixing up Mrs. King's house, Canada don't play too much cricket, so I can't think of anything to ask you to bring fuh me."

"No man," Mr. Lashley says. "You right 'bout the cricket and Canada. Still, I'll try and remember you when I coming back down. Tell your Grandmother that for me. And Mrs. King too."

"That would be all right," I say. "She'll be glad to hear. Plus I don't know if you'd ever get to see my mother."

"You never know," he says, looking off into the dark. "Still, it is a big place and not so easy to see anybody so. Still, what you doing there sitting down on the steps all night long by yourself?"

I stand and brush my pants off. "You getting to be a big man now," Mr. Lashley says, "and by the time I get back down, I'm going to be sure you would already have a woman of your own. Some woman woulda already br'ek you in good as cent by the time I get back down here. I mean when I was your size, I was already thinking of going on the program. So, come inside the bar and hold a drink, like a real man. I ain't telling you it gotta be alcohol or nothing so right now, but come here and get a drink too. Show them you is man, just like everybody else. You is family. You's almost a brother to Stephie."

I enter the bar and take up one of the already opened sweet drinks on the counter. I take a long swig straight from the bottle and feel the fizz in my mouth and then the cold liquid running down the back of my throat. Still holding the drink by the top of the bottle between the third and fourth fingers of my right hand, just like most men handling a beer bottle, I prop up against the door of the bar, positioning myself so I can easily hear Grandmother or Mrs. King call to me. I too am ready for any performance the situation requires.

The good news soon reaches us in the night. First comes the announcement on the radio, reported as a special bulletin that is repeated every half-hour. The men in the bar receive every repetition as eagerly as if they are hearing it for the first time. When it comes on, they pause in their talking, quiet the jukebox, turn up the volume of the radio to its highest setting and listen to the entire announcement. When it ends, they turn the volume of the radio back down. Between announcements, they proudly relate to any newcomers what they have missed and encourage them to stick around for corroboration next newscast.

Cyrus and the group of men who went into the city to witness the announcement first-hand return and report that the mammoth crowd was so excited, especially when the prime minister took to the microphone. They tell the men in the shop and the curious women who have come up to the door of the bar to peer over on to this hallowed ground where the men are piss-parading with excitement how sweet it was to see the flags waving and how, as the announcements were made, there was a projector showing pictures on a large white screen.

Everette Pinder, the local politician, pulls up in his car and takes a big TV with long rabbit ears out. He hooks it up in the rum shop so we all can see what they are showing on TV. I stand transfixed, wishing I had been where all this activity had been happening. And then I remember why Ursula and her family were driving out: she told me on our way to the bus stand that they were going to this political outing.

This is the first time I am watching TV, and I smile to myself, for apart from Grandmother and Mrs. King, I doubt anyone around me had to wait this long to set eyes on this progress. Everything appears so beautiful on the TV screen. First there is a quick panorama of scenes going back to what must have been the days of slavery on the plantations, the riots, and the statues of the heroes and places of historical note. All of these come together in a flourish of images and words. I look around and it appears that everyone, maybe even Grandmother, but not Mrs. King, for she is still sitting by the coal pot, is crowding around the television set. As a group, only Pastor Wiltshire and his crew continue unmindful of everything else.

"*We write our names on history's page with expectations great.*" Everyone on the TV is singing the national anthem. The words appear on the screen along with images of young children, boys and girls of five, six or seven years, healthy looking and with smiles as broad as their faces, some of them with their front teeth missing. They are running across fields of grass and flowers, under clear blue skies, wearing the uniforms of the various primary schools. A big national flag flaps high in the air, almost as high as the sun. Then it looks to me as if something, maybe the flag, is beckoning to all the children. As the camera moves, it appears the children are not actually running to anything. Instead the children are aging. They appear in the uniforms of the middle schools, and then they become like me and Stephie in high school colours. Then they are older and are passing through iron gates, arriving at buildings with the word *university* on the walls. I feel the excitement in my own belly. Everybody around me is breathing hard.

All the while, in the background, an orchestra is playing the national anthem. The tune rises to a pitch, with the cymbals and percussion crashing at the height of the music. I feel the goose pimples on my arms and back, and I remember how we all felt this way when at school they paraded us out for church services and had us sing all the patriotic songs with one voice rising up in praise and hope. And I remember how loudly Stephie always sang, and I wonder what has become of Desmond Smith's plans to put boys and girls to sing on TV every Saturday evening.

On the TV now I see fast-moving pictures: older people sitting together, playing card games, dominoes and draughts, some of them on benches with the white sand and blue sea behind them. Smiling nurses take the old people's arms and wrap a black cuff around them. Women in uniform bring them meals on trays, and the old people smile and talk a lot. Next come pictures of women working at those factories that are springing up almost every day around the place. There are pictures of men and women working in fields and wearing big brimmed straw hats against the sun. And then there are the cruise ships arriving at the harbour. We see foreign-looking people stretched out on chairs, on towels on the beaches, as if bleaching themselves in the sun. There are pictures of young men running up to the cricket wicket and bowling, of batsmen executing gracefully all sorts of shots. Seeing the cricketers makes me smile and think of myself. There are pictures of young men and women running around asphalt tracks, dancing and singing on stages with big speakers and lots of lights.

These are the images of progress and development, a voice is telling us, the same one that spoke over the large speakers situated around the square to mark independence. These, the prime minister is saying, are the dreams and aspiration of a people who are now independent and who can take their future in their own hands. And the people in the square on the TV, as if in one voice, are responding in approval, shouting over and over: *"Forward ever, backward never—for we's now people too."* Even some of us at Mrs. Watson's shop are joining in, and I look across and see Everette Pinder, the politician, smiling. The band on the platform in the square strikes up one long, long medley of local songs, both Christian and wuthless ones, so that everybody begins dancing and holding on to one another and just jumping up to the sweetness. Everybody knows that Desmond Smith, even if we do not now see him on TV, must have been right there in the midst of things, on hand with that big-able recorder, to capture everything, especially the music and the singing. I have never seen anything like this.

Looking away from the TV, I see a solitary figure slinking away, as if drawn in the darkness to another time now gone forever. It is Mr. Lashley, and I think he's probably going home to watch on his own TV these promises of independence.

Finally, the politician unplugs his TV and packs it back into his car in order to head off to another rum shop for the next repeat of the special announcement. Before leaving, he makes sure Mrs. Watson has replaced the bottle on the counter for the men to keep drinking. "Just keep listening to the radio for the details of what we just witness," he says over his shoulder. "Just keep listening, for you ain't see and hear anything yet. Just wait."

Grandmother returns to Mrs. King's side and they fan the coal pot. The announcer on the radio begins to explain the specifics of the government program. Even though the men are eager, they control themselves and remain silent while the radio confirms what they know. Now that the crop season is in full swing, the government is proposing a number of new benefits for the people. The plan is to make the most advances for people while world commodity prices are high. This way, the government is giving real material meaning to independence so the people of the nation can take control of their lives and their future.

First, the government announces free secondary education for all school-age children and a hot meals program for them so no student will go hungry and be unable to learn because of an empty stomach. All of their books will be provided by the government free of charge as of the next school year and all students will get to travel on the government-run buses at a greatly reduced rate. Starting immediately, the government will provide free health care for the young and the elderly, and those of working years will be required to pay only a small fee. The government is looking to increase the weekly pensions of the senior citizens, and as soon as the required legislation is passed in Parliament, everyone working will be paid a minimum wage. Everyone will be entitled to severance pay when fired or if they lose a job for whatever reason. The prime minister says that this is a government looking for a clear break with the past and to a brand new future. "Better must come," he says.

Everybody fires another drink. "Better must come," we all repeat, as the radio breaks into a sweet-sweet medley of calypso, ska, mento, some new music that mixes in all these different sounds and beats, and a little bit of music like what Pastor Wiltshire and his congregation are always singing.

"So where we're going to get all this money for all this freeness from?" Henderson Brathwaite asks. "I mean, I's the first man to accept a good freeness if it comes my way, but can we afford all these things?"

Nobody answers. Everybody is just hoping he'll shut up and let all the niceness of the night play itself out without interruptions.

The new week at school brings the news I've been hoping for. My name is on the list posted on the notice board for the senior cricket team. Ursula sees it first and then takes me over to see for myself.

"Well you know who will be spending Saturday afternoon watching cricket now," she says, hugging me.

"Who?" I ask, not clueing in.

"*Me*, nuh," she says and smiles. "And you know *who* it is I coming to see play." I smile too. At assembly, the headmaster reads out the names of the senior cricket team and there is a cheer from my form when he gets to my name.

Cyrus seems to be of mixed feelings when I tell him the news, which surprises me. He congratulates me but seems sad when I tell him I will now have to practise every day after school with the team. I will no longer be able to attend his training sessions. After our last practice together, and after I tell the rest of the cricketers my good news, Cyrus asks if he can buy me something to drink or if I would like to come over to his house and spend a little time talking with him. But I am not in the mood for talking and I still have my homework to finish. Grandmother has taken to staying late over at Mrs. King's, so I have to be home to light the lamp and prepare for school the next day. I thank Cyrus for his help and decline his offer. He walks me home. When I tell him goodbye for the last time, he takes my hand and kisses the back of it. This is strange, something I would not expect from another male, but I say nothing as I quickly pull my hand away.

Two weeks later, Desmond Smith gets his big news too, or rather Leila does. Now construction is starting on the medical complex he is building near the district hospital. Mrs. Smith comes by to report the good news to Grandmother and Mrs. King and to tell them her son is also negotiating a big contract with the government. The medical and dental services in his building will be part of the delivery of health care to the children of the nation. Leila will be running the business.

"He calling it a *polyclinic* or something so," she says. Mrs. Smith says this is the realization of a dream for her son. It is the reason he decided to come back home to be where his navel string is buried. And Mrs. Smith says, from the way things are working, it was a good decision after all. All of which makes her so happy that God has shown her a way to help her son borrow the money from the bank to help set him up in business. For that's the way life should be: she helps Bertie to use his land to help his very own son, and now this son is going to help the government to help the people. Everything is turning out good, good, one hand helping the next. Leila is already talking about building a house that she and Desmond will live in. "And as soon as that house done build, Leila give everybody notice," Mrs. Smith says. "She two children joining *she*. No more waiting."

"And Desmond okay with that?" Grandmother asks.

"I guess so. In any case, these are the best of times for everybody," Mrs. Smith says. "It is good we are alive to witness these times as we become more develop and independent. We only have to pray God don't deliver us into evil for His name sake."

"True, true, true," Grandmother says. Mrs. King is silent and there is a slight scowl on her face. Grandmother has been saying lately that she does not like how long it is taking Mrs. King to find a way back to her old self. Grandmother says something in her bones tells her things aren't all right.

Though we don't talk about Stephie much, she is never far from our thoughts, at least not from mine. The house across the road from us is in darkness. Mr. Lashley is long gone.

I am getting off the bus after a long evening of practice when I see Desmond Smith walking alone with something in his hand. He steps into the gutter by the side of the road and waits until the bus moves off again.

"Ah, there you are," he says when he recognizes me. "I was just taking this over to leave with your grandmother for you. Stephie sends it for you. She says that since you are a big boy in cricket you can use it to listen to commentaries."

"So she heard," I say, laughing. "I was wondering if she did know about me and the pick for cricket."

"Everybody knows everything on this island," Desmond says, also laughing. "It is not like over-'n'-away, where you can live in the same town or city and don't ever see or hear anybody else you know. On this island there ain't nothing nobody don't know." I wonder if this is his way of acknowledging that people are talking about how he and Leila don't seem to want to walk about much together of late.

He hands me the radio Mr. Lashley brought back for Stephie. I take it by the leather handle. It still looks new, with the dials and the chrome latches that keep the speakers attached and the various parts together.

"Stephie says that she was thinking of sending it for you a long time now," Desmond says. "She says she doesn't have much use for it since her Auntie Dorothy has a radio in the house that anyone can listen to."

"Oh gosh," I say. "Tell her thank you for me. She's okay?"

"As to be expected," he says. "Always asking how you doing whenever I drop by to see Dorothy, 'cause you know Leila don't like a week to go by without we going to see Dorothy. I don't know why Leila is that way. And when she goes she always taking something for Stephanie."

I hold the radio by the handle and heft it. "When I see her I will thank her myself, you tell her that. But I glad to hear she's doing okay."

"She wants you to listen to cricket and for you to stop worrying about her. She says to tell you she is okay, that you and she will talk in your own good time."

"Is that what she'd say?" Everybody knows how much I have been thinking of her, even planning how to defy Grandmother and go and see her.

"Me, for my selfish part," Desmond says, continuing to laugh, "I just hope you find time to sing. 'Cause when I get my competition going, I coming for you and for Stephie too first thing. Just remember that. As I keep telling Leila, this island is full of natural singers." And he walks off, puffing on a cigarette and, to me, just looking lonely.

Since Grandmother spends most evenings over at Mrs. King's, I will be able to listen to the radio and turn up the volume as high as I wish. The only problem is that this radio eats up batteries. We do not have electricity, and the radio runs on six large batteries at a time. I decide to save my drinks money to buy batteries so I won't have to burden Grandmother with this purchase. Ursula makes sandwiches for me every day, and now that I have a radio, I'll be able to talk to her about different things she hears on her father's radio. I keep promising I will come by and visit her. I tell her someday soon, I am just too busy right now. But she keeps on inviting me and it is becoming harder to say no. I keep telling her tomorrow, maybe.

Chapter Seventeen

To hear Grandmother tell it, the dream was her first tipoff. For some time, she had been having the same dream, and it was why she knew in her heart that something was not right. In the dream, she would be brushing her teeth, or just talking to someone, when she would feel something loose in her mouth. When she searched for it with her tongue or fingers, a tooth would come out. There was no blood and no pain. And though she would turn the tooth over in her hand and examine it, she could never find anything wrong with the tooth. Not even a speck to show that it was beginning to turn rotten. Just a tooth, looking like it had been shaken from the skull of some long-dead animal. In the dream, she would know what losing the tooth meant, for her heart would beat faster, almost to a flutter. It could only be a harbinger of evil. Because she was already so concerned about Mrs. King, she did not tell anyone about the dream except for Mrs. Smith, who understood such signs. Grandmother did not tell Mrs. King because she did not want to frighten her or make her think she was some kind of oracle.

The day in question did break as usual. Grandmother called to Mrs. King before tending to the turkeys and chickens and Mrs. King called back to her. Grandmother says Mrs. King's voice should have alerted her, for her response was not as robust as usual, but sounded a bit papcie, papcie, as if she didn't have much strength. Grandmother blames herself for not continuing the conversation, but she was pre-occupied with minding the stocks, and too besides, her mind was on that little girl, whose time was drawing near. Nobody had heard one word from that wuthless man Wendell Lashley since he went back overseas.

Of late, Grandmother and Mrs. King had been hearing complaints from men and women about how Wendell Lashley had let them down by not sending the television sets. If he had had such intent and was of such a bad mind toward them, he should have told them straight up to their faces, not leaving them holding a big rock in a paper bag. While the men simply asked Mrs. King if she had heard anything from Mr. Lashley, the women tended to speak their mind. They did not hes-itate to tell Mrs. King of their growing disappointment and who they were holding responsible; ultimately, it had to be Mrs. King's fault. If she had taken Wendell Lashley in hand early on, he would be piss-ing straight, he would be under proper manners for a long time now. They grumbled that they had taken to boasting to one another about the TVs they were expecting any day now and had told the children that should they behave themselves, carry out their chores around the house and study hard at school, and they would get a television to watch in their very own home. The women complained, particularly to Mrs. King, since she was the closest thing to family that Wendell Lashley had in the area, that you can only promise a child something for so long before having to produce what was promised. The children were now humbugging them, and some of them were even dropping word and giving them a lot o' back chat about whether they were ever going to set eyes on this television that they had been hearing so much about and for so long. When the parents tried to explain to the children about Mr. Lashley, the children asked why they didn't just go down in town on Broad Street and buy one of those televisions down there, as if they believed money grew on trees or something so. The women couldn't believe how there is no justice in this world.

As a result, poor Mrs. King was under stress and strain. Anyone who knew her well could see the botheration on her face, how she had started holding her head on one side in a strange way and how her clothes were dropping off her because she was becoming so thin and poor-rakey. But really, it was what had happened to poor Stephanie, and the fact that the little girl did not come back even once to visit her grandmother, so she could see with her own two eyes how this child that was the apple of her eye was doing, that was upsetting Mrs. King the most. She never stopped asking people who knew Dorothy or who passed through the area where she and her husband lived if they had set eyes on Stephanie and, if they did see her, how they thought she was doing.

Grandmother said she was always hearing the same old story from Mrs. King. "She would always be saying," Grandmother told Mrs. Smith, "that nobody don't know what it was like, the pain and the sufferation that it caused, to have people talking yuh name bad, bad, bad all the time." She knew that all the people were saying that Mrs. King was responsible for what had happened to poor Stephie, that she did not keep an eye on the little girl and bring her up as a young lady the right way and keep her in the church at night instead of in some hard-back man house. Now that Wendell Lashley had gone back up on the program and his house across the road was all boarded up and locked down as tight as a drum, nobody had heard one word from him, and Dorothy was telling people that she knew Wendell Lashley ain't no use and that he did not even bother to send one thing for the little girl now that he should have a few dollars well in his pocket, and that he didn't even send back down "not even a little bit o' soap money from time to time for she to wash up her self, for it was nobody but he that did make she so."

Mrs. King was always explaining to whoever would listen that she had taken the little girl as a baby from her mother out of the goodness of her heart and had sacrificed all she had for that little girl, so that if she had only salt to suck, that child sucked the same salt as she, and that she had only the best of intentions and hopes for the girl, that she had sent her to school and had told her to open her brains and to take in a learning, and she even had her in Sunday school from an early age. But what can you do when children grow up and don't want to go to church no more, or not as regular? She had told little Stephie she was going to become a young woman in a time that was different from that of her grandmother and even her mother, and that in a country that got independence, the women of the future can make something of themselves, especially now they were getting the same education as any boy.

Grandmother told Mrs. King countless times to stop worrying her head and leave everything in the hands of the Lord. "The best you do will always come to nought," Mrs. King lamented. And it was when she started talking that way that Grandmother started dreaming about the teeth falling out of her mouth.

Grandmother said she was in the house and I had already left for school when the thought occurred to her to give Mrs. King a shout. When she did, there was no response, but Grandmother did not think anything of it at the moment. Maybe Mrs. King was minding her own business and needed some time for herself.

However, things were too quiet, and Grandmother didn't feel right. She decided to give Mrs. King another shout. When again she heard nothing, and she could not remember Mrs. King telling her she was going anywhere and planning to leave the house, she decided to go over to the house, all the while calling to her and joking that after all this time together, she had decided not to answer she back and was now hiding from her. Still, no answer. Grandmother said she went around to the back door and looked into the house: there was Mrs. King, stretched out on the floor by the table, the tot with the tea she was drinking still on the table. Grandmother broke open the door with her foot, for it was latched from inside, and rushed over to Mrs. King, calling her name. She did not respond at all; she wasn't even groaning. Grandmother took the smelling salts from off the ledge where Mrs. King kept them and passed them under her nose. Mrs. King just groaned, and Grandmother knew she was in a bad way, but nobody was around to help her: not Stephie, not me and not even Mr. Lashley.

Grandmother managed to drag Mrs. King into her bed and decided to make a dash for Enid Watson's shop to call the hospital in town for an ambulance—that is why, Grandmother said, the politicians are right when they say there should be ambulances stationed at the district hospital too, at what Mrs. Smith say Leila is calling polyclinics, just in case of emergency. Anyway, Grandmother said, you should have seen her at her age running pell-mell all the way to the shop; she did not know she could run so fast and so long without being out of breath. Anyone seeing her running so fast would think she had thief something and was running to get away from whoever was chasing her. At the shop, she tried to explain to Mrs. Watson what had happened while catching her wind. Luckily for her and Mrs. King, Boysie Watson had not yet gone 'long about his taxi-driver job. Mrs. Watson called to him to put on a pants and shirt and come quick, quick from out of the bedroom, because it was an emergency. Boysie took Grandmother back to Mrs. King's house in the car, and Mrs. Watson sent along the young woman who was working in the shop; she said it was a good thing it was a weekday and that business was light so she could take care of everything in the shop sheself. The three of them rushed back into the house and lifted Mrs. King into the back seat of the car, where she stretched out with her head in Grandmother's lap. Grandmother held her hand and told her everything was going to be okay, that she shouldn't be afraid, for she was there with her and they were taking her to the hospital. Grandmother said she could not tell if Mrs. King was understanding one word she was telling her, but she knew she had to keep talking. All the while, Mrs. King's eyelids fluttered fast, fast, fast and she groaned.

The orderlies at the hospital helped to remove Mrs. King and, because it was an emergency, they took her right in to see the doctor. By then, they all knew that Mrs. King had had a passover. Her entire left side was paralyzed and she could not talk.

When school finished, I was surprised to see Grandmother waiting for me outside the school gate. She explained to me what had happened. Mrs. King was in the intensive care room at the hospital. She said Boysie Watson had waited around until the doctors explained the situation, and then she had asked him to drop by the hotel and tell Dorothy about her poor mother. Grandmother said she had already returned home to pack some decent clothes for Mrs. King, because in her proud self, she would not want anybody seeing her in some old hospital gown. She wanted me to take home the clothes Mrs. King had been wearing when she came to the hospital. She said that if anyone came by and asked what happened, I should tell them what she had told me. She would be staying with Mrs. King in the hospital until visiting hours were over. Grandmother wanted to be there should Mrs. King wake up and find herself in a strange place without anyone she knew around her, but the hospital did not allow anyone that wasn't direct family to stay all the time. In any case, Grandmother said she would stay outside the ward, reading her Bible and talking to others in the same situation as she. There was a nice woman who was the matron of the ward, who said she understood certain things and would allow Grandmother to slip in and out of the ward every now and then to be with her good, good friend, as long as Grandmother respected the rest of the rules and didn't get in the way of the doctors and nurses.

I took the package with the clothes from Grandmother and we began walking toward the bus stand. As I was about to board the bus, Grandmother said there was one thing she had forgotten to tell me: when I got home, I was to try and make something for myself to eat, and maybe something to drink as well, but that if I could not find anything in the house, I should go to Enid Watson's shop and ask her to trust me a few rock cakes and coconut turnovers and a sweet drink for my dinner. She said Mrs. Watson would understand. She told me to feed the turkeys and chickens and collect any eggs and to latch up the house and go to sleep at a good time. I should not wait up for her, because she would stay at the hospital for as long as they would let her, and, for all she knew, she might not even come home that night.

As the bus pulled away, I saw Grandmother walking slowly in the direction of the hospital, her head down. Soon the bus turned the corner onto the main road, and she was gone from sight.

Mrs. Watson asked me if I had any news about how Mrs. King was doing, and if I knew when Grandmother was likely to come home.

Two other women in the shop listened attentively, passing careful glances to each other and clucking their tongues. Everyone was talking about the suddenness with which the passover had struck, about the frailty and uncertainty of life, and how in the midst of life there is always death. They felt sorry for Mrs. King. I told Mrs. Watson that I did not know much more beyond what her husband would have relayed to her or when Grandmother was coming home.

"And how she's holding up when you'd see she?" Mrs. Watson asked.

"She look' fine to me," I said, not knowing quite what to say. "She looked okay. Just a bit worried. And tired."

Mrs. Watson nodded her head knowingly and sighed yet again. The women stood pensively at the counter. She said, "You go straight home and now your grandmother ain't here to watch over you don't get yourself in any trouble, you hear me." I nodded my head. "Remember, you's a big boy now, almost a man, if you know what I mean, and you should be doing the things of a man, especially now that your Grandmother have other things on her mind, now she has her trials and tribulations to bear. This is a testing time for her, just like in the time o' Job. That is why we must all pray for she, and for Mrs. King too."

"True, true," Sister Mavis Thorpe said. "That is why we starting with this prayer vigil tonight. Right there in the church, right Mrs. Brewster? We're going to pray Mrs. King back to good health if that is the wishes of the Father above."

"I gine be there," the older woman said. "You can count on me."

"Praise the Lord," Sister Mavis Thorpe said.

"Praise the Lord, indeed," Mrs. Watson added. "As for me, I gine try to see if I can get away from here and come to the pray' meeting. From the time I did hear the news this vigil was on, I did be spreading the word far and wide, telling everybody coming into this shop today, especially the women, 'cause you know the men and how foolish they can be about praying, that is until something up and happen to them. And everyone I talk to tell me they gine be coming." Mrs. Watson pushed the groceries toward me. I took them up and placed them in a canvas bag. "You be good, now," she said, not looking up from the book in which she was entering the new amount we now owed her.

Inside the house, I hear the creaks and pings of the galvanize roofing and the flapping of the breeze wandering through the house, ruffling the curtains at the window. I hear the silence that comes from Mrs. King's house and also from Mr. Lashley's across the way. This is a silence that carries the strong message that all is not right in the world. I can feel it in my bones, this quiet, which is like nothing I have ever known. I do not feel like eating anything, not even a cheese cutter, and anyway, slicing the cheese and placing it in the bread seems too much for me to do right now. I don't even feel up to turning on the radio and listening to anything. But I force myself to, if only to have some company.

Chapter Eighteen

The knocking at the side of the house wakes me up. I must have fallen asleep at the table. Out of the stillness, I hear a male voice calling out to me. I jump up and realize the light from the lamp is getting pale, even though I filled the lamps with oil before closing down the house for the night. The radio plays softly. I had been reading *A Midsummer Night's Dream* for English literature class the next day when I decided to rest my eyes for a little while. In the fullness of my freedom, I would have remained like that until morning, for Grandmother is not here to wake me and send me to bed.

"Christopher? You still up? Open the door, bwoy, I got a message for you from your grandmother."

I open the door and Boysie Watson comes into the light. He is wearing his taxi-driver uniform and he takes the black sailor-type cap from off his head and holds it in his hand. A lighted cigarette clings to the corner of his mouth, and he breathes out a plume of white smoke that swirls around his face and disappears into the air over his head.

"You okay?" he asks. "I ain't waking you or nothing so, ain't I, eh?"

"No. No. No," I stammer and try to suffocate a yawn. "I was in here just doing my homework for school, just a little bit o' reading, but I must have nodded off." I switch off the radio to save the batteries.

"Good, good," Boysie Watson says. "What a day it's been, eh? Lord have mercy. Anyway, my missus send me over here to give you a message from your grandmother. She say that your grandmother manage to get a phone call to her." He pauses to take a deep drag on the cigarette before flicking the stub into the darkness. "So she's asking you, that when you coming in town tomorrow, first thing in the morning, to put a few clothes in a bag for she so she can have a change o' clothes, since she won't be able to make it home tonight." He coughs into his hand and reaches for the cigarette box in his shirt pocket. "She said you should also go into Mrs. King house and go into the bureau in the bedroom and to take out some more clothes, night-gowns, undies and things like that, for Mrs. King too, and you should put the two set o' clothes in two separate bags and bring them down to the hospital tomorrow. You understand?" His face looks ghostly in the lamplight.

"Uh-huh," I say,

"'Cause if you don't understand," he says, sitting in the doorway and blowing smoke into the darkness, "the missus say I should tell she and she would come and do it for you. I mean, you don't have to feel no way if you don't understand, for I is a man myself and when it come to them women things, to tell the truth, if it did be my own missus that did send me such a message, I don't think I would know what to do. But you know what to do, right?"

"Yes, I know," I assure him.

"Good. Good." Boysie Watson takes another deep puff on the

cigarette. "Too besides, my missus say to tell you that you should go to your bed right away and tomorrow, before you go along to the hospital, after you pack the two bags for your Grandmother and Mrs. King, and she says that quiet so, you should stop by the shop and have a word with her. You understand that?"

"Yes, Mr. Watson," I say.

"How old you's now?" he asks.

"Fourteen," I say.

"And you not afraid alone in this house, eh?"

"I don't think so," I reply. Only then does it occur to me that I haven't even thought of being afraid, not like the times I could not wait for Grandmother to get back home at night or needed Stephie to keep me company. Thinking of Stephie, I wondered how she was taking the news of her grandmother's sickness. She must be taking it hard, poor thing.

"You and I know it would be a lot better if Mrs. King's grand-child, Stephanie, did still be here." He stands up and dusts the back of his pants.

"True," I say softly and immediately begin to miss Stephie more.

I am up early in the morning, even before all the chickens and turkeys are out of the trees and waiting for their scratched grain. I rush out to begin counting them, to feel the safety in numbers. By counting, I am making sure the world is indeed as it should be, that no unexpected additions or deletions have occurred in the darkness of the night. It is so quiet that the noise of the wind in the trees and what is left of the cane fields seems rowdy, as noisy and disruptive as the sound of the waves rudely bashing against the rocks some distance away. The quiet of the morning is broken only by the sound of the first bus roaring and barking its way through the village.

I feed the fowls and the pigs, and then pack the clothes for Grandmother and Mrs. King. Then I make a tot of hot cocoa for myself.

Through the side door to her house at the back of the shop, Mrs. Watson takes the bags of clothes from me. She has not yet opened the shop to business. She inspects the contents of each bag and then says, "Come. Let we go back to the house." Boysie Watson, standing by the door and smoking a cigarette, hunches his shoulders to me in resignation.

At Mrs. King's house, I stand looking at the picture of Stephie mounted on the wall while Mrs. Watson enters Mrs. King's bedroom. In the picture, Stephie's hair is in long plaits and she is wearing a white dress with white socks and black shoes. The picture was taken a long time ago, when Mrs. King wanted to show Stephie's mother how she was growing. She had asked the photographer for one for Esmeralda and an extra one for herself. This is the Stephie who at such a young age had a strong will, who was always smarter than me and always guiding me. As I stare at the picture, it is as if Stephie wants to step out of it and tell me which are the clothes her grandmother has set aside for circumstances such as these. But all we have is the instinct of Enid Watson.

After a few minutes, Mrs. Watson reappears from the bedroom with a bag of folded clothes. She gives it to me and says, "Now let's see what we can do for your Grandmother." I follow her without speaking. I have learned that there are times when nothing can or should be said, especially by men, and I think this must be the beginning of wisdom.

Soon I am waiting at the bus with the two bags of clothes and my books, including the copy of *A Midsummer Night's Dream* with the upper edge of the page folded over to mark where I fell asleep while reading last night. On the way into town, I hope to finish reading the play. I hope that when I meet up with Grandmother, she'll have enough money to buy me something to eat, for I am truly hungry.

"Mrs. King ain't doing too good," Grandmother whispers to me even though nobody else is around. "She ain't doing too good *atall, uh, uh, uh.*" She tells me that the doctor said Mrs. King would need a lot of care and attention, but she is not sure whether he is telling her the full story. At first he declined to disclose any information at all about the patient to Grandmother. It was only after she insisted she be told *something or the other* before all the worrying and tension sent her crazy that the doctor relented and said Mrs. King is not doing too good. She has to remain in the intensive care unit for some time, but he is hoping that she will eventually be able to talk and walk again. She would, however, have some paralysis for the rest of her life. The doctor asked if she has any family at home to help her. Grandmother says that at the moment, Mrs. King is virtually no use to herself.

Grandmother takes the clothes from me, yawning. Her usually neat afro is uncombed and misshapen, as if she had slept on one side, and I can smell sourness on her breath. She must notice the look of concern on my face, for she wets the tips of her fingers with some spit and cleans the corners of her eyes. She pats her hair, yawning again, deeply, ending with a loud hissing sound, which she does when she is really tired.

"What you put in here?" she asks, peering into the bags.

"Not me," I say. "It was Mrs. Watson. She came and . . ." I realize Grandmother is not paying attention. She folds the bags and puts them under her arm. Her eyes dart around and then settle on a woman about her age, dressed in a green uniform with a white nurse's cap on her head, walking toward us. She is with a group of younger nurses.

"Still hanging in there?" she asks, as she is going by.

"Yes, dear heart," Grandmother says. "Still holding on in the name of the Lord."

"You must try and get some rest, you hear me," the woman says. "Otherwise you won't be any use to yourself or Mrs. King if you let yourself fall to pieces."

"Yes," Grandmother says. "I know. I know. But you know how things is."

"Yes, I know, but I don't want to have to put you in a cot in there beside Mrs. King, you hear me," the woman admonishes. "Anyway, I will let you come in and see her as soon as we're finished the rounds this morning, after the doctor comes through."

"Yes," Grandmother says. "Faith indeed, I really thank yuh, mistress. The Lord knows, I really do thank you. You's a good woman. The Lord bless yuh, dear heart."

When the nurses move on, Grandmother whispers to me, "That is the head matron, the one in the green uniform. She's the one that's been so kind and nice to me. She is who let me use the hospital telephone last night."

I watch the women walking away from us down the long corridor, past the gurneys by the side of the wall and the piles of dirty linen in canvas bags, until they disappear through a door.

"She's right," Grandmother admits. "I got to get something to eat. The gas in my stomach already beginning to affect me." As she speaks, she massages an area below her left breast. "It was only last night when I was trying to sleep there in the little room the nurses does use, I realize I didn't even let a dry biscuit cross my lips all yesterday. I didn't even have time to think 'bout eating anything so. And by then I was full o' gas. The gas was riding my stomach and sticking me in my back real bad."

She shifts the bags with the clothes from one side to another.

"All I could say is I thank God I was able to get to Mrs. King. The doctor done say if she did stay alone in that house without any medical attention just one bit longer it would have been good night, nurse, she might even be a goner. Still, things ain't looking too good. And then yesterday evening that Dorothy turned up in the people hospital, crying and bawling at the top of her voice as usual, claiming she is the next of kin and only she got any right to say what treatment her mother should or shouldn't get. And then the doctor and the hospital administrator tell me such is the rules, that Dorothy is the one they would have to consult about anything when it comes to Mrs. King, and they ain't bound to tell me anything. And that I's just a friend, which mean I don't have any rights. And all this time Dorothy bawling down the place, making me think what use she'd be to Mrs. King if she'd be bawling and crying all the time. So I realize what was what and I tell everybody I don't care who gets to make any decision for Mrs. King, whether it is Dorothy or whoever, that all I care about is that Mrs. King get the best treatment and, if it pleases them, I will be around for her. I'll leave everything else in their hands and in the hands of our Father who is up above so that when she wake up, she'd see a face she knows and she won't be afraid and she would know I am here for her as always. That is what we agree, so if they want they can even stop me from going in to see her. But I don't think Dorothy would do that. She can't be that spiteful to her own mother. Anyway, I have to go and clean up myself and give these clothes to the nurses and to check on how Mrs. King doing this morning."

"And Stephie?" I ask. "How she's doing?"

"Don't know," Grandmother says. "She hasn't come to see her Grandmother yet. Dorothy saying some foolishness about not letting the chile come to see her grandmother in her pregnant state. So she ain't come to see her yet."

"Oh," I say.

"So that it is my voice alone Eudene hearing most of time," Grandmother says. "I sit there and talk to her, tell her a few jokes and even read from one o' them Gideon Bibles they have there in the hospital. The matron tell me that is what I should keep doing, talking to Mrs. King and seeing how she responds to a voice she know. So, I sit and hold her hand and talk to her."

She looks into the bag and picks up the comb and brush before putting them back into the bag and refolding the top. "This morning, they are going to let me comb her hair for her. I *gotta* go and make myself ready."

"Okay," I say. "I'll come by after school and see if you want anything."

But Grandmother is already walking away, tugging at her dress to straighten it around her behind. As I walk away, I feel something within me fall. Grandmother looked tired and said she is hungry, and now she has to contend once again with Dorothy. I too am hungry, but with all that is happening, I did not have the heart to tell Grandmother I do not have any lunch or lunch money. I know she has bigger things on her mind. It's going to be a long day. I wonder, where would *my* mother be if her mother should need her? If I should need her?

When I stop by the hospital after school, Grandmother looks more relaxed. She has changed her clothes and her hair is combed. She says that she managed to get some sleep, maybe an hour or two, when the nurses were tending to Mrs. King in the afternoon. Mrs. King is still in a bad way, but Grandmother says she and some of the sisters from the church gave her a good, vigorous 'nointing down. They had pulled the curtains closed around her bed and, while praying and interceding to God, stripped Mrs. King as much as possible and gave her a good rubbing down. By the time they finished, Mrs. King was groaning, which they knew was a good sign.

Grandmother says she will stay at the hospital for as long as possible tonight and take the last bus home, which means I will be in bed already when she arrives. She tells me to go straight home and look after the stocks and feed and water the pigs, and be there in case anybody should come around asking for she or for Mrs. King. She has arranged with Mrs. Smith for me to drop by her house for a bite to eat. She tells me to eat whatever Mrs. Smith gives me and not to skin up my face if she cooks something I don't like, for beggars can't be choosers. I should let her know I am grateful for what little morsel she gives me. "I tell Mrs. Smith you won't be any trouble, that she only have to give you a little share of whatever she cooking, to just add you into the pot. So don't let me down now."

"Okay, Grandmother," I promise. "You think they'll let me see she?"

"Who?" she asks.

"The nurses and them," I say. "You think they would let me see Mrs. King?"

"Okay, come with me," she says. "Keep close to me."

We enter a wide room with many cots and little tables and chairs. People are standing around the cots, some sitting at the foot of them and others sitting in the chairs. As we go by, people call out to Grandmother, for already they have built up a line of friendship and caring in the ward. Three women I do not know are standing near Mrs. King's cot. Grandmother nervously explains who I am, telling them I am her grandboy, that Mrs. King treats me like a son and helped her to raise me from a little baby, and that I only want to have a look at Mrs. King. I see her stretched out on the cot with the sheets and blankets up to her chin.

"Okay," I say quickly. "I going now."

I start to walk away and hear the sound of Grandmother's skirt behind me. The women I pass look bewildered at my rapid exit. Grandmother walks with me to the main door of the hospital, and as we are saying goodbye, I notice Stephie, her belly swollen, entering through another door. I don't know if she sees me or even recognizes me. Grandmother smiles. "That would make Eudene feel really good. Faith it would," she says, and then as if realizing I am still there, says, "You go 'long now. And you try and be a good, responsible boy for me."

Grandmother always told me that "come and visit me" is very different from "come and live with me." I never understood what she meant as much as when I started visiting Mrs. Smith for dinner. The first day, I went to the house as soon as I got home, and Mrs. Smith said I was too early. She said Mr. Smith liked to have his meals at the same time every day. On regular weekdays, he had his lunch at 12:00 noon, not a minute later, and when those piping sounds began on the radio to indicate 1800 hours GMT, or 6:00 p.m. our time, he must have his dinner on the table. On Sundays, he would put on his tie and preside over the most important family meal of the week at 12:00 noon, demanding that everyone eat with a knife and fork. Keeping regular mealtimes and never varying from them was the way the people he used to work with in America always ate. Eating regular meals, Mrs. Smith said, helps the digestion and aids metabolism, for you are never too full or too hungry, and you always have the strength the body requires at any time in the day.

She said I could wait around there for the hour or so while the pot finished cooking, or I could return just before she was ready to dish the meal, but in whichever case, the meal would be dished at the appropriate time. I really would have preferred not to return at all, but

I could feel the pangs in my stomach and my belly started to grumble. As Mrs. Smith talked, I noticed Leila sitting inside the house. It looked like she was preparing something, but I could not tell exactly what she was doing. Mr. Smith was sitting at the opened front window, looking out on the road. He looked as glum as usual. His face was always set up as if he was expecting rain to fall. None of us youngsters ever felt comfortable to as much as say hello to him. Not when we'd see him sitting there, staring into space and looking angry at the world.

I told Mrs. Smith I would return at the time she suggested and went home. Since it was still too early to feed the stocks, I sat in the backyard, watching the ants crawling across the ground in straight lines, coming and going, carrying things into a big nest they were building near a rock. I noticed that the yard was becoming filthy from all the chicken and turkey droppings, and I decided to use the scraper to clean up. Soon this job became too tedious. I decided to concentrate only on the wet droppings, not on those dried by the sun and no longer catching flies. Time was passing too slowly. So I found a long piece of string and took an old ball from my school bag and tied the string and the ball to one of the tree limbs in the backyard. I decided to pretend I was playing cricket and one of the spin bowlers from India, the land of all great spin bowlers, was confronting me on the final day of the test match to decide the series West Indies versus India. With the surface of the pitch dusty, full of cracks and taking spin as if from a magician who can trick the best batsmen in the world, I watched as the ball on the string spun in front of me and moved in a zigzag. I pretended I was moving my feet to get to the ball on the full. Just then the bowler made a mistake and spun one of the balls too short, something like a long hop, and I was ready. I swung hard and long, and watched as the ball left the bat and broke the string. The next thing I heard was a crash and splintering sound. The ball made contact with one of the new panes of glass Mr. Lashley had installed at the side of Mrs. King's house and disappeared inside. I stood leaning on the bat, wondering what had got into me to make me want to hit out. Why did I not have the good common sense to know this was only make-believe, pretend cricket? What a fool I was.

Looking around, I noticed there was nobody else about but me, no witnesses. So it would be up to me alone to decide whether to tell Grandmother and to take responsibility. I removed what was left of the string from the branch and returned the bat to the inside of the house.

When I arrived at Mrs. Smith's house, I recognized Desmond's big red Zephyr parked to the front. Everyone was already eating. Desmond Smith asked me how I was doing and Mr. Smith grumbled that I must be doing really well to be able to turn up for free bittle when everyone else was already almost done eating, when I knew, for he had heard his wife explaining to me, that he, as a man, likes to have his evening meals at 6:00 sharp and does not like anyone to keep him waiting.

"Dad," Desmond said, "you don't have to beat up on the little boy so. He's a good boy. Suppose you had to deal with some o' the children up north. In fact, what you're going to do when you have to deal with Leila two children?"

"What you mean by that?" Leila asked. "And why are they now only my children and not *our* children?"

"What I mean," Desmond began, putting down his fork and picking up a piece of pigtail with his hand. He hunched over his plate, elbows tucked in close to his ribs, and began tearing bits of flesh off the bones with his front teeth, spitting the excess fat and bones onto the plate. "What I mean is you know how the children up in North America stay. They ain't got much manners and you know nobody can't tell them anything. That is one of the things that got me a little worried when your two children come down here to live all the time. I mean they are not like even this little boy here, at least he has a little manners. Not like you know who, and that is what got me worried now you say they coming fuh good. But down here, they will have to change, that is one thing I know. They will have to change as good as I am sitting here at this table this evening."

"I don't know what got into you lately," Leila says. "If you didn't want the children to come down here, why didn't you say something earlier and before I made all the arrangements? Why didn't you say so when I was still up there and before you got me to agree to come down here and to start life all over down here, where I can't even find anything good for me to do, not like before I decided to give up *my job* and *move* down here with you and to support you in getting your business started."

"Okay, you two," Mrs. Smith says, "this ain't the time nor the place for this *kinda* behaviour. I don't know why the two o' you always have to be going at one another so. You got to remember that you's man and wife and you should live in togetherness and love. And too besides, remember, we got a guest eating with us."

"Yes," Mr. Smith says. "Not that he's eating anything. He's just sitting there watching the food on the plate that you put in front o' he. Maybe he don't like your food, Maisie. Is that it, bwoy? You don't like the way we does cook over here?"

"No, sir," I say. "Not at all. It's just that I ain't too hungry right now. I eat something when I was waiting at home, and now I feel a little full."

"What you'd eat?" Mr. Smith shoots at me. "And why'd you'd go and full up your guts and now can't eat the little food we giving you out of the goodness o' we heart. What'd you eat?"

"I . . . I . . . I . . ." is all I can manage.

"Dad, leave the boy alone," Desmond says. "If he ain't hungry, then he ain't hungry. What's the big thing anyway?"

But I remember what Grandmother said about not embarrassing her by appearing as if I was ungrateful and did not appreciate Mrs. Smith's cooking. So, gingerly, I cut into the rice and peas and begin eating. I chew and swallow, and chew and swallow, and when I open my eyes again, the mound of rice and peas is still as high. Flakes of salt fish float in the butter sauce. With time and persistence, the heap starts to disappear. As Mr. Smith watches me keenly and Mrs. Smith takes up the plates and scrapes the ends of the food for the dog in the backyard, I finish my plate and ask Mrs. Smith for some water to drink. Then I say I have to return to the house to see if everything is all right with Grandmother's stocks and to feed the pigs and light the lamp. I bid them all good evening.

"Tomorrow, you can come back for a few more spoonfuls of food," Mrs. Smith says. "That is the least I can do to help out, with your Grandmother spending every living minute at the hospital."

"Yes, Mrs. Smith," I say. "Goodbye." And I leave, trying not to show how anxious I am to be gone.

Chapter Nineteen

Saturday morning I awake and realize that I have overslept. I jump up and quickly begin to bundle up my bedding until I notice the unusual calm around me. Instead of the singing I expected to hear in the backyard, there is a deep and rhythmic snoring, and I realize Grandmother must have come home late in the night after I had gone to sleep. She is sleeping so soundly and snoring so deeply, I decide not to wake her just yet. She must be tired. For the first time that I can remember, there was no Friday night planning, no need for me to collect and store the ground provisions in anticipation of doing business today. If Grandmother still plans to go into town for her usual shopping, she's going to miss the first bus. I decide not to wake her until I hear the second bus of the morning going up, so that she will be able to sleep for as long as possible. She'll still have time to ready herself before the bus turns around and comes back down.

As quietly as I can, I push the bedding under the bed. My eyes fall on Grandmother stretched out sleeping, still in the clothes she was wearing the previous day; she didn't change into her sleeping clothes. I step into the backyard, and as soon as I am outside, the chickens start running around me, fluttering their wings. One of the big turkeys flies down from the clammy cherry tree, lands at my feet and begins a loud chorus of gobbles. I close the back door to keep the chickens and turkeys and their noises in the backyard and take out the brown paper bag with the scratched grain from underneath the larder. My return is met with much noise as I throw handfuls of grain into the yard, and the chickens and turkeys form small groups and begin to peck away frantically.

I watch them, calculating in my head, so that I don't overfeed them. I know they are quite capable of eating all the scratch grain in one go, if I am foolish enough to feed it all to them. I take up the bowl and go around to the nests to pick up the eggs; I find five or six in almost every nest, and take care to leave at least one egg in each one, for Grandmother says the chickens and turkeys will not return to lay in a nest that has been robbed of all its eggs. They will come back only when they feel there is safety for at least one egg. I take two buckets of water, mix in the brown growener and serve the pigs their morning mash. They too are as noisy as ever.

I hear the bus coming back down, but Grandmother continues to snore. When I call to her, she rolls over on her side and continues to sleep. Grandmother does not wake until about midday, and she is slow to move around. She starts preparing a pot of soup, and when it is boiling down, she washes her hair and takes a bath. We eat and Grandmother tells me she will be returning to the hospital in a little while. A group of women are planning to go down together to give Mrs. King another 'nointing. She says she does not know what time she will return, or even if she will come back tonight.

"I want you to warm the pot o' soup and eat it when you get hungry," she says. "Don't you leave the soup there and let it turn sour on you, you hear. You know how funny soup is: if you don't drink it, it will turn sour on you quick, quick, quick. It ain't like dry food or even rice that you can keep and fry up the next morning."

"Yes, Grandmother," I say.

"And you be a good boy and keep yourself outta trouble," she says. "Is it today that you start playing the cricket for the school?"

"No, Grandmother," I say. "That is next week."

"Good." She seems relieved. "'Cause you'll have to get your things ready and, perhaps, you can start preparing from now. Since what happened to Mrs. King, I ain't even had the chance to have a good little talking with you. But I hope you don't mind. You know I was sitting there last night at the hospital and I did hear the last bus going down into the stand to turn around and come back up for the night. And I said to myself, I wonder how Christopher doing, and since they weren't going to let me spend any more time with Mrs. King for the night, I just took up my two tackling there and I hurried out and catched the bus on its way up. Boy, was that bus ever full. I don't know where all them people did be coming from. Must be all them young men and women who went to the theatre and catched the last show."

"The cricket is next week," I say, "so I might be coming home late in the night, and next Saturday you might have to get somebody to help you with the trays and things 'til I come."

"Not like with Mr. Smith, eh," Grandmother says. "Like he's running a' army or something. Everything got to be on time. He set yuh right eh, *ha, ha, ha.* He set yuh straight enough 'bout being late. You didn't listen to me, did you?"

I look quizzically at her, wondering how she knows. She places some hairpins in her lips as she continues to comb her hair and twist and pin it into bumps. "Mrs. Smith tell me," she explains, still holding the pins between her lips. "And I said to myself, well, that is one lesson you would never forget. You now know how different people have different rules and thing, and how you always have to respect a man and find out what are the rules he set even for himself in his house."

"Nobody don't mind Mr. Smith," I say.

"You can't say that," she says sharply, still holding the pins between her lips. She takes some brown Vaseline from the cigarette box and applies it to her scalp where she has parted her hair. Then she combs the square of hair. "If you gine be going in a man house, you'd have to mind him." And she chuckles some more. "But, all the same, and getting back to the cricket next week, you shouldn't worry too much about me and when I get back from town. To tell yuh the truth, I don't know what we gine do from now on to keep a few coppers in we hand. With Stephie gone, it was already getting to be a problem, but we did be just getting through, even though we'd miss her hand on Saturday morning. But now with Mrs. King sick, I just don't know. It might just be too much for just me and you, especially if you also got to be spending half the day playing cricket."

"Yes, Grandmother," I say.

"That is why," Grandmother continues, finishing the last twisted roll of her hair, "I didn't worry my head with getting up early this morning and going 'long down to town. In the first place, I ain't got the money to buy the things with, and what li'l money I have I got to try and stretch and to buy a few things for Mrs. King, things I know she gine need when she come out of the hospital. Somebody was telling me I should get Mrs. King to ask the welfare people to put she on the list of indigent people, but I don't know if she'd like that, 'cause both o' we's very proud people. We don't like getting welfare like some pauper, especially when you have a child living over-'n'-away, and you have to keep explaining they don't send anything for you."

"Stephie does come to see her grandmother, right?" I ask.

"Not really, only the one time we did see she," Grandmother says. "But I think it is that aunt of hers stopping her. 'Cause she might not like too much having Stephanie and her pregnant self coming to the hospital. You never know what she might see and frighten the little infant in her belly. Then the baby'd be born with some defect or just looking ugly."

I wonder what it will be like when the baby is born, especially with Mr. Lashley away and nobody hearing from him. I would like to see Stephie and talk with her, to hear from her own mouth how she is managing.

"I think I will have to put off doing the business we does do on Saturdays until things settle down," Grandmother says, "until at least I catch my hand again, and I can figure out what is and isn't with Mrs. King. So you shouldn't worry your head too much about how I'll get help next Saturday. Just concentrate on playing your cricket, and God will take care of everything else."

Grandmother takes up her bag and sprays some perfume on her neck. Mrs. Smith calls to her from in front of the house. Grandmother answers, quickly brushes some brown powder on her face and on the top of her bosom and rushes outside. I watch the group of women walking down the street toward the bus stop. The rain clouds are beginning to set in, with a shadow moving across the land. I wonder if the rains will come before the bus. As I watch, I notice the swirly developing just pass Mrs. King's house; bits of paper and dust twirl on the ground and then rise into the air. The swirly moves in the direction of the women walking toward the bus stop. It looks as if it is running after them, with the paper, dust and grit rising and even overtaking them, buffeting the skirts of the women. Within half an hour, the rains come. By then, however, the bus has already passed back on its way to the city.

My visits to Mrs. Smith's house after school did not get any easier, even though I made it a point of arriving on time and sitting quietly at the table. Most of the time, Mr. Smith glowered at me and demanded that Mrs. Smith bring him a malt to drink. In addition to insisting his meals be served on time, Mr. Smith always demands a malt. Even when Mrs. Smith had placed the bottle and the glass with the ice in it on the table, Mr. Smith still asked for his malt.

What saved me was cricket. Everyone knew I was selected to represent my school in the senior division. I told Mrs. Smith that I had to attend practice sessions after school. I also told her that the school was providing us with a snack after practice, which was not true, and that I would not need to rely on her for dinner. For two weeks now, I had been relying on Ursula. She was bringing me two and sometimes three sandwiches each day, even though her mother was starting to ask why the loaves of bread and meats that usually lasted a full week were now disappearing so fast. I made sure I stayed at school so late that it was not only dark when I got home, but also well past the appointed time for eating at Mrs. Smith's. Most nights when I got home now, the chickens and turkeys were already nesting, missing out on their regular evening meal. In the morning, I would try to compensate by throwing more scratched grain to them. The pigs didn't care how late it was; I discovered I could feed and water them at any time. The result was that I avoided having to go to Mrs. Smith's until the last day of the week. Everyone knows there is no cricket practice on Friday. As well, Grandmother appears to have caught on to what I've been doing, and she tells me not to make Mrs. Smith feel slighted by not showing up for her food and not showing my appreciation.

So Friday evening, I join Mrs. Smith, her husband and Leila at the table. Desmond is not expected home until late. We sit and eat in silence, and when the plates are being cleared, I say that with the big game happening the next day, I have to get home and finish up the work around the house for Grandmother and go to bed early.

"That makes sense to me," Mr. Smith says. His agreement catches me by surprise. "Makes a whole lot of sense to me. In fact, it makes more sense than what you grandmother, a big able woman like she's doing these days. From what I hear, she's still hotting up the people chair at the bedside o' the sick every day, like she's there keeping watch or something. I don't know why people like your grandmother have to be that way. I don't know why she doesn't realize if anybody around here needs care and attention, it's you, her grandboy, and that a mother's place is with her children or grandchildren."

"But he isn't sick," Leila says.

"What?" Mr. Smith shouts.

"I said he isn't sick," she repeats, raising her voice as if speaking to someone hard of hearing. "He looks to me like he's in good enough health. So I don't see why he needs his grandmother to take care of him."

"You don't have to be sick to need taking care of," Mr. Smith says. He pours into his glass what is left of the malt in the bottle and returns to his usual position at the window. While sitting, he reaches up and increases the volume of the radio.

"Good night, and thank you," I shout before stepping out into the evening.

"Good night," Mrs. Smith says.

"Night," Leila says, and then I hear her sighing.

Grandmother is not home when I get up and get dressed, so I pour myself a big tot of mauby, making sure it contains a lot of sugar, and drink it down. Even though I do not feel hungry, and although I am so very anxious to get to the cricket ground, I know Grandmother will notice if I leave home without having anything to eat or drink. Later, she would quarrel with me for going into such a big day with nothing in my stomach. In no time, I finish off two Julie mangoes, placing the skin in the food for the pig. I am full. I take my bat, pocket my bus fare and set out for my first game at the senior level.

I am the last of the teammates to arrive, probably because I am coming the farthest and, unlike some others, by public transportation. As I walk onto the playing area, I notice my teammates have already changed into their whites and are waiting for me. Several spectators, many of whom look like students from our school, are also staring in my direction. Both the headmaster and the games master have asked all the students to come out, if possible, and cheer us on. Indeed, the headmaster said we would need all the encouragement we could get, for it was our misfortune to have as our opponents in the very first game of the season the team that convincingly won the championship for two years running and has its sights on a hat trick.

We form a circle in front of the club, and with the captain in the centre, start limbering up by catching the balls he hits to us. The captain of course hopes to win the toss, which would give him the chance of sending in the opposing team to bat first, thereby delaying having to expose such a young batting lineup to bowlers with such, as Mr. Jones would say, ferocity, guile and experience. As we practise, the opposing players place on display their bats and pads, which carry the scars of the battles they have found themselves in over the years. Several of the players are wearing their sleeveless pullovers and their maroon caps with the crest of the West Indies Cricket Board of Control on them. They joke with one another and talk loudly so we can hear what is in store for us. I look at their main fast bowler and he looks mean as he flexes the muscles of his bowling arm for his teammates to see.

One of the umpires signals for our captain to follow him and they are joined by the captain of the opposing team as they make their way to the pitch in the centre of the field. The other captain flips the coin in the air and we watch nervously from the distance of the pavilion as the coin glints in the sun and falls. From the slow manner in which our captain makes his way back to the pavilion, we have a strong feeling we lost the first strike in this battle.

"We batting," the captain confirms when he rejoins us. "They won the toss and they are asking us to take first knock." He reaches into his pocket and pulls out a sheet of paper. "Harewood and Clarkie, pad up as the openers, with Harewood, you taking the first ball strike. All the best to you both, boys. See what kind of a start you can give us. And, Christopher, you pad up too, you're going in at number three."

"What?" I ask, not sure I heard correctly.

"I said to pad up," he repeats. "You batting number three, with Bynoe following at number four. Bynoe, you may as well pad up right away too, for you never know."

"But *geez*," I say, mainly to myself. "One down. I going in at one down."

I walk over and sit on the bench beside Harewood and begin strapping on my pads. I choose a new pair of batting gloves and, for my penis, a protective box that is still in its wrapper. Already I can feel the thumping in my chest. I mean, I did not expect to be sent in as a key batsman. I thought that as a new member of the team, I'd be sent in around number six or seven, that they would be playing me as an all-rounder and a fielder, as someone who could bowl a bit and bat a bit. Cyrus told me that you always send your best batsman in at the number three spot, so he can control the game.

I sit behind the official scorer and glance over his shoulder for confirmation. There it is beside the number three: *Lucas, Christopher.* The rest of the team is listed from one down to the number eleven.

A noticeable buzz rises from the spectators, and I look up and see the fast bowler already at the top of his mark. So vigorously is he polishing the ball, there is already a red streak on the front of his pants. The shine is supposed to make the ball swing more, making it harder to hit. Harewood settles into the crease and taps the bat rhythmically. The umpire raises his hand in a gesture to the scorer and the scorer waves back. Then the umpire crouches and signals for the first ball of the season. Harewood gingerly negotiates the opening ball. It makes a deadening *klunck* sound as it jumps ferociously short of a length and cannons onto the bat. The ball skittles away involuntarily to the slips, where the opposing captain picks it up, polishes the ball on the leg of his trousers and returns it to the bowler. The second ball sends Harewood's middle stump cartwheeling from the pace. The speed of the delivery breaches his defensive prod with the bat. He is out. The bowler punches the air and is immediately surrounded by the rest of his teammates. At the far side of the ground, the scorer makes the adjustment to the board for public viewing. Under the sign *batsman*, he replaces the number one with a three, my number to go to the wicket.

"You up, Chris," the captain says. "Best of luck, man. See what you can do."

As I walk out, I pass Harewood, who is still taking off his gloves. "Wicket fast as *shite*," he says. "Really fast. I didn't see that one *atall* once it left the bowler's hand."

"I see," I mumble. Suddenly I am on the grounds where so many championship games have been played, and I know everyone is watching me. The captain is adjusting the fielding team, putting even more men closer to the wicket, perhaps to further intimidate me into playing too cautiously and making a false shot that would cause my downfall. We are off to the worst start imaginable. Now I will have to try for as long as I can to remain at the wicket and to hold on with Clarkie, my batting partner. We have to make sure we don't lose too many more wickets too quickly. I notice the outfield looks exceptionally smooth, as if the groundsmen pulled out all the stops to produce a perfectly green and level lawn for the opening day. I feel the wind blowing in my ears and hear the hum of the noise in the distance, and I know that what I am doing is the most natural thing in my life.

I arrive at the wicket and nod to the wicket-keeper, who says something that I do not hear clearly but that causes everyone else to laugh loudly. I take my guard, asking the umpire to allow me to guard two wickets and expose a bit of the third to the bowler. This ritual complete, I settle in to receive my first ball. The next thing I see is the umpire waving the bowler in; he's running fast, gathering speed as he approaches, his shirttail flapping. And he jumps and then the ball is in front of me, for me to do anything I want to it. It looks as if it is coming in slow motion and I could hit it anywhere I chose. But since it is full of a length, I gently lean into it, keeping my head low in my crouch and drive it. I hear the gasp of the fielders as they see the bat making contact with the ball. And I hear so loudly in my head Mr. Jones saying, "*Perfect!* What a perfect cover drive!" The ball seems to explode out of a cannon and races across the field. We do not even attempt to run, for it is clear from the time the ball leaves the bat that the cover fieldsman will not get to the ball before it crosses the boundary.

The umpire frantically waves his hand in front of his waist, signalling the first four runs of the season. The attendant on the public scoreboard makes his adjustment. The fielder runs all the way to the boundary, recovers the ball from a bush, tosses it to the bowler as he storms back toward the top of his run-up and waits for the fieldsmen to retake their positions. I settle in again, and the umpire signals for us to continue.

The second ball is short of a length and rising at my body, though it stands there seemingly suspended in the air. I have enough time to shift my weight onto my back foot and hook the ball. I position it so that the ball drops midway between the two fielders, before running to the boundary for another four. The third ball is short of length, and I square cut for another four. By then, my heart is running free, but then I remember Cyrus telling me that it does not make sense to play each and every ball as if it were a bad ball, that I shouldn't try to play all my shots at the same time, that I should respect the bowlers by treating every ball based on its merit, and that it is no use giving away my hand by getting out rashly.

I look up at the bowler running in and see the anger on his face. He jumps, seemingly higher than usual, and so much quicker, the ball is on to me. I reach forward, my bat and pads together, and I feel the impact as the ball hits the dead centre of my bat, and rolls out to the fielder at silly mid-on, only steps away from where I am standing.

I have survived the over. The fielders change over for the first time for the day to allow the other over to begin from the other end. I look up at the scoreboard: Runs: 12; Loss of Wickets: 1. Beside batsman number 3 are all 12 runs.

This is the champion team on the island, I tell myself. Some of these fellows have played all over the world representing the region. They are heroes I have read about in the newspaper or heard Mr. Jones talk about, which means that we still have a long ways to go. We can't afford to lose any more wickets too soon. No matter what, I must keep my bat and pads close together.

Within a short time, I have established the rhythm of play. It is necessary for me to take most of the strikes, as the other batsmen are always in trouble with the bowlers. Yet I feel free. I feel like I am the only person that matters on the field. Each ball is an opportunity for me to create something. More than that, I feel there is an order, cause and effect; if I do one thing, something else is going to happen, promptly, precisely and with certainty.

And the execution is so easy. I see the ball leaving the hand of the bowler and I see myself playing a stroke, and I feel the ball hitting the centre of the bat, just as I wished, and then hitting the ground exactly in that part of the field I wished to place it. Shifting my feet and adjusting my weight makes whatever I wish happen, just as I envisioned it. The results are always as I intend and desire.

Soon I am fully caught up in this creation. Within a few overs, my score has passed the twenty-five runs high point, and then it just speeds on to the half-century marker. I raise my bat to recognize the ripple of applause from around the grounds, but by then I have lost two more partners. I know our team has a long tail of players who are picked for their bowling rather than their batting, so I decide to concentrate on counting the balls in the over. This way I can try to get a single as close as possible to the sixth and final ball of the over, so that the next over will begin with me on the striker's end, thereby allowing me to shield my partners from the opposition attack. Meanwhile, I am dispatching the loose balls to the boundaries, even occasionally hitting one or two straight over the boundary, through the air, for six. Each time I do this, the umpire stands up straight and waves his hand above his head as if he is doing a strange dance. By keeping a check on the balls remaining in each over, I have to be on the lookout for quick singles when they come available. I remember Cyrus telling me that batting is strategy, like life itself. You have to have a plan and the patience to carry it out, no matter the odds.

I am concentrating so intently, I am not even aware of my own score, not until I hit a ball near a fieldsman that is almost caught, and my partner comes down the wicket and whispers that I should not take any chances of getting out now that I was only eight runs away from a well-deserved century. I keep quiet for an over or two, picking up a few singles and bringing my score into the nineties. Then a medium pace bowler sends down three really bad balls at the beginning of the over; hitting them along the ground, I put them straight away across the boundary to bring up my century.

I cannot believe it. My partner comes down the wicket and we shake hands, as the opponents applaud grudgingly. But I know that any of the top order batsmen on the opposing team is capable of wiping out not only my score but that of the entire team by the close of play if I do not continue to bat for as long as I can and collect as many runs as possible. Now that I have passed my own milestone, I do not bother to consult the scoreboard; I just bat, and all the cares of the world are somewhere else. Only occasionally am I interrupted for a water break or once to go off for tea, where we are served cucumber sandwiches and guava jelly sandwiches and hot tea in little dainty teacups, or aerated drinks that are kept in an icebox.

With these interruptions out of the way, and trying my best to slow the pace at which I am still losing partners, I resume my battle, sending the ball speeding off to the boundary with another well-timed stroke: a square cut when I pounce on a ball and send it straight to the boundary, or a flicking off the pads when pacers float the ball too close to my legs, or one of the many late cuts through the slips, strokes I play off the spinners. My favourite stroke of all is the back drive off the fast bowlers, which sends the ball screaming back past the bowler even before he finishes his follow-through. There is, indeed, an order to things, and I am in charge.

Just when my head starts to hurt from all the thinking I'm doing,

I notice the shadows on the fields are now much longer. I have long passed the century mark with one hundred runs beside my name on the scoreboard, and I don't even know how long ago that was. All I know is that we are up against the champions of the island and they have the strongest batting lineup. We have to keep our heads about us and give them a good target to chase, especially if we are to give our bowlers a chance.

The umpires collect the bails and pull the stumps. It is the end of play for the day. I suddenly feel so tired, as if I have been running all day with iron balls on my legs. My mouth is dry. I look at my bat and notice the fresh red marks, all near the centre of the bat and none that would indicate snicks, edges or indeterminate strokes. I kiss the sweet spot of the bat. The opposing team stands to one side and applauds as my partner, a senior player named Holder, and I walk back to the pavilion where the members of my team are there in front holding bats high in the traditional cricketer's salute and applauding.

"Great knock, Chris," my partner says. "I don't think anybody ever did do this before. Not against this team. Not on the first day of season. Not in their very first innings at this level."

"Thanks," I say, looking at the scoreboard and noticing the number 188 beside the number 3.

"Twelve more runs and you would have a double century," he says. "You really tamed them bowlers today, man."

"I didn't know that I'd score so many runs," I confess. "I was just playing my hand, that's all."

The applause follows us into the pavilion. The captain of the opposing team shakes my hand once more. My captain slaps me on the back several times. My teammates lift me in the air, and camera bulbs explode as someone snaps pictures. I sit down and start to unbuckle my pads. It is a relief not to have to carry those pads any longer. I rub a few painful spots on my arms where I was struck by the fast bowlers, and look through the window. The spectators are gathered around, looking inside at me and talking excitedly. Though I do feel so tired, I am happy with myself. This is one day like no other: a day when I knew what I wanted to do and then was free enough to just do it, just as I desired.

On the bus, I sit by the window and place the bat between my legs. The bus pulls out of the stand and I feel the evening breeze on my face through the open window. As we pass by the hospital, I wonder how Mrs. King is doing and if Grandmother is still there, for it is about the time that visiting hours finish. If the doctors say there is a need for more tests or anything so, Grandmother won't leave. But if Mrs. King is doing well, Grandmother might come home to sleep in her bed, though not before ensuring that Mrs. King is comfortable for the night.

I wonder if Stephie ever went back to see Mrs. King. Grandmother said it was one visit that did not go down too good. Stephie was frightened because of what she had heard the people saying about why a pregnant woman should not be in a hospital. And Dorothy was crying and bawling and not agreeing with Grandmother on anything concerning Mrs. King.

I think about Ursula and how much she and I will have to talk about when I see her next week. Maybe she watched the game, as she'd promised. Maybe her father was even watching me bat, for he is a big fan of cricket and I know they had talked about me.

The street lamps are on as we drive though town, but once we hit the country, we are plunged into darkness. There are few lights along the highway out here, especially when we pass between the sugar cane fields. Now that the sugar cane has been harvested and turned into sugar, the fields contain only the brown trash leftover. Sugar prices, as

Mr. Smith knows so well, are mysteriously falling on the international markets, as are the prices for bananas, pineapples and nutmeg. Prices, it seems, are falling for everything our island sells abroad, but rising for the things we import.

The bus driver seems to have the pedal permanently pressed to the flooring, for we are roaring along the highway. Soon it turns the corner and we begin the drive up the long road with the houses on either side. I can see Pastor Wiltshire and his flock already assembled a little ways from the shop. I reach up and press the stripe running the length of the bus to let the driver know my stop is next. I exit through the back door. As the bus pulls away, the conductor calls, "Great knock, sonny. Great knock, man. I can't wait 'til next week."

I watch the bus leaving and then I hear a voice shout, "Look he there. He just got off the bus."

I look in the direction of the voice and see a young boy standing in front of Mrs. Watson's shop, pointing at me. The boy runs toward me and grabs my bat and slings it over his shoulder as if it were a rifle. He marches beside me, and no matter how I try to take back the bat, he will not allow me. In the shop, everyone is waiting. They make a path for me. Cyrus slaps me on the back and pushes me up against the bar.

"Drinks for our conquering hero," he says. "Mrs. Watson, give this boy here anything that he want tonight. Man, everyone o' we so proud o' you, as proud as if it did be any o' we own self. And to hear how they talking about you on the sportscasts after the news on that radio there. Every hour on the hour. How you went to the home turf, the home ground, of the hardest team on the entire whole island and nobody coulda get you out. You withstand them all. They could not get the ball to beat your bat not even once. They could not get you to play one false stroke for an entire day. As them politicians like to say down where I does work, you are the man. *You's* the measure of all things, now. How did you do it?"

"I just bat," I say. "They gave me a chance to play for the school, and all I wanted to do is to just bat, to make sure we didn't lose too many wickets and get bowled out so cheap that it'd be a shame to the school and everybody else, 'cause them pace bowlers did be bowling really fast. So I just do what I had to do: I just bat and bat 'til the umpires pull up the stumps."

"'Til the cows come home," Cyrus says. "And then next week to come. That is what we got to look forward to, next week Saturday."

"Here, here," somebody shouts. "And bat you did. They keep saying on the radio there in the corner that they never did see so many strokes from a schoolboy, not the way you went after that bowling. Turn up the radio there some more," he says to nobody specifically, "so we can hear what they're saying when the news come up again."

"We already have the radio volume up to all," Michael says, but he still tries to turn the knob. "Nothing so never happened to one o' we before, not where we have the whole bloody nation talking about one o' we."

"Give the boy a drink," Cyrus says. "What you having?"

"I'll have a Kola Champagne," I say, and everyone starts laughing. The music is blaring away as we await the next newscast.

"Still very much a boy, eh," Henderson Brathwaite says. "Still a youth even though performing feats of men. If he want a Kola Champagne, then we shouldn't push him to drink anything harder. But all the same, as man, I gine be firing a good rum for myself. We'll do the hard drinking fuh he, and he can do the batting fuh we. That's life."

"And I will second that," Mr. Jones says, pushing his way to the centre of the crowd. "My son, what you have done today is more than I could ever hope to achieve with a thousand lessons or lectures to your school. You have made your school proud. You have shown us with actions what we mean when we talk about virtues and about performing virtuously. The actions speak for themselves."

Everyone applauds. Mrs. Watson asks me if I want anything to eat to go with the Kola Champagne and I tell her I'd like two coconut turnovers. She takes them out of the glass case, wraps them in a thin white sheet of paper and hands them to me.

Outside, Pastor Wiltshire is going to each point of the compass and ringing his bell, proclaiming the good news to all points of the earth. Off to the side off the road are two women preparing to fry fish to sell, now that an unexpected business opportunity has opened. On the other side of the shop, women are buying their groceries, and whenever I look up, I see one of them looking at me and smiling. But in the midst of all this life is still a void, a noticeable absence whose presence remains fixed and haunting.

I prop myself against the bar so I can be at the heart of the noise and celebration. I want to hear all the things being said about me. The sports announcer on the radio talks about how a schoolboy embarrassed the defending champions on the opening day of the senior level cricket season.

As the night wears on, the radio reports become repetitive, and the men turn on the jukebox. "Born to Lose." The American bluesman is singing this favourite song. The initial enthusiasm of the men wanes, though some of it returns every time someone new comes into the bar and sees me. Cyrus asks me what I am doing later and if I would like to join him and a few friends over at his house to continue the celebration. I tell him I am too tired from all the batting and ask him if we can put off the celebrations until another time. I tell him I really appreciate what he has taught me about batting and that some day I will show him my appreciation. Cyrus places his hand around my shoulder and pulls me to him in an embrace.

I say goodbye to everyone in the bar, take up my bat and leave. Grandmother does not come home during the night. The next day, she sends word through Boysie Watson that I should resume going to Mrs. Smith for my meals and that she will explain things to me when next she sees me.

Chapter Twenty

"Caramba, Maisie," Mr. Smith says as I come through the door. "Look who is here. The very said same person that we've been talking about all morning long."

"You mean *you've* been talking about," Mrs. Smith corrects him. "Lord, I haven't heard your clappers going so non-stop since the two o' we did be young yams together."

Even before entering the house, I could smell the fried chicken Mrs. Smith and Leila are preparing for Sunday lunch. I overslept this morning, after the excitement of the day before, and only woke up when Boysie Watson came by with a message from Grandmother, which was what I should do for Sunday lunch. Mrs. Smith would have started preparing the meal after returning from the morning church service. Leila is standing in front of the kerosene stove sticking a fork into some beets in a pot.

"Come here, son," Mr. Smith says, pulling up a chair at the table.

"Come and sit down here with me and tell me what it was like yesterday. And Maisie," he calls, "give this boy here a malt for me, please. He's going to need the strength from a malt or two, the way he's going."

"Morning," I say to everyone, and I sit on the chair Mr. Smith offered me, stretching my legs out and crossing them at the ankles. I start to rub a sore and swollen spot on my right hand where a ball struck.

"Morning, son," Mrs. Smith says. "You sleep good last night?"

"Yes, Mrs. Smith," I reply.

"And your poor Grandmother," she says, "I didn't see she at church this morning, so that must mean she's still at the hospital, right?"

"Yes, Mrs. Smith," I say.

"Lord, Maisie," Mr. Smith says. "Stop all the talking and bring one o' them malts for the boy. And bring one for me too. And two glasses with some o' the ice which you did get not so long ago from the ice truck." Everybody hears the clanging bell when the ice truck comes through every Sunday morning after church. A chunk of ice costs five cents and, once purchased, is placed in a wash pan in one of the coolest spots in the kitchen and covered with some salt and a big crocus bag to stop it from melting away too soon. "Do you drink malts, boy?"

"Now and then," I say. "When Grandmother can afford it." I feel like explaining that sometimes, for a treat on Sunday, Grandmother mixes a malt with evaporated milk. Or if not a malt, she mixes a fruitee drink with the milk. But I decide not to say anything more.

"Well, you better start drinking them regularly," Mr. Smith advises. "Especially if you plan to continue to be a first-class batsman like yesterday. You'd need the strength of them malts, and once in a while, a good stout or two with a few raw eggs in them."

Desmond Smith comes out of the bedroom wearing only short pants and looking as if he is planning to go to the beach for a swim.

Passing behind me, he stops and presses my shoulders. "You see the newspapers yet, boss man?" he asks.

"No, man," I say.

"Your face all over the newspaper, front and back. Everybody talking about that performance yesterday, man." He yawns loudly and begins scratching his head. "I'm proud of yuh, man. Real proud."

"Thank yuh," I say, and we slap palms together.

"Well, give him the newspaper and let him read for himself," Mr. Smith says.

Desmond goes back into the bedroom and returns with the newspaper and a shirt that he is putting on with one hand. He places the newspaper on the table in front of me. The front page carries a picture of me driving a ball. When I turn to the sport page, there is another picture of me, this time sitting in the pavilion, looking a bit tired but smiling broadly.

Just then, we hear a rapping on the side of the house and a voice calling, "Mistress, anything from me today? You want anything?"

"Sure, Trevor," Mrs. Smith shouts. Turning to Leila, she asks her to pass her purse, which is on a shelf in the kitchen. "It's the lettuce man," Mrs. Smith explains. "How much for a bunch?" she calls out, while reaching into the purse. "How much you robbing people for this Sunday morning when these days we can get lettuce from over-'n'-away almost for free in the supermarket?"

Leila lifts the pot off the fire and throws the beet-red water into the pig food bucket. She pours cold water into the pot. The lettuce man comes up the step to the open door. He puts down his cardboard box of lettuces and looks up.

"But wait," he exclaims. "That is *you*, the star batsman, sitting there, boss? Man, I have to shake your hand." He steps over the box, extends his hand to me and draws up a chair. "For what you did do yesterday, man. Everybody talking about it. Everybody who stopping me asking me to sell them a head or two o' lettuce to go with their nice Sunday dinner-lunch talking and talking. So, let me shake your hand again."

We shake hands once more. The lettuce man signals for Mrs. Smith to pick the bunch of her choice, and when she asks him his price, and whether it is going up just like everything else poor people have to buy, he shakes his head and says today's bunch is on the house. "My gift to this boy here so," he says. "With an innings like that, and you helping out his grandmother now she spending all her time at the hospital with Mrs. King, this boy here shouldn't have to pay for anything. We should be paying he just to watch he bat." Turning back to me, he asks, "So what you plan for next week? Just 200, 250, how much runs you think you can get this Saturday coming?"

"I don't know," I say.

"Of course, he don't know," Mr. Smith says, casting a glance at Leila, who is smiling broadly as if amused by the antics she is witnessing. "It all depends on his partners. How much he can make must depend on if anybody gine stand up at the other end for him, and if he don't run out of partner."

"I know that," the lettuce man says with a bit of annoyance. "But we talking here about a real *tactician*, as the commentators like to say on the radio. Don't let his age fool you. He already got them fellows figured out good, good, good. And to tell the truth, I was waiting for this day to come when somebody would put some good lashes in that team that think because them is the championship team they're really bad and nobody can't control them. Well, believe you me, I like how my boy here draped them up. He showed them that because them is schoolboys don't mean nobody can't bat like a man." And with that, the lettuce man takes up his box and leaves. We hear him calling at the house next door and reporting how he just talked with me over at Mrs. Smith's house and that I told him I would not be settling for anything less than a score of 250 runs on Saturday, and how I said that with a score like that, I would not only be putting that so-called championship team in its place but sending a clear message to the national selectors that I am ready to represent the island. And we hear him saying that as far as he is concerned, it is about time somebody that did grow up in our area was on the national team and that, yes, the price of the lettuce is the same as last week, 'cause there is no way that a poor-arse grower like himself can compete otherwise.

"Maisie," Mr. Smith says, "where is the malt you keeping there in the kitchen? I keep telling you to bring some malts here for me and my friend to drink."

"You know we have only one left," Mrs. Smith finally says. "I was saving it for your Sunday lunch today."

"Don't mind," Mr. Smith says. "Bring the one malt then. I can drink water with my lunch. Maybe Desmond can climb the coconut tree and get some coconuts so we can have coconut water with the lunch today. Yes, coconut water, with the jelly in it, with a sweet drink. But bring the one malt and two glasses and let me and my friend drink it down. Then he can tell me in his own words exactly what happened yesterday."

Mrs. Smith brings the bottle and the glasses to the table. Desmond sits at the table too, and Leila puts an enamel cup of tea in front of him. Mrs. Smith says that once she and Leila wash the lettuce, they will be ready to share the Sunday meal for us. And she agrees that Desmond should take out the ladder from underneath the house and climb the trees in the backyard for a few water coconuts, remembering he isn't exactly a young boy anymore when it comes to climbing and he should exercise proper care not to fall.

I decide to stay with the family long after lunch. With my bat in hand, I plan to return for dinner this evening and every evening of the coming week. I see myself walking to the bus stand during the week with my bat hanging at my side, my book bag over my shoulder, and Ursula at my side talking about what could happen next. She and some of her girlfriends might even come to watch me carrying on. I cannot wait for play to resume.

Chapter Twenty-One

"You know how it is," Grandmother says as she is about to leave the house for the bus stop. "You know my heart and my spirit will be there on that cricket field with you when you go back out to bat, 'cause the Lord knows I want you to continue to do good. But you know my mind would be some place else the whole time."

With Mrs. King having her relapses all the past week, Grandmother might come later rather than at the beginning of play. This way she will at least see me passing any milestone there might be in the works for me, rather than coming at the resumption and then having to leave. She's planning how she can kill two birds with one stone, she says, so she won't feel as if she is always torn, always having to choose between two things equally important to her, always feeling guilty no matter what she chooses.

"It's okay," I reassure her, joining her in the doorway. We look at each other and smile foolishly, and I see that Grandmother's face looks drawn, like she is losing weight. Her eyes are dull, like she could use more sleep. I place my hands in my pocket, as I do whenever she is about to look me over to see for herself how I am doing.

"So, I am going to be honest and come over to see you when everything is okay with Eudene," she says, hugging me. "'Cause the time they starting the cricket match is a funny time around the hospital, when they starting to prepare patients to receive visitors a few hours later."

"That's okay, Grandmother," I repeat. "I understand. I understand."

"Thank you, son," she says, "and God will bless yuh. You go and do your best."

"It's okay." I try to comfort her. "I'll be okay." And I feel the water welling up in my eyes. Still, I look her straight in the face rather than looking away to avoid these feelings.

"But I have to go 'long now," she says, hugging me again, and she reaches to pick up a canvas bag from the floor. It contains the clothes for Mrs. King she had brought home, washed and ironed. She tucks her dress and steps out. "God guide and direct yuh, son. I gone. But I'll try to come by and see you bat." And I watch her hastening down the road, the sound of the approaching bus causing her to scamper.

For the resumption of play, I make sure to arrive early. I pad up, taking care to locate the same pairs of pads and gloves and the same balls protector, and I get some of my teammates to bowl a few balls to me while I loosen up. This practice is primarily for show, for the photographer from the newspaper and for all those who have come to see the outcome of the day's play. Interest in the game had been ratcheted up when the main fast bowler told the newscaster during the week that he would quit playing cricket at all levels, including international or test cricket for the West Indies, if a schoolboy were to make 250 runs against him. He had heard the talk, especially from certain parts of the island, about how I had spent the week boasting about what I planned to do. I did not tell anyone I wanted to make 250, but as we got closer to the resumption, the idea of achieving such a score started to grow on me.

The umpires indicate they are ready to resume play. I take a final drink of water from the cooler and adjust my pads one last time as the opposing skipper leads his team onto the field. From what I can see, the crowd has swollen in the final minutes leading up to the game. I can see more people arriving, still. The radio commentator is in a van with a large aerial on it. I can see him standing, in his open-neck white shirt and black pants, at the side of the van, with the stub-nose microphone in his hand.

There comes a loud ripple of applause as my partner Holder and I walk out of the shadow of the pavilion onto the sun-drenched playing field. Somebody turns up the volume on the hi-fi, blasting the bass vibes and drum. I look under the trees where most of the spectators are sitting and see Desmond Smith at the turntable with Trevor the lettuce man, who is waving with one hand and holding a beer bottle in the other. Holder and I walk together side by side, the music driving us on.

"*Christopher.*" I hear a familiar voice and look over to see Ursula waving and clapping. She is with some girlfriends from school, standing in a huddle. I raise my bat in salute and hear the girls squeal and giggle. I am to resume at the striker's end. The main fast bowler is already at his mark.

As I come to the receiving end of the wicket, I notice that the pitch looks even smoother than the previous Saturday, an indication of the efforts of the groundsmen, who watered the pitch and used many different rollers with different weights to prepare it. The pitch has a sheen, as if it was polished and buffed. With the surface so hard, I know the wicket will help the fast bowlers and provide more bounce and variation for the ball.

I take my usual guard of protecting leg-side two wickets and I settle in. As the fast bowler moves in, I hear the din of the crowd rising. The first ball is pitched up outside the off stump, and once again, everything looks so easy. I lean into the ball and steer it through the gully area to the boundary for four.

The crowd applauds loudly and I hear someone calling out my name clearly. Someone retorts, but I cannot make out what is said. Obviously it is funny enough to produce a general round of laughter amid the spectators. The scorekeeper adjusts my tally to 192, and as the bowler begins to move in again, I hear a rhythmic slow clap, a salute from those who believe my first stroke is a sign I am merely picking up from where I left off. They believe it could be another day of hard toiling for the champions. I am now confident that making a double century might not be too difficult at all. Then I can build the score to 250, then to who knows what, especially if my eyes continue to sight the ball the way they did with the first one, as long as my reflexes are just as fast, as if there is no break between last Saturday and now. I am feeling good.

The bowler jumps and delivers and I see the ball pitched in line with the centre stump. I play back and cross, keeping the bat and pad close together, a moment of indecision, for I possibly should have gone onto the front foot. I hear and feel the *klunk* as the ball hits the inside edge of the bat and careens into my pads.

"*Howzat.*" The bowler is jumping in the air and punching the air as he shouts his appeal to the umpire to claim my wicket. I look to the spot where the ball pitched and imagine how I would play a similar ball differently: the better stroke would have been to shift my weight and stance so as to play from the front foot. I hear the roar from the crowd. I look up and, with the greatest feeling of dread that will ever come over me, I see the umpire slowly raising his finger.

How could he be giving me out? Only the bowler appealed to get me out. None of the other fielders had seriously supported him in asking for my dismissal. Everyone except the bowler must have seen and heard the ball hitting my bat first, so it isn't fair for the umpire to give me out, my innings ended just like that. Such judgment would only be fair if the ball had struck me directly, if it had not first hit the bat. Those are the rules. In this case, everyone but this bowler must know what really occurred. But still, there is the umpire, the final arbiter of the game, standing alone from all others in the world, index finger raised, indicating I am out. My innings over, sudden so, like some death that in a twinkling of an eye extinguishes. All my great plans and hopes are now gone. So much is now unfinished. Tradition dictates I have to walk. And I must. I cannot even grumble or show any displeasure, for otherwise it would not be cricket. Mr. Jones is watching my sportsmanship. To me, this is a death.

I look at the captain of the opposing team, and when our eyes meet, he lowers his head. I look at the bat and the red spot where the ball hit before colliding into my pads. The faster bowler is now screaming at me, and some of his colleagues are shaking his hand. I look again at the umpire, but I know that because this is cricket, I have no choice but to walk back into the pavilion. I have to let the game go on without me. I feel the tears running down my cheeks. This is unfair. And I am getting angry and angrier by the second. I pass my replacement, who whispers that they thief me out, for everyone heard and saw what really happened—everyone, that is, except the umpire and the bowler, who is still celebrating.

Inside the pavilion, I throw down my bat, fling my gloves into the pile of equipment and begin taking off my pads. The crowd roars again and I look up to see my replacement following me back into the pavilion. The umpire repairs his shattered stumps, and the same fast bowler celebrates with his teammates. The music is still blasting away, but I do not see any reason why anybody should be dancing.

Just then I look up and see Grandmother and another woman making their way into the grounds. They stop to look in the direction of the pavilion. Cyrus is pointing to where we are, obviously telling them what happened in the less than five minutes after the resumption. Grandmother waves, even though I am sure she can't make me out in the shadow of the pavilion.

This time our team is not the one celebrating. It is the end of the day, and the champions are performing just as everyone expected. Everything now appears to be back to normal. The captain called on me to bowl a few overs, but my heart was not in it. With exacting vengeance, the champions have piled up the score on us and it looks like there is nothing we can do to redeem ourselves. The first Saturday of the season now seems like something random, nothing more than a pleasant dream. This performance on the second day is the real indicator of the true and genuine cricket. On my way home, I purposely sit at the back of the bus. I am ready to sneak home, but when I get off at the bus stop, the same little boy is standing in front of the shop and pointing me out to everyone.

There is no celebration this evening, and barely any interest when I try to explain I was robbed. The men drink what rum there is and talk mainly about what will become of the island now the government has announced that a team from the International Monetary Fund is visiting.

With the men talking about politics and nobody seeming to care I was cheated out of a double century, I decide to go home to be alone. I slip out the side door of the shop with my bat and walk the long route home, which means I do not have to pass in front of the spot where Grandmother and Mrs. King sat in better times, or near where Pastor Wiltshire is preaching and prophesying about good times now and in the future.

"Christopher, you in there, boy?" I hear the voice by the side door and recognize it as Cyrus's. "Open the door, boy, and let we talk."

I turn down the radio, open the door and make to sit at the entrance. Cyrus pushes pass me and enters the house. This surprises me, for I expect somebody coming by so late to visit me when I'm alone, and with everybody knowing how grandmother feels about her privacy, to stay outside. Cyrus flicks the end of his cigarette into the yard, just beyond the rim of the light from the lamp. The cigarette bounces several times and settles in the darkness, the red glow facing me.

"Things didn't work out too good today, eh," he says. "That umpire is as blind as the three blind mice."

"I know, I know," I say, standing up and facing Cyrus, glad for the opportunity to get some things off my mind. Until now, I didn't think anyone fully understood my hurt and disappointment. Not even Ursula waited around until the end of the day's play. She and her girlfriends were long gone, probably preparing for their Saturday evening.

"That's why I come over to cheer you up." Cyrus places his hand around me. I smell cologne and rum. "I thought, you know, with your grandmother not coming home, that I could come and spend the night with you, and nobody don't need to know anything, just you and me."

"What?" I ask.

"Come, man, let we sit together here on this bench." Cyrus pulls me closer to him and I feel the tips of his fingers digging into my side as his hand starts to caress my neck and then my back. Cyrus takes my hand and places it around his neck.

I realize what is happening. Without thinking, I dart through the door into the darkness.

"Wait, boy," Cyrus is shouting. "What yuh doing?"

But I am running. All around me is darkness: Mrs. King's house is shut tight and so is Mr. Lashley's. I just know that I have to get away. I keep running my feet, which seem to have a mind of their own, taking me toward Mrs. Watson's rum shop. But I am not ready to tell anybody in there what happened, and the shop will soon be closing. I continue running and running, and I start to hear the first vibes of the music, growing louder the farther I run. The road is deserted; not even a car passes. Up ahead I see a lone figure passing under a street light and then continuing into the darkness, both of us drawn to the same place.

"Why you look so out of breath?" Desmond Smith asks as I settle in beside him. "Where you going this time o' the night?

"I don't know," I say, gulping loudly. "Just that I don't want to go back home. I don't want to be in Grandmother house alone tonight." I decide not to explain further. I can sense from how he is walking and carrying himself that something is bothering him.

"Well, come with me," Desmond says, sounding happy for the company. "I'm going over to the dance hall."

"Where is Leila?" I ask. "She not coming with you?"

"Leila, *cheee*," he says and sucks his teeth. "I don't know about Leila anymore. These days she ain't have no time for the dance hall. No time now for me and my plans for the music around here. Other things on her mind. So I don't know about Leila."

"Oh," I say.

"But she's at home sleeping," he says. We walk on in silence, drawn by the heavy bass beat, which is pounding just as hard as my heart, and by the light and the voices. I think Desmond would probably think his problems are bigger than mine, so I should not unload on him. It would not be fair. I just have to learn how to manage my own problems and leave Desmond and everybody else free to deal with theirs.

"Why you decided to come back down here to live?" I ask.

"Why I come back?" Desmond says. "Hmmm. These days sometimes I ask myself the same thing." He pauses to light a cigarette. "You see me here?" Desmond pulls heavily on the cigarette. "Well, I was sitting in my apartment up there, and I got to thinking 'bout life and independence, thinking how I had come along as a boy and heard the old people saying certain things. And I tell myself, you know what, Dessie boy, everything them old people did say is right, for it is true the grass is always greener on the other side and that anyplace you find yourself is always hell itself. So I tell myself, Dessie, it's true: hell is wherever you happened to be. And I am up there thinking how so many o' we people for the longest of time long before independence come going to all parts of the world and how they always catching hell, for they always starting at the bottom and can never get to the top. They always building other people country for them, but getting fart in return. They and even their children's children are always the outsiders. So I say if that is the way of the world, if you have to catch hell, why not go back amongst your own people. I say to myself, why you, Dessie, sitting around up here just like all the others talking about going back home *eventually*, maybe when you getting old, retiring. Why not go back and help build now? And that is when I decided to come back. It's as simple as that."

"You mean my mother," I ask, "and Stephie's mother too, them catching hell?"

"Why you think they don't write?" he asks.

"I don't know," I say. "I just think they just don't write."

"Why they don't send for you two?" he says. "I mean you yourself see how Leila in my arse all the time for she to get back her two children. How she always comparing her daughter, Clarice, to Stephanie and saying how she won't want the boy, Henry, to grow up like you without mother far less a father, for you and Stephie remind her so much of the two children, only that the two of you older. So why you think your mother or Stephie's mother will be any different? Aren't they mothers the same?"

I do not have a response. Desmond has given me many answers to questions I've had since my earliest memories of me and Stephie playing in the backyard. I try to control my breathing.

"But don't get me wrong," Desmond says after some time, as if he's been thinking hard. "'Cause I ain't saying that your mother or Stephie mother can't send for the two o' you or that it won't be a good thing if they did. So don't go and tell your grandmother anything that I didn't say. Especially knowing how Mrs. King is these days. It's just that you asked me a question that everybody keep asking me, that even Dorothy keeps asking me, and with Leila the way she is, even getting my mother on my arse these days. Plus I like to tell young people the truth when they ask me anything."

We walk in silence. Beyond the music and voices are the sounds of the ocean beating against the shore. The waves sound as if they won't stop there but will come and get all of us too.

"Once you leave here, you become an outsider when you come back," Desmond says. "In the end, you are an outsider, either up there or back here among your own flesh and blood as people. Sometime it is like they are more willing to accept somebody like a Leila than like me. But I ain't giving up yet. Not yet." He sucks his teeth again. There is something about Desmond, the way he carries his shoulders and looks and sounds so alone, that I do not like.

"Christopher," a familiar voice calls, just as we arrive on the scene. "What you doing out here so late? Your grandmother knows that you are out here?" Ursula is standing in front of me, smiling as if she is the most surprised person in the world. Desmond walks off as if anxious to leave me on my own with Ursula.

"Why you so *stiff*?" Ursula says, shaking her waist and stepping away from me to show me how it is done. "Loosen the shoulders, man, move your waist. You acting like you is really some grandmother chile and don't know nothing." She bounces against me, winding, pushing her groin up on me, bouncing fast and then slow. I am trying to keep up.

"Put yuh hands in the air; act like you don't care," a man on the platform is reciting into a microphone, over the music. He is waving what looks like a towel over his head and prancing, then hopping from one foot to the other. "Now bend down low; touch your toe." The DJ mops his brow. His face and arms glisten with sweat. "Now rub up, rub up; shake yuh body line." I look around and everybody is responding to his call, the young girls showing the way, as if in competition, as if seeing who can be the most outlandish, winding their waist sometimes all the way down to the ground and back up, hands in the air, laughing and sweating. The dance hall itself seems to be bobbing and bouncing to every beat, as if everything is moving together, the bass beat linking everyone, and the drumming pushing us into a greater frenzy. I mimic everybody around me and lose myself too, trying to bre'k-out just like everybody else.

The music changes from a calypso to a soft ballad. Ursula steps in closer. My heart is beating fast. I feel I am being tested and there is no escaping. What she just said grates me, because it might be true. This is not the first time I've heard people talking about somebody acting like some grandmother chile, how people like me are always out of fashion, how grandmothers dress us the wrong way, make us spend all our time at church and cut us off from what the other boys and girls are doing, how we always going through life acting so frightened—frightened as if everything in the world will bite us. I know this is how Ursula was thinking when I surprised her outside the dance hall and she blurted out her question about my grandmother giving me permission. I wonder, is this how everybody sees me? Is this how they saw me and Stephie when we were on the bus, or walking to the beach for sand or sharing books? How the two of us were cut off from the rest of the world, even from the children who used to come by on Saturday to share the pot of black pudding water. Is that why people always think-ing they can unfair us?

Ursula is now asking me to prove I am not just some grand-mother chile, that I can dance, or at least hold my own while she leads the way; that I am as regular as anybody else. "Every man fuh grab a woman," the DJ screams. "Every woman fuh grab she man. 'Cause we feeling nice, nice, nice." Ursula pulls me closer. I smell the burnt Vaseline in her hair that she must have straightened for the weekend. *"We feeling good, good, good. We grinding slow, slow, slow."* I look across the room and see Desmond. He smiles in approval and moves to the foot of the stage where the DJ has a stack of LPs and forty-fives. I feel Ursula's belly against mine. I know I am not much of a dancer, but I tell myself I do not have to be an expert, I only have to balance my feet and grind slowly against her. I hear Ursula breathing and snuggling even closer into me, her left hand around my neck and her right hand on my bottom tapping, encouraging me to sway with her as she taps with each beat, as she teaches me timing and how to dance. I have no choice but to hold her close and stay on the floor, for otherwise how can I hide this big bulge in my pants? We dance until someone shouts to Ursula that her father has arrived to take her home. She kisses me on the cheek and walks toward her father's Hillman Hunter.

I walk over to where some young men and older boys are in a ring, dancing and trying to outdo one another. Some have unbuttoned their shirts while others are shirtless. One of them has a big towel, which he uses for mopping the sweat from his face and twirling in the air above our heads. Young women move in and out of the ring, showing their motions, matching the men with their moves. Everybody is *carrying on bad* to the music. And I like it. For the rest of the night, I am just one of them in the ring, in the dance hall. Every so often, I think of Grandmother and Mrs. King and what they would think of me here with all this slackness, me acting so vulgar. What would Stephie say if she saw me here acting like some wild beast?

I decide not to dwell on my problem from earlier in the night. I feel certain now that I can handle the situation on my own. As Ursula tells me, I can't be some grandmother chile anymore. And I know who would be the first to agree with her: Stephie.

By the time I walk back home with Desmond, we can see the first sign of the sun rising somewhere over the ocean. The lamp is out in the house, but the door is closed. I am tired. Ursula is probably long in her bed. I don't think I've ever had a day like this. I'm thinking maybe I won't tell Grandmother anything that happened, so that nothing I did or was done to me will upset her. As I settle into my bed, I think about what Stephie would say if I told her I spent most of the night in the dance hall. I could see her laughing. I wonder too what she would say if I told her about what happened with Cyrus and me. In my mind, I hear her saying that even if I did run away, at least I wasn't crying like some little baby. I can't wait to go walking with Ursula. If she asks again what I want to be, I can say DJ in addition to something in sports.

When I wake up the next morning, Grandmother is already starting to cook. She came home even later than me but still managed to get out to church with Mrs. Smith and the other women while I slept. Grandmother tells me I should go and visit the Smiths today to thank them for being so kind to me. To my surprise, Mr. Smith was asking about me, and she says I should go and see what he wants.

"You know, this morning was the first time I could go to church with so much of the burdens of life lifted off my shoulders," Grandmother says. "I have to thank God for the wondrous work he is doing when it comes to Mrs. King, what the Almighty and the doctors are doing."

"So, Mrs. King might be coming home then?" I ask.

"I hope so," Grandmother says. "One way or the other that would stop me from having to spend so much time at the hospital, time I could better use by starting to decide how we are going to make a living from now on, 'cause I can't see, no matter what, me and Mrs. King continuing with the business like before. Both o' we going to need some money to see us through. So, I guess, we may have to start thinking of killing one o' the pigs and seeing how much money it will bring us."

"So what you're going to do?" I ask. "Sell the pig whole?"

"Not so fast," Grandmother says. "I ain't deciding nothing yet, not before I have a good long discussion with Mrs. King as my business partner and who own a full share in them two pigs we got there. We can either sell the pig whole to a butcher, or we can hire a butcher to kill the pig for us—in which case we would have to sell the meat we own selves. That might be a lot of trouble going around from house to house asking people for orders and then having to run down the said same people to collect our money afterwards. Or I can sell off a few of my stocks to raise a few dollars to help me to get by. In any case, come tomorrow, God willing, I will be taking the few eggs the chickens does lay down to the supermarket and ask them to sell the eggs for me."

"If it was me," I say, as I am leaving, "I'd sell the pig whole and cut out the trouble."

"What he did wasn't fair," I explain emphatically to Mr. Smith. "And the captain on the other side should know better too. It wasn't fair at all. That isn't the cricket I know."

"Fair," Mr. Smith almost shouts, standing up to turn down the volume of the radio. "What you mean by fair? Did people storm the field and stop the play when they gave you out?"

"No," I say, not sure where Mr. Smith is going with his argument.

"Did they continue play as usual?" he asks.

"Yes," I say.

"Did the prime minister we got declare a state of emergency and send in the defence force boys to correct things?" he continues.

"What you mean with all this questioning?" I ask, baffled by the foolishness he is asking.

"I just trying to understand what you mean when you say it wasn't fair," Mr. Smith says, laughing. "What is fair?"

"I mean it was wrong the way they got me out," I explain. "They thief me *outta* my hand and stopped me from making a higher score, that is what I mean, and I am still vex about what they did to me."

"But what you'd expect in cricket?" Mr. Smith asks. "I mean, that is life, and as long as you're playing, there will be times when you will be given out when you shouldn't be and times when you should be given out when you won't be."

"But we don't expect that in cricket," I say. "You don't expect the umpire to give you out when he done know you ain't out, or for a bowler to claim a wicket when he ain't deserve it. I mean everybody I know now saying thiefing out my hand is the only way they could stop me from making a double century or more."

"How old you's, boy?" Mr. Smith asks, grinning.

"Fourteen," I say, puzzled. I am playing for the schoolboys' team, after all. "Why?"

"Humility, my boy," Mr. Smith says. "Remember that word. You are getting to be a man now. When I was your age I was already working. Life's tough. And if you hear anybody saying you *woulda* make so much and so much runs, you should ask them if that was guaranteed, and if they say it was, ask how come then you didn't make the score. How do you know you won't get out fair and square with the very next ball? I mean, I *gotta* be asking myself as well where all this talk about this double century coming from, 'cause if I can remember right, you weren't thinking about nothing so last week. You were just thinking of staying at the wicket and helping out the schoolboy team, but now all I'm hearing from you is about what was good for you, what *you* want."

"I know, but how you would feel if you did be me and you could go on and set a record?" I ask. "Nobody would be happy getting out like I did, especially when according to the rules I wasn't even out. I didn't expect that at all."

"That's right," Mr. Smith says. "You don't *expect* that just as you were saying if the umpire or bowler *know* you ain't out. But suppose they don't know. Suppose they really *believe* you did be out fair and square. As I must ask you, in life how many things we do out of good intentions?"

"I don't understand what you mean," I say, struggling to hide my annoyance. "Everybody that's got eyes to see did see the ball hit the bat first and then the pads. Everybody that got ears to hear did hear the loud knock when the ball hit my bat."

"Don't get angry, sonny," Mr. Smith says. "All I am suggesting to you is life is like that. Everybody else in the world mighta did see and hear the ball hit your bat, but most important, the umpire didn't, and we gotta operate on the basis the umpire intended to be fair and to do what is right and that he wanted to be fair and right to both sides. But he is a human like me and you, and in the moment, we don't know what happened."

"I always look to the umpires to make right decisions, or for the captain to do the right thing, such as indicating when he knows someone isn't really out when they are given out. That is what I understand to be cricket, a gentleman's game."

"If that is true,' Mr. Smith says, "that it ain't got nothing to do with luck, then you should not now be holding a grudge 'gainst the umpire who gave you out."

"What you mean?" I ask.

"I mean," he says, laughing some more, "that it ain't no use complaining about one bad decision, a decision that is bad only because it went against you. I am sure the previous Saturdee all the players did appeal to the same umpire countless times and each time he did make what you'd call the right decision. He turned them down, even when some of them were close. I am sure all the other fellows on the other side did go home thinking the umpire was favouring you."

"But he wasn't," I say. "The fact is I was hitting everything clean with my bat. Or at least everything but that one ball."

"And that is all it takes," Mr. Smith explains, "one misjudgment, one blemish, one false stroke and then one big calamity taking place."

"I see," I say, even though I don't quite understand or believe him. "I see."

"So, my boy," he says, "you *gotta* stop fretting up yourself because of one decision. That is now part of the past, a decision that you cannot change. Call it a mistake or whatever, but you should let it go and go out and play cricket knowing that things will not always turn out the way you want them, and when they do, if they ever do, that you should enjoy it when it is happening." Pausing, he smiles broadly at me. "What I just tell you is the same thing I am telling this boy here in a different way," he says, looking over at Desmond, "and to his wife too. I keep telling him that we have to always start off by having good intentions and hopes. The same with your mother and Eudene King's daughter and anybody else going over-'n'-away, leaving everything behind. They have to always expect that good would come no matter what."

"I see," I say. I feel funny in his stare. Mrs. Smith moves around the kitchen, and I know she is listening. No doubt she has an opinion too, but she is keeping it to herself for now. I will probably hear it later from Grandmother when Mrs. Smith reports to her how I am taking this chastisement from an older head.

"You say you's fourteen years old, right?" he asks.

"Yes, sir," I say, recognizing that he is reminding me with his voice and grin that he is much older than me.

"Well, you're a big man now," he says. "Many o' we when we were your age were already working, as I done tell you. And we did still be helping out in the house like you'd have to do more and more with your grandmother. You have to stand up." A part of me feels good hearing Mr. Smith say this. It is good to hear this from a man, since there is no man in the house. Cyrus said these things too, but Cyrus is different.

"The same thing with you staying down here and learning to become a man standing on your own feet," Mr. Smith says. "'Cause one of the things independence doing for we is to make sure that we learn to be strong and from early to stand on we own feet in good times or bad. So that we ain't relying on no brother or sister, aunt, uncle or cousin, or no friend looking after his own interest, to take care of us. We *gotta* learn to cut and contrive, make the suit according to the cloth we have, to use what we have to get what we want. It ain't no guarantee of the good times only. And that is why I hope that a young boy like you with so much talent and ability would no longer feel bad if his mother over-'n'-away don't send for him, if he has to be his own man, in his own country."

When I am leaving, Mr. Smith says I should not be a stranger, that I should come by and visit him every now and then, to share a malt or a stout with him. And he tells me I can take his copy of the newspaper, as he is finished with it.

As I walk home, I feel angry with Mr. Smith for not understanding the point I was making about the cricket game. I feel that much of what he said did not really apply to me. Clearly, he was spending too much time secluded in the house, listening only to the radio and receiving everything second-hand; he was therefore out of touch with what is happening in the real world. What he claims to have learned from living overseas such a long time ago seems to be of no relevance to what is happening around us.

Yet, as I reflect on the specifics of what he said, I begin to have a different image of the stodgy old man who I used to see through the window of his house merely looking out on the world like some kind of prisoner, now too old to be of use to anyone. I am beginning to have a better understanding of him and his mind, which is obviously much sharper than I had expected and from what Mrs. Smith had led us to believe. I wonder why she would give the impression that her husband is almost dotty in his old age, suffering with maladies of all sorts and from indigestion, which made him a picky and finicky eater. I now understand why he insists on having his meals at specific times: so he can take his medication with them in order to control his diabetes and high blood pressure. I think that he and Mrs. Smith both want to show that they are the boss of the house; neither of them wants to be the slave. And I am noticing the same thing between Desmond and Leila. Maybe no two people can always be getting along together. Maybe that is why Grandmother and Mrs. King's friendship is so special.

I am still angry with Mr. Smith for not understanding the way I feel, and for suggesting I was sulking. How was he to know what I really felt, when he was not even at the cricket grounds and had to rely on what the commentators said? No sooner do I think this when I realize the contradiction in my thoughts. Mr. Smith was trying to tell me that even though he was not at the grounds to witness what happened for himself, he was assuming that I was acting with good intentions, that everybody was acting that way. Otherwise it would not be worth his, or anybody else's, time to follow the game. I guess that is part of what Mr. Smith is trying to tell me: in the end, each and every one of us must try to give meaning to our lives and to what is happening in them. Maybe that was what the leader meant on independence night when he said we should become firm craftsmen of our fate and even seek to write our names on history's page in our very own hand, so the writing would be exactly what we want. Otherwise we would either be longing for a past we cannot change or facing a future rushing to meet us without any of us having a say about what that future should be.

Suddenly I realize that Mr. Smith was telling me in his more mature way the same thing Ursula told me on the floor of the dance hall, what Stephie's been telling me for as long as I've known myself, about not being just a grandmother chile. In these changing times, every last person on this island has to step out on his or her own and make a life. When I get home, I do not turn on the radio to keep me company. I just want to hear myself thinking.

Grandmother is ecstatic when she comes home.

"So, you hear Stephie's baby born this morning?" she asks.

"No," I say, impatient for her to tell me more.

"Yes, man, a beautiful little girl," Grandmother reports. "She came in this morning seven pounds something or the other."

"Yeah?" I say. "How she doing, I mean Stephie and then the baby?"

"She's doing as to be expected," Grandmother says. "You know with her age and everything. But she and the little angel seem to be okay from as far as I could tell. I even went up on the maternity ward and had a look at Stephie and the little angel."

"She named she yet?" I ask.

"What yuh mean?" Grandmother asks. "The baby just born. Nobody 'round here don't name no baby until we give it a little time so you can tell what is the best name for her. In fact, Stephanie already say she will be giving nobody but her dear grandmother who did raise she the honour of naming her baby. She says the infant will be known as Baby King until her grandmother is up to the task of naming she. Well, that news, both of the baby borning and the honour Stephie is giving her grandmother, was enough to make Mrs. King look a good ten to twenty years younger. You shoulda see the smile on her face and the look in her eyes. The news was enough to bring about such a change on she, the hospital people say they definitely will be discharging Mrs. King from the hospital later this week."

"Where you think she's going to go when she gets out?" I ask.

"I think she will be coming back here," Grandmother says, "although there is a side o' me thinking she would want to go to Dorothy to be near Stephie with the baby."

Grandmother is right. Mrs. King indicates she wants to return to her house. Grandmother makes arrangements to have some jobs done before her return. She asks Cyrus to come around and give her a hand putting up a piece of cardboard where somebody broke the windowpane. And she gets the wiring, which Mr. Lashley started, done as well as the electrical hookup. Grandmother, me and Cyrus go into Mr. Lashley's house and lift out the television set. She plugs it into the outlet in Mrs. King's front house, so the two women will be able to sit together every evening and watch it.

Chapter Twenty-Two

Mrs. Smith says she hopes nobody will hold her responsible, for it looks like nothing good is ever going to come from Desmond and Leila. Indeed, Leila has moved out, as is reasonable and expected, for she is a woman and sooner or later needs a home of her own, especially with her two children expected to arrive in a month's time. However, when she left, she did not even tell Desmond where she would be living. She told him that all she needs from him is the regular support to which he is committed. She does not want him around her quarrelling all the time and criticizing her two children, even though he has not lived with them in a long time and does not know how much they have changed. It seems that Desmond and Leila have broken up because she wants them to concentrate on the polyclinic business and he wants to devote all his time to developing a music recording business. Without agreement on this issue, everything else has broken down.

I look at the clock to judge how much longer it will be before Ursula arrives. Every evening she comes by and I walk her home.

"And you know I was thinking," Mrs. Smith says, "if this is the same thing that does happen to we young girls when they leave their children down here and go over-'n'-away to make a life for themselves in a foreign country."

"What you mean?" Grandmother asks. Mrs. King sits in a high back chair and stares at the television, banging her good foot, as if unaware of what is happening around her. This is how we have come to accept Mrs. King since she returned home. Most nights Grandmother keeps Mrs. King company, the two of them not talking, until it is time for Grandmother to put her to bed. I notice that Grandmother is becoming as thin as a rake.

"I was thinking about this boy here mother and of Stephanie mother," Mrs. Smith explains. "The both of them living overseas, with these two children here, but you don't ever hear anything from them."

"Yes," Grandmother says. "True, but I still don't understand the point you're making."

"What I was thinking?" Mrs. Smith asks softly. "I was thinking if that is the reason these girls don't follow through on what they know they should be doing. I mean, I was thinking that when they get up there over-'n'-away most likely they will have a man friend, for they ain't going to be living alone forever, and that being so, they will have to make a life of their own with the man friend, whoever he be. And I was wondering, you know, with these women in a strange country, having to make life with a man most likely from another place and different from them, and then they have to think if they want a child they left behind to come and join them in all this comess, and that might be the reason they never get to send for the children they left behind. The time never get to be right, where they're happy with the strange man in their life, and where they could bring up the ones they left behind."

"But even so," Grandmother says, "they could still write. They still got the two hands God did give them, and they could still send back a letter even if they still have to sort out things."

"I know, I know," Mrs. Smith says. "But you know the point I am making. When I look real close at what happening to my own son, Desmond, and to Leila, a nice girl but still a foreigner and different from we at doing some things, I started thinking about your two girls and all the other girls from down here that went out to make a life for themselves."

Grandmother and Mrs. Smith lapse into silence. Mrs. King continues to stare at the television. I step outside and close the door and notice the bluish light seeping through the various crevices of the house in the darkness. Ursula said she would be passing by at the end of her training run, and she is right on time. As we walk back to her house, we plan for the weekend, for cricket and then the dance hall. But I feel strange. Something Mrs. Smith said stands out in my mind, reminding me of the feeling you get struggling against sea waves. Everybody seems so hopeless, those that are here on the island and those that flee overseas. Nobody seems to expect much from tomorrow or any other day. And feeling this way, I realize how much I am caught up too, just like everyone else, in whatever is washing over the island. It is like what people call the Devil and his wife fighting, when there is sunshine but also rain. Neither can dominate the other, and that is just life for them. Except that this time it seems the old way of doing things is fighting with the new way, except that independence is about starting anew. It dawns on me that I have a choice: I can be swept away too, or, as Mr. Smith says, I can become a man—my own man.

Pastor Wiltshire makes his way past the boys and girls who are assembled outside Mrs. King's house to watch television and knocks on the half-opened door. Even with the windows fully open, the heat in the house was baring down on us, prompting Grandmother to open one half of the door to help cool us.

"Good evening, sisters," he says, as he pushes his head in.

"Well, good evening, Pastor Wiltshire," Grandmother says, standing up to greet him. "Fancy seeing you out at this hour in the evening. What you doing out so late?"

"I just dropping by to say hello," Pastor Wiltshire says. "I was meaning to do this for a long time now, but you know how things are these days, how they don't seem to be enough hours in one day to do everything. Can I come in?"

"Sure, man," Grandmother says. Pastor Wiltshire enters the house, looks around and sits between Grandmother and the silent Mrs. King. He places the leather bag he is carrying at the foot of the chair.

"And how is Sister King keeping this evening?" he asks, raising his voice as if speaking to someone hard of hearing. He takes Mrs. King's hand and, when there is no response, looks at Grandmother and asks, "How is she doing these days?"

"The same way," Grandmother reports. "No better, no worse. Just sitting there, hardly talking to anyone. Just watching the TV until she gets tired and I have to help her to her bed. Three times a week the nurse does visit and give her treatment by rubbing her down and I does do the rest."

"How *you* making out on your own?" he asks, turning to look directly at her.

"*Me?*" Grandmother asks, surprised. "I don't even think of myself.

It's just that I try to make sure Mrs. King is comfortable and then there is the boy to look after and his cricket that is taking up so much of his time and I still want him to concentrate on his books and school work, and you know I was just sitting here more so with the TV looking at me rather than I watching the TV and I was thinking—"

"Lord," Pastor Wiltshire says, letting go of Mrs. King's hand, "you sound like you got it a bit rough. You should try and take care of yourself, take some time off for yourself. If you want, I can get some of the church sisters to come and spell you off from time to time during the week so that you can get away now and then. Maybe try and get out to yuh own church, bearing in mind you are always welcome to come and worship with us. I am sure Sister King would want that for you. Right, Sister King?" Again there is no discernible answer.

"Well, I glad to hear you say that," Grandmother says, and she starts to cry. "But you know some people around here keep saying what me and Mrs. King doing ain't right in the sight of God or man, how as a woman with a next woman we ain't a good example, so we might be getting punished by the Lord himself, and to hear a church man like you say—"

"Lord, Sister Lucas," Pastor Wiltshire says, "it ain't me to judge anyone. 'For my thoughts are not your thoughts, neither are your ways my ways, saith the Lord. For as the heavens are higher than the earth, so are my ways higher than your ways, and my thoughts than your thoughts.' So who am I to judge anyone?"

"Thank you," Grandmother says, wiping her eyes with the back of her hand. "Still, I try my best. I try to make sure Mrs. King is comfortable and that she takes the medication on time, even though the price for the medicine keep going up every day and the supply we did get from the hospital for free run out a long time ago and the hospital saying that now it have to charge for every single tablet, and sometimes, she like she doesn't even want to take the medication, or to eat and drink anything and I have to be gentle and force her a little bit and—"

"I know," Pastor Wiltshire says, taking Grandmother's hand in his. "Still, I admire your strength. You are better than even me."

"What you mean?" Grandmother asks. "How I could be better than you?"

"In a way *nobody* is like me," Pastor Wiltshire says, and he starts to laugh. "Sometimes I think I am just like the man that has to roll a big able stone up the side of the mountain every day and to then wake up the next morning and have to be doing it all over again."

"I know what you mean," Grandmother says, and she too starts to laugh for the first time in a long while. "That is the only hope that we have."

He laughs some more. "Right, Sister Lucas. I still have faith and I have hope things will change. I have expectations great. Some day, we will wake up and find the rock has not rolled back down, and then, as human beings, what we'll do? What will we do?"

"I know," Grandmother says, sighing at the thought of the relief. "What would we be without the trials and tribulation, eh? For that is life self."

"'Yea, though I walk through the valley of the shadow of death,'" Pastor Wiltshire recites, "'I will fear no evil: for thou art with me; thy rod and thy staff they comfort me.' I drop by to give you comfort and to give you the assurance there is, indeed, honey in the rock in the Lord our Saviour, and that God knows what each and everyone of us is going through."

"Amen," Grandmother says. "Amen, Pastor Wiltshire."

"Anyway, I'm going to be leaving now. You hang in there, and if you don't mind, let me say a prayer for both you and Sister King before I leave and to ask God's blessings on all of us and to give us patience and hope." Grandmother and Pastor Wiltshire look at Mrs. King, who shows no reaction. Pastor Wiltshire places one of his hands on each of the women and says a short prayer.

"Amen," Grandmother says.

"Amen."

Pastor Wiltshire picks up his black bag, and Grandmother walks him to the door.

"Good night, Sister King," he says. "And may God bless and keep you, you hear. And you too, Sister Lucas, hang in there and don't give up."

At the door, Pastor Wiltshire stops and digs into the bag. He takes out an envelope. "This is a one-time gift," he says. "A special collection from members of the church for those who we feel we should be helping. We got a little bolster for it earlier when them two foreigners made a donation after interrupting with their motorbikes." He presses the envelope into Grandmother's hand.

"Thank you," she says. "Thank you, Lord."

Then he looks in my direction. "Next time, the double century, you hear me."

"Yes, sir," I say.

When Ursula arrives, I am waiting for her in front of the house. There is a cool breeze as I walk her home. We are not talking much, but when we get there, Ursula turns to me and asks, "Why don't you go and see her?"

"Who?" I ask.

"Stephanie," she says. "If I was you, I would go and see with my own eyes how Stephanie is doing for myself so that I can settle my own mind. And if I was Stephanie I would want you to do that too.

That is how I see it." And she kisses me on the cheek and walks away. "Good night, Christopher," she says.

"Good night, Ursula," I reply.

In the darkness of the fore-day morning, I go into the backyard to pee.

"You hear them dogs in the distance howling and howling, like they seeing spirits?" Grandmother asks. I hadn't heard her snoring but I had assumed she was sleeping. Until she drew the howling to my attention I had not been aware of it. "I don't like it at all," Grand-mother whispers from behind the curtain that separates her bed from the rest of the room. "All night I laying down here just listening to them dogs howling and carrying on and I remembering how the old people would say it was not good when these things happening. They are a sign. We *gotta* be prepared."

Back in my bed, I listen to the dogs. To me, the howling doesn't sound any different than usual, but because Grandmother discerns something special in it, I cannot get back to sleep.

The next day after school, I am walking back to the bus stand with Ursula when I see Grandmother waiting. Her head hangs down and her hair is rumpled like when she runs her hands through it. She says she was at the hospital all afternoon sorting out things. "Mrs. King," she says, "is finally at peace. They send out a van to tell Dorothy and Stephie." I feel Ursula squeezing my hand. Grandmother does not even blink as she stares straight at us.

"What a friend we have in Jee'sus."

As the words come out, I feel a chill. Every hair stands on end. The clarity of the voice seems to hit the rafters, then to bounce back to the flooring, filling up all the space within. In the church, it is almost as if someone has let out a big sigh. Desmond Smith keeps adjusting the knobs on the recording machine and every now and then he exchanges a reel of tape.

"*All our sins and griefs to bear!*" Grandmother's voice is strong, and there is purpose in her singing. I notice her reflection in the fine polish of the coffin, right beside the silver handles and the nameplate.

The undertaker and his attendants pushed the coffin on a set of wheels up the aisle, stopping when it was beside the pew where Grandmother and I were sitting. I look around and notice the church is full. Across the aisle from us are Dorothy, who is closest to the coffin, and her husband, Arnold. Other members of the family, who I never heard about until the official death announcement on the radio, fill out the seating. Everette Pinder and the other men who are offering themselves as candidates in the next election are all present; so is Mrs. Watson and her husband, Boysie, and Mrs. Smith, who is sitting with some other women. I cannot spot Mr. Smith or Leila anywhere. But I see most of the women who came to visit Mrs. King in hospital and 'noint her down. With the singing, everyone is looking straight ahead, as if he or she is momentarily in a special place. On the altar, the pastor and officials of the church are sitting, dressed in their robes of white. Behind them, the windows are open, and I can see the breadfruit tree next to the church and in the distance the houses and the other trees, stretching as far as I could imagine.

"*What a privilege to carry . . .*" Grandmother is singing as she has never sung before. Every word of the song seems to come from her heart and to have a special meaning. It had been a long struggle since Mrs. King came home from the hospital, and when the end came, even Grandmother said it was for the good. Mrs. King, she said, had left this world of pain and sorrow, where Grandmother could no longer be of any help to her, and she is now in a land of joy, where there is no pain and where the choir of hosts is always singing. *Everything to God in prayer.*

Still, there is ambivalence, for Grandmother knows she will miss her special friend. But the Mrs. King of late was not the same person she had met and come to love, who had been a sister and best friend to her, and who would not want to hang around when there was nothing more of life to enjoy. Grandmother said that Mrs. King had squeezed every ounce of life out of her living and she had fought strong and brave to the end, even when the stroke had robbed her of the best things of life. Grandmother told me she had noticed the wood doves on the roof cooing and knew it was a harbinger. And now Mrs. King is passing over, where she can be with all our ancestors, especially those of our recent memory, who still are almost alive to us.

"O what peace we often forfeit."

I look around the church some more. I cannot help but notice that someone is still missing. And then, just as Grandmother is ending her tribute, Stephie slips into the church. Wearing a black dress and hat with matching high-heeled shoes, Stephie walks up the aisle and stops at the coffin to kiss it. Sobbing, she wipes her eyes with a handkerchief. Stephie looks at Grandmother and her head moves in an almost imperceptible nod. Grandmother makes room for Stephie to join us in our pew and holds her as she, Stephie and I cry throughout the rest of the ceremony.

At the graveside, Dorothy and her husband lead Stephie away. She is crying so hard, they almost have to lift her. I do not even get a chance to talk to her.

Grandmother leans against the side of the house as Henry, the butcher, a tall, slim man dressed in soiled khaki overalls, gives one of the pigs a slap. The animal grunts, jumps forward, wiggling its tail, and starts rubbing its back against the side of the carts. Henry closes the door and, with the rope, lashes the two pigs to the side. His assistant is a young man, perhaps only a few years older than me, wearing a baseball hat. As he fastens a knot and pulls the rope tight, one of the pigs starts squealing; the second one soon joins in. Everyone in the area must hear the pigs. As his assistant climbs into the cart with them, Henry walks back to where Grandmother is standing.

"I'll fix you up once I have them weighed," he says to Grandmother. She looks at him as though measuring him from his feet up. "I'll come back and fix you up." She nods her head. The pigs are grunting and squealing as if they have realized what is happening to them.

"As you know, the price I am paying per pound is lower than if you did sell to me at least a month ago," he explains. "Still, I am a businessman and I got to tell yuh that even the people that buying pork from me looking to get everything for next kin to nothing."

"I understand," Grandmother says. "See what you can do for me. As you know, I have to pay off some o' the funeral debts from Mrs. King."

"Yes, I understand." Henry looks around. "Who own the house?"

"Which one?" Grandmother asks

"This one here," Henry says, gesturing toward the closed-up house. "This house that did use to belong to Mrs. King before she dead."

"As far as I know, it belongs to the family," Grandmother says.

"You know if they're planning to sell, or if they planning to keep the house buttoned down and boarded up all the time?" Henry asks.

"I don't know," Grandmother says. "You would have to ask them."

"I guess so," Henry agrees. "All the same, a house ain't got no use if it's going to be closed up all the time. A house is for the living, not for the dead." He wipes his hands on his pants, leaving a greasy black stain. "But as I was saying, in terms of me and you doing bidness, I'll come 'round, perhaps in the middle of the week and settle up with you fair and square. By then them two pigs in there would be long time on some people tables." Henry laughs at his joke, but when he realizes Grandmother is not joining him, abruptly stops.

"See yuh during the week," he says and starts to walk away.

"See yuh too," Grandmother says. "See the best price you can get for me."

Henry gets into the truck, places it in gear and drives off. When he is gone, Grandmother says, once again, that she had no choice. The turkeys and chickens are all gone. She had held on to the pigs for as long as possible, perhaps to her detriment. She had no choice but to sell Henry the pigs alive. Butchering them on her own would have been too much trouble and too much work.

"But what anybody would want me to do?" she asks. "Things tough, real tough around here. Things brown, brown, brown. Eudene would understand. She'd do the same thing if it was she who did be in my place and position. It's the right thing to do."

"Suppose your mother did actually send for you, what would you do?" I ask.

"You mean if she did send for me and Eudene Margaret?" Stephie asks. "'Cause I done know there ain't no place on earth I'm going that I won't have this little girl with me."

We are sitting under the tamarind tree in the pasture across the road from Dorothy's house. I feel this visit is one of the first things I must do to take charge of my life so I won't end up washed along like a piece of dried sugar cane caught on the sea waves. Stephie appears as happy to see me as I am to be visiting her and the baby. She threw her arms around me as soon as she opened the side door to the house and saw me standing there with the paper bag in my hand. Inside it was a shak-shak toy I had bought for the baby. Eudene Margaret shakes the toy, raising it to her face.

"You want she to be a musician from early," Stephie says, laughing, as she tries to stop the child from putting the toy in her mouth. "You want me to train her so she can get one o' them contracts Desmond Smith still talking about? You don't think she too young?"

"As they say, you never too young." But in truth I had not thought about making her a musician like all the young boys and girls who were forming bands and playing in every corner of the land. I just wanted to give her a gift.

With the temperature inside the house rising from the strong afternoon sun, Stephie suggested we take a cardboard box with a blanket out under the tamarind tree. The baby looks sleepy, and Stephie places her in the box. For the first time, we can really talk about all that is happening at school, now that I've become "a big man in cricket," she says, and everybody on the radio is talking about when I'll be selected for the national cricket team for the regional Shell Shield tournament.

"Plus don't let me have to go and scratch out Ursula's eyes for she," Stephie says. "'Cause if she not treating you good, I would have to come and fix she up good, good."

"No, man," I say, smiling at her joke, for Stephie still thinks she is the big sister having to protect me. "Ursula's cool. She's good. In fact, she thinks a lot about you."

"Oh yeah?" Stephie says. "Why is that, so tell me?"

"I think she misses you," I say. "I think she did like when you and she did provide competition for each other. But now you're gone."

"Well, I ain't gone for good," Stephie says. "Tell her I am still around. I ain't done with running yet. And I ain't done with you yet."

"Maybe you and she can run together for one o' these athletic clubs they have around here," I suggest.

"That don't sound like a bad idea," Stephie says. "But I definitely ain't done with running. Nor with singing either. I've been talking all the time with Desmond when he comes by to talk with my aunt, and he keeps saying that as soon as he gets his recording business up and running, we—you and me—can come and try out with him. And we should."

"Can you imagine me and you singing together? Just like old times, even before the radio."

"You mean me, you and Eudene," Stephie says.

"Mrs. King?" I ask, wondering what Stephie is talking about.

"No, you big fool. Eudene here." She points to the baby.

"Oh, that's right," I say, and we laugh at each other.

Again I ask her if she still longs for the chance to join her mother, especially now that Mrs. King is gone.

"Sometimes I think about what I would do if my mother did send for me," she admits. "But it ain't like before. I don't feel so excited about going away anymore, not now I have little Eudene Margaret. 'Cause one thing I know, I ain't leaving her anywhere. Not like what my mother and your mother did to the two o' we. If I have to suck salt, Eudene will be right there with me to suck it. I ain't ever leaving her to go nowhere. Not after hearing what Desmond Smith does be saying about living abroad."

"What about Mr. Lashley?" I ask.

"What about him?" she says. "I guess he's somewhere. I don't hear anything from him and I guess for all I know he'd be coming back down some time soon. Besides that, I don't know anything. In any case, I don't like to think about him anyway."

"I really hope things work out for you," I say. "I hope if it is what you want that your mother will send for you and—"

"Well, as I just said, I don't know if I would be going anywhere on my own." She pauses for a long moment, while waving away a fly from the box. "'Cause in any case, I don't know who I would leave Eudene with. It ain't like how my mother and your mother did have Grand and your grandmother to help them out. If I had to leave Eudene, I would leave her with only one person I know."

"Who that?" I ask.

"You, nuh," she says, smiling. "I would only leave her with you. 'Cause I know I can trust you. You'd be good with her. You'd be responsible."

"But *me*," I say, "I'm too young."

"Too young," she repeats. "How much older you think I am than you?"

I laugh and, maybe because of what she is saying, I reach into the box where Eudene is curled up in her white vest and diaper and pick her up. "But I would take care of her for you if you had to go."

"I know you would," she says. "But then what would happen if it is then, at that very same time, you get sent for, especially if that is what you still want? Who would take care of Eudene then? I guess I would have to come back home and take care of her, 'cause I won't want her left with anybody else."

"Maybe I'd bring her up for you," I suggest. "Maybe you would be settled in and it would be better off for me to bring her with me. Then we would all be in the same country, me and you, just like we used to talk about it when we did be smaller."

"Yeah," she says. "But I am not counting on that. I am planning to be staying around here on this island and making something of myself. I've made some decisions of my own and I am comfortable with them. I don't have to go anywhere over-'n'-away to make a life for us. I know we can get along if I keep my head about me. And when I catch my hand and can find some place of my own to live, 'cause even if I could, I don't want to live in Grand's old house across from that *other* house of so much trouble. I'll be all right. I plan on taking some o' them courses to prepare for university the government offering. For as sure as I done tell you, I planning to take back up my running by training with all them boys and girls looking to make the national team, 'cause I know I good at running; that could be the future for all o' we. Somehow I'll make a life for me and Eudene and I won't have to depend on nobody. Nobody will unfair me again, neither me nor that little girl you holding while she sleeps against your chest."

"I know you will," I assure her. "But still, it's always a lot of fun sitting with you and dreaming and thinking about what could be, just like when we were younger."

"I know," she says. "I know. And I miss talking with you. And besides, who's to say you and me can't keep dreaming now we older? I hope you don't ever find yourself in a position where anybody's unfairing you no matter the circumstances. I won't want that for you. Plus we *gotta* start learning from the mistakes of the past."

"I know." Imitating Stephie, I rock Eudene Margaret in my arms. We sit in the shade listening to the breeze rustle the top of the tree and the grass in the pasture. And even though we do not talk much, it feels just like old times. In some way that I may never fully understand Grandmother and Mrs. King must have thought they were protecting us by keeping me and Stephie apart all this time. Perhaps they were waiting until we were ready to better handle the world. Maybe they did not realize that we had already begun to learn about hurt and disappointment. I am finding that even though there is a rhythm to life, there isn't always a clear rhyme or reason.

A car pulls up in front of the house. Desmond and Leila are in the front and Dorothy is in the back. They are all laughing. Seeing them so happy, I think of Mrs. Smith. She must be feeling better now.

Her hope for Desmond and Leila must be restored. And I feel good for her. Dorothy gets out and waves goodbye to them. As the car drives off, she enters the house. They did not see us under the tree.

The sun setting, Stephie eventually says it is time for me to head back home, since I am still a schoolboy after all, and not yet a man to match how she has become a full woman; but she hopes I come back to see her and the baby real soon. I know she is teasing me, just like old times, and that she must be having the same thoughts as me about what has become of us. So I say nothing and pick up the box with the blanket. We are almost back at the house when Stephie stops and looks straight at me.

"Can I tell you one thing that I hope you don't mind?" she asks.

"Sure," I shrug my shoulder, "you know you can tell me anything."

"Well, I think with the way you performing at cricket and thing," she says, talking while looking at the baby, "well, I don't think you should be thinking of leaving down here no more for over-'n'-away. I mean, everybody is now saying music and cricket is the future for we here in the West Indies for the next ten, twenty years. They say that's how we'll make our mark in the world. Since you have the talent, you should stay, be one o' them cricketers on the world stage."

"Oh," I say, feeling my cheeks burn. "Maybe."

"Me the runner, you the cricketer, this *l'il* one here, as *you* suggest, the musician. All o' we singing together."

We look at each other and smile for a long time. Finally, she breaks the moment. Placing Eudene over her shoulder to free a hand, she slaps me lightly on the shoulder. "Try and go along," she says. "Go before you miss your bus."

"Yeah, I should," I say, placing the box on the step. "Goodbye, Steph. I'll come and see you and Eudene soon."

"Walk good," she says. "And tell your grandmother I say hello to she and that the first chance I get I'll come and see her real soon. Me and the baby. So you take good care of her."

I put my hands in my pockets, for what else can I do, and walk away. I look back to see her standing on the spot holding Eudene, watching me. In the distance are the sounds of the waves breaking on the shore as rhythmically as ever. Tomorrow.